THE ATHELSONS

For nearly a thousand years the Athelsons have owned
the estate of Clere Athel, on a remote stretch of the
north-west coast of England, and have administered it
according to patriarchal custom. Successive generations
of their tenant farmers have tried to buy the land they
work, and by 1903 it is clear that the commercial
pressures of the outside world are closing in; yet Old
Athel still fights to hold back the tide of change, determined that his grandson shall succeed him in the
traditional way. Then, to the Dower House comes
Antonia Athelson, widow of a discounted second son,
with her daughter, Justine. The seasons pass, and a
boy and girl fall out of friendship and into love. But the
blood of the Athelsons runs deeply in young Athel and his
cousin, Justine—their every action and emotion bound by
a sense of duty and honour to the house of Athel. Over-
shadowed by the brooding presence of Old Athel, they
face the painful challenges of love. The story of the
Athelsons is a saga of love: the tender love of man and
woman, the dutiful love for the people of Clere Athel,
and the all-consuming love for the land and the house
of Athelson.

THE ATHELSONS

★

JOCELYN KETTLE

**THE
COMPANION BOOK CLUB
LONDON**

This edition, published in 1973 by
The Hamlyn Publishing Group Ltd,
is issued by arrangement with
Barrie & Jenkins Ltd

THE COMPANION BOOK CLUB

The Club is not a library; all books are the
property of members. There is no entrance
fee or any payment beyond the low Club price
of each book. Details of membership will gladly
be sent on request.

Write to:

The Companion Book Club
Odhams Books, Rushden, Northants.

---

*Made and printed in Great Britain
for the Companion Book Club
by Odhams (Watford) Ltd*
600871665
9.73/266

For
Jane Aiken Hodge

Part One

Part One

CHAPTER ONE

THE ROAD TO CLERE ATHEL crossed an old province of the sea, a desolate place with a salt wind sighing and soughing over coarse marsh grasses. Weary with the round trip to Lancaster, the horses began to pick up their feet more briskly, flaring their nostrils at the pine forest ahead, knowing a feed of hay waited just beyond it.

Antonia Athelson leaned her head back against the worn upholstery of the old travelling carriage and closed her eyes against the unsympathetic view. She was not a woman for the country. She was at home in Paris. She was at home in London. And yet that morning, entirely of her own free will, she had placed herself and her daughter on the nine o'clock train at Euston and headed for this bleak-looking part of the northwest coast of England, intending to make her home there.

'I must have taken leave of my senses!'

'I beg your pardon, Mother—did you say something?'

Antonia opened her eyes and looked at the girl sitting opposite her. Justine. Her face softened. Such a quiet, serious child. It was for Justine's sake that she had finally accepted the invitation to occupy the Dower House at Clere Athel.

'No, I didn't say anything. I was just thinking aloud.'

'I imagine we shall be there soon. Isn't it exciting? I

9

wonder what they will be like, Grandfather and Grandmother and my cousins.'

Antonia regarded her daughter with wonder. She seemed to have no misgivings whatsoever about their introduction to the family they had never met. But then at fifteen years of age one took so much for granted. Justine was going to her father's family and could anticipate only a loving reception. Antonia prayed that she would not be disappointed, but it was impossible to share her confidence.

'My dear, I just don't know. The only member of your father's family I ever met was his brother, your Uncle Athel, who was killed in the war in South Africa. The Athelsons never leave Lancashire if they can help it, and we were not pressed to visit them . . . not until now, that is.' Antonia hesitated, considering whether she ought to have attempted a fuller explanation. But how to explain a situation of which she herself had only a partial understanding? And could she say to a girl of Justine's age, 'When your father was alive, we were not welcome here, but now that he is dead your grandfather wants you?'

It had all to do with the land and the inheritance of it. Lucian, as a younger son, had been expected to make a career in the army. He was not suited to service life, however, and, unable to live on a subaltern's pay, left the army and tried to set himself up in a business career in Paris. It was then that he made the mistake of asking his father for help. He had half expected a rebuff, perhaps, but never the manner of it, which was extremely harsh. That much and no more he had confided to Antonia when they first met and were planning to marry. 'He made me feel as though I were trying to rob my brother and as though simply by asking for a loan I had done something so dishonourable that I could never live it down.'

Once, when they had been enjoying a phase of particular prosperity—for Lucian's business affairs were subject to remarkable fluctuation through all the years of their married life—she had suggested that they might visit his parents, taking Justine who, then turned five, was of an age to travel. Lucian's face had hardened at once in the way she so much disliked because it meant a mood in which she could not reach him, and he had answered curtly. 'No. You wouldn't care for my family. They're not your sort of people. You would find them very rough in their manner.' She had laughed at him for that. 'You are an Athelson and nevertheless I *love* you.'

'You don't understand. My father and my brother would think we had come a-begging.' And when she had persisted gently that they could remove any such misunderstanding with a letter before they went, he had grown angry and left the room.

Had she been wrong to disregard Lucian's warning now that he was dead? The trouble was she had very little choice in the matter, for although they had contrived to live with reasonable comfort while he was alive, he had left her with no more than the value of the lease on their Paris apartment, and her own income was only a pin-money annuity.

It had been a hard decision, and she delayed making it for more than a year. Yet she reasoned that Athel Athelson was an old man. He had lost two sons in the most unforeseeable way inside a year, and when he had written offering his protection and pressing her to occupy the Dower House, there was a note of sadness and regret that seemed to indicate a change of heart. He wanted his grandchildren about him, he said, and he was full of concern for her circumstances and Justine's welfare. Moreover, even knowing that his elder son had left an heir and two other children, Antonia could not stifle the hope that once her father-in-law met Justine and come to be fond of her he might find some way to make provision out of the estate for her future, for the marriage settlement that must surely be found one day. In the meantime there was a rent-free home and their keep. Yes, for Justine's sake they must go to Clere Athel. In the end she had given herself no time for second thoughts, had immediately concluded the sale of the lease and the contents of their home, said good-bye to her friends, and here they were, three days later, covering the last few miles in the shabby conveyance which had been sent to meet them at Lancaster station.

'I only hope I am doing the right thing for you,' Antonia said suddenly. 'I have explained to you how awkwardly we were left. Your father had this tendency to be more hopeful than events, financial events, justified.'

'I know,' Justine said quickly. She did not want to hear again how improvident her father had been.

'I doubt if we shall meet the family tonight. It is getting quite late, and we shall be going directly to the Dower House. But if, when we do meet them, you should find their manner a little . . . bleak . . . try to make allowances. Their ways are sure to be different, to seem strange after the life we have been used to in Paris. But it is really very good of your grandfather to offer us a home—a whole house to ourselves.'

The pine trees were thinning out. Justine lowered one of the windows and saw a finger signpost with the half-obliterated name of their destination. Just below it there was a much newer sign with the words DANGEROUS MARSH in bold black letters, and abruptly the road changed from the shingle surface on which they had been driving to a wooden construction, crossing an expanse of matted vegetation.

'Don't worry about the noise,' Justine said cheerfully over her shoulder. 'We're on a kind of bridge, going over a marsh.'

'How reassuring. You will please not trouble to tell me whether the bridge is in a good state of repair.'

'We'll be clear of it in a minute. I can see a cobbled road ahead and the ground is rising. . . . There's quite a steep hill in the distance, and I can see fields and a farmhouse. This must be Clere Athel. We're here at last.' Justine turned back from the window, her grey eyes alight with anticipation.

The road continued between two rows of cottages. There was a small shop with a cipher to show it also served as post office, an alehouse, and a smithy. Some children were trying to round up geese at the edge of a pond. They stopped to stare with curiosity at the carriage and waved and called to the driver. And here and there a woman with a ladle in her hand, another dusting flour from her elbows came to their cottage doorways to watch them go by. Just past the pond the road turned over a humpbacked bridge. A low white-washed building on the left seemed to be a schoolhouse, since its double doors standing open revealed rows of benches and a blackboard, and directly opposite this was a rather handsome church with an adjacent vicarage of matching sandstone.

The entrance to the home park lay ahead, its tall wrought-iron gates fastened back to admit them. They had an impression of a tiny lodge house, of a wealth of fine, old trees, of pools of light and shade across broad, sloping grass-land, and of a wide, beech-lined drive curving away before them until it was lost to sight. But the carriage followed the drive for only a short distance and then wheeled sharply to the left, stopping on the circular gravel sweep before an elegant Georgian house.

The building did not appear very large, yet it seemed to Antonia that the harmony of its exterior features at once promised accommodation that would be gracious and well proportioned. Justine, watching anxiously for her mother's reaction, saw her eyes widen in surprise, and then she smiled.

'Oh, you like it, don't you, Mother?' The girl's voice told her relief. 'I am so glad. We can be happy here, can't we?'

'Let us wait and see what it is like inside.'

'It will be beautiful. I know it. I can feel it.'

Their driver, having rendered them the minimum assistance in alighting, turned at once to the task of unloading the luggage.

'Just give that bell a pull, and Bessie Rimmer will be out to see to you.' He directed Justine with a jerk of his head. 'I canna keep yon hosses standing about.'

The door was already opening without any summons

being necessary, however, and a smiling, country-faced woman, plump and neat in black twilled silk, presented herself.

'Good evening, Mrs Lucian, Miss Justine. I'm Bessie Rimmer, housekeeper to the Dower, if you please. I hope you have had a comfortable journey.' The quick, bright eyes—like the eyes of some small furry animal Justine thought, like a squirrel—were taking in every detail of Antonia's fashionable travelling costume.

Antonia glanced wryly at the carriage. 'Well . . . as comfortable as could be expected.'

'Aye, yon's an old bone shaker, right enough.' The housekeeper nodded sympathetically. 'Come away in then and rest yourself. Ellen will fill baths for you in your rooms, and I've supper ready for you whenever you want it. And how many hours have you been travelling. . . .' Antonia allowed herself to be shepherded gently into the house.

Justine, pausing to collect the small dressing case, which her mother would certainly want the minute she removed her hat, felt that the driver was offended by the criticisms levelled at his vehicle and sought to make amends.

'Thank you for fetching us from Lancashire. It was a long drive to do twice in the one evening, I am sure.' Justine faltered shyly.

The man's scowl was deterring. 'Tha's best pair of carriage horses in the county—aye, in England, like as not.'

Justine considered the horses carefully. 'I am not surprised to hear it. . . . And I thought you drove them very well.'

'Not easy to handle,' the man conceded. 'There's spirit there.'

'Yes, they do look lively.'

Having unloaded the last box, he climbed up and unknotted the reins. The horses stopped resting their feet and came to attention, quivering as they waited hopefully for the gentle slap of the leather.

'They're restless now. They know they've done their turn. They're sweatin' and they want a feed.'

'Then you mustn't make them wait any longer. Good night, and thank you again.'

The driver smiled down at her suddenly. 'By God, tha's got the look of our people, right enough. My name is Harry Thorpe. You need anything, you come to stables up at the house and ask for me.'

'You're very kind. I will remember that.'

The hall was empty. Somewhere upstairs the murmur of voices and the opening and closing of doors indicated that her mother was losing no time in exploring the bedrooms.

Justine put down the dressing case and moved slowly into the centre of the hall, clasping her hands in pleasure at all she saw. Directly ahead double doors stood open to a long drawing room with a terrace and the garden beyond. The soft light of the late summer evening hung like a gold mist through the house and everywhere picked out the beauty of polished wood, the glow of old gilt, the subtlety of time-worn colour. There was such a stillness that petals falling from a full-blown rose in the bowl on a table close beside her made her turn her head sharply. . . . Her mother's quick, light step to the head of the wide staircase was followed by her anxious inquiry.

'Ah, there you are, child. I wondered whatever had become of you. Hurry now and take your bath and change. I have told Mrs Rimmer we will be ready for our supper in half an hour. . . . And would you please bring my little dressing case up with you, dear?'

Antonia's bedroom ran almost the width of the house with windows looking across the park.

'But you still can't see the big house because of the trees. Mrs Rimmer says it is over in that direction. Isn't my bed fantastic? I think it must be Louis the Fourteenth, don't you? The hangings are dropping to pieces with age, but I suppose it would cost a fortune to renew them. Go and see your room. You have a pretty view of the garden.

Justine found the young woman called Ellen spreading towels around a small hip bath enamelled with roses and thought how much more fun to bathe this way. There had been a small *salle de bain* in their apartment in Paris, a dank, rather dispiriting little room with a great deal of mahogany and a marble tub that made one feel like a fish on a slab. But still her mother might miss it. Now she was anxious again. Somehow she felt responsible for Clere Athel because it was her father's home and her mother had not wanted to live there.

Left on her own, she went over to the window and opened it. A thrush was singing in the jasmine that grew against the wall beneath, and dusk was beginning to blur the contours of the garden. If she was very quick, she might just have time to slip out and take a closer look before supper.

Antonia was still dressing when Justine tapped at her door twenty minutes later.

'Come in, dear. What are you wearing? The shantung? Oh, well, I suppose it will do, since Mrs Rimmer assures me none of the family will call on us before morning. But really it is past its best, you know.'

'It was on the top of my box. I just took the first thing I could find. . . . May I go and look at the garden until you are ready?'

'Yes, but be sure to put a scarf round your shoulders. These summer evenings cool down quite suddenly.'

As soon as she stepped out on to the terrace, Justine knew that this stipulation had been unnecessary. The high walls sheltering the garden seemed to have trapped in all the scent and warmth of the day. There was just sufficient light left to distinguish a profusion of roses and clematis hung upon the broken pillars of a miniature colonnade and, at the centre of the small lawn, the pale shape of the fountain she had seen from her window. It had looked pink—or had that been merely the reflection of the setting sun? She went to examine it more closely, a wide, shallow basin of translucent marble set on a pedestal with three claw-shaped feet. And yes, it was a very pale pink. The slender jet of water leaped high in the air and fell back in a delicate, shimmering loop.

Instinctively Justine held out her hand and let the cool water trickle through her fingers. It was then that she became aware of another sound that had nothing to do with the rhythm of the fountain, a gentle rattle of small stones somewhere behind her.

She looked around. There was no one on the terrace. Where else? The bushes? The wall. There was a figure, a man, sitting astride the top of the high wall. She began to edge cautiously towards the house. But in an instant he had swung himself down by the creeper and stood directly in her path.

'Who are you? What do you want?'

He laughed softly.

'Did I frighten you, cousin? I am sorry, but I was curious and decided to come a-calling.'

'It doesn't seem a very proper way to arrive—over the wall.'

'Why not? My land this side of the wall, my land that side of the wall. My wall.'

Justine felt that this was not the sort of observation one ought to make, but it was delivered without arrogance, as a simple statement of fact. And there was even a note of polite inquiry as though he would be interested to hear a better argument.

'Then you must be Athel. Won't you come inside? My mother will be down any minute.'

'Your mother? I didn't come to see your mother.' He seemed surprised she should suggest it. 'I daresay I'll meet her tomorrow. That's soon enough. No, it was you I came to have a look at.'

'Well, really!' Justine's sense of propriety was outraged. 'And do you always come to spy on your guests?'

'I wasn't spying. An Athelson doesn't spy, he reconnoitres.'

'I am an Athelson, too, but I wouldn't consider it any excuse for that sort of behaviour.'

He was silent for a moment, considering this criticism.

'I startled you. That's why you are getting so cross.'

'Not at all.'

'You don't care for the idea of being watched without knowing it,' he suggested.

'No, I don't. Nobody would.'

'I liked the way you were going round touching things . . . as if you were greeting them . . . as if everything you saw pleased you. Do you like this house?'

'Oh, yes! Yes, I do.' She smiled suddenly.

'That's better. You're better-looking when you smile. Give me your hand, Cousin Justine. I will promise never to make you angry again, and you must promise you will smile at me all the time.'

'I don't think I can promise that.'

'I see that you are a very difficult child,' he said with mock severity.

'Neither am I a child. I am fifteen, only a year younger than you, so I understand.' It was hard to believe, she thought. He was so tall and strong-grown like a man. Only the outline of his face was boyish. 'Nevertheless, I will shake hands with you, and I hope we will be friends.'

He took her hands in both of his. 'Welcome to Clere Athel.'

'My mother will be down any minute. I shan't say that I have seen you. She would think it very odd of you not to introduce yourself to her, you know.'

'Yes, I suppose you are right. Then we shall have to meet tomorrow as if we were strangers.'

'That will not be difficult. I cannot see you well enough to be sure of recognizing you again. And we have to learn to know one another.'

'Oh, no, you're wrong. There's nothing one Athelson has to learn about another. We're all alike. It's in the blood, Grandfather says, in the very nature of us. I can tell it's in you by the way you speak back at me.'

Justine was inclined to resent the easy confidence of this pronouncement. For how could it be true when she was her mother's child as well as her father's? 'And something more besides,' she thought, 'I am the person I have the will to be.' But it was no time to argue. The chandelier had been lit in the drawing room, and she could see her mother talking to Mrs Rimmer.

'I must go. Good-bye until tomorrow.'

'Good-bye, then.' He still seemed to hesitate.

'Oh, quickly . . . my mother is coming out on to the terrace.' She slipped past him and ran across the grass, not daring to look back to see whether he was still visible.

'I was just coming to call you,' her mother said. 'I have told Mrs Rimmer she may dish the savoury. I am sure she has gone to a great deal of trouble, so we must try to do justice to her supper. Are you hungry? I declare I am almost too tired to eat.'

They ate supper in near silence, which was partly due to their own preoccupations and partly the inhibiting presence of the manservant, Pegger.

'This is Pegger,' Mrs Rimmer had said before retreating to the kitchen. 'Pegger lives at the lodge. Pegger waits.'

He was a thin, stooping man of melancholy expression. 'Aye, Pegger waits,' he echoed gloomily as he drew back their chairs for them. 'But Pegger does a sight more than that,' he added, seating them tenderly. 'Pegger chops wood and cleans chimneys and Pegger polishes silver and does the garden'—he shook out napkins of fine old linen and presented them with a bow—'and Pegger mends this and fixes that and runs errands for Mistress Rimmer. . . .'' He left the room still muttering.

Justine had giggled, and Antonia had raised her eyebrows and said, 'Well, really the servants here are quite remarkably free in the way they express themselves. Ellen was telling me while I dressed that most of the families on the estate have been here as long as the Athelsons have. I suppose they feel that gives them right.'

She did not sound as though she agreed with them.

Justine was glad that her mother did not seem to expect her to make conversation. She was thinking about her cousin Athel and the way he had spoken and what he had said and there was a quiet, pleasurable excitement within

19

her at the thought of the next day and meeting the rest of the family. She felt enfolded by the quiet of the countryside, by the house, by the sense of coming to a place she belonged.

'Justine! Justine!' Antonia was shaking her gently by the shoulder. 'Why, child, you are positively nodding off over your plate. If I leave you any longer, you will be asleep, face down in the pudding. Come along. I have asked Mrs Rimmer to bring you up a cup of warm milk. Let me see you to your room, and then I shall go to bed myself. We want to be at our best tomorrow.'

Yawning, Justine was glad to climb the stairs with her mother's arm about her waist, glad to be assisted with the fastenings of her dress and tucked in the four-poster bed as if she were a little girl again.

'Will you draw the curtains back, please? I would like to have the sun wake me in the morning.'

'Oh, very well.' Antonia turned out the lamp and did as she was asked. The creamy moonlight poured across the room. 'This will keep you awake,' she said. But Justine was already asleep.

Sleep did not come so easily to Antonia, although she was in active pursuit of it half the night, turning and groping after it through the handsome proportions of her canopied bed. Pointlessly she relived the strenuous efforts of the past few days. The frantic packing in Paris, the Channel crossing, the mislaid luggage and the misunderstood timetables, the eight-hour train journey to Lancaster with a change at Rugby. And all the time one thought was struggling to the surface of her consciousness, a thought she had repeatedly pushed down since the invitation to Clere Athel first arrived. Now it would no longer be denied, and in the sad hours before dawn she lay and wondered whether her father-in-law blamed Lucian for his brother's death.

Now, when it was too late to retreat, she must recall in ever painful detail the occasion on which Athel had come to see them in Paris. War had been declared in South Africa, and Athel had obtained the promise of a commission for his brother in one of the Lancashire regiments. Lucian, refused help when he had asked it and left to go his own way for so many years since, was outraged at this sudden interference in his life. She had not witnessed the scene, but she had heard it. 'Even now after all these years you can't rid yourself of the fear that I might want a piece of your inheritance,' Lucian had roared, and in his anger he had gone on to give the shape of words to feelings better never owned. What a fateful encounter between two brothers that had been, and what vein of Athel's nature had been breached that made him take the commission himself and go to fight the Boers, while Lucian, determined to prove that he could make a fortune in foreign trade, had gone rushing off to book a passage for the Philippine Islands?

Antonia's eyes filled with tears over the futility of it all. The pride and the possession and the unforgiveness. For Lucian had been killed, stabbed as he left some waterfront café for the sake of his wallet and a gold half hunter that had never kept very good time. And Athel had died trying to dislodge a tenacious Dutchman from the top of a barren ridge that neither of them wanted.

CHAPTER TWO

THERE WAS NO GARDEN to the front of the Dower-House. Its carriage sweep, leading off the main avenue through the home park, formed a total circle, and whether or not by design, the effect of the expanse of gravel enhanced the dignity of the house, forcing those who approached to admire its expression of self-sufficiency. At the centre of the gravel circle, a stone mermaid sat desperately marooned upon a rock, listening with rapt face as though to the memory of some sonorous sea.

'It's rather a good piece of sculpture, I think,' Antonia said. 'There's a great deal of expression in the face'

'I don't like it. It's sad.'

'That's because you are very young,' she told Justine. 'There has to be a little sadness in art. Even when the subject is entirely a joyous one, the artist's own yearning for perfection will impose it.'

It was the afternoon of their second day in Clere Athel. The morning had been fully engaged in the supervision of Ellen unpacking their trunks. It had been a morning of much running up and down stairs with armfuls of dresses and skirts and jackets and blouses; a morning of the flat iron and the goffering tongues; a morning of discovering that the hanging cupboards in Antonia's dressing room

22

and the drawers of the dressing chests were haunted by Eugenie Athelson, who had built the Dower House—or rather by her patchouli scent, which the passage of well over a century had failed to extinguish.

'It makes me feel quite sick,' Antonia said. 'I cannot possibly put my clothes in there, Mrs Rimmer. We must give the cupboards a thorough airing and spray them with eau de cologne.'

'Won't do no good, ma'am. I've had them airing for weeks, and Ellen scrubbed them out. Can't understand how it do cling so. Old Athel's mother—begging your pardon, Mrs Athelson, your father-in-law's mother, I should say—when she were here, had pine cones and camphor in 'em because she was mortal worried about moths. That kept the scent down right enough. But after her things were taken away, the scent came back again!'

'Well, really, Mrs Rimmer, we cannot allow ourselves to give in to a perfume distilled before our grandmothers were born. And I decline to accept the smell of camphor as an alternative.'

So now the cupboards and drawers were damp from a fresh scrubbing, and Antonia's clothes hung over screens and chairs in the bedroom, while the dressing room was a battle-ground for the reek of soap and damp wood and the jasmine and eau de cologne that Antonia had splashed liberally in every direction.

'But you mark my words'—Mrs Rimmer shook her head darkly—'that scent'll come up again. It keeps on coming up. My mother knew it in her day here at the Dower, and she used to say as how she had been told it were a concoction brought from Eastern parts. Eugenie had it added to the powder used on her hair, and the powdering was always done in the dressing room. It must have sifted everywhere, into cracks and between the floorboards. We'll never get rid of it!'

There had still been no word from the family so after lunch Antonia and Justine took a brief walk under the great

23

trees flanking the Dower House and came at last to examine the lonely mermaid.

'Eugenie!' said a voice.

'Oh, no!' Antonia turned sharply to stare at the woman who was watching them from the avenue. 'I'm sorry. That sounded very rude. It is just that I have had rather too much of Eugenie for one day.' She walked quickly towards the tall stranger, holding out her hand, and received on it a touch as dry and fragile as a pressed leaf.

'Are you Mrs Athelson?'

'I am Great-Aunt Ivlian.'

'Great-Aunt *Ivlian*,' Antonia said in a voice of determined pleasure. 'Justine—come, my child, and be presented to your Great-Aunt Ivlian.'

The woman gave an impression of vagueness, which was dispelled when she said, 'I see you never heard of me. I thought Lucian might have spoken of me, but no matter. I am Athel Athelson's sister, Lucian's aunt.' She nodded past them to the statue. 'I saw you looking at Eugenie's mermaid. They say she is a symbol. Eugenie was always a fish out of water in this place, and the mermaid was a sort of bitter pun on her own situation. After the building of the Dower House was completed, she spent a year travelling in France and Italy, looking for works of art with which to add the final touches. That was when she brought back the mermaid and decided to put her there as a defiance and a reminder to the Athelsons.'

Antonia frowned. 'We are beginning to feel rather uncomfortable about Eugenie. What did the Athelsons do to her to make her dislike them?'

'I do not believe that *we* did anything,' Great-Aunt Ivlian said, and Justine noticed the odd acceptance of a collective identity. 'I think Eugenie was disillusioned with human relationships before she came here. . . . She was the only child of Lord Carle, you know, and one of the richest brides who ever came to Clere Athel. They say her mother and father detested each other, though, so it is my guess that her childhood had not been happy, and that was what made Eugenie the way she was.'

'And how was she?' Antonia pursued, reluctantly interested.

'Cold,' said Great-Aunt Ivlian. 'Beautiful and bored and cold. She was an unfathomable enigma to the Athelsons all her life. She lived among us for half a century, and still we never knew her. Even her own sons never got close to her. The two older boys—she had three children, all boys—exchanged a number of letters about her which survive. It seems that shortly after her husband died, she announced her intention of building the Dower House and retiring into it for the rest of her life. She was then about forty years of age, and her oldest son had just married. There never was a Dower House at Clere Athel before, and the poor young man could not understand why his mother should want to live by herself when the family home is so large. He pointed out that as his wife was very young and inexperienced in household management, she was looking to Eugenie for guidance. But Eugenie was not persuaded. She had, she said, always disliked the family house and considered a "twenty-year martyrdom to its discomforts outside of enough". Those were her exact words and I fancy I know just how she spoke them.'

'When was this built?'

'Well, it was finished about 1740. I couldn't say how long they took to build it. Of course the labour wasn't local. Called in master craftsmen from all over the country. I always think the architect must have been an extraordinarily sensitive man because in some subtle way the house *suggests* occupation by women, don't you think?'

Antonia nodded. 'Why, yes. A pleasing fancy. A place of women . . . in their quiet years,' she added, and a faint frown shadowed her smooth, pale forehead.

'I must be going,' said Great-Aunt Ivlian suddenly. 'I only came to deliver the message for Cecily.'

'A message from my mother-in-law?'

'Well, she would have come herself. My brother told her

25

to come, but she couldn't leave Barbara. Barbara's in a delicate condition, you know, and it's touch and go because of her age. . . .'

An air of confusion had come over Great-Aunt Ivlian, as though in talking about the present she had lost the ability to marshal her thoughts coherently.

'Indeed I am sorry to hear,' Antonia began, politely concerned, 'er, who is Barbara?'

'Oh, dear, silly of me! Barbara is Cecily's favourite brood-mare. Very valuable and with child . . . I mean, in foal. Cecily really did not want to let her try again, but, well, it's a matter of money. . . . However, Cecily asked me to come in her place to deliver Athel's message. You don't mind, do you?'

Antonia made a dazed attempt to sort out the explanation. 'You mean there is a message for us?'

'Didn't I make that clear at the beginning?' Great-Aunt Ivlian asked somewhat sharply.

'No,' said Justine frankly. 'You didn't. Are we going to meet Grandfather?'

'Certainly,' said Great-Aunt Ivlian with increasing severity. 'Of course, you must meet your grandfather. Should have done so long before now. Should have been born here, come to that.'

Justine was about to protest that she had been given small choice in the matter when Antonia silenced her with a look.

'Are we to expect Athel Athelson to call on us here, then?' she asked.

Great-Aunt Ivlian laughed with a return to good humour. 'No, no, child! Athel would never dream of such a thing! That would be most unfitting. No, you are both to come and dine with us up at the house this evening.'

There was no question of their convenience, Antonia observed. It was not so much an invitation as a summons. For one moment she battled with a desire to refuse, to say the arrangement did not suit her, to announce their imminent departure from Clere Athel, to utter any defiance, however irrational. She choked down the inclination. After all, where was the sense to come this long journey, this long, long journey that was measured in more than miles, only to turn on her heel without a confrontation?

*   *   *

A little governess cart was sent to the Dower House to fetch them at exactly half past seven o'clock. Justine, watching out of one of the windows in her mother's bedroom not knowing what to expect, was charmed. The cart appeared freshly varnished and upholstered, and the boy holding the pony's head winked amiably when he caught sight of her.

'Oh, look, Mother! It's like a pretty toy. Will you drive it yourself?'

'In a dinner gown? Certainly not!' Antonia went back to her dressing table and settled a fan-shaped tortoiseshell comb over the smooth chignon of nut-brown hair at the nape of her neck.

'Are you nearly ready?' Justine asked anxiously. 'We shall be late, you know.'

'It is my intention to be late,' Antonia said firmly.

Mrs Rimmer came in with a spray of pale-pink roses.

'No, those won't do with this dress, I'm afraid.' Antonia shook her head. 'I told Pegger white, Mrs Rimmer, white roses.'

'I know, but Pegger says you'd do better to have these, ma'am—the white roses he got out there, they don't die well!'

'Who does?' Antonia sounded gay, almost reckless. 'Never mind, I won't bother with a corsage.' She stood up and twirled around before the mirror. 'How do I look?'

Mrs Rimmer and Justine stood back to admire the gown of rich coffee-coloured lace with its skirt caught back into an echo of the bustle and the delicate scalloped tracery of the neckline just clinging to Antonia's elegant shoulders.

'My! You look beautiful, ma'am!'

27

'Justine, I'll take my white ostrich fan, I believe. It's such a warm evening again, I shall be glad of it. Look in the drawer of the little inlaid table by the window. There's a flat blue leather case. . . . Ah, yes, there! Now that is just right. The flowers would have been too much.'

'You're going to be terrible late, ma'am.'

'Well, we are ready now. Justine, let me look at you. Perfect! I know of nothing so becoming to a young girl as crisp white taffeta!'

With the pony stepping out briskly up the avenue, it was only a matter of minutes before they had their first view of the home of the Athelsons.

Justine whispered, 'Oh, Mother! Isn't it beautiful,' and unaccountably, Antonia felt herself too moved to answer with a steady voice. It would have been hard to identify the quality in the house that inspired such a response. Antonia supposed vaguely that an architectural purist might have found it outrageous, a historical hotchpotch, a mongrel of many eras. Yet miraculously, differing tastes and times had weathered together, and each new portion had sprung, like a fresh shoot on the old wood of a rose tree, belonging where it grew.

The central part of the house, where the pony came to a knowing halt and they were invited to climb down, was a long, crenellated stone structure, with a heavy iron-studded door set in a vaulted porch. Two deep oriel windows mounted guard over the entrance, and away to the far right a Tudor gable end advanced, with long mullion windows red-gold in the setting sun.

There was no time to take in more, since the wooden door was already in a weighty, opening swing as they alighted and a manservant stood back for them to enter.

'Good evening, ma'am. And Miss Justine. If you would be pleased to follow me.'

They made their way along a wide, panelled corridor and down half a dozen shallow stone steps into a lounge hall, furnished with high-backed settles covered in ageing tapestry and a wealth of armour. A slender silver-haired woman in black lace was standing by the window.

She turned when she heard them and crossed the stone floor with a strong stride that contrasted oddly with her fragile appearance.

'So you are my Lucian's gel, Antonia.' She shook hands as vigorously as she walked. 'Yes, got style. See why he chose you. Lucian, too. He had style. Fine boy. . . . Always liked 'im,' she added as an afterthought. 'And you're Justine. Not like your father. Chip off an older block. Athel will be tickled to death.'

Mrs Athelson's rapid manner of speaking left no opening for the usual introductory courtesies.

'We are so very happy to meet you at last, Grandmother,' Justine said with simple directness. 'We often wondered what you were like.'

'Justine!' Antonia protested.

Cecily Athelson's eyes darted with a sudden, sharp amusement.

'Oh, you did, did you? Well, you're honest, and I don't mind that. But we mustn't stop and talk now, Athel's waiting to see you, Antonia. Alone. Justine can come with me and meet the children. . . . Alfred! Al-fred! Drat the man!' She peered about the room suspiciously. 'He's sure to be listening.' Alfred manifested himself from behind a stone pillar. 'Ah, there you are! Will you take Lucian's wife to Athel Athelson now, please?'

Alfred inclined his head. 'If you will come this way, ma'am. He is expecting you.' He glanced across significantly at Mrs Athelson. 'And to tell you, ma'am, that *he* has ordered dinner put back again.'

'Heaven defend us! I never before remember dinner being held back one minute for anyone who was a member of the family. I don't know whether you should be pleased or alarmed, Antonia.'

The room to which Antonia found herself escorted was the library, and at first glance she thought she was alone in it, noticing only the enormous—and vacant—carved oak chair at the head of a long table and recognizing it as an exact partner to one she had seen in the hall.

She walked forward into the room, and a voice spoke startlingly behind her.

'You are very late!'

It was a voice accustomed to be heard and attended, not loud, yet somehow identifiably arrogant.

Antonia forced herself to turn slowly to face her father-in-law and with the same control made herself regard him steadily, determined not to show how thoroughly he had cheated her expectations.

Old Athel they called him. Antonia did not know how old he was, but he had to be in his seventies. And it had not seemed unreasonable to presume that he would be a little stooped perhaps, a little infirm, a little crabbed and short-sighted, in short a little like the grandfathers of one's general acquaintance, like other people's grandfathers. Only Justine's paternal grandfather had to stand about six feet four inches tall, a broad-shouldered, powerful man with coarse-textured hair and beard of a handsome greying gold, close-cut to subdue the thick springing curl.

'So! You are Antonia,' he said, drawing the name out lingeringly. 'This is the face that launched Lucian into disobedience and robbed me of my Athel in his prime. . . .'

Antonia stiffened, resenting the strange greeting, yet uncertain of its tone. Was it an accusation or an attempt at raillery from a man without taste or sensitivity? She could not bring herself to answer directly. But neither could she permit herself the social gaucherie of standing there, tongue-tied, while the minutes ticked by in the heavy silence.

'I have brought Justine to see you as you asked.'

'You think I am a rude old man.' It was not a question but a statement, and the voice carried not the slightest shade of interest in her opinion. 'Come, sit here across the table from me.' He signalled her abruptly to a chair. 'You

30

did not think we two could meet without there being something to be said of Lucian and Athel?'

Antonia felt confused. These Athelsons. Really, they were far worse than she had imagined. She stammered, 'Why, of—of course I h-had expected we would speak of Lucian but——'

'My way is to come at the heart of the matter without hesitation. I asked you here because I want my family about me. Is that wrong for an old man—to want his grandchildren about him?' He did not wait for her answer. 'But I must know what manner of woman you are, because you are Justine's mother and the wife of a son who brought much grief upon me. I want to know about Lucian. I have waited a long time for the answers to questions that plague me.'

'What questions? If you had questions to ask about Lucian, why did you not write to me? I would have told you whatever you wanted to know if it was in my power.'

'Would you? I wonder. I wonder if you will tell me the truth even now. Will you tell me what happened when Athel came to see you and Lucian in Paris? Will you tell me what it was Lucian said that made Athel go in his place to fight the Boers?'

Antonia could find the courage to answer back at last. 'I think you are being unjust to Lucian. Why was it his place to go and fight the Boers? Lucian had decided to leave the army long before he met me. He had never been able to manage on his pay, as you must very well have known, and he believed he would do better in business.'

'Business! Lucian! Pah! Well, we know where that led.'

'For a time he was very successful.'

'He wrote to me to pay his debts!'

'That was when he was getting started and he had been a little . . . a little unlucky. But he didn't want to go back in the army.'

'He should never have left it. What did he expect me to do? He knew I hadn't any money, never have. Sophie's uncle was prepared to give him a commission, and in wartime

31

he could have got promotion quicker, better pay. Might have made a splendid army career.'

'He didn't want an army career,' Antonia said, exasperated. 'He wasn't a little boy any longer; he didn't want to be ordered about.'

'Well, what did he say to Athel that made him come bolting back here like a man demented and then dash off to South Africa? Athel was a farmer, not a soldier. He knew nothing of fighting and wanted nothing of glory. And he would never have gone to fight other farmers in South Africa, but for some mighty dreadful words of Lucian's. You were there—what passed between them?'

'I was not there . . . at least I was not in the room with them all the time they talked.'

'But they quarrelled . . . you must have known they quarrelled?'

Antonia said hesitantly, 'I knew there had been some unpleasantness, yes. But Lucian didn't want to talk about it afterwards. He told me only what you know. About the offer of a commission in one of the Lancashire regiments and that he had refused.'

Old Athel's eyes, grey as a frozen sea, flickered over her with renewed intensity. 'You are not being truthful with me, woman. Do you think I don't know my own sons? If they had hard words, voices would be raised. You must have heard something.'

Antonia had a sudden urge to strike back. 'Very well, then. I do not understand why you should want me to put into words what you cannot fail to have guessed. It is painful to me, it is painful to you, I am sure. But I will tell you Lucian's parting words to Athel. He said, "Clere Athel has always stood between us. Go back there! I am disinherited, but I will be free to live my own life".'

'So!' Old Athel sighed, and the cold eyes were turned from her towards the window and who knew what distant vision. 'It is, as you say, what I already knew. . . . I had no brother to resent my birthright, but this land must have come between brothers before. Perhaps Lucian always resented Athel, but you'd never have known it when he was a lad.' He shook his head. 'Well, well. What's done is done. God alone knows what Athel hoped to prove by joining the army. When he left you in Paris, he came back here a stranger to us, bitter and silent. I couldn't talk to him, couldn't reason with him. I blamed Lucian in my heart then, cursed him. And in the act of cursing him I get a letter from you telling me he had been robbed and murdered in a back street of some South Sea port. How do you think I felt then?'

Antonia shook her head, hopelessly. 'I don't know, I don't know.'

'Within a matter of months Athel was killed in action. You think it was a judgement?' He darted the question at her suspiciously.

'No, of course not!'

He nodded. 'You're right. We must not look for the hand of God in every human accident.' He stood up. 'Athel has left sons. Life goes on.'

Antonia looked at him doubtfully, rising to accept the arm which he now offered her with unexpected grace.

'I am at a loss, sir, to know why you wanted me to come and make my home here.' She spoke hesitantly. 'It may be as well after all if we do not stay above a few days.'

'Nonsense. Where else should you be? This could have been your home from the time of your marriage. If Lucian had been overseas with the army, I should have expected you, at least, to make this Justine's childhood home.'

'She is no longer a child, however.'

'Indeed! Is to be fifteen to be a woman?'

Antonia smiled slightly for the first time.

'Not quite.'

'Then it is "not quite" too late to make amends. Come, we will go in to dinner.'

As they made their way along the wide stone-flagged passage, Antonia was aware of a bowing footman, who turned to pull a bell rope as they passed.

'Heavens, what is that!' She had been unprepared for the sudden shudder of roof and walls under the weight of four great strokes from a bell directly overhead.

'Do not be alarmed. They call that bell the Voice of Old Athel. It tells my people I am going to my dinner. If they are out in the fields, they say, 'There's Old Athel gone to table; time I turned for home too," or the man who's just sat down to table says, "Come on, woman, dish up! If Old Athel's eating, why aren't I?"'

Antonia looked at him curiously, wondering at a man so arrogant and autocratic, who could drop effortlessly into the homely dialect and idiom of his farm labourers.

They could hear voices now and the soft chink of cutlery and glass. Around yet another turn in the wandering passage and they came to an arched doorway with double doors standing open. Antonia hesitated, unconsciously tightening her grip on Old Athel's arm, as the eyes of the company turned towards them.

'What's to do? It's only the family, y'know.' He patted the hand on his arm reassuringly, as he led her to a seat at his left hand. 'Now then, everybody, introductions while they serve the soup. Alfred! About your business, man, I'm famished.'

At the head of table, Old Athel occupied one of the throne-like chairs, which seemed to be set in every room of the house, while his wife took her place at the opposite end with Sophie, Athel's widow, at her right hand and a clergyman on her left.

Next to Sophie there was a grim-mouthed man. Antonia felt sure he *was* a stranger to her, and yet there was a stirring in her memory.

Then, for the first time, her attention was drawn to the boy standing beside his chair, directly opposite her.

'Antonia,' her father-in-law was saying, 'allow me to present my heir. This is young Athel. What do you think of him?'

Antonia stared. 'It's incredible. He could be Justine's brother!'

34

Old Athel nodded down the table to where Justine was sitting. 'I see that. Go on, boy, go and stand beside your cousin.'

Athel walked around the table and stood behind Justine's chair. The same straight, thick, wheat-coloured hair, the same level grey eyes, even the same carriage of the head.

The company considered them gravely.

Then Old Athel threw back his head, and the roar of his laughter contracted the vast room about them.

'Come to me!' He threw his arms wide. 'Come to your grandfather, my children.'

In any other man it might have seemed extravagant, but not this man. And Antonia saw with surprise and some prickling resentment that Justine, who was never demonstrative in the usual way, ran willingly to share the embrace with her cousin.

'There now,' Old Athel said, kissing Justine soundly and slapping his grandson affectionately on the back, 'away to your seats.'

Between courses Antonia talked to the amiable boy next to her. This was Hugh, Sophie's second son, not yet fourteen but well endowed with the Athelson assurance. Antonia noted with private amusement the way he divided his attentions scrupulously between Justine on his left and herself on the right.

The dinner progressed in a unique blend of ease and almost lordly formality, six footmen waiting with silent skill and Alfred, a field marshal, summoning reinforcements from the kitchen and cellar, here bridling impetuous game pies seeking to assault the company before their time or there loosing a salvo of champagne corks with the signal of an eyebrow.

While they ate, Old Athel continued in an offhand manner to make Antonia acquainted with the company. Sophie's daughter, Charlotte, sitting next to her brother Athel, was acknowledged to be only twelve years old and allowed at the dinner table in token of the occasion. The gentleman of stern expression, who listened more than he talked, was introduced as Fenn Haldane.

'Think well of him, Antonia. Fenn's our steward, and more to us than that, eh, Fenn?' Old Athel said—an observation which seemed to amuse the entire table and even won some knowing reverberations beyond the swinging baize doors that led to the kitchen.

The clergyman was the Reverend Cuthbert Rainbird, Cecily's third cousin, who tutored the children in addition to his pastoral duties at Clere Athel.

'They take their lessons from nine to twelve in the mornings,' Cecily Athelson put in, 'and I know my cousin would be pleased to instruct Justine, too, if you should wish it.'

'Yes, indeed, Cousin Antonia,' Cuthbert Rainbird said earnestly. 'It would be most gratifying to have another pupil.'

'What does Justine say, though?' Old Athel wanted to know. 'Perhaps she don't want to do lessons. Perhaps she's had enough of being cooped up over schoolbooks, eh? You wrote me that you'd put her to school in Paris some time back, did you not, Antonia?'

'That is so. Justine attended classes at a convent near——'

A sudden stifled shriek from Great-Aunt Ivlian froze the company.

'Now what the devil was that?' Old Athel demanded in a voice of thunder, deliberately looking the other way as his sister rose in confusion and distress. The next instant Great-Aunt Ivlian had whisked herself so precipitously out of the room that only the napkin she dropped in the middle of the polished oak floor could testify to her ever having been there at all.

Antonia, bewildered, looked to her mother-in-law for some explanation and was surprised when she put a warning finger to her lips.

Old Athel's eyes scanned them suspiciously. 'Must have been one of your damned peacocks, Cecily.'

'No,' said Hugh, 'it came from Cousin Cuthbert's pigeon pattie! When he stuck his fork into it.'

'Shut up, Hugh,' his brother told him.

Charlotte giggled uneasily.

'I think,' Cecily Athelson concluded, 'that if Sophie and Antonia are ready, we will leave you menfolk to your savouries and dessert and go and take our coffee where we can look on the garden.'

The silent footmen stepped forward to move back their chairs for them and the men stood with raised glasses while the women left the dining room.

'Walk with me, Antonia. And Justine. You will need to know about Ivlian if you remain at Clere Athel.'

Cecily Athelson led them into the summer room which looked out on to a paved walk and lawns sloping down to a small lake.

'Can't sit in here beyond September. Catch your death! None of the confounded windows fit. Always on to Athel about it, but he just says choose another room to sit in. After all, got plenty of rooms but no money to change the windows. Logical,' Cecily admitted.

The coffee was ceremoniously borne in by one of the footmen, and Antonia noticed, now that they had the last of the daylight as well as candles, that his livery was threadbare. Yet it was hard to reconcile the monstrous weight of Queen Anne silver he supported with the frayed cuffs or balance the draughty windows against the number of servants one sensed as well as saw about the house.

'That's all right, Warrener, you may go. Sophie, will you pour the coffee? And, Charlotte, you may kiss me and go to bed. Good night, child.'

Charlotte made a dutiful round of kisses and left them.

'And now,' Cecily Athelson continued, 'about Ivlian——'

'Is it'—Antonia interrupted delicately—'is it suitable for Justine to hear?'

Cecily chuckled. 'Think you're going to be shocked, do you? No, nothing like that. Damned silly business, really. Sort of situation only the Athelsons could get themselves into. Quite puts me out of patience!'

'But, Grandmother, you're an Athelson,' Justine said, laughing.

'Nonsense! I'm a Hamlack. Got more sense. Anyway, don't interrupt, child. As I was saying, when Ivlian was young, she really was quite handsome. Athelson women are never pretty, carry too much of the family likeness, but often handsome. Wealthy husband found for her, doting young man, only son, good North Lancashire family. Name the day. Only she wouldn't!' Cecily paused to sip her coffee.

'Name the day,' Sophie supplied helpfully.

'Thank you, Sophie, I can tell the story without your assistance. . . . Well, as I was saying. . . . It seems Ivlian had been reading a book about some young woman who threw up the chance of a happy marriage in order to enter a convent. Guess the rest.'

'You mean she actually entered a convent? Then that's why when I said "convent"—' Antonia looked astonished. 'But the Athelsons——'

'Aren't Roman Catholic,' Sophie said and then clapped her hand over her mouth.

Cecily Athelson's eyes riveted her accusingly. 'Now you're doing it to Antonia. Really, it's an abominable habit, Sophie. Do try to curb it. Pour more coffee. . . . Yes, Antonia, she did. Her father was dead, but Athel did everything possible to stop her. Argued, bullied, raged. No good. Ivlian locked herself in her room. Refused food. Very stubborn, you know. Wouldn't think it to look at her. But just like her brother underneath. In the end he had to let her go. Went rushing off to Ireland and, as if that weren't enough, took the bulk of her mother's jewelry with her and handed it over as a dowry. Have to have some sort of dowry to get into a convent, apparently.'

'Yes,' said Antonia, 'so I understand. But if she went into a convent, what's she doing here? Didn't they think she was suitable?'

'Don't know about that. Might have been Mother Superior by now if she'd stuck it, but she didn't.'

'Stick it?' Justine asked.

'My God, is Sophie's habit catching?' Cecily said irritably. Sophie giggled. 'I think it's the way you talk, Grandmother.'

Cecily glared at her. 'So back home Ivlian came. Only by this time her rich suitor had married someone else, and she hadn't bargained with Athel keeping so strictly by his word. You see, before she went. Athel told her, once inside the convent she was dead to him. He would have *no* sister. When she returned to Clere Athel, he ignored her. He just looked straight through her as though she weren't here.'

'But how very cruel,' Antonia said.

'Well, I think at first he was only waiting for her to say she was sorry she'd defied him and that she had been wrong. Only she never would say that. After a while it became a habit. He pretends she doesn't exist and refuses to listen when anyone mentions her.'

'And for how many years has he maintained this—this charade?' Antonia wanted to know.

'Oh, let's see . . . she's the same age as me . . . going on fifty years, I suppose.'

'It's inhuman.' Antonia shook her head.

'Well, I must say it doesn't seem to bother Ivlian very much. Of course, I've tried over the years to get them reconnected as it were. Useless. To tell the truth, I think they both enjoy it now. Ivlian rather fancies herself as a tragic heroine and Athel—why, it's enough for Athel that he's never given in.'

'I noticed Grandfather never introduced Great-Aunt Ivlian at table,' Justine said slowly. 'I thought it was because he must have found out we'd met.'

'No. Always like that. Never would introduce her to anyone. As far as he's concerned, she simply isn't there.'

'We have a terrible time squeezing money for her clothes out of our allowances.' Sophie sighed. 'She doesn't have any money of her own, of course, and the convent kept the jewelry, since she never liked to ask for it back.'

Antonia set her coffee cup down delicately. 'Forgive me . . . I should most dislike to give offence . . . but I wish I understood the . . . circumstances of the Athelsons more precisely.'

Neither Cecily nor Sophie seemed offended, so she continued more confidently. 'It would seem to an outsider that you live in a very grand manner for these modern times, and yet——'

'Feudal,' Cecily said, 'it's the feudal principle. The Athelsons are still trying to live by it. Kept it going about four hundred years longer than anyone else. Got to give them that.'

'But I remember Lucian told me that every inch of Clere Athel belonged to the family and all the farmers were tenants. Surely the income from rents must be considerable?'

'Rents?' Cecily smiled faintly. 'They are paid in kind and in labour for the most part. Oh, yes, we are rich in butter and milk, cheeses and eggs, and pork and poultry and vegetables and fruit. We also have a considerable credit balance of work-hours from carpenters, ditch-diggers, and seamstresses. We should have done very well in the Middle Ages, I don't doubt. But in the year 1903 one needs money, and money is what we lack.'

'Yes, you see, Antonia, the only income in cash is from a tiny capital investment or the surplus produce from the home park, which goes to the nearest market. And Cecily's horses . . . when she can be persuaded to sell any of them,' Sophie explained with a sidelong glance at her mother-in-law. 'In the past money has come into the family through marriage. Eugenie's inheritance lasted for the better part of a century after her death in the 1770's, and then later there was my portion. All gone now.'

She shook her head.

'The Athelsons must have consumed a great many heiresses over the centuries,' Antonia said dryly.

'Not at all,' Cecily retorted. 'It is precisely because they have not consistently hunted fortunes that the family is in its present plight. The criterion for any Athelson bride has always been a good old English bloodline, sound in body and mind. It's what kept 'em going. Never a barren woman in a thousand years. Father to son, father to son, it has gone. Or father to second son in the case of accident. Same with horses. Bloodstock. That's what counts.'

'Grandmother, herself, had no dowry at all, did you?' Sophie prompted eagerly.

Cecily chuckled.

'Never a single penny. You might even say that I won Old Athel in a wager. But that's another story.' She frowned reflectively. 'Mark you, I had my inheritance later on. M'father left me the finest stallion in Yorkshire and three mares.'

Alfred, announcing the arrival of the men of the party, put an end to any further revelations and left Antonia in two minds whether she was glad or sorry that she had no fortune to pour into the Athelson coffers. Since these must be insatiable, it was probably just as well she had not. Yet the thought of Old Athel, grateful and humbled, was an undeniably pleasurable daydream.

The next few minutes shamed this unworthy speculation. Her father-in-law joined her immediately and set himself to please with questions after her comfort at the Dower House. Did she find Mrs Rimmer satisfactory? Would she like to alter any of the household arrangements there? Had she a fancy to play croquet, because if so he would immediately order a lawn to be rolled on the parkland alongside the Dower?

More coffee was served, this time with a rare old liqueur brought up from the cherished cellar by a triumphant Alfred. Old Athel considered the bottle, venerable with cobwebs and pendant seals.

'Ah, yes. You will like this, Antonia. It is like liquid moonbeams in the glass. I brought it back to England myself from ... from ... devil take it! Where did I get this stuff from, Alfred? Well, anyway it was one of those benighted middle European countries.'

'Indeed!' Antonia was curious. 'I had no idea you had travelled in Europe.'

'Oh, my father had a notion I should make the grand tour, y'know. Complete waste of time and money, of course.'

'Surely not! You must have seen many memorable sights.

I think travel is an excellent experience,' Antonia suggested agreeably.

'Smelled a great many memorable smells, I can tell you that! Yes, indeed. That's what has stayed clearest in my mind, the stink of some of those foreign inns upon the road. . . . You speak to me about the gaiety of France, and I will tell you about the sullen peasants I saw, hardly raised above the level of the wasted beasts grubbing on their poor, wasted land. . . . Talk to me of the great art treasures of Italy, of Florence and Rome, and I can remember only the pitiful children, clawing beggars waiting for a coin or a kick in the garbage at your feet. . . . Well, I saw it and I came back to Clere Athel and rejoiced in our land, which is sturdy and healthy like our people. I gave thanks that no woman was dishonoured in order that she might feed a family, no man brought so low that he must beg, no child unclaimed.' All the company had fallen silent to listen to him, and seeing this, Old Athel checked himself with a sudden laugh. 'There now! I have fallen into the grave social error of speaking from the heart—I have done worse, I have made a speech. Antonia, you must forgive an old man, who forgets his manners.' He waved Alfred forward to refill their glasses. 'Come, let us drink a toast. Cousin Cuthbert, you have said little enough all evening—call a toast to fit the occasion.'

The Reverend Cuthbert Rainbird, Antonia was pleased to note, had a merry eye. He advanced the ample proportions bestowed by fifty years of good, if somewhat secularly self-indulgent, living to the middle of the room and performed a graceful pirouette.

'Ladies, gentlemen, I ask you please to raise your glasses to the grace and beauty which newly adorn our company. To Antonia and Justine. May we deserve the favour of their long continuing presence among us.'

'Well said!' Old Athel nodded. 'And now let us have some music. Antonia, do you play upon the pianoforte? Come, I am very sure you do.' He led her to a handsome rosewood instrument and folded back the lid from the keys. 'This used to be my mother's greatest treasure, and it has been kept well tuned, I understand.'

Antonia seated herself on the embroidered bench seat and fingered the keys tentatively.

'What would you like me to play?'

'Well, let me see. . . . Suppose I were to permit myself the luxury of another cigar and I stepped through those doors to watch the last of the light fall across the surface of the lake what would be sweetest to hear?'

Antonia smiled.

'Something by Brahms—this perhaps. . . .'

She loosed a soft fall of golden melody, and Old Athel nodded, satisfied, passing out through the long windows.

Antonia played well, losing herself in the music, scarcely aware that Young Athel had set candles beside her, wandering from one theme into another as she explored her own mood. How strange that she should be here, in Lucian's childhood home, surrounded by his family, making music at the whim of this singular man who was his father. Lucian had liked Brahms, liked to hear it, as now, in the dusk at the end of a quiet day, and sometimes they had laughed together to think they were rehearsing how it would be when they were an old, old couple. There had not been so many of those quiet evenings. Life in Paris had been too diverting, and Lucian, who had said, 'We will never be middle-aged, but one day we will be venerable,' had left the party unexpectedly early. Suddenly irritated with herself, recognizing that she was deliberately invoking painful memories. Antonia allowed the piece she was engaged on to wind away under her fingers to its close.

And Alfred, entering purposefully at that moment, broke the spell, which appeared to have extended over everyone in the room. He was followed by a footman, who lit more candles, and brought Athel Athelson the terse message that Old Tom had something to say to him.

'Old Tom? What's to do, then? Bring him in.'

'He says he's not fit for company.'

'What company? This is family. Bring him in.'

43

When the man came, Antonia was bound to agree with his own assessment. He was not fit for company. Yet no one except herself appeared to have the smallest concern for the silky Persian rugs under his sand-caked thigh boots or to find anything unacceptable about the ragged shirt and knotted neckerchief, the unkempt beard, and harsh sea smell of the man.

'Come in, man, come in,' Old Athel greeted him, strong and warm. 'Never say you've walked up from the Moss?'

Old Tom nodded gravely.

'Then you're a fool,' Cecily Hamlack told him roundly. 'You've no business trekking such a way on that leg.'

'Come to tell you about the hay.' Old Tom glared back at her. 'Dorrie Latchitt's youngest was along after drift and says you reckoned to have done with t'hay on Monday.'

'Aye, well what of it? Won't it do?'

'No, thee mun do it tomorrer, or thee'll likely lose it. There's devil o' rain on t'way.'

Old Athel thought with a deep scowl.

'Right then! We'll have every man out tomorrow. Alfred!' Alfred was waiting. 'Have you got Jed there? Good. Tell him to go down for a sup as usual and turn them off early to their beds. Pass on what Old Tom says.'

'I'll come up again in t'morning and help thatch.'

'You will not,' said Cecily quickly. 'You'll stay the night here.'

'Ah, reet you are then. I'll sleep over t'stable.'

'You can have a bed like a Christian man for once.'

'Not on thee life. Alfred's woman won't have yon dog in t'house. And where I go, that dog go.'

'Daft old thing!' said Cecily severely.

Old Tom's fierce light eyes crinkled suddenly in his gaunt, weathered face. 'By heaven, Cecily Hamlack, Old Athel's never tamed thy tongue, has he?' Without another word he nodded to the company and limped out of the room.

The tone of this exchange was so unlike anything within the scope of her experience that Antonia resolved to ignore

44

it altogether and remarked to Cuthbert Rainbird that as it was Sunday next day, she looked forward to hearing him preach.

This, however, was not the way to turn the conversation.

'There'll only be the womenfolk in church, then, Cuthbert,' Old Athel said.

Cuthbert accepted this complacently. 'The Lord will not begrudge you the harvesting of His gift.'

'Anyway, if He wanted us in church tomorrow, He would have kept the rain off until Tuesday,' Hugh said, looking particularly cheerful at the prospect of a day in the fields.

'Perhaps He will,' Justine suggested.

'No.' Hugh shook his head. 'Old Tom's never wrong. He lives in a hut down on the Moss, and he reads the signs from the sea and the sky and the birds.'

'Where is the Moss?' Justine was intrigued. 'It sounds . . . eerie.'

'That's what we call the land that used to be a tidal marsh. You must have driven across it on the old pier road when you came. We'll take you there. We often go, and Old Tom tells us terrific yarns about the days when people used to get sucked down into the mud and were never seen again.'

Antonia's face tightened with disapproval. 'I really don't think . . . that is, Justine——'

'Oh, don't worry, Aunt Antonia,' Young Athel said quickly. 'We won't take Justine anywhere that isn't safe. Charlotte comes with us when we ride down to the shore, and we're used to taking care of her. Besides, it isn't a marsh any longer. The stories Tom tells are generations old.'

'But the sign on the road,' Justine broke in, puzzled, 'that said DANGEROUS MARSH and it looked, well, quite new somehow?'

Her cousins laughed.

'Ask Grandfather!'

Old Athel drew down his thick brows in mock ferocity, but his eyes betrayed his amusement, and there was a chuckle in his voice when he said, 'Let alone, impertinent young puppies! Don't you think it fitting I should warn strangers who might chance on my land?'

'Aye, warn them off,' Athel said, looking at his grandfather very straight.

'And will you not do the same when your time comes?' Old Athel growled. 'We don't want every jack rover, every footloose vagabond on the highway to come among our people, do we?'

Justine watched the exchange with interest. There was something here, said and not said. A sense of conflict. But that was only on the surface. Adolescence is a good time for listening to the meaning behind the words, and perhaps Justine alone confidently judged the deeper understanding that flowed between her grandfather and her cousin.

Antonia certainly was not aware of it. For her, the evening had been discomforting, even painful. She was accustomed to the protection of more conventional manners, and the directness of the Athelsons seemed outrageous—almost a physical assault. She did not know where this exchange between the old man and the young one was leading, but there had been revelations enough for one encounter with her husband's family.

'Justine, my dear, I believe you are looking tired. I think we must ask your grandmother to excuse us.'

Cecily Hamlack nodded, her sharp eyes understanding.

'Do you hear, Athel? Antonia says she's ready to leave.'

'Eh? Oh, yes, to be sure.' He turned to Antonia with quick approval. 'There's no good comes out of keeping late hours. You may be sure we do not keep late hours here in the country. The land requires more sense of a man. Will you want the cart? It's a fair night, and you'll have Cousin Cuthbert to light the way for you if you've a mind to walk along the avenue.'

'Not that I am personally incandescent, you understand'—Cuthbert Rainbird made his little joke apologetically—'but I shall be most happy to carry a lantern for you.'

Antonia gladly agreed to this arrangement, wanting only to

46

be away as soon as possible. And since Old Athel was clearly anxious to break up the party, she escaped thankfully on Cousin Rainbird's arm, down the warm, earth-scented cavern of the tree-lined drive, heedless of the gravel underfoot tearing her satin pumps to shreds.

Part Two

CHAPTER ONE

IN THE DAYS THAT FOLLOWED, my mother did her best to understand and adjust herself to the ways of my father's family—or so she is clearly going to maintain for the rest of her life. And I am not going to judge her because she failed. There is something exotic about my mother. She is lovable, gay, witty, accomplished, and elegant. She needs to be cherished and admired. Now that I am grown up, I can see why it was inevitable she should hate everything about Clere Athel. Perhaps she is even right when she says it would have killed her if she had stayed there.

But for me it was quite different. Clere Athel—such a place. Good land. Generations past counting have worked it and lived off it. Men have poured out their sweat and their tears and their seed upon it like ardent lovers, and in the spring they lift handfuls of the fine, rich tilth and fondle it with languorous eyes.

Yes, the men of Clere Athel are all alike. They are in thrall to broad fields and the drills in the vegetable garden. They test their manhood on these acres and are not found wanting, and they pity lesser men who work at barren trades and sire no harvest at the end of the long, sensual summer.

The place they are settled is locked off on the landward side by the encircling arm of the pine forest. There is just the one

51

road in, to the south, where the land is low-lying about the marsh. But the ground rises through the village, gentle and easy, until it climbs a hill where Godwin's field hangs like a carpet upon a wall. The main street is cobbled and runs between two rows of cottages. Five large farms and ten small-holdings lie tucked away up cart tracks that tunnel through sprawling hedges of maythorn. They are great hedgers here on the northwest coast of England. They know the strong arm of the prevailing wind and set thorn slips to a broken hedge as soon as they see it. For the same reason a man will prize a span of beech or elm on his boundary and, provident for the future, replaces what is lost by storm and time.

The fast-flowing stream they call Little Rip waters the cattle in the meadows, feeds the ditches and the village duck pond, and finds its way out to sea at last by the channel it has scored across a mile-wide shelf of sand. It was once possible to sail a fishing boat out from Clere Athel, but the tide has built a barrier in its own path over the centuries and can no longer climb it. Only the old men and children still net shrimps from a rowboat or dig for cockles in the wet sand. For the rest, they have turned their backs on the sea. They smell the salt in the wind, but they are realistic. Those days are done with, they say. And it is only the land that matters to them now.

I understand that very well. I believe I must have been born understanding it, for my early experience of the earth and what grows in it was limited to the gardens of the Tuileries, which was close to our Paris home, and an occasional visit to the Jardin des Plantes. But though no acre of Clere Athel has ever belonged to me, yet I have such a passion for the place. I know I am a part of the people there and they of me. I knew this the first time I saw Clere Athel. I felt I had come home.

Although I never saw much of my father when he was alive, I think that after he died, I was lonely. Perhaps I was just at the age of self-recognition, and being more than ever alone in my mother's company, I sensed that we were not as alike as I wanted us to be.

I began to be afraid that I was not a credit to her. When I looked in the mirror, I saw that I was very fair, very pale, rather tall, and rather plain. A line from something I had read ran in my mind: 'She is not pretty and she wears no rouge.' I used to wonder if when I was a woman, I at least might try the benefits of rouge. It was in this mood of self-doubt and in my fifteenth year that I began my life at Clere Athel.

Looking back now, I cannot recall much of that first summer, except how happy I was. Cecily Hamlack gave me a sturdy little mare to ride, and Athel and Hugh and Charlotte and I would gallop across the fields and down along the shore as though we had harnessed the northwest wind that blew in over the sea. I remember the first time I climbed on this mare —she was a grey and her name was Cobweb—and Athel, who was alongside me, said with deceptive politeness, 'You did say you had done some riding before, didn't you, Justine?'

'Certainly,' I replied firmly, thinking of the sedate morning canters I had taken in company with other girls from the convent school.

'Good! Then off you go!' Athel cried, and brought his hand down with such a thwack on Cobweb's hindquarters that she was startled into a bolt. 'You did say you could ride,' Athel shouted after me.

'Never like this,' I thought, desperately scrambling about for the stirrups and reins. By the time I had struggled into an upright position we had reached the edge of the home park, and there was this great dense hedge looming up. I had never been over a jump in my life, but I instinctively leaned forward on Cobweb's neck. Heaven alone knows what would have happened if she had jumped the hedge. She thought about it. I felt her check fleetingly and then lengthen her stride. But she was a canny mare, and I am thankful to say that she solved her problem by charging straight through it instead and, without animosity, deposited me scratched and torn on the other side.

I was still lying there when the others rode up and peered

53

anxiously over the broken hedge. And Grandmother was with them, scolding Athel.

'I saw everything, you stupid boy. How could you do such a thing? You know how dangerous it is for a horse to jump with an inexperienced rider. Cobweb could so easily have been lying there now with a broken leg!'

'Or Justine could have broken her neck,' Charlotte pointed out in her solemn, practical way.

'Yes . . . even that,' conceded my grandmother, the thought not having previously occurred to her.

Athel helped me up and worried over my scratched face and bruised, shaking limbs, while the others comforted the trembling Cobweb. Athel's expression was so contrite that I could not be angry with him, and it was all I could do to stop him from carrying me back to the house. He couldn't do enough to make amends. Athel was always like that. He could be thoughtless; he could be unbelievably arrogant; sometimes he could even be cruel. But there was a largeness about his nature, and he knew how to be handsome in apology, which is not a general virtue.

Anyway, after that Cobweb and I arrived at a good understanding. She knew my inadequacies, and when the others took a fence or a hedge, she learned to look for a gate. In time we had a well worked-over route of our own, and since she was fast-paced and surefooted, we kept up pretty well, even gaining some advantage in the loose sand of the dunes, or when we made our way across the stones of a shallow stream bed.

And so the days slipped by, easy, sunny days, into autumn. I suppose it is commonplace to say this of one's childhood. To see the time spent waiting to be an adult as a continuous stream making islands of small events. Every morning between nine and twelve we took our lessons with Cousin Cuthbert. I usually breakfasted with my mother in her room, and then I walked up to the house, unless it was raining, when the governess cart was sent to fetch me. I went back to the Dower to lunch with my mother.

The afternoons we spent in a variety of ways. At first we nearly always rode out together, Athel, Hugh, and Charlotte calling for me, with Athel leading my mare. But, increasingly, Grandfather wanted Athel to spend the afternoons with him on estate business, and I imagine Hugh became fed up at being left to tag after a pair of girls, for he very soon left us and went to work with the Hamlack horses.

Mother did not care much for riding. In her opinion the only civilized forms of exercise for a lady were a stately promenade on a fashionable thoroughfare and a drive in a well-sprung carriage. She could have neither at Clere Athel. The promising discovery that there was a very reasonable-looking landau in the coach house remained unfulfilled.

'Thee can't tak it on't road,' Harry Thorpe had said, relishing his bad tidings when my mother spoke to him.

'Why not?'

'There's work needs to be done on it. T'aint in right trim.'

'Well, it doesn't look as if there is much the matter with it to me. Can't you mend it?'

'I can, and then again I canna. There's smithy work needed for one thing, and smithy time's money.'

It was a fact of life that one soon learned at Clere Athel. Grandfather disliked any project which involved the services of the blacksmith, Bartholomew Tyte. And for the very sound reason that alone among the men of Clere Athel, Bartholomew Tyte insisted on being paid in good, hard coin for his work.

'Tyte by name, tightfisted by nature,' Grandfather would snarl at him in their recurring confrontations. But it was no use. The smith had small premises and considered he met his rent amply by keeping the Athelson horses shod without charge. Other work had to be paid for, and he would not accept produce as a fee.

'The labourer is worthy of his hire,' he would roar back, a mountain of a man, standing toe to toe with Old Athel. 'I'm a good craftsman. I sweat blood over my fire to keep your old farm tools hanging together. And how I do it I'll never know, for tha's been needing new ones for forty years nor more.

Sometimes I have to take a fowl or two from other folks hereabouts, for they've no' but that to give me. But I'll not barter wi' thee! Thee'll give me brass or thee'll do the work theeself!'

I never saw any man in the village stand up to Grandfather as Bartholomew Tyte could. But then in a community like Clere Athel, which aims at being largely self-supporting, a skilful worker of metals knows his value right enough. Not a farm tool, or a cooking pot, or a door latch on the estate, I daresay, but surrendered themselves sooner or later to his anvil.

My mother did not easily give up hope of getting the landau repaired, even when the subtleties of the relationship between Grandfather and the blacksmith had been explained to her. Finally, she asked Old Athel outright if she could have the use of it. He countered by suggesting that the old travelling carriage—the same museum piece which had first brought us to Clere Athel—would do very well if she wanted to make a journey and that she might have the horses put to whenever she chose. Gently persistent, my mother said that she did not feel the travelling carriage was at all the thing for driving about the countryside.

'Driving about the countryside!' Grandfather was outraged. 'You surely don't want to tire a pair of horses just driving about the countryside? Well, let me tell you, Antonia, folks hereabouts either go somewhere or they stop at home where they belong.'

Unexpectedly Aunt Sophie found the courage to support my mother and said that she, too, would enjoy the use of the landau.

'We might take Justine and Charlotte on an outing occasionally. It would do the girls good to get beyond the limits of Clere Athel just once in a while.' But this wistful appeal had only the effect of strengthening Grandfather's opposition.

'No, no. It won't do. Now if you tell me there are some women's folderols you need to buy, then drive into Lancaster by all means, and the old carriage will serve very well. Indeed,

56

if you wait a week or two, I will escort you myself, like as not. I could do with seeing m'tailor. . . . But let you go gallivanting off like a cartload of gypsies for folks to stare at in every highway and byway? No, the devil I will!'

'Your mother used to do it,' Cecily Hamlack countered. 'That's what she bought the landau for. Drivin'.'

Old Athel glared at her. 'Things were different then. There weren't so many strangers about. Besides, we had a larger acquaintance in the neighbourhood, and Mother used to go calling.' He turned to Antonia, shaking his head regretfully. 'So many of our old friends hereabouts died out, sold out. Gone away.'

And so, adroitly, my grandfather had turned the discussion to other times and other circumstances. And we never did get permission to have the landau repaired. Not that I was in the least concerned either way. But I should have been, for Mother's sake. I have blamed myself since for my selfishness, as I have blamed my grandfather for his. The old and the young can both be heedless and ruthless in the prosecution of their own will. The middle years are for giving.

Perhaps if I had been more companionable to Mother in those early months at Clere Athel, the story would have been a different one. But I doubt it. And anyway, what is the use of trying to relive one's life in speculation?

Charlotte and I did often spend our afternoons with her, and Sophie could come over from the house to the Dower and sometimes Great-Aunt Ivlian would join us, too. There would be needlework to occupy us, and there would be the ritual of tea, prolonged because it was a diversion. Sophie was avid to hear about the gay life my mother had known in London and Paris. When she learned we had seen the coronation of Edward VII the previous year, I thought she would choke with excitement, and I cannot count the times my mother had to relate the details of it. Charlotte and I used to get very restless and long to be out with the boys.

Tuesdays, Thursdays and Saturdays, Mother and I dined at the house, and on Sundays we went there to lunch after church. Not that we were always in church. The Athelsons had, on the whole, a proprietorial attitude to God, confident that His benevolent interest followed them wherever they went. If some matter to do with the Athelson property or their people needed attention, it was assumed that God would want it to be dealt with first. And if Cousin Cuthbert disapproved, he never said so in my hearing.

Until our coming, I believe Cecily Hamlack was the only member of the family who unfailingly occupied the great carved pew—well, I say pew, it always reminded me more of a box at the opera. One entered it from a door opening off the centre aisle and once inside could not see or be seen by the congregation. Carved, vaulted screens guarded us from the draughts on three sides, and a moulded canopy sheltered our heads, which was a merciful providence because the roof leaked just above us, and in very wet weather the intermittent pat-pat-pat disturbed our silent prayers. Inside, there were two individual prie-dieus, used by Grandfather and Grandmother, and for the rest of us there were upholstered benches with armrests, which I thought a great luxury. The kneeling stools and the cushions of the prie-dieus were tapestries, which Eugenie had worked. They were faded and threadbare in places, of course, but you could still make out the beauty of the design.

For my mother it was one of the important conventions of life that one went to church on Sunday morning. She was shocked to hear that Sophie did not always go and that it was an even rarer occurrence for her to take her children with her. In fact, the boys never went unless Grandfather did, and Charlotte, who did not see why she should be the only dutiful one, had made a lifelong practice of losing herself directly after breakfast on Sunday mornings.

'Well, it's difficult, you see,' Sophie explained in her anxious way. 'I would like to come myself, but Grandfather gets so angry if any of the children are late for lunch, and he won't have them coming to the table untidy. You know what children are! They can't keep themselves clean and neat through a whole morning. I have to be at home to call them in in good time to wash and change for lunch.'

'Athel,' my mother pointed out, 'isn't a child any more, and Hugh is quite old enough to look after himself, too. Besides, if they spend Sunday mornings with Grandfather, then it is up to him to see they come punctual and tidy to table. Certainly you should consider yourself free to attend church if you wish. And a girl of Charlotte's age. . . .' She left the rest unsaid.

'Well'—Sophie fluttered indecisively—'perhaps I ought to make the effort for Charlotte's sake. . . . It won't be easy, though. *She* won't want to come. She always copies what the boys do, and for all she seems quiet and biddable, there is more will in her than one would think. . . . Still, if it's only matins. . . .'

'Naturally, only matins.' Mother looked pained. 'One wouldn't go to evening service as well. That would be excessive.' I think the implication of her faint frown was that such an obvious display of piety would be vulgar.

And so it came about that our arrival in Clere Athel helped swell Cousin Cuthbert's congregation. For now with five Athelsons in the family pew, the tenants were also encouraged to field a better proportion of their numbers at matins. Cousin Cuthbert's gratitude to my mother was touching, even embarrassing, since he fell into the habit of consulting her for the choice of hymns, and, worse still, practising his sermons on her.

The selection of psalms, however, by long custom, remained Grandfather's exclusive province. I wondered at first over his apparent relish of the obligation—he would make a great business of the choice, always sending for his psalter directly after dinner on Thursday evenings, writing out his decree in a bold, straggling hand, and presenting it to Cousin Cuthbert on a folded piece of paper.

I did not have to wonder long. Grandmother had been pressing Grandfather to attend church ever since our coming. Not that I think she was a deeply religious woman herself.

Athel said she always went to church because she was superstitious, and the boys had a private joke that she only prayed for horses.

Anyway, at last Grandfather agreed that he would come one particular Sunday, and we were all quite surprised at his abruptly giving in to her. It was not in the least like him. The pew seemed almost overcrowded that Sunday. For one thing, it seemed to shrink the minute Grandfather stepped into it and took his place at the prie-dieu next to Grandmother, and then there were Athel and Hugh with their legs everywhere at the back.

I thought Grandfather looked very pleased with himself, turning every now and then to regard us with a curious sort of smile about the eyes.

The service proceeded uneventfully, until it came to the singing of the first psalm. It was number 147, and I noted that it was unfamiliar. I do not recall that I had ever read it before, and I have certainly never been called upon to sing it since.

'Praise ye the Lord: for it is good to sing praises unto our God; for it is pleasant; and praise is comely . . .' we began. The cadences of the chant fell softly, the words beneficent, comforting. . . . 'Who covereth the heaven with clouds, who prepareth rain for the earth, who maketh grass to grow upon the mountains. He giveth to the beast his food and to the young ravens which cry. . . .' All unsuspecting, we were plunged into verse ten with Grandfather's voice suddenly booming out twice as loud to lend point to the words. '*He delighteth not in the strength of the horse*. . . .' All eyes in the family flew to Grandmother. She had turned to look at Grandfather, her psalter lowered and the words dying away on her lips. My cousins were shaking with suppressed laughter, and even my mother and Aunt Sophie were exchanging smiles. The voices of the rest of the congregation wavered, and one could tell from the changed tone that the joke had been generally appreciated. 'The Lord taketh pleasure in them that fear him . . .' they sang with a quite inappropriate degree of cheerfulness. Grandfather looked straight ahead, his confident voice not stinting to give credit where it might be due. 'Praise thy God, O Zion. For He hath strengthened the bars of thy gates; He hath blessed thy children within thee. He maketh peace in thy borders and filleth thee with the finest of the wheat.' It was his moment of triumph. He was leading his people in song, and he had scored off Grandmother.

Later Athel told me that there had been other occasions when Grandfather was suspected of injecting a personal message into the service. But it is to be doubted if he ever found another reference so suited to his purpose.

*　　　*　　　*

I do not know whether Cousin Cuthbert was a good tutor or not. Having little formal education myself, I am in no position to assess him. Certainly he was the only teacher Athel ever had, and Athel never appeared to me to be at a disadvantage in any discussion. Our curriculum was not a strict one. 'To each according to his needs,' Cousin Cuthbert would say. So he set Charlotte to work to improve her grammar and her handwriting and gave me the essays of Montaigne to ponder over, while he took the boys to a far corner of the schoolroom to struggle with a little Latin or Greek. History, geography, and English literature were his favourite subjects, and he saw them as inseparable from one another. Thus we would begin with the study of the Alps on a relief map, digress to the character of Hannibal, dispose of Livy's reputation as a historian (Cousin Cuthbert did not like Livy), stand back to admire the Emperor Augustus (who regarded Livy as a friend but had no other flaw in Cousin Cuthbert's eyes), and return home to Britain via Julius Caesar. Or again we would come close to studying the history of Spain, but Pizarro would take us to Peru and on the way remind us that Sheridan had written a tragedy about him which showed a marked decline in style (Sheridan's style, that is). There was a terrible moment of indecision for Cousin Cuthbert, astride two continents, Pizarro pointing the way to the Incas and Sheridan tempting him with *The Critic* and the impeachment of Warren Hastings. I remember this occasion particularly well, because in the end it was a draw. And Sir Joshua Reynolds, entering the lists late with the recollection that he had painted several excellent portraits of Sheridan, brought his friends Johnson, Goldsmith, and Burke with him and stayed the rest of the morning.

It may be that we were sometimes confused by this method of teaching and that we acquired no very firm grasp of any one subject. But at least we were never bored or inattentive, since to let one's mind wander was to be left a thousand miles, if not three thousand years behind.

I think Cousin Cuthbert is a natural lifelong scholar. He came to Clere Athel after a short curacy in Somerset, summoned by Cecily Hamlack when the living fell vacant, and it would be hard to imagine a better choice of post for man or man for post. Jovial, benevolent, tolerant in his interpretation of doctrine, yet diligent in his duties, he settled down to a contented life. I really think him one of the most contented men I ever met. He inherited with the living and the comfortable proportions of the vicarage, an excellent library, to which a number of predecessors had contributed. If he was born a scholar, he was surely born a bachelor, too. But he appreciated a comely woman and fine fare on the table, so Providence had thoughtfully provided him with a cottager's handsome widow to keep house for him. He does very well. And although there is as yet no second generation of the family for him to tutor, I hear from Charlotte that he drops in on the little village school three or four times in the course of a week, and his Scripture classes have a way of progressing via Egypt and Ptolemy's geographical treatise to his influence on fifteenth-century mapmaking and the voyages of Columbus.

But more fascinating to me than any history that came out of books and dearer to me than any classic fables are the stories, part fact, part folklore, of Clere Athel itself. They have been written nowhere but told by one generation to the next over the centuries, and some of the oldest are sung in a language that is strange to me. I do not know for sure, but I think it has something in common with the language of Beowulf. The people of Clere Athel understand what the words tell, but they cannot write them down for you. They frown when you ask it of them and shake their heads. They say it is an old tongue used only for the singing of songs and the telling of tales and cannot be shaped with letters. And when you tell them that if the songs are not written down, they may one day be lost, they laugh at you. 'No, no,' they say, 'folk in Clere Athel have long memories. . . . Now if you were to write the songs down on a piece of paper, you might lose *that*!' Perhaps after all they are right. If they could read the words, they would stop learning them by heart. Perhaps this has happened before, and many an ardent research scholar has destroyed what he most wished to enshrine by simply destroying initiative to remember.

The most haunting song the people sing—and every child in the village has been cradled to its chorus at one time or another—tells of the men who came in a longship at twilight looking for gold to steal and blood to shed. The chief of the village told them the only gold they had was buried in his father's time to keep it from earlier raiders and no man could find the spot because it had been hidden on a dark, storm-ridden night. In a fury, the men from the longship had slain the chief and those about him and would have cut down the other men of the village with their axes had it not been for his young widow, the beautiful Isil.

Now Isil, so the song tells, was as lovely as the dawn over the sea and as cunning as a fox in a thicket. Seeing what slaughter was about to be done, she called out to the leader of the raiders to hold his men and the gold might yet be unearthed for them. It was known, she said, that the cache lay in one of their fields, but not which one. When the crops were harvested and the stubble burned off, all would be turned over until the treasure was found.

This interruption was not ill received by the war party, and though some were still for wetting the blades of their axes, others reasoned that if there was digging to be done, they might use the labour of their prisoners.

Then their leader, Aethel, spoke out, and the voices of the singers conjure up his mighty presence, leaning on a two-handed battle-axe that no other man could lift. The scene is awesome, lit by the burning homes of the villagers, hazy with the bitter smoke of wood and thatch. Aethel tells Isil that if the treasure can be found, they will spare the lives of the women and children, but what need to wait for harvest when their torches are already kindled?

At this Isil pretends indifference and disdain. If he wishes to burn the crops, so be it. But do the northmen not eat? Does grain not have its price in gold to a hungry man? She grows bolder. Only a barbarian and a fool could fail to see that the treasure that stands thigh-high in the fields is a sure prize, while the trinkets that lie buried beneath have still to be found.

Aethel is not enamoured of the lady's tone. But he reluctantly agrees that there is reason in what she says. Moreover, as it happens, his people are hungry and their ship needs repair. He decides to wait the two weeks which Isil promises will bring the harvest to perfection.

And it happens sometimes with fighting men that when there is no fighting to be done, they become bored. So with Aethel's men. They drink two days and nights away, and they make free with the fairest of the women. Then they spend a further three days putting their ship into good order. Then they look about them, and they see that the depleted manpower of the village is making poor shift at rebuilding the houses, so they are not above lifting one or two beams into place to show off their strength to the admiration of the women. They play with the children, who begin to gather about them with less fear and more wonder, and they feel that the land is good and steady beneath their feet. Oh, look well to your treacherous feet, men of Aethel, or they will put down roots in this place and never again tread the rolling decks of your warship!

In all this time no man touches Isil, but Aethel's eyes are

64

heavy upon her, especially when she leans over to fill his drinking horn, and he scowls a good deal. Oh, Aethel, the singers mock, are you now the conqueror or the conquered? Will you let yourself be bound by two ropes of golden hair?

A moon comes and goes before the harvesting is done and the grain is stored. At last the men of the village begin to dig over the fields, and the northmen labour beside them. They work from first light to darkness, day after day, and only when they are turning over the last strip of land do they find the hidden casket.

The villagers wait anxiously to watch while it is opened. They know there cannot be a great deal of gold in it. Will it be enough to satisfy the raiders and buy their lives? And some of them lose heart, for are the crops not also promised, and even if the northmen spare them, how will they live through the long winter without food?

Aethel stares into the casket, and his scowl is fiercer than ever. He looks at Isil. 'Little gold and much bronze,' he says. 'Is this the treasure you promised us, woman?'

'As I told you, the better half of our wealth grows up out of the ground each year. We do not have to search for it, and we do not have to steal it or kill for it either. We only have to work for it. We are a farming people, and we work a good earth. Our purses are slender, but our bellies are full, and our granaries overflow.'

For once Aethel is unsure of himself. He looks at his men, but they, too, are doubtful. He looks again at Isil, his eyes narrowing suspiciously.

'Am I cheated?' he mutters.

'Is there gold in your ship?' Isil asks.

'Aye, there is much gold.'

'Then if you were to offer us your gold in exchange for our grain, do you think we should have a good bargain?'

'Aye, that you would!'

'Not so!' says Isil firmly.

Aethel is perplexed. He is more accustomed to bed women than to talk to them. He cannot follow the way Isil's mind works. She confuses him. He strokes his plaited yellow beard and growls, 'Not so! How not so?'

'If you took our grain, most of us would starve in the coming winter. We could not eat your gold, and our neighbours may have little to sell. But you could grow fat on our food and would live to raid many another coastal settlement.'

'You could slaughter your stock.'

'We have little enough left. You have eaten most of it this past moon.'

'You could fish.'

'You do not know the waters of this coast. When the winter brings storms, we could not catch enough to feed even the children.'

Aethel ponders this. He understands then that if he takes the promised grain, the villagers may starve. He consults with his men. They withdraw to the beach and sit around a drift-wood fire, talking.

At last the northmen return to the village, where the women are preparing supper.

'This is a poor place,' Aethel says.

'It is a good place, provided we are left in peace,' Isil answers.

'You need better men to protect you. Your men do not know how to fight.'

'They know how to farm.'

'A man should be able to do both. We will teach them to fight, and they shall teach us to farm. Have we not already helped to dig over the fields for the next planting?'

Aethel has fixed a nail to a beam in the house of Isil and hung his winged helmet upon it, and Isil is no longer a widow. The warship is beached, and the village prospers on its cargo of gold. Alas for Aethel that he learned the names of the people of this place, for then he could not destroy them. Alas for Aethel that Isil had a secret, knowing smile. But well for their children.

CHAPTER TWO

ATHEL and I shared the same birthday month. I was born on the second of March and Athel on the twelfth. It was a very special year for Athel, that spring, since by custom the Athelson heir was said to come of age on his seventeenth birthday, and Grandfather planned to give a dinner party. Some of the Hamlacks were invited over from Yorkshire, and a number of other old Lancashire families were bidden to send representatives. A particularly large contingent would be coming from just the other side of Stonethwaite in Cumberland— eight members of the Saward family, including four daughters, from whom Grandfather was hopeful that a future wife for Athel might emerge.

It was Sophie who told my mother this, confiding it over the seating plans, the wine list, and the half-completed dinner menu, which was causing her so much anguish.

'Though what advantages there would be in the match, I can't see! There certainly wouldn't be much in the way of a settlement. The Sawards run sheep. I suppose they are better off than we are, but with four daughters and two sons. . . . They do have very rich connections in America, I understand. There's an uncle who went out and made a fortune in beef as a young man. Now he's in banking and has millions, so they say. I don't know whether *he'll* do anything for his nieces, but

67

I doubt it. He has children of his own. . . .' Aunt Sophie would run on happily this way for hours, prompted by suitable exclamations of interest from my mother. I don't know whether my mother was always as interested as she pretended to be. I have never thought of her as a woman who very much enjoyed family gossip, but she got on well with Aunt Sophie, admiring her thoroughly amiable nature and probably prepared to suffer a little boredom on account of it.

Whatever my mother's reactions, I at least was highly intrigued by this particular revelation, however, and I lost no time in finding my cousins to break the news.

Athel frowned when I told him. 'Oh, yes, I had heard something about it. The Sawards say they are a very old family, I know that. Like us, they believe they came from Danes or Vikings or whatever. We had their eldest boy here to visit a couple of years ago, and he said their name meant "sea lord" though I don't know what that proves. They've settled a mighty long ways inland!'

'They all have sticking-out teeth,' Charlotte put in. 'Athel won't marry a girl with sticking-out teeth, will you, Athel?'

'You've never seen them, silly. How do you know what their teeth are like?'

'Well, Edward Saward had sticking-out teeth, and when I asked him why they stuck out, he said he didn't know, but his sisters had them, too.'

'Oh, Charlotte! What a thing to have said to him. It isn't done to make personal remarks, you know.' I had cast myself in the rôle of elder sister and felt obliged to mind her manners for her.

'I didn't make a remark. I asked a question. Anyway, at least I talked to him about something. Athel and Hugh wouldn't talk to him at all. They were angry with him because he said Grandmother was silly keeping peacocks if we couldn't eat them.'

'Well, don't let's waste time going on about the Sawards,' Hugh said. 'We've got better things to do. We're going to the old quarry, aren't we?'

68

'What quarry?'

'Come on then,' Athel agreed. 'Let's go and get the horses. If we don't go at once, we'll never be back in time for dinner.'

'But why are we going to the quarry?' I demanded. 'Besides, I can't come. I haven't got my riding skirt on.'

At that time I wore a divided skirt and rode astride. But Athel waived aside the objection.

'We'll borrow one of Grandmother's saddles, and you'll just have to hold on tight.'

It was the first time I ever rode with a sidesaddle, but I managed to stay on, so I must have been a much improved rider by this time. Athel led the way at a good pace, and we took the old pier road until we were clear of the pinewoods and heading for the nearest village three miles north, which was Upstrand. Before we reached it, however, we turned due east and climbed up and around Beacon Hill, until at last we came to a stop at the head of a disused quarry and stood looking down a sheer cliff of smooth yellow sandstone.

'Keep well back from the edge! Look, we'll tie the horses over there.'

'What are we doing here, though? No one has told me why we've come up here yet.'

'You'll see. Now you start looking over that side, Hugh. I'll try round here. Remember the grass will probably have grown over the cover. Charlotte, you stay back with Justine, out of the way.'

The two boys began to pace up and down on the top of the cliff, prodding the long grass with sticks.

Suddenly Hugh dropped to his knees and began to tear back a mat of weeds. 'This is it! Here, Athel, I've found it. Help me get the cover off!'

Together they lifted a sheet of rusting metal and stared down at their find.

'At last! Now perhaps you'll explain.' I moved over to join them. 'What is it, then?'

'We think it's an old borehole,' Athel said.

'Yes,' I said, irritable with ungratified curiosity. 'I am sure

69

you're right. I imagine it's quite the most boring hole I have ever seen.'

Charlotte obliged me with a giggle. 'It's special, though.'

'Grandfather told us about it,' Hugh put in quickly. 'It has an echo.'

'Try it, Hugh,' Athel said.

Hugh leaned over the hole and shouted, 'Halloo, there.' Nothing happened.

'Perhaps you need to put your head right inside.'

'Thanks very much,' said Hugh, 'and dive in!'

'You couldn't fall down it.' Charlotte made her practical contribution. 'It's only about the size of your head. Your shoulders wouldn't go through.'

'I'm not relying on your mathematical theories,' Hugh assured her cheerfully. 'Besides, the edge might give way.'

'No, it feels pretty firm to me.' Athel lay down flat on the grass and wriggled forward until his head was just over the hole. 'You hold my legs, Hugh. . . .'

'Hugh . . . Hugh . . . Hugh . . . Hugh,' said the hole duti-fully.

'It does echo!' Charlotte clapped her hands delightedly. 'Go on, Athel—say something else.'

'Is there anybody down below?' Athel called.

'. . . 'low . . . 'low . . . 'low . . . 'low. . . .'

He wriggled back from the hole, and we all sat down beside him on the grass.

'Well, it's a good echo,' I conceded, 'but it still seems a long ride just to shout down a hole.'

Athel grinned. 'Aye, we mak oor pleasures outa simple things here in t'country.'

I knew it was said to tease, because Athel was always on about my town-bred ways and my failing to understand them. But his eyes were smiling, and I did not mind.

'No, but there's more to it than that,' Hugh explained earnestly. 'You see Grandfather was telling us at breakfast how he found this hole on the morning of his seventeenth birthday. His horse nearly put a foot down it, as a matter of fact, and

70

that's why he had it covered. Anyway, it seems he was feeling pretty pleased with himself one way and another, coming of age and all, and when he found there was an echo, he shouted that he was Athel, son of Athel, and the echo went on as though it were telling of all the Athels since time began. He told Father about it, and just for fun on Father's seventeenth birthday they rode up here and did the same thing again.'

'Oh, heavens!' I groaned. 'And so another Athelson tradition was born.' That was my way of teasing Athel in return, but just in fun and in affection. 'You're not seventeen for another week, though.'

Athel shrugged. 'It is a fine day. We thought we might not get the chance next week.'

'Go on, then, Athel,' Hugh said impatiently. 'Do it.'

'Yes, do it, Athel,' Charlotte urged. 'We shan't get back for dinner if we don't hurry.'

Athel looked at me, and I nodded encouragingly.

'I suppose,' he said slowly, 'it would be silly not to, now we're here.'

He edged his way back to the borehole again. We waited. He took a deep breath and shouted as loud as ever he could: 'I am Athel, son of Athel. . . .'

'. . . Athel . . . Athel . . . Athel . . . Athel . . .' cried the echo. Ringing as though down a long corridor of years.

*   *   *

For weeks the house had been in a turmoil of preparation. Nearly all the guests had to be accommodated overnight, and the Hamlacks would probably stay several days, which meant that bedrooms not slept in for twenty years or more must be spring-cleaned and aired. Presses were searched for linen, and an army of tenants' wives and daughters sewed frantically in the crossfire between Aunt Sophie, who pronounced it unusable, and Grandfather, who insisted it would do very well. In the end it seemed neither of them was right. It would not do *very well* . . . but it would just *do*.

71

Old oak chests, brooding darkly in corridors and attics, were ravaged without warning and plundered of brocade testers, fragile with age, faded velvet drapes, and wall tapestries rolled in black paper.

'Most of this stuff is in a really dreadful condition, you know,' my mother told Aunt Sophie. 'Look at this! Moth! It ought to be burned.'

'I know. But the Athelsons never throw anything away.'

My mother sighed. 'Well, at least we ought to do better by the dinner table.'

The burden of the organization had fallen largely on Aunt Sophie. Grandmother had never liked housekeeping, and when Athel brought Sophie home as a bride, she had given it up altogether.

'Two women in one kitchen makes trouble. I shall leave everything to you, Sophie, as I have always done.'

Thus she had resigned all responsibility for the dinner party.

'And as a matter of fact, I should be surprised if she knows where the kitchen is!' Aunt Sophie confided to my mother with uncharacteristic asperity. 'When I came here first, old Mrs Brett—you know Ted Brett, the baker, his mother—did all the housekeeping. When she died, everyone just looked to me to do it. But, of course, Mrs Carr is a wonderfully capable cook, and I really leave everything to her.'

Certainly, Annie Carr knew how to fill a larder and her husband, old Alfred—he was nearly thirty years older than his wife, and I think theirs was a marriage of careers more than anything—knew how to look after a wine cellar. This most important part of the arrangements well in hand, therefore, and the dining hall itself shining in such panelled magnificence that no one could find fault with it, Aunt Sophie came at last, with my mother's assistance, to the choice of the tableware.

Knives, forks, and spoons, these were no problem. Eugenie had provided the best and most beautiful when she brought her wedding silver to Clere Athel, and two footmen were speedily put to work upon it in the butler's pantry. The china and the glass took rather longer to select.

'It really is a question of one's personal fancy.' My mother resigned the decision. 'This service is more elaborate, but the other one is older and in better taste. And the same thing applies to the glasses. I like the weight of these and their feel in the hand, but the set over there, on your far left, have a handsome shape.'

Aunt Sophie ticked off items and made little notes in her pocket book. 'There are some silver-gilt dinner plates we can use for the main course. . . . Oh, and I thought the Charles the First chalices would be interesting for decoration. . . . Then there are the candelabra still to be chosen, and I thought we might use the half dozen glass ones we have. They're really very pretty and not so obstructive to conversation across the table. . . . Now for the serving dishes, I suppose the plate——'

'The plate?' my mother interrupted in sudden surprise. 'Well, of course, Sophie dear, you know best. But I should have thought that if one has the real thing, it would be a pity not to give it an airing on a special occasion like——' She faltered, discomforted in the realization that she might be causing embarrassment. 'Of course,' she added hastily, 'what you have may be too old and precious to use.'

Aunt Sophie looked doubtful. 'I'll have to ask Grandfather. I don't know what he'll say, I'm sure. He keeps it all locked away; the plate, too, for that matter.'

My mother clearly thought this rather odd, and I thought it odd myself. I was supposed to be counting table napkins with Charlotte but not giving much attention to the task, and there was the table before us weighted down with solid silver. So whatever was Grandfather about to lock up a few serving dishes when no door in Clere Athel was ever bolted, no window latched, no cupboard, seemingly, with a key to fit it?

The riddle was not solved that day, but on the next, when Charlotte and I were again pressed to be useful bringing in the fresh-cut spring flowers to arrange for the bedrooms, Grandfather was at last cornered by Aunt Sophie in the kitchen. My mother was there, and Mrs Carr, of course, bustling in and out of her vast pantry, and three kitchen maids, and two gardeners' boys with baskets of vegetables, and a man with four hares kicking inside a tied sack.

'So Antonia doesn't think we ought to use the plate, eh?' Grandfather growled.

'No, no!' my mother protested. 'It isn't for me to say. I only suggested that if you had something better——'

'Something better than the plate! Who could want anything finer than that, I'd like to know! There's no royalty coming that I'm aware of. I suppose you haven't invited an emperor or two without my knowing, have you, Antonia?'

My mother became slightly pink with annoyance.

'I have invited no one, as you are very well aware,' she said tartly. It was a matter of some resentment to her that although I was supposed to be sharing the dinner party, by right of my birthday being so near, we had not been asked if we would like any guests of our own choosing. Not that any of them would have cared to make the long journey, nor would she, I fancy, have cared to introduce them to Clere Athel.

'What do you think about it, Alfred?' Grandfather asked unexpectedly.

Alfred was warming himself a midmorning cup of ale, mulling it with an iron from the kitchen range. He looked twice as dour as usual and shook his head, refusing an opinion.

Left alone with his decision, Grandfather stroked his beard, considering us darkly.

'I'll tell you what,' he said at last. 'Perhaps if Antonia sees the plate, she'll fancy it well enough. Alfred, man, leave off cossetting yourself and get two strong 'uns to bring up the boxes. . . . Bring them all up. . . . I'll take a look at them all before I decide.'

They were a long time about it. It took Alfred with a lamp to guide them in the dark country of his wine cellars, and Grandfather with the keys to his vault, and Harry Thorpe, and Simple Sam, called in from the harness room in a hurry and without his shirt, and even, in the end, the man who had brought the hares in a sack—'Poached, I presume?' Grandfather would say when the dish was presented. 'No hare tastes like a poached hare.'

And so they brought these heavy hide cases up to the dining hall at last, struggling on the cellar's narrow stair and squeezing awkwardly through the low arched doorway, to set them down with a thud at our feet. We watched with interest as Grandfather unlocked each in turn and threw back the lid.

It was rather a dull morning, and the mullioned windows only half lit the large room. I do not know how long I stared at Grandfather's treasure without realizing what it was. I remember thinking how lavish the crimson velvet-lined boxes looked and that the silver was yellowish and doubtless needed a good clean. Then my mother gasped.

'Is it—is it gold?' she asked faintly.

Grandfather snorted, 'Well, it isn't brass!'

My mother groped her way around a chair and sank reverently to her knees before one of the boxes. She examined the contents closely, touching the rim of a huge dish with awe.

'That's the gold plate you're looking at now; the real stuff is over here.'

'I simply had no idea!' My mother shook her head in bewilderment. 'I thought Sophie was talking about *silver* plate.'

'*Silver* plate?' It was Grandfather's turn to be astonished. 'Silver plate's for shoe buckles!'

'Well,' my mother said weakly, 'the possibility of anyone having a choice between gold plate and solid gold serving dishes never crossed my mind.'

Grandfather thought this showed a limited imagination and said so. 'Nothing better than gold to put your money in. Safer than any of these banks with their little scraps of paper and clerks putting figures in the wrong columns. The Athelsons have always put by gold, at least in the past they have. Can't say I've added to it myself. I couldn't afford to save even a sovereign piece, and that's the truth.' He paused, biting his lip reflectively. 'Changing times, you know.'

'You must have great wealth here at least.'

'Aye.' The acknowledgement was complacent. 'But it's only for the holding, not the spending, you understand.'

'Naturally. There must be many old family treasures here that you would be reluctant to part with in any circumstances.' Mother cast an appraising eye over the collection, clearly thinking that some of its value at least ought to be realized without delay.

Grandfather shrugged his heavy shoulders, pursing his lips. He was watching my mother, and I felt that he made at least as good a guess as I could what was passing through her mind. I knew myself to be blushing painfully. I do not think I had ever been so conscious of our circumstances before that time. And was it wrong of her to covet some of that gold if it might buy independence in her widowhood and provide a satisfactory settlement for an unmarried daughter? This, after all, was what we had come to Clere Athel hoping to receive. I had understood that. And if this was what she wanted, I wanted it for her, too. But somehow—I cannot tell why—I seemed to sense in that moment that she would be disappointed.

The next few days were full of diversion and excitement. The party really began with the arrival of the Hamlacks the evening before Athel's birthday. They were the only relatives we were expecting since all living Athelsons were already assembled. I liked the Hamlacks. There were two of Grandmother's nephews—her elder brother's sons, Howard and Heywood—and their wives and an assortment of second cousins, but they were the sort of people one is immediately at ease with, steady-eyed, comfortable sort of folk with a wry Yorkshire humour and a keen enjoyment of living.

Of course, like Grandmother, they were obsessive about horses. But although Aunt Sophie complained that there was nothing but stable gossip when the Hamlacks got together, I could not see any fault in it myself. I like people with great enthusiasms. I like the way they become illuminated when they talk. One can enjoy that without sharing the passion.

The rest of the guests began to arrive just before luncheon the next day and tracked the newly raked gravel of the drive with every conveyance imaginable until the late afternoon. Some had come part of the way by train and broken the journey with a night in an hotel, others had travelled shorter distances in a convoy of gigs, and some people called Stannard won the distinction of bringing the first motor-driven carriage into Clere Athel—I think it was a Napier or a Daimler perhaps. I know Grandfather was thrilled when they let him try it out.

Towards the end of the afternoon there was an undignified scramble to get the latecomers' trays of tea and pitchers of hot water in their rooms. Mother and I slipped thankfully away and went back to the Dower to make our own preparations in leisurely comfort.

'I have suddenly a great liking for Eugenie,' my mother said.

'Oh? Why?'

'Well, only think, if there were more than two principal bedrooms, we would certainly have had to take some of the guests here. So pleasant to be able to escape from the crush and have Mrs Rimmer to ourselves to help us dress.'

Ellen was on loan, but there was still Pegger to stagger up with our bath water, and I am sure Mother was right and we were the only people in Clere Athel that night who took a well-filled bath.

Dinner was to start at seven thirty. 'Very prompt,' Grandfather said, and for once we did not keep him waiting. He wanted the immediate family to be first in the hall, ready to receive their guests as they came downstairs to dinner. We looked our best. Mother wore the emerald her Uncle Simon had given her, which made Grandfather stare, and Cecily Hamlack was wearing a formidable pearl collar which had been left to her by her mother. Later it paid for Hugh to go to college. Even Great-Aunt Ivlian, who was customarily as vague in dress as manner, was made quite presentable in brown velvet with her hair dressed high and a small curled ostrich feather to set it off.

The meal was rather grand. I know it seemed to go on a very long time. Charlotte, who was sitting just below me, grew restless and giggled too much and later became glassy-eyed with fatigue, poor lamb. Hugh kept giving her a kick under the table to keep her in order.

In the end it had been decided not to use the gold patens because of the risk of their being scratched, but the plate gleamed richly enough under its burdens of oysters and turbot, the gravy roasts, the guinea fowl and the ducklings, and the pigeons in pastry.

As there were not enough regular house servants for such a large company, a number of tenants' sons and one or two of the men from the home farm had been brought in to wait at table. There was an unexpected bonus from this arrangement, since the men of Clere Athel always spoke their minds freely, and it made Grandfather roar with laughter to hear one of his guests told by a stern-faced footman: 'Tha's not done justice to that bird . . . pick thee bones like a man!' and to hear: 'By God, Heywood Hamlack, tha's got hollow legs, for I've filled yon glass seven times. Tak note there's Madeira and brandy still to come, man!'

It was gone ten o'clock when Cecily Hamlack at last gave a peremptory rap on the table and we were able to follow her thankfully from the dining hall, leaving the men to mingle cigar smoke with the heavy odour of fruits and spirits and two hundred wax candles in need of a trim.

'I don't hold with dancing,' Grandfather said later. 'It's unbecoming in a woman to grow too warm and a man looks a fool when he capers like a bear.'

Nevertheless, we polkaed and waltzed to the best that the village musicians could give us. And I waltzed with Athel. I remember I waltzed with Athel more than once.

There were games too. Now Grandfather did approve of games. We played blindman's buff, where each of the young men was blindfolded in turn and caught a partner for a tableau that had to represent a title of a book. Hugh caught me, and we tried to be *Pride and Prejudice*, but it was impossible to act prejudice, and we gave up and were jeered out of the competition. But one of the Saward girls, Elizabeth, and a boy

78

called Roger Hesketh did very well with *The Cloister and the Hearth* and were held to be the easy winners.

We had naturally been all agog to see the Saward girls, looking them over for Athel, you might say. They were jolly creatures, to be sure. I think I never met more friendly girls. But not even their own mother could have thought them pretty.

'Well, have you made your choice?' I asked Athel when we were dancing.

'What choice?'

'The Saward girls, of course.'

Athel smiled down at me lazily. 'You really need an answer to that?'

'What about Grandfather, then?'

'Grandfather's already married.' Athel pretended to be shocked. 'What are you thinking of, Justine? I tell you what. I'll give *you* to Edward Saward, that will serve just as well!'

'I shall marry whom I please.'

'Ah, but then you may please no one and I dread to have you left on my hands, a penniless spinster,' Athel teased.

'I shall not be penniless.'

'Not if you marry Edward Saward, no. You will be very comfortable. Were I head of the family I would see you settled right away.'

Suddenly it seemed that Athel had grown quite serious, and I did not like it. My eyes found Edward Saward across the room, a cheerful, gangling, unlovely boy with a receding chin and these remarkable teeth. Could Athel really mean to push me into a marriage with him? Edward Saward saw me looking and stared back. The next thing I knew, when the dance had ended, there he was beside me, claiming a dance and Athel handing me over with a slight smile and unreadable eyes.

Edward Saward haunted me for the rest of the night. I could not turn any way without coming face to face with him.

'You appear to have made a conquest,' my mother said dryly.

Other recollections of the party only survive in a vague and disconnected way. A man, whose name I do not remember, telling of some family where a traditional presentation party was held on the heir's eighteenth birthday. 'They present him to the tenants, d'ye see. Gives them a chance to meet and get to know him. Makes quite a ceremony.'

'Present him to the tenants! God above, man, don't they already know the feller?' Grandfather was outraged. 'Can't imagine such a thing! Athel was dandled on every knee in the village while he was still in skirts. The folks here have watched him grow, aye, and seen him beaten when he was at fault. They're part of him, and he's part of them. But I would not care to introduce a stranger to master our people . . . not now, nor seven hundred years gone for that matter. There's all the world between what a man will do for love and old times' sake and what he'll let you force upon him.'

The other man nodded sympathetically. 'I am sure you are right. But of course the family of which I speak has a number of estates. The heir cannot be raised on all of them, and so he must come as a stranger to most of his tenants.'

'Aye, and I expect they cheat him whenever they can, and good luck to them. That sort of landholding degenerates into a mere commercial enterprise. There's no justice in it, no security for the men who work the land. It's no way to live at all . . . no way to live.'

I hardly understood the meaning of what was said then, but I listened because of the passionate way Grandfather spoke.

And then there was Great-Aunt Ivlian saying to me, 'My dear, I have not given you anything for *your* birthday. You must accept a very pretty fan. I'll get it for you directly. It is painted on chicken skin, and I think it must have belonged to Eugenie.'

But Aunt Sophie whispered, 'Don't be disappointed, Justine. I heard what Ivlian said and I'm afraid she gave the fan away years ago. She made it a wedding present to somebody . . . I forget who.'

My mother summed up the occasion in a letter to Aunt

Mathilda. 'It was the most singular social event I ever attended, somewhere between a mediæval banquet and a children's treat. We played strenuous games, if you please, on top of a dinner where twelve courses were served. And the drinking that was done! My dear, you never saw anything like the way these countrymen in the north can drink, yet they are neither the better nor the worse for it. I confess that it would be asking a good deal for them to grow wittier or more gallant in their cups, but when they will not even give me the satisfaction of seeing them become a little foolish. . . . Nevertheless, it was a diversion to have company about the place. Now we are very quiet and dull again. . . .'

CHAPTER THREE

I ALWAYS THINK of that second summer in Clere Athel as
the coming of the Barb. I never saw his like before or since,
and though many score more horses may pass through my
life, I shall never forget him. He has gone to his grave now—
somewhat prematurely dispatched—with a roll call of broken
human bones to his credit and a couple of attempted murders
on his conscience. I only hope he lies more quietly than he
lived.

Naturally it was Grandmother who was to blame for bringing the Barb among us, although Grandfather attached some
discredit to Hugh and even to me, because we had been there
at the time of the purchase and 'ought to have stopped her
from doing such a damn fool thing'. I should like to have seen
him try to stop her.

Grandmother and her horses. It is to be doubted if any
other living creature came as close to her heart. I have heard
it said that Pegger's widowed mother raised her children for
her, since her own lack of interest bordered on neglect.
Apparently she had never forgiven my Uncle Athel for
screaming when she put him up on his first pony. My father
fared better with her because she thought she detected some
of the Hamlack flare for judgement, and she liked and fostered
Hugh's interest in the stables.

But she had no opinion of the Athelsons as horsemen.

Grandfather rode the most ungainly-looking cob about the estate. He had stubbornly picked out this animal for himself at Bowland Horse Fair, and Grandmother was never done taunting him.

'Cecily, the cob seems to be walkin' lame.'

'Really?' says Grandmother. 'How can you tell?'

Grandfather regarded her under lowering brows. 'Just look to it, woman, and tell me what's amiss. Do you think there's a tendon pulled?'

She shrugged. 'I'm sure I don't know. Does it have tendons? I always imagined it held together by pieces of string and a packet of pins.' Nevertheless, she allowed that the cob must have one redeeming feature. It must, she said, have remarkable stoutness of heart to take such a rider upon its back, day after day, without showing a marked inclination to bolt at the sight of him.

The horses were always given the best of the grazing, prime grass on the lower slopes of the home park. They would never have been there without Grandfather's consent, but this did not prevent him from continually complaining that they 'ate their heads off to no profit'. The winter feed accounts were better still. 'Oh, yes. To be sure. Any little delicacy they fancy. Sturgeon or a couple of hogshead of best claret, perhaps?' He would measure Grandmother's small, slight figure with his eyes, and she looking back at him with a faint smile, quite unmoved.

But I think that they both derived a good deal of secret enjoyment from these skirmishes. A man of Grandfather's temperament could never have relished a woman who gave him no opposition at all, and he knew well enough that everywhere outside the stables she was the staunchest upholder of his authority.

One of the biggest events in Grandmother's year was Bowland Horse Fair, equivalent in its delights to her as a day spent in the shops around the Madeleine was to my mother. Sometimes she would take along a couple of three-year-olds to sell.

Not the best, because these were sold through the Hamlacks or on private recommendation to buyers she met by arrangement at Beacon Cross.

Mostly, however, she went to hunt a bargain and back her own judgement.

'You must come with me, Justine. It's fine country about the Trough of Bowland. Not so beautiful as Yorkshire, of course, but in the same style.'

'What Grandmother means to say,' Hugh explained, 'is that it's real dragon and giant country, wild and bleak. The truth is she's afraid to go there on her own.'

I had hoped the fair might make a diversion for Mother, but the journey put her off because we had to leave at six in the morning and travel in the carriage. In the end there were just Hugh and I of the party, with Harry Thorpe to drive, one of the stable lads up beside him, and a mounted groom following to lead back any horses we bought.

It was a perfect July morning, with just the faintest veil of mist promising the fine, warm day that was to come. I thought Grandmother's claim for the views we saw far too modest. There is a quality to the beauty of certain parts of Lancashire that calls forth silence rather than praise. But Harry Thorpe found a few words that do well enough when we stopped for a late breakfast at a place called the Game Cock Inn and looked across the boulder-strewn fell towards the Pennines. 'By heck,' he said mildly, 'it puts a man in mind of his maker.'

Romany horse traders came from all over the country to Bowland, and as we drew near the site of the fair, we could see their gay-painted caravans diminished like a child's playthings against the scale and sweep of the scenery.

The road over the last few miles was thronged with conveyances of every kind making for the same destination as ourselves.

'There! Now you see why it was necessary to get an early start,' said Grandmother, fretting at our reduced speed among the carts taking farmers and whole families on the jaunt.

'Not early enough, by the looks of things.' Hugh grinned

and winked at me. 'There'll only be knackers' meat left by the time we get there.'

Grandmother stuck her head out of the window. 'Harry! Harry! What the deuce is the matter with that cart ahead of us? Have they got a pair of oxen in the shafts? If they can't make better speed, tell them to shift over and let those who can come by.'

I felt myself blushing for the attention she was drawing upon us, but Hugh was vastly amused, and I must admit that these vigorous directions were not unfavourably received by our immediate neighbours. A gentleman rider, who had just drawn level with us, was even so considerate as to slow his own pace and explain that there appeared to be a wagon with a broken axle farther along and we were reduced to single line to pass it.

The minute we reached the fair, Grandmother was out of the carriage, practically dragging me by the hand.

'Come with us, Harry, I may want you to bid for me. Bob can see to the carriage.' We were breathless trying to keep up with her as she made her way from one roped enclosure to the next, her sharp eyes raking the rows of horses. A chestnut mare caught her fancy for a moment, and then she was away again. Was there something about a skewbald yearling? No, there was not. We hurried on.

'Look!' Hugh said suddenly. 'There are the Tarletons come all the way from Cartmel.'

We were nearly upon them. The man was raising his hat. The lady on his arm and two little girls in muslin dresses stood ready with expectant smiles.

'How d'you do.' Grandmother nodded curtly, passing them without even a fractional loss of speed. And Hugh and I could only smile apologetically and hurry after her, leaving the Tarletons open-mouthed with amazement.

'Why didn't you stop and speak to them?' Hugh asked, when we caught up. 'They were quite put out, you know.'

'The Tarletons may have come here to gossip with every acquaintance they see, but I haven't. Now do keep up. I don't want to have to waste my time looking for you if we get separated.'

So we trotted on obediently for another hour, following the neat figure in faultless black, as it flitted ahead of us through the whirling, colourful crowd. There was colour all around us that day—in the restless, gleaming bodies of the horses; in the Oriental extravagance of the Romany clothes, the hard, primary colours of their travelling homes, and the drift of blue woodsmoke about their campfires; farmers' wives with chip-straw hats like cornucopias and handsome daughters, beribboned as maypoles; ladies of the county, requiring one hand for a flounced parasol and the other for the support of a gentleman, surrendering pastel silk hems to the springing green turf.

It was long after noon when Grandmother relented and allowed us to locate the carriage and our luncheon hamper. We ate chicken pasties and raspberry sponge and rested thankfully in the shade.

'My feet in these new boots!' Hugh groaned. He glanced hopefully at Grandmother. 'Daresay you've seen all you want to now, eh? We could just take a look at some of the sideshows perhaps. . . .'

'No, I'm not done yet. I haven't been over there—behind the wrestling booth. We'll go now. I'm quite ready.' She dusted crumbs from her lap and stood up. 'You can buy a trinket or two afterwards. . . . Now, Bob'—she turned to the groom—'here's two shillings for you and ninepence for the lad. You can take turn about to leave the carriage during the next hour; then we must be on our way home to avoid the crush on the road. Keep out of mischief, mind, and should anyone ask you if you can find the lady, say you haven't lost one!'

This made the men laugh. I puzzled over the secret of the joke as we set off once again in Grandmother's wake.

'What did it mean, Hugh,' I asked, 'about the lady? Find which lady?'

'Oh, that. It's a card game the sharpers play. They put three cards face down and show you one of them's the queen.

Then they shuffle them about and bet you can't find her. . . .
Only you never can because they palm her.'

'Palm her?'

'Yes, keep her hidden in the palm of the hand.'

'But if people know they do this, they wouldn't bet, surely?'

'Ah, they don't all know. That's the point. Plenty of
greenuns like you around. Of course,' he added kindly, 'you're
a girl. Mightn't be expected to know.'

'If you see a sharper, point him out.'

'All right. Hey, looks as if Grandmother's found something
at last.'

We hurried up to join her where she stood with Harry
alongside a particularly large caravan. They were staring at
a horse tethered to a stout wooden rail, quite alone. It was a
black stallion, and even I could tell it was something quite
out of the ordinary.

'Well, Hugh,' Grandmother said at last, 'let us see how
bright you are. Tell me what you think.'

Hugh took his time. 'It must be a devil to handle.'

The horse was standing quietly enough, and I was astonished
to see Harry Thorpe nodding approval of this opinion.

'Whatever makes you say that?'

'Gone to the trouble of driving great, thick posts into the
ground for the tethering. Then again, look at the space around
him. Other horses well out of reach.'

'Good.' Grandmother clapped her hands sharply, and the
horse turned to look at us.

'What a small head. Is it an Arab?' I asked.

'A Barb. And I would call the head refined.'

I tried to see it that way, but the laid-back ears and the
small eyes which seemed to direct ill will upon us were dis-
couraging. Accustomed to the large, kind, sometimes quizzical
eyes of the English Bloodstock horse and the general expression
of intelligence with pricked forward ears and deep brow, I
simply could not adjust my attitude.

'You don't want that one, Grandmother, do you?' Hugh
said.

'Solid bone, good broad feet, good slope to the shoulder.'
She sounded wistful. 'Harry?'

'Powerful neck.'

There was an old woman sitting on the steps of the caravan,
smoking a clay pipe. She turned and called over her shoulder,
and a man came out and strolled languidly towards us.

He did not speak immediately but took up a position beside
us as though he, too, had merely come to admire the horse
from this angle. He looked like a very prosperous Romany.
His riding boots and well-tailored breeches were as good as
anything Athel owned, and if a hacking jacket in brown velvet
is unorthodox, it was in this instance most effective, worn with
nonchalance and a gold ring in one ear.

'You like the horse, lady.' It was not a question. 'He's a
Barb.'

'Yes,' said Grandmother agreeably. 'There's a sight too
much Barb in him.'

'Not a ride for a lady.'

Grandmother chuckled.

'I believe you. Can you ride him?'

'Surely.' The man's eyes did not waver. 'But I have hurt
my back bracing a wheel. Tonio will ride him for you.' He
put his fingers inside his mouth and gave a piercing whistle,
which brought a ragged boy of perhaps twelve years scrambling
from under the caravan. They exchanged a few words in their
own language, and the boy went over to the horse and offered
it something in his hand. It accepted with a snap. He seemed
to be talking earnestly to the creature, and it was clear that
there was some understanding between them.

I had not expected to see that horse ridden, but anyway
saddle and ride it he did. The Barb was continually weaving
his head from side to side and looked as if he would devour
the bit, given time, but there was no attempt to dislodge the
young rider. Grandmother persisted that the weight of a child
was not the weight of a man, but I could see she was favourably
impressed.

The dealer maintained his air of indifference, hands thrust

in the waistband of his breeches, but his eyes had narrowed intently upon her face.

'Do you go into Yorkshire?' Grandmother asked with seeming irrelevance.

'Yes, lady.'

'Ever sold to the Hamlacks?'

'Yes.' The man's expression was more alert.

'I'm a Hamlack.'

The dealer's manner underwent immediate change. He began to talk volubly, giving Grandmother the Barb's history in detail, extolling his soundness, the interesting qualities he might impart at stud. She listened, interrupting from time to time to say that of course this was all very well, but what about temperament, and what if he didn't prove himself, and anyway there was still too much Barb in him. Harry made a closer inspection of the creature and so many disparaging remarks that it seemed to me there could be no more question of Grandmother's buying him, but in the end it seemed she would give the dealer twenty guineas to take the stallion off his hands.

The Romany smiled thinly. All the Hamlacks liked to make a good joke. One *hundred* and twenty guineas would be closer to the value of the animal, but to see him well placed, he would accept ninety. He held out his hand for Grandmother to slap it and make the bargain. It was her turn to smile, and she shook her head, turning away. It was, in any case, time for us to leave.

The dealer said the Hamlacks were hard bargainers; he knew that and respected them for it. But for a ride that a prince of Barbary might covet none of them would insult him by offering less than seventy guineas.

In that case, said Grandmother quickly, she would leave him the stallion since no doubt a Barbary prince would happen along at any moment. She could not bring herself to insult him with the thirty guineas which must be her final bid.

'Lady, at fifty guineas I should be giving you an expensive present. Now do you want the horse or do you not?'

Harry intervened firmly. 'I'd forget it, ma'am, if I was you. Here we have a genuine difference of opinion on the merits of this horse. Myself I don't favour 'im. Can't think of none of the mares would be the better of a visit from 'im. And if we don't use 'im, what are we left with? Not even a ride.'

In the end the Romany said he had paid forty guineas and he would take forty, although his children would go hungry and curse the day they were born. And Grandmother said thirty-five *pounds* would be her last word, and the Romany said guineas. So they struck hands on the bargain.

We had several false starts leaving the fair, as the Barb made repeated attacks on the hindquarters of the groom's horse. In the end we had to tie him on the back of the carriage, and that slowed us down considerably.

Just as we were clearing the ground, Hugh tugged at my sleeve. 'There, Justine, you wanted to see a sharper. Reckon that's one.'

I looked out the carriage window. A little man, in a checked suit, holding his bowler hat on his head with both hands, was sprinting along the road at an astonishing speed with three young farm lads in furious pursuit. A shower of small change fell out of his pockets as he ran, but he did not stop to pick it up.

'Obviously wasn't sharp enough, was he?' said Grandmother.

So we brought the Barb home to Clere Athel.

'Ye gods!' said Grandfather. 'Is this a stables I'm keeping or a menagerie? Why, the damned thing's half wild.'

'No, he's not,' Grandmother snapped. 'We've seen him saddled and ridden this very day by a lad far younger than Hugh.'

There was quite a commotion going on in the stableyard since Grandmother could not decide where she wanted the Barb housed. Horses were being led about in different directions while she tried to weigh the merits of giving him one of the larger loose-boxes, which would afford him the freedom he had been used to, against the danger of his rolling and getting cast. Harry was in favour of a stall and a halter for better control until the stallion had calmed down. This latter course being decided upon, the most suitably isolated stall was found to be the home of one of the carriage horses, just settled down with a feed.

'You've gone mad, woman,' Grandfather roared, seeing the carriage horses making a reappearance. 'Do you realize it wants five minutes of eight o'clock? We've none of us had supper, and there's upwards of a dozen horses cavorting in the yard.'

'Hold his head steady, Bob. Right, now lead him in. Watch out for his heels, boy. Don't get behind him.' Grandmother was uncharacteristically flustered. 'Get out of the way! I said *keep away from his heels——*'

It was too late.

One of the stable lads was kicked and fell with a cry and a thud on the cobbles.

Grandfather swore and strode forward to pick up the limp body. 'Now I hope you're satisfied, Cecily. He's killed the lad.' In fact he had not. The damage was three broken ribs as it turned out. But it gave us all a terrible fright.

It was a grim end to the day.

I wish I could say for Grandmother's sake that the Barb redeemed himself in time. She found some comfort in the fact that he 'threw two very fine colts and a filly'. But not, as Athel pointed out, before he had thrown everyone else within reach and had accounted to our certain knowledge for two broken arms, one fractured thigh, Harry Thorpe's collarbone, and a piece bitten out of Jed in a place he did not care to discuss. Perhaps it was this final lapse that decided Grandmother to part with the Barb. At very least it assured the stallion of a place in Clere Athel folklore because within a week of the incident unruly offspring were being threatened 'with a leathering where the Barb got Jed'.

The Hamlacks took the stallion readily enough, but age in no way mellowed him. He was said to have deliberately attempted to roll on Howard Hamlack. In the end they put him down, after he had cornered a groom in a loose-box and

—as Grandfather would relate with relish—'tried to hammer him into the ground like a tent peg'.

*   *   *

'Athel has worked hard and done well! We've all done well,' Grandfather said. 'Even the blasted asparagus begins to look as though it may pay for its keep. We'll celebrate. We'll take our lunch in Godwin's field tomorrow if the weather holds . . . make what Antonia here would call a *fête champêtre*.' He winked broadly at Mother.

The family greeted this statement with a rapture that would have been unaccountable to an outsider. The truth is we were relieved for Athel. It was no light responsibility to direct the entire harvesting and market operation for a community like Clere Athel, which had such a diversity of crops and such a perversity of people, and it was the first time Athel had been put in sole charge. Ordeal by harvest, Hugh called it. But Grandfather had no fault to find with the way things had been done. And now even the little asparagus farm, pet project of the moment begun after Grandfather had read an article in the *Countryman's Journal* praising the properties of our sandy soil, was beginning to flourish. God was surely in his heaven.

The next morning promising a fine, warm day, we set off at about eleven o'clock to walk up to Godwin's field. Everyone was in a gay mood. It was the first and last time I ever saw Grandmother using a parasol, and as we walked along, I saw Grandfather offer her his arm, and moreover, she accepted it. Cousin Rainbird was with my mother, while Fenn Haldane seemed to fall in easily alongside Aunt Sophie.

I had come to understand the family's sly jokes about Fenn Haldane by this time. 'Fenn's our steward, and more to us than that,' Grandfather had said when he first introduced us. The Haldanes had always been stewards to the Athelsons, the post inherited father to son in a tradition almost as old as the passing of the land itself. But as Grandfather had hinted, there was more to the relationship than that. The first steward had been a favourite natural son, so the Athelson bloodline was as strong and true in Fenn as any member of the family and ill betide any tenant who would have forgotten it. Not that the Haldanes wanted respect in their own right. They had always been known as just and honest men, and their unique position with regard to the family—of it but not precisely in it —had benefited the entire community. Not all the Athelsons would have been fair masters. Some must have been greedier than others and would have oppressed the tenants if they could. But when they spoke to a Haldane, they spoke to an equal, and since the Haldanes had married into tenant farmers' families, they also spoke to a man who had sympathies and loyalties on both sides.

Fenn Haldane had not married, however, and now turned forty, he seemed less likely to do so with every year that passed. I had a sudden romantic notion that morning, as we were on our way to Godwin's field. Nonsensical, of course, but I thought Fenn Haldane was in love with Aunt Sophie. It was something about the way he helped her down from a stile. Surely he held her hand longer than was needed, and she, laughing at him as she stepped down, seemed almost pretty.

To reach our picnic, we followed a footpath through the best farmland on the estate and at last came to the trampled stubble of Godwin's field. The ground rose slightly here, and we were breathless when we reached the top.

'Now look at the view,' Grandfather said. 'You can see the whole of our land from here. You're standing on the highest ground in Clere Athel, Antonia.'

'I didn't realize we had climbed so high.'

'No, you wouldn't. The fall of the ground deceives the eye. It is a very gentle gradient.'

We stood a while longer, shading our eyes against the noon sun, looking directly across the fields and village to the far distance, where the old pier road wound away to disappear in the pinewoods. The Dower was lost in the tall trees of the home park. But it was just possible to make out two wings

of the house, locating them by the shimmer of the little ornamental lake, now no more than a fragment of broken mirror
on a green and gold patterned carpet.

Directly behind us the slope wore a coronet of windswept
trees, and in their shade rugs and cushions were being arranged
and luncheon set out on lace cloth, very much as it would
have been in the dining hall. It seemed that everything—even
the ceremonial salt cellar which was twenty-two inches high
and never used because of its tremendous weight—had been
transported to Godwin's field. Only Alfred was missing.

'Couldn't manage the walk, y'know,' Grandfather said.
'Gout in his feet.' He chuckled. 'A man gives a lifetime of
devoted service to another man's wine cellar, and that's what
he gets—gouty feet!' He was very fond of Alfred.

If a picnic cloth spread upon the ground can be said to have
a head, then that is where Grandfather sat and saw nothing
out of the way in having a manservant on his knees beside
him to hand shrimp savouries, cold soufflé of duck with
cherries and spinach, timbales of veal, and apricot pudding.

We finished the meal with coffee prepared over a spirit
burner. I took a lighted wooden taper from one of the footmen
and held it while Grandfather lit his customary cigar. This
was an attention that it pleased him either Charlotte or I
should perform. My mother did not approve—she disliked
seeing women wait on a man 'as though they were hand-
maids', she always said—but I was happy to comply. There
are some men who can make a women feel privileged to wait
on them. And Grandfather was such a man.

I was about to blow out the taper when Grandfather
suddenly leaned forward and took it from me, touching it to
the dry grass close beside him. A small flame kindled almost
directly.

'See! Dry as thatch.' He emptied the remaining contents
of his wineglass on the tiny blaze he had started. I looked into
his face inquiringly. 'Do you know the story of this field where
we are sitting—Godwin's field?' I shook my head. 'This whole
field was once set ablaze to make a man's name a legend.'

He saw that he had intrigued me and settled his back against a tree, clearly in a mood to enjoy the telling of a story. 'It's an old tale. It takes us back to the fourteenth century and more precisely to the year 1349. The view from here would have looked rather different then, of course. There were fewer houses, and the woods grew right up to the edge of the home park yonder. It was still possible to put out fishing boats with a shallow draught, and sometimes the last surge of a heavy sea could just cover the marsh with a thick brown scum. But the sandbank was already treacherous, and there was only one channel deep enough to cross it at the neap.

'In those days much of the land was farmed in strips . . . you've learned something of the manorial system from your history tutors, no doubt. But this field was always arable land and rotated with two other open fields, the one just below it where we climbed the stile and another that is now part of the Warrener farm. Once in three years this would be wheat-sown, as it was this year and in the year I am telling you of, and believe me it is good earth. I defy anyone to show me another piece of land that yields more bushels to the acre.

'Well, as you may know, in 1349 a great plague was running like fire through the countryside. The Black Death they called it, and they say it killed one in three of the population. But because of its isolated position, Clere Athel had been spared, and you may imagine our people stayed away from market as long as they could or stood well back when they bargained!

'Now there were three sons to the Athelsons of that day, and the youngest—dearest to his father so men say—was Godwin. It happened that one August morning the boy wakened early, before the dawn and before anyone else was astir, and for what reason no one knew he walked up here to this field. Perhaps he came in search of a lost arrow or a stray hawk, or perhaps he just wanted to climb the hill and exult in the morning as any young man in good spirits may do from time to time.

'The sun came up, however, and Godwin had not returned to the house, and by then his father learned of his absence and was angry because the boy was neglecting his tasks. But when Godwin did not come to his meat and the day wore along towards noon, anger gave way to anxiety, and everyone began to search about and call for him. Then at last a cotter's boy ran to Athel and said that Godwin was up in this field and shouting that his father must be fetched but no other one must walk that way.

'Picture the bewilderment of the father and Godwin's brothers, who, together with other men of the village, hurried up the way we walked this morning, and imagine their astonishment when they see Godwin apparently unhurt and in good cheer waving to them from the midst of the wheat field . . . just . . . about there. . . .' The butt of Grandfather's cigar indicated the place, and we looked to it. In the shimmering haze of that hot afternoon it was easy to conjure up the figure of a boy, waist-high in waving wheat. . . .

'"Come no nearer, Father, nor let anyone else by," Godwin calls. 'I have found a sick man lying here, and I fear he has the plague!" Strong men recoil, but Athel exclaims for his son and starts to walk towards him. "No, Father!" Godwin cries. "Think of our people. None must come near until we see whether this man dies or recovers. I have touched him and must stay. Bring meat and drink and the wherewithal to build some shelter about us. Leave these things at the edge of the field and then go away and ask again how we do tomorrow."

'Now, loath as Athel was to leave his beloved child in such a plight, he understood that Godwin spoke with wisdom beyond his fourteen years. It was not unknown for a whole community to be wiped out by the plague and none left to bury the dead. So he answered, "It shall be as you say. Watch this night, and mayhap rest and food will revive the man, and he will be able to tell you what ails him and how he came to Clere Athel." "Why, as to that," replied Godwin, "he is a pedlar, for he has his pack with him. And he came in by the footpath through the woods at the back of the ridge. I have looked and found some of his wares scattered along the way. He has not passed through the village, of that I am sure."

96

'The next day Athel again hurried to the edge of the field and called to his son. "Nay, he is no better," says Godwin. "He moans, but I cannot tell what he would say, and I fear he is dying. Send strong wine that I may try if that will aid him." "No, by the true cross," Athel roars. "I can see you no longer in this peril. Strip off your clothes for fear of the infection and come away." But Godwin pleaded for another day, and in the end his father left him, in great agony of mind, yet still hoping that it might not be the plague after all or that if it were, Godwin, being both young and strong, would resist it.

'On the third morning, however, Godwin told his father that the man was dead and that he was certain it was the plague. 'We must burn the wheat, for the pedlar stumbled and threshed about in it before he fell, and the taint of the plague is all about." Now, when news reached the villagers of what was to be done, they made their way to the edge of the field and stood before Athel in great consternation. It was no small thing to sacrifice the wheat crop, and there was a very proper fear that such a fire would impair the soil. After all, it is not like burning off a bit of stubble to fire a whole crop. But Athel agreed with Godwin, and since our people dreaded the Black Death more than hunger, it was finally accepted that the grain must be destroyed. Torches were sent for, and Godwin called out that he would leave the pedlar's body in the midst of the field to be burned along with the rest of his belongings.

'The field below was fallow, but it was necessary to cut a wide swath round three sides of the field and drench them with water so that the fire should not spread. While this was going on, Athel kept calling impatiently to Godwin to delay no longer but take off his clothes and come out of the field. When at last the torches were brought, Godwin directed that everyone should move back to a position of greater safety, declaring he himself would fire the wheat nearest the body and a light fickle breeze would then carry the flames out to the dampened edges of the field. There were some who insisted this was not the way to do it, but Athel said well enough and let it be done as Godwin said, only let it be done quickly.

'It was the work of a minute or so for Godwin to start a column of flame leaping in the midst of the dry, ripe wheat. "Have a care, my son," Athel shouted. "Run out quickly while you can!" Then before the horrified eyes of our people the fire began to snake out erratically from the centre, running one way and then turning back upon itself, gathering strength and forming walls of flame that grew into a maze about Godwin. They could just hear his voice above the roar of the fire. He cried, "I have been infected by the plague, and I must perish that you may be saved." Then a great cry was wrung out of Athel, and he started into the blazing wheat, and Godwin's brothers after him. But the men of the village leaped upon them and dragged them back to safety. And our people waited there, huddling about them, until the fire burned itself out.

'They found what was left of Godwin and the pedlar and buried them where they lay. But the strange thing is that although the earth was burned, it proved more fruitful than ever. People said Godwin's self-sacrifice had blessed it, and for many generations after, prayers were said on that spot in the middle of the field whenever the stubble was burned.'

'But the prayers are not said nowadays?' I asked.

'Well,' said Grandfather, 'men hereabouts carry Godwin's story in their hearts, and if that isn't a prayer, I don't know what is.'

*　　　*　　　*

I have no favourite season of the year. In England, it seems to me, all are beautiful. But that being said, one must occasionally admit a rogue season, one that declines to play its part as it should, and just such an autumn now closed upon Clere Athel, dragging in a dank mist off the sea to wreathe the trees of the home park and drip melancholy from every gutter and sill about the Dower.

Mother seemed peculiarly affected by the mood of the weather. At first I only noticed that she sighed a good deal and complained frequently of headaches because it was too wet for us to take a walk. Then gradually I noticed that she appeared to have lost all interest in letter writing, had given up her needlework and her chats with Mrs Rimmer about the household affairs. Aunt Sophie remarked how quiet Mother was when they took tea together. But she was far worse when she was alone with me. I would search around desperately to find something to say that would cheer her. She seemed to find it an increasing effort even to answer me with a listless yes or no. Sometimes she would add a slight vague smile, as though to reassure, but I found this quite painful, it was so unlike the dazzling warmth of her own, true smile.

I could see Mrs Rimmer beginning to dart anxious little looks at her, and even Pegger muttered in a concerned way when he removed her plates at dinner and saw the food scarcely disturbed. In the end I could bear it no longer and went to talk to Grandfather about it. Grandmother was with him, and they both listened to a long recital of my alarm.

At the end Grandfather shook his head. 'Well, it makes no sense to me. What's amiss with your mother? Is she ill? Seemed fit enough at dinner t'other night.'

'No, she did not,' Grandmother snapped. 'Hasn't looked herself for months. Been very quiet. You haven't noticed because you never do. You and the children do all the talking.'

'Well, if you noticed, why didn't you mention it?' Grandfather said irritably. 'Can't be seeing after women's megrims myself, that's for you to do!' He turned to me and added in a kindly tone, 'She must see a doctor. I'll send for Bruce McIntosh. He's over at Upstrand, y'know. He can be here tomorrow morning.'

Later I told Athel about Mother and how Grandfather was sending for the doctor.

'I don't know what she will say when I tell her. I'm afraid she will say I should not have mentioned it.'

'I shouldn't worry. A visit from the Bruce may be just the

99

thing to reassure her. He's a plainspoken man but a good doctor. And anyway I don't believe she *is* ill, you know. I think she just isn't happy living here.'

'You think that's all it is.'

'Yes, I do. But it isn't a small thing, to contemplate living out your life in a place you don't like.'

'How very understanding you are. I wish I had the imagination to see Clere Athel as she does, but I haven't. And I'm selfish. I can't bear to think of leaving. That is why I have kept telling myself she would get used to it.'

'Don't be ridiculous! You won't leave Clere Athel—Grandfather won't let you. You belong here!'

'Oh, but I must go if Mother goes.' I felt confused and tearful at the thought of either parting.

'We'll see,' Athel said comfortingly. 'Don't think about it now. Wait until Dr McIntosh has been.'

Mother accepted the news of the doctor's coming visit with protest. I thought she seemed relieved that I had taken matters out of her own hands. But watching the arrival of Dr McIntosh next morning, I was again wishing I had not meddled. Some slight acquaintance with the medical profession had accustomed me to the image of tall silk hats and discreetly smart carriages. The rough-looking fellow who slid from the saddle of a fat roan gelding in sou'wester, saturated waterproof cape and mud-splashed thigh boots was a disquieting substitute. Nor did the language in which he instructed Pegger to see after his horse offer much comfort.

Unwrapped in the hall, however, he proved slightly more presentable. His tweed suit was at least neat and clean, and he produced a pair of pumps to replace the thigh boots.

'So, missie! It's not you I've been called to. Your mother, I take it? Antonia Athelson.' He rolled out the words with an aggressive Scottish accent. 'Where is she?'

'My mother is in her room. Will you come up?'

Mrs Rimmer stayed with Mother while Dr McIntosh examined her, and I waited in my own room and tried to read a book. It seemed a long time before Mrs Rimmer tapped on the door and said I could go back in. Her face beamed cheerful news. 'Everything is right as right can be. Doctor says there's nothing the mattter with her that a change of air can't cure.'

Dr McIntosh had just finished washing his hands when I went in. I thought Mother's colour rather high, as though she were embarrassed or irritated or both.

'Yes, I always list three requirements for good health,' he was saying, 'regular food, regular exercise, and regular bowels. And the best tonic in the world is cheerful company.'

Mother was not favourably impressed by the simplicity of this prescription.

'You're a widow, Mrs Athelson, I believe?'

'I am.'

The doctor pursed his lips and shook his head.

'A very dispiriting condition, widowhood. You should marry again.'

He scooped his equipment into an ancient bag with a broken handle. 'I'll say good-day to you then and be on my way, Mrs Athelson. Take my advice now—try a change of scene and a new husband!'

'What a graceless man!' Mother exclaimed, as soon as the door had closed behind him, and resentment had restored some of the old energy to her voice. But later I found her crying silently, staring out at the stone mermaid, and the heavy tears chased down her cheeks like the rain on the window.

'Why are you crying? Can I do something for you?' But she turned her head away from me and would not or could not answer. 'Please, Mother, you must tell me. What is the matter? I shall not leave you until you tell me.'

After a minute or two the dreadful, silent tears ceased, and she patted at her face with a fragment of damp handkerchief. 'I'm lonely.' It was only a whisper; I rather guessed than heard it. I wanted to say, 'You aren't alone. I am here,' but I knew these words would be a mere convention between us and that she could quite easily be alone when she was with me and I with her. So I just stood looking at her and feeling terribly sorry that I was her only child and she was my only parent and that wasn't enough, and that I could love and admire her and she could love and care for me, each after our own fashion, and that wasn't enough.

I said, 'You could go and spend Christmas in London with Aunt Mathilda and Uncle Simon.'

'Would you like to go?'

'I think you would enjoy it more if you went alone. There are always invitations you don't accept because of me. You could see all the risqué plays! And I . . . well, to be honest, I would have more fun here at Clere Athel . . . that is if you didn't mind my not coming. You know I am always rather tongue-tied at parties.'

Mother smiled slightly. 'What an admission from a carefully brought-up girl.' She considered me. 'Still, you are young yet, and I suppose it is natural for you to enjoy the company of your young cousins.' She was perfectly calm now, and her manner grew more resolute. 'Yes, I will think it over. I might talk to your grandfather and see what he thinks . . . whether you should stay here at the Dower or move up to the house. I am sure Mrs Rimmer might look after you as well as Sophie could . . . and anyway it would only be for a few days. . . . As I say, I will think about it.' And she added with something of her old sparkle, 'It would be fun to see a play.'

The next day she wrote to Aunt Mathilda, and then I went with her up to the house, to see Grandfather.

'I'll go in alone,' she decided suddenly, when we were waiting for an answer to our knock on the study door. 'You go and talk to Grandmother, Justine.'

Mother's spirits were certainly picking up now that the prospect of escape was before her.

I found Grandmother in the harness room.

'Well, what did the doctor have to say about your mother?'

'He said there was nothing seriously the matter with her . . . that she needed a change of scene and a new husband.'

Grandmother snorted. I think she was the only person I have ever met who genuinely snorted and very much in the manner of an outraged horse, as you might expect.

'How typical! It has always seemed to me that doctors have a great contempt for women. Only time they'll pay any attention to 'em is when they're deliverin'. . . . Then it's only self-glory. . . . Heave-ho! Like pulling a rabbit out of a hat and you'd think they'd done it all themselves!'

This second opinion both alarmed and confused me. 'Do you think Mother really is ill, then? Do you think we shouldn't rely on Dr McIntosh's opinion?'

Grandmother spread the pale, fragile hands that were so strong on the reins. 'Well, it is a singular diagnosis! Heard doctors recommend folks to take some funny things in my time, but never a husband. Now if you ask me, it's her corsets!'

'Her corsets?' I repeated in astonishment.

'Yes. Women who are in the fashion will wear their corsets too tight. . . . Always have. . . . Did myself when I was young. . . . More sense now. Then, of course, she don't ride. Can't promenade in the country, so a woman must ride.'

'But Aunt Sophie rarely rides,' I pointed out.

'Sophie's different. A fidgety woman. Gets her exercise fidgeting about the house and the dairy.'

I considered this. It seemed to me that what Grandmother said made a good deal of sense.

'Well, I do think a change would do Mother good. She's thinking about going to Aunt Mathilda in London for Christmas. She's gone to talk to Grandfather about it now.'

Grandmother was beginning to lose interest. 'Has she? Then she could always see another doctor in London. Anyway, tell her from me she shouldn't pay too much attention to McIntosh. . . . Only got to look at that roan he rides to see his judgement ain't sound!'

*   *   *

Mother went to London two weeks before Christmas, intending to return for the tenants' party on New Year's Eve. It had been decided I should stay at the Dower, and she had left some interesting parcels for me with Mrs Rimmer. 'But the shops in Lancaster are so poor. I shall be able to send something much more exciting from London,' she said. I gave her my present to take with her. It was a little chamois leather buffer for polishing the nails, and it had a silver and tortoiseshell handle. I got it from the only silversmiths within miles, and Athel helped me choose it. The price had been too high for my purse, but I wanted to give Mother something special because she was going away, and I asked Athel to lend me some money.

'No.' He had been firm. 'I won't lend it to you. But I'll give it to you.' I protested, but he explained. 'If I lend you the money, you will find it hard to repay, and then if you need money again, you won't like to ask. Or worse still you'll go to someone else for it. This way it's over and done with.'

I found it hard to accept the gift, but Athel would not allow any argument. All Athelson men seemed to have an inbred distaste for money transactions, and I have often wondered if that was why my father was not a success in business.

It was an attitude that was certainly a trial to their women-folk. Many a time I have heard Aunt Sophie, practically on her knees for the housekeeping, 'I wonder, Grandfather, if we might possibly have some money for necessities that must be sent for this market day,' and Grandfather roaring back, 'Confound you, woman, must we have this haggling at the breakfast table.'

Athel was never kept short of money, though. I think Grandfather gave him most of what he had in the way of ready funds, and certainly it was more than Athel wanted or needed for his own use, since he had no personal extravagances. Aunt Sophie said she thought it was because Grandfather had never had an allowance when he was young, but had had to ask *his* father for every penny.

'He seems to have resented that more than anyone guessed at the time . . . the sheer humiliation, you know. He told me once, that when his father sent him to tour Europe, his tutor was instructed to hold the money and letters of credit. Grandfather even had to ask him for a few coins to tip a waiter. I suppose he made up his mind there and then that his own heir would never be in that position,' Aunt Sophie told me. 'Certainly he was always very generous to Athel's father when he was young. But as soon as we married, he expected us to manage on what I brought with me! No wonder it went so quickly. And nothing to show for it now but the Red Poll herd on the home farm . . . oh, yes, didn't you know? It was my money that bought the foundation stock for that herd. I always think of them as my cattle . . . well, in a way.'

New Year did not, after all, bring Mother's expected return. She wrote first that the daughter of an old friend from our days in Paris was to be married there the third week of January and she was being pressed to attend. Would I mind if she delayed her return, or better still, could I not tear myself away from Clere Athel and travel to London at once and join her on the visit? I liked the idea and would certainly have gone. But even before I could reply, Charlotte caught scarlet fever, probably in Upstrand on a market day. We were all quarantined and under suspicion. I, especially, since I became feverish two days after Charlotte went down.

As it turned out, I was only suffering from a chill, but there were four other cases of scarlet fever in Clere Athel, and Dr McIntosh sternly forbade any movement. We were imprisoned in our houses.

Mother was for cancelling her plans and returning, but I begged her not to since I was well looked after by Mrs Rimmer and Hugh had moved into the Dower with me and was occupying Mother's bedroom. It was diverting to have Hugh for company, and thrown so together in this way, we formed a special bond of understanding that time and change have not undone.

By mid-February we were returned to normal. Mother was due back at the beginning of March, and Mrs Rimmer had insisted upon spring-cleaning the Dower from attic to cellar. I was keeping myself out of the way as much as possible, which meant that I was up at the house most of the time. I could always find something to interest me there.

One afternoon I was in the gallery, looking at a rather sparse collection of family portraits in the last of the light, when I met Athel.

'What are you doing? Trying to find a Raeburn or a Reynolds? Don't waste your time, we haven't any. Only rubbish left now. The best of the pictures went years ago. And you don't need to rely on my judgement, they've been valued!'

'How do you value your ancestors?' I asked. 'Surely not through the eyes of an auctioneer. You shouldn't expect anyone else to be interested in our relatives.'

'I don't. In fact I'm not very interested in them myself. After all, I see the same face every time I look in the mirror. It's a bore to have a family face, and I don't want reminding of it by them.' He gestured disrespectfully at a pair of Athels—one in a full-bottomed peruke and the other in a neat tie wig. 'Besides, I expect the best of them never bothered to get themselves painted. It's a damned silly thing to do anyway, to commission one's own portrait!'

The shafts of light from the mullioned windows were grainy with the dusk. We drew together before a bare wall at the end of the gallery, where a subtle difference in the tone of the panelling betrayed the fact that some large picture had once hung there, dominating the others.

'Was there a portrait here?'

'Yes. That was Eugenie. She was wearing a revel costume, and she had a mask on a stick in her hand. I remember her from when I was a child. Grandfather sold her. We were quite sorry when she went.'

'Was she very beautiful?'

Athel shook his head. 'I was too young to make a true appraisal. I think she had a rather triangular little face. She wasn't exactly smiling, but there was something about the eyes and the mouth that made you think she was faintly amused.'

'Mocking perhaps?'

'Is that how you imagine her? Yes it might have been mockery. . . . Pity we had to part with her picture. . . .

Ought to have kept it at the Dower. I wonder where she is now?'

'Well, by all accounts, she never liked Clere Athel, so maybe it was fitting that her portrait, at least, should escape,' I said, smiling at the notion.

But Athel did not like it. 'You make it sound as if she was a prisoner here. It would have been more fitting for her to stay where she belonged. At the Dower.' And there was a strong look of Grandfather for a moment, a look I did not care for, which filled me with unease.

'You are not like Eugenie, are you?' Athel turned to me with sudden suspicion. 'You don't want to leave Clere Athel?'

'No, of course not! I love it here. You know that.'

'Do I? Your mother brought you here because she hopes Grandfather will give you a marriage settlement. Perhaps that is all you want. Would you go if you got the money?'

'I—I don't know,' I faltered. 'I should have to do what Mother wanted me to do.'

Athel laughed unkindly. 'Well, you'll have to stay here forever if you are waiting for money. Grandfather won't give it to you because he can't.' He had hold of my arm and pulled me with a sudden roughness towards one of the windows. The rest of the gallery was swallowed up in shadows now. 'Listen to me, and listen carefully. What I am saying can make a difference to your future, your life. Grandfather will never tell you, because one of his strongest feelings is for the family and he hopes to keep you and your mother here, in expectation and hope, if not in love. Everything is mortgaged except this house and the home park. And the gold plate and the gold patens just about cover the mortgage, which Grandfather was forced to raise when he inherited. We have lived on that money ever since. There is nothing left now.' He spoke slowly and deliberately, as though to a child, and I seized the opportunity to interrupt.

'But why not sell the gold and free the land? Then you could sell the bigger farms to the tenants. I have heard it said that some of them are very anxious to buy.'

107

He shook his head impatiently. 'We can't sell the land to these people who have farmed it for hundreds of years. They asked Great-Great-Grandfather in his time and Great-Grandfather in his, but we have always given them the same answer. We will never sell the land. . . . But one day . . . one day . . . we will give it to them.'

'That is ridiculous,' I gasped. 'You will be ruined.'

'Not necessarily. It is a question of finding the right way to do it. We could not keep up this house, of course, but it ought to be possible to live off the home farm. Grandfather could not make these changes, but I could.'

'Have you talked about this with Grandfather?'

'No.' Athel spoke fiercely out of the darkness. 'He knows change must come one day, but he could not bear to think he was the last of his order . . . that would be as if he were somehow to blame by bringing it to an end. He hopes I will marry an heiress and keep the estate going for at least another generation.'

'And will you—will you do this to oblige him?'

'I don't know. . . . I honestly don't know what I would do if the time came and he was pressing me. You see I understand so well how he feels about Clere Athel, because I feel the same. It is like a trust holding this land and holding these families together on it.'

'Why doesn't Grandfather at least sell the gold and pay off the mortgage?' I asked, striving to find some practical suggestion to stave off the feeling of hopelessness which had overtaken me.

'He was going to do that, but the war in South Africa has caused prices to fluctuate. He hoped to profit by waiting for the right moment.'

'I don't know what Mother will say when I tell her. I am sure she will never believe me.'

'Then keep it to yourself for the time being. You are no worse off than before, and you both have a home here if you want it. I shall do no less for you than Grandfather, and whatever I have you shall share . . . always.'

CHAPTER FOUR

'THIS AUNT MATHILDA we hear so much about—I take it she's your mother's elder sister.'

I was not in the least surprised that Grandfather knew so little about Mother's family. This was the first time I had ever known him interested enough to ask.

'No, Aunt Mathilda is Mother's aunt, my great-aunt really, but I never call her that. Mother was an only child.'

'Have you any other family on your mother's side?'

'No one as close as Aunt Mathilda and Uncle Simon.'

'And they've no children of their own, I think.'

'No.' I waited, prepared for what came next.

'Will they leave your mother their money? Seems as if they're a well-feathered pair, with a house in London and a place in Oxfordshire and all this gadding about foreign parts they do. . . .'

Aunt Mathilda and Uncle Simon were going to Baden-Baden and had just written to invite us to go with them, which was why Grandfather was giving them his attention.

'I suppose Uncle Simon is very comfortably off,' I answered cautiously, 'but I don't think he will leave Mother any money. He has a younger brother with five sons.'

Grandfather frowned. 'No, no! Daresay he won't in that case. After all, you're not blood kin to him, are you?' He

109

thought for a bit. 'Has your mother's aunt nothing of her own to leave?'

I suddenly felt very defensive about Mother's family. They had not been landowners like the Athelsons, but gentle people, living quiet, unassuming lives on modest incomes. Perhaps they had only left small annuities and a love of the fine arts to their children, but it seemed to me that Grandfather was in no position to call them to account for that. And my loyalties were so confused at that moment that I even found some satisfaction in the sure knowledge that Mother's father— that other kindlier, frailer grandfather remembered from early childhood—would have thought the Athelsons a rough crowd.

Grandfather on Mother's side had suffered from ill health most of his life. A chest condition led him to live in the south of France shortly after he married, and there, with a small inheritance from his father who had been rector of a country parish, he purchased a pretty little white-walled house with a huge mulberry tree shading the courtyard. I remember him well, for we used to visit often, and we would find him sitting in a big wicker chair with a rug over his knees. He would always be painting. Over the years he had earned a respectable reputation as a water-colour artist and occasionally sold a few pictures. And once when we were watching him, a huge, ripe mulberry fell from the tree on to his paper and he brushed in the juice to make a sunset sky. I liked that. He wasn't at all cross, although the painting was nearly finished. 'One must accept any gift that falls from above and do the best one can with it,' he said. His hands were very small and delicate for a man. I see them always busy, working away with brushes and paint while he talked. He died when I was nine. Mother felt the loss. I don't know that there was any remarkable closeness of understanding between them, but she adored him because her mother died when she was born and he had been both parents to her.

I knew little of my maternal grandmother, who died when she was nineteen, save that her name was Justine and I was named for her. But Aunt Mathilda had once told me they were the daughters of a classics scholar, who owned a preparatory school but could never make it pay.

'No,' I said. 'I don't think Aunt Mathilda will have anything of her own to leave.'

Grandfather sighed and shook his head. 'Well, it's damned unfortunate. . . . Still if they take you about a bit, you may find a husband who'll have you without prospects. . . . Not that I like you leaving us and going jaunting off, mind. Like to have you ride round the estate with me, like the way you get on with our people, like almost everything about you.'

I restrained myself from asking what he did not like. Being Grandfather, he would certainly have told me.

'Anyway your mother has it set in her mind that you *will* go, so there's an end of it. . . . But this place, Baden-Baden'—he scowled heavy disapproval—'they tell me folks go there for the water . . . well, it may be all very fine for bathing in, but don't you go drinking any of it. You can't trust the drinking water anywhere outside the British Isles. Stick to the wine and you'll do very well.'

I did not attend to Grandfather's advice too strictly and nevertheless contrived to do very well indeed. I have pleasant memories of Baden-Baden, of a certain elegance about its buildings, of wide, well-kept lawns made pleasant with fountains and shady trees, and of agreeable drives in the surrounding countryside. Like all fashionable watering places, it exists principally to cosset and divert rich tourists, who have grown tired of the cossetting and diversions they have at home. That is not to decry it. One may take the waters and bathe by day, and then in the evening the cuisine and the pale-gold German wines both reward and undo these endeavours. Aunt Mathilda and my mother soon contracted a lively acquaintance, and we made up card parties or danced. Indeed, now I come to think of it, the most vivid recollection of that vacation is one of us revolving endlessly to the *valses* of Johann Strauss. I enjoyed it all very much, just that once, for the experience. But I am out of my element in what is generally called society.

Autumn found us in Paris, and Aunt Mathilda led us on a grand shopping expedition, filling our wardrobe with the fashions for the new season. We went to the opera and visited old friends, had our hair restyled by Antoine de Lannier, who was then the rage, and attended a series of musical soirees, where we kept hearing the same currently popular lieder singer.

I began to get homesick for Clere Athel.

It was then that Athel wrote to me, the first letter I had had from any of them in all the months of my absence, for the Athelsons are not letter writers.

My dear cousin,

What a very long time you have been away. We begin to wonder if you are ever coming back. Charlotte and Hugh and I miss you very much, especially when we play tennis or croquet, and Hugh says he is fed up with having Cousin Rainbird for a partner! Furthermore, Charlotte says what about the dress you say you have bought for her in Paris. It will be historic costume by the time she wears it. Grandfather misses you, too. He says that if you are back by the twenty-first of November he will let you attend the witenagemot. I told him that would bring you home if nothing else would, and he said write it then at once, which is why I am here now, signing myself yours affectionately. . . .

Athel

And Athel was right, of course. Nothing on earth would have made me miss the opportunity of going to the witenagemot, for this was the annual parliament of Clere Athel, a tradition as old as its Anglo-Saxon name, and normally women did not attend, unless they were senior members of the family or widows who had been granted tenancies in their own right, which was rare enough. Aunt Sophie had never been invited, and Mother was discouraged when she expressed a mild interest in attending. Occasionally Grandmother and Great-Aunt Ivlian went. They had been the previous year when

Athel, being seventeen, had taken his own place for the first time. Grandfather saying I could go must mean he really did want me back at Clere Athel, and I went at once to show the letter to Mother, hoping she would agree to make plans for our return journey.

She was not pleased. 'Oh, Justine! I don't want to go to Clere Athel now, just at the beginning of winter. You remember how dreadful the weather was this time last year. . . . I couldn't stand that again. I thought we would travel with Aunt Mathilda and Uncle Simon and spend Christmas in London. You surely don't want to go back just for a dreary meeting.'

'But I do,' I said. 'The witenagemot is so very special, and Grandfather may never give me the chance again.'

'Oh, nonsense! Even *he* could not be that unreasonable. If he says it is permitted for you to go this year, then next year will do just as well. And really now you are seventeen—nearly eighteen—you can benefit so much from a London season. It will give you confidence, more poise,' Mother persisted. 'And only think of the lovely dresses Aunt Mathilda has bought you . . . to be wasted in Clere Athel!'

'Perhaps I could go back for the witenagemot, then, and afterwards I could be with you in London . . . please, Mother. I should love to see them all again.'

'But this travelling about is so expensive! Your grandfather really is the most tiresome old man to be tempting you with this, just when I had written to him that we might stay away until after Christmas. Quite treacherous! And he knows perfectly well what he is doing, trying to put you at odds with me.'

However, I finally persuaded her to let me go on condition that I did not waste more than a week of the season in Clere Athel.

The hall in which the witenagemot was held was the oldest part of the house, dating back to the beginning of the eleventh century. In the late fifteenth century a handsomely proportioned manor house had obscured it from view by the park approach, but it was allowed to remain as a jutting wing at the rear of this building and continued to be used for meetings, the storage of arms in times of danger, and the customary harvest and Yuletide hospitality to tenants.

Further building in the Elizabethan style usurped at least two of these functions, providing the large dining hall, where tenants were now entertained in greater comfort, and the gallery above, where they danced on New Year's Eve. The early Georgian Athelsons, making their contribution of the drawing room with the long windows, to say nothing of additional bedrooms, better kitchens, and a dairy, had thoughtfully incorporated a gun room in the design, so that now the antique arms were displayed there and the old hall had only the witenagemot left to justify its continued existence. It was enough.

Folks said, 'Hold witenagemot in Old Athel's dining hall? Why, we never 'eard of such a thing. Witen's always been 'eld in t'old 'all. There's no virtue in change for change sake. Got wood beetles borin' away at it, has it? Well, Old Athel will just have to sit up nights and bang 'em on t'head when they pops out.'

I had never seen inside the old hall, because by tradition it was kept locked until the meeting drew near, when it was given an airing for the occasion.

'I think Grandfather believes that keeping the door locked stops the beetles getting through into the rest of the house,' Hugh said, when we went in to explore.

'My goodness, it's gloomy, and what's that smell?'

'Age. None of the windows open. The women will be in to polish directly and that helps to kill it.'

'Does Grandfather sit in this big chair?'

'Yes . . . at least he will if it's still safe.' Hugh sat down gingerly. 'Look how these pieces of carving just break off in your hands. The wood's rotten . . . just powder . . . holding together by force of habit.'

An enormous panelled screen of some dark wood was set a little way behind the chair, and I moved closer to examine it in the dim light. There were traces of lettering upon it, but the surface was worn, and I could make no sense of it.

I was suddenly aware of a faint stirring in the stale air of the room. I looked around and saw that the door was slightly open and Great-Aunt Ivlian was standing in the middle of the hall.

'I startled you,' she said. 'I am already my own shade. Soon I shall whisper in the dust of this room and no one will even see me, let alone hear me.'

Hugh and I exchanged a look. Great-Aunt Ivlian had begun to talk a good deal about her death, and we never knew how to answer her. To change the subject, I asked her if she knew what had been written upon the screen.

'*Sumus sunt.* Very inelegant Latin. One might say it was a family motto.'

This surprised me since the family had steadfastly resisted the temptation to record an achievement of arms, and I remembered how scathing Grandfather was when I innocently asked about the crest on the carriage door. 'Crest on the carriage door?' he had repeated incredulously. 'Well, I cannot say I have ever noticed such a thing, but it may be so. There have been Athelson brides flaunting coats of arms, I shouldn't wonder, but only from their own families! They never had one from us.' He made heraldry sound like some hereditary disease. 'And what use would an Athelson have for a coat of arms, who, in the days when such things had a purpose, took precious good care never to go and fight in other men's wars?' He chuckled wickedly. 'Many's the messenger who rode in here seeking to raise men for a king's army and our people drove them, horse and rider, on to the marsh at pike's end and swore the call to arms had never reached them. . . . No, Justine, banners and devices are for men far from home and among strangers. We have no need of them.' Here, my mother had incautiously observed that a friend of hers claimed descent from Norman times and had a number of interesting coats of arms in her family. Grandfather's lip curled. 'Normans! Don't mention Normans to me! Didn't we have to buy our own land from them to be left in peace here? Nothing but a pack of johnny-come-lately adventurers!'

Great-Aunt Ivlian moved nearer the screen and traced the dark scored marks with a reflective finger. 'Not carved, I have always thought. Burned. Probably with a poker or maybe a mulling rod used to froth the ale. Alfred says it was done by Thorold Athelson, a younger son, who went with other Lancastrians to fight for Henry the Sixth against the Yorkists.'

'How does Alfred know?' I asked curiously.

'Alfred's family has always been in service in the house. They know more about our ancestors than we do ourselves and remember everything. Alfred's great-grandfather lived to be over a hundred years old, and it is said there never was such a teller of tales. Anyway it seems the night before he set out this Thorold took a good deal of wine and vowed he must have a war cry to lead the half dozen men he was taking with him. He chose "We are, they are." Quite appropriate for an Athelson.'

'And what happened to Thorold?'

'He was killed and all his men with him.'

'Grandfather told me no Athelsons ever went to war.'

'Did he?' Great-Aunt Ivlian frowned. 'Well, I conclude he meant none in the line of inheritance. I certainly do not know of any Athel Athelson who went to war until your poor uncle took it in his head to fight in South Africa! But younger sons must have gone on occasions, looking to win themselves some fortune. Why, I should not be at all surprised if a number of them ended their lives as mercenaries in Europe.'

'Well, you won't catch me doing that!' Hugh interrupted suddenly. 'I'm going to be a veterinary surgeon. I'm going to learn how to mend horses' legs, when they break them, and all the great racehorse owners, even the king, will pay thousands of guineas for my services!'

Great-Aunt Ivlian and I looked at him in astonishment.

'When did you get that idea?' I asked.

'Oh, I've had it a long time,' Hugh said airily. 'I've talked it over with Grandmother, and she says she will find the money for fees. She's all for it, and thinks I may be able to study at Liverpool. They just got their royal charter, you know. . . . Anyway Grandmother is going to find out about it.'

The delivery of this communication had left Hugh rather flushed, but obviously well pleased with himself, so I could not bear to dampen him with any doubts about Grandmother's ability to get money for his studies. It gave me real pain to think he might be disappointed.

Great-Aunt Ivlian said vaguely, 'I daresay it is a reasonable notion. It would not have been so in my young days, but they tell me everything has changed. They are always telling me that. . . . I sometimes think there is nothing constant now *but* change. There! I have made an epigram . . . at least I think that is what it is.' She looked about her as though suddenly struck by the recollection of something mislaid and then drifted out of the room as silently as she had come.

I went over and put my arm around Hugh and gave him a squeeze.

'It's a wonderful idea, Hugh. I think you would make a very good veterinary surgeon, and you must have a head start because of what you have learned from Grandmother. Have you told Athel what you want to do?'

'Not yet. Grandmother said not to talk to anyone about it yet. . . . But I have now, haven't I?'

'Never mind! Great-Aunt Ivlian has probably forgotten already and I won't say anything to anyone. But Athel might help you.'

'I doubt it. He has problems enough of his own. And besides, I don't want to ask him for a slice of his patrimony. It's not done, you know.'

I have ever since had this picture of Hugh in my mind, of him sitting in a worm-eaten chair of old seignorial rights, which his brother would inherit and he would not. And the formal word 'patrimony' seemed as natural to him as if it were a simple, nursery noun he had known all his life, his use

117

of it dignifying the disparity of fortunes. 'Hugh was just born gallant!' Charlotte once exclaimed, when she was really calling him a fool.

* * *

The witenagemot was held in November because it was the quietest month on the land. But there was no such thing as a day without work in Clere Athel, so even at this season the meeting could not begin before six o'clock in the evening. A great log fire had been lit in the early morning to air the old hall. An hour or so before the meeting pine cones were being added to scent the woodsmoke and candles set glowing in a dozen iron candelabra, which stood on the floor and matched the height of a man.

'God alone knows when we shall dine,' Grandfather said, dispatching the last crumbs of a providentially large tea. 'You never can tell how long it will take when folks get arguing.' He directed a nod at me across the darkening room. 'Well, Justine! I've no doubt you will find it hard to follow our proceedings this night. You'll likely hear words your mother wouldn't wish you to hear and learn a hard fact or two she would rather have kept from you, but I'm not about to apologize for that. Life isn't all soirees and morning calls. You're a grown woman and my granddaughter, and I'm not going to have you wrapped in the sham innocence that says it is. Now if you go to the window and look out down the drive, I believe you'll see a pretty sight—a line of lanterns bobbing along towards us through the dark. And that means our people are coming to us with their grievances, claims, and appeals, and now, as always, we are going to try to give them justice.'

Alfred came to tell us that there were some forty people settled on the benches of the old hall and no more expected. Athel and I followed Grandfather at a respectful distance, and when we reached the door, we heard Fenn Haldane's voice.

'Will you receive Athel Athelson, Athel who is to succeed

him, and Justine Athelson, a well-loved daughter of this house?'

There was a general murmur of assent, but no one rose. It was one of the good things about the relationship between the family and the people in Clere Athel, perhaps even a unique thing, that none of the traditional signals of fealty was ever expected or offered. Perhaps this, more than anything else, lay at the root of the community's long existence. The people of Clere Athel had always accepted and followed the leadership of the Athelsons, but not without the right to question and never without pride and self-respect. No tenant of ours was ever seen to tug a forelock, and the man who bent his knee even in Great-Great-Great-Grandfather's time could only have been tying the laces of his gaiter. So our people sat when we entered the hall, for the very good reason that they were already sitting, and we walked to our places at an ancient trestle board covered in books and records and sat down facing them.

'Now,' said Grandfather. 'We'll take the reassignment of the tenancy of Orchard Farm, first . . . the request of Katherine Leigh. . . . Is Kate here? . . . Ah, yes, there you are, Kate. . . . As you know, the Leigh family are always giving us a great deal of trouble on account of a lamentable tendency to beget twins.'

A gentle laughter stirred around the hall.

'Not always,' Kate protested.

'Often enough. However, we don't blame you, Kate, never fear! Anyway, in this generation there was some added difficulty on account of it not being known which of Kate's two sons was eldest born. Poor Mrs Rush, who assisted at the birth, is no longer with us. But you will remember that when she had bathed and swaddled the boys and put them to lie in their cradle side by side, she could no more tell t'other from which than she could fly over the moon.'

A deal of murmuring and nodding confirmed this.

'Now, as the boys have grown up, we have always looked towards the time of their mother's resigning the tenancy with some concern. There have been those among you who suggested a joint tenancy ought to be granted, as the most fair and just way of dealing with the matter. But with a little thought you see this could not possibly serve. What of *their* children and their *children's* children? Orchard Farm is good land, but we cannot see it supporting a whole tribe of Leighs!'

'Especially not if they are twinning in alternate generations!' put in Athel.

'The good Lord has foreseen our problem, however,' Grandfather said, 'and He was already at work making provision against this day when it was necessary for us to give a judgement. William Leigh has fallen in love with Ellen Thrustleton, and they are to be married. And as you well know, the Thrustletons of Little Meadows have only their daughter, Elly, left to them, since their boy, Roger, died two years ago.'

'Pneumonia!' Athel whispered to me.

'Ted Thrustleton, here, is well content that I shall set it down in writing now before you all'—Grandfather took up his pen and drew a vast leather-bound book towards him—'that William Leigh shall work Little Meadows with his father-in-law and inherit the tenancy of same at his death . . . and this being so, Kate's other son, Harry, shall now become the tenant of Orchard Farm, his rights never to be disputed at any time. For William and Harry being agreed to this decision, so their heirs must abide by it.' Grandfather turned to Athel, who was sitting at his right hand. 'Have you anything to say?'

'Only that Harry will need to employ help at Orchard Farm now, to replace William.'

'Aye, that's rightly said. Think on now, Harry.' He directed a nod across the hall, to where the Leighs were sitting alongside the Thrustletons. 'Orchard Farm is land we expect to see well worked. Don't think to save yourself the hire of a man's full-time labour. Or two lads giving half-time, if you'd rather. There's Richard Warrener with four sons set about him; be glad to see at least one of them placed, I shouldn't wonder.'

It was plain from Harry Leigh's scowl that he had hoped to work a single-handed miracle, but I saw Athel jot down 'Get Leigh and Warrener to terms,' and I didn't doubt he would.

'We'll take the permission for the Leigh-Thrustleton marriage as granted since I have already consulted the Blood Book and all's well. But in the question of the application to marry made by Elizabeth Coppin and Arthur Parr, I'm none too happy in my mind. The affinity is closer than I like, no more than six generations past, and neither the Coppins nor the Parrs seem to have married with any outsiders for centuries. . . . Has anyone anything they would like to say that might help us reach a favourable decision?'

I had never heard of the Blood Book until then and thought this strange talk about a marrying. In fact, the Blood Book was a record of every family in the village, kept for more than six centuries, its object being to protect the community from the consequences of inbreeding. Many people might find the concept of such a book outrageous. I know my mother did for one, when I told her about it. But all in Clere Athel upheld it as a strict necessity in their lives, saying that in the past there had been 'those who had flown in the face of its wisdom and gotten witless and crippled children.' That had been God's punishment, they said, for breaking His natural laws and no one in the village but dreaded to do such a thing 'for very shame'.

The village being isolated and the people seeming deliberately to hold themselves aloof from the outside world, inhabitants of Clere Athel might well have degenerated without the guidance of their records, for it had been a very rare thing over the years when a newcomer to the village was accepted and permitted to settle, infusing new blood.

So there were sighs and murmuring regrets, but no one had anything good to say for a match between the unhappy Elizabeth and Arthur if the book did not favour it.

The rest of the meeting was concerned with plans to rebuild a row of six cottages, a heated discussion about hedging and ditching, and the settlement of annual accounts. The last item gave Fenn Haldane much work, writing furiously in a vast ledger, though I noted that no money changed hands. It seemed that whatever was owing was either in somebody's barn or in their byre. Sometimes it was merely in their good intentions or their optimism. I even heard it confessed to be in their stomachs. It was never in the bank.

'Now,' said Grandfather, 'if no one has any other matter to raise, we'll be going to our—all right, Muriel, what's the matter wi' thee?'

A handsome young woman, with a dawn-pink complexion and a windswept sort of beauty about her, had stood up at the back of the hall and was waving energetically at Grandfather.

'If you please, sir, I was wanting to ask whether you couldna do summat to make my Jake marry me!'

There was a roar of laughter, and although Grandfather did not join in, it was clear he was mightily amused.

'Well now, Muriel, that isn't exactly the easiest commission that ever was put upon me.'

'No, sir. But I know you can do it if you've a mind to.'

Grandfather shook his head. 'I doubt Rabbity Jake will pay any heed to what I have to say. He's his own law and his own conscience.'

'But he will, really he will! He sets great store by your opinion,' Muriel cajoled prettily.

'Tush, woman! You're talking to a man who has been buying his own rabbits and hares back from Jake for nigh on twenty years. If he'd any respect for my opinion, do you think he'd make his livelihood by poaching my game?'

'Ah, now that's the curious thing on it, sir! He canna see it that way hisself. He always says them rabbits is wild and rightly belong in t'forest. But they burrow along and 'appen up in yon park.'

'Oh, he says that, does he?' Grandfather growled. 'And when he pops a sack over one of the fowls in my yard, he reckons that's wild, too, and has just flown in and settled there by chance, I suppose?'

Muriel could find no defence for this, it seemed, but Athel unexpectedly came to her assistance.

'I imagine Muriel is worrying about the children. You have a second one now, haven't you?'

'Why, that's it exactly, Athel.' She beamed. 'I mean it ain't right for them. Jake and me not being married. There's the girl three now. Soon she'll be old enough to understand, and other folks' children won't spare her. The lad's no' but four months old, but what'll it be like for him growing up without a name?'

'All very fine to think about this now,' Grandfather interrupted impatiently, 'but you never found yon children on a pumpkin patch! Now if it had been rape, we'd have made Jake wed thee or turned him out of Clere Athel. But when you were expecting your first and I talked to you about it, you told me very plain that you loved Jake and had a mind to live with him even if he wouldna make an honest woman of you.'

'Aye, tha's made thee bed, and thee mun lie on it, me dear!' Mrs Leigh said roundly.

'But I always thought Jake'd change his mind,' Muriel wailed.

'A man never changes his mind when you expect it of 'im, only when you don't.' Mrs Leigh was implacable. 'Tha's a pleasant lass in many ways, and I'm sorry for thee. But children should be made in a lawful bed and not in a hayloft. There's a lesson in thee for every girl in t'village, and I only hope they pay heed to it!'

Mrs Leigh's judgement, not being untempered with kindness, was given a respectful attention by the meeting. There was plainly good-natured sympathy for Muriel in her predicament, and all eyes turned hopefully to Grandfather, who was deep in thought.

'Suppose,' he said at last, 'just suppose I was to threaten to turn Jake out of his cottage if he willna wed Muriel. . . .'

'What! Turn him off our land! Oh, thee couldna do such a thing, Athel Athelson!'

'No! No! He dunna deserve that!'

'Oh, no, sir, please!' Muriel cried. 'I never asked for such a thing! He's a simple, good man in his way. . . .'

'Hush up!' roared Grandfather. 'Of course I wunna turn him off. Tha knows that. I know that. But does Jake know it? He isn't here. I said suppose I were to threaten it. . . .'

The meeting digested this thought.

'It might serve,' Ted Thrustleton said thoughtfully. 'No one loves the countryside hereabouts more nor Jake. It'd break his heart to think of leaving.'

'Aye, he loves my parkland,' snapped Grandfather. 'And his isn't a trade you can carry everywhere. Other folk bring the law on poachers, though it may surprise you to hear it!'

'It'll never work,' said Mrs Leigh. 'The men'll never keep the secret. They'll tell Jake it's no' but a plot to get him to t'altar!'

'Now then, Mrs Leigh, tha's already put in thy two penn'orth this evening. It's worth a try for Muriel's sake,' said Fenn Haldane.

Grandfather turned to Athel. 'What do you say?'

'I think Fenn should tell Jake tomorrow that you don't like his irresponsibility towards his children and that if he doesn't put up the banns by the end of week, he goes. I think further, that anyone here who lets us down should forfeit four fat geese at Christmas, the imposition of this fine to be witnessed and approved by all present.'

There was some doubt about the size of the fine, but—
'Come, come!' said Grandfather. 'No one will have to pay it unless he cheats on us. Only think of Muriel and her children and hold your tongues. We'll give Jake a week to think it over, as Athel says, and see what comes of it.'

'Right,' said Fenn. 'I'll tell Jake in t'morning. Like I'll not find him home tonight since I saw that lurcher of his along the low footpath and——'

'The low footpath! shouted Richard Warrener, leaping to his feet. 'Was it heading towards my place?'

'Aye.' Fenn grinned. 'Now I think on it, it was.'

'Damn you, man! Why didn't you say so afore? Tha knows that dog never leaves Jake's side.'

Fenn chuckled. 'But then I didn't reetly see Jake, only t'lurcher slipping along under t'hedge.'

'Tha knows full well Jake would be t'other side of hedge. Tha might have warned me! I'm off now, any road. The thought of Rabbity Jake loose among my fattening turkeys fair drives me mad!'

The sequel to the meeting was awaited by the entire village. At first Jake had scoffed at Grandfather's threat, and unable to confirm, but suspecting Muriel's attendance at the witenage-mot, he boxed her ears a time or two for any guilty part she might have in the business.

As the days passed, he began waylaying folks, testing public opinion. 'I canna understand Old Athel—what's it to him whether I'm wed or not? Do I ask to see his marriage lines? He'd never turn me out of the cottage I was born in, though . . . would he?'

He even stopped Athel and me when we were riding over to a Saturday fair at Upstrand.

'You're a rogue and a thief, Rabbity Jake,' said Athel. 'Happen Grandfather thinks this as good a way as any to rid Clere Athel of you.'

Perhaps it was this encounter that finally broke Jake's nerve. Anyway, the following day being Sunday, the banns were called. The thunderous applause that filled the church was not seemly.

CHAPTER FIVE

WHEN I WENT back to London at the end of the week, I noticed a change in mother's mood. There was a sort of breathless catch of excitement when she laughed and a graceful significance in the way she carried herself, which stirred childhood memories of the days when my father was alive.

I asked Aunt Mathilda, 'Has Mother got a beau?'

'Goodness,' said Aunt Mathilda, 'aren't we growing up! Yes, she has, and I think him very charming, whatever your Uncle Simon may say. Don't you be the one to discourage her, either! Pierre Aucassin has everything to recommend him to your mother . . . as an escort or even as a husband if he asks her.'

'Doesn't Uncle Simon like him, then?'

'Oh, you know what men are! If you ask me, my dear, he's simply jealous! Pierre Aucassin is very distinguished-looking and very rich. He also happens to be a foreigner and therefore knows how to turn a compliment to a woman. That is quite enough to make any Englishman distrust him.'

Aunt Mathilda busied herself impatiently with the coffee tray. I could sense an issue, and since we were alone—Uncle Simon having dined at his club and Mother away to a theatre and supper party—determined to fortify myself with the facts.

'Is he French?' I asked, pondering on the name Pierre.

'Well . . . half French.'

'And the other half?'

'I understand,' Aunt Mathilda said carefully, 'that his father was of Oriental origin—Egyptian I believe . . . or was it Turkish? He was educated in France anyway, and he has travelled very widely. The family has banking and tobacco interests.'

'And you think he means to ask Mother to marry him?'

'As to that I cannot say, of course. Antonia met him—oh, it must be a year ago now—at an embassy reception. Just the once. But he sent her a magnificent gift of flowers when he left London. He was on his way to Cairo, you see. They haven't seen each other since then. Now he has come back. Terribly romantic, really. I am sure he only came to England to find your mother again.'

'Has Mother said anything to you about him?'

'Not much. But I can see she likes him. Indeed,' she added with a sigh, 'I don't believe any woman could fail to do so. He's forty-five—such a suitable age—has never married, and has just built the most palatial villa in Lebanon. He brought a sketch of it to show us.'

I thought Aunt Mathilda seemed to have catechized Mr Aucassin very well.

'Anyway you will get a chance to meet him yourself. He's dining with us next Friday. I have seen to that.' Aunt Mathilda nodded triumphantly. 'All very well for your Uncle Simon to be dithering on about whether foreigners make reliable husbands, the fact is there aren't many eligible bachelors in their forties, and he don't consider that Antonia is left very awkwardly placed with no money of her own to speak of. And no help coming from your father's family by all accounts.'

The idea that my mother might be about to throw herself into the arms of a dubious foreigner to recoup our fortunes teased me for a long time before I slept that night. But in the end I resolved all the evidence cheerfully since Mother was clearly in better spirits and looks than she had been for years, and Aunt Mathilda was too sound-headed to give her blessing lightly.

I looked forward to the Friday dinner party with impatience, taking particular pains to make a good appearance at this important meeting. When I at last presented myself in the drawing room, I felt that Mother's inspection was peculiarly searching, but she nodded, satisfied, and I was at liberty to take a suitably retired chair with a good view of the double doors standing open to the entrance hall. Mother had still made no mention of Pierre Aucassin to me, and I wondered what she was thinking, what she was hoping, while I watched her rise with Aunt Mathilda to greet the first guests.

I had a direct view of the large gilt mirror in the hall, which it seemed no gentleman could pass without some nice adjustment of his collar, a caress of whiskers, or a darting of cuffs. In this way I was introduced to each male guest in turn, looking over their shoulders at their little unconscious vanities before they made their entrances. I almost missed Mr Aucassin's arrival, because he was the one man who did not look in the mirror. He stood with his back to it, giving his cloak and hat to Patterson. But his height and breadth of shoulder in an impeccably fitting jacket attracted my attention. Then he was entering the room, easing his way through a party of women who had just come down from leaving their wraps and now stood blocking the doorway while they found their escorts, paying his respects to Aunt Mathilda and Uncle Simon, saying what was proper to the acquaintances in his path, and yet his eyes hardly left my mother.

Mother was trying to make conversation with a comfortably bosomed woman in violet silk, but she had seen Mr Aucassin, and her attention wandered. When he finally reached her and I watched them talking together, I knew instinctively that they were in love and just as surely that all would now be well for her.

It had been contrived that Mr Aucassin should take me in to dinner so that we could get acquainted. Mother introduced us but gave no sign that there was anything special to her about this man. I wondered if Aunt Mathilda had told her of our conversation.

'So you are Antonia's daughter, Justine.' His voice was pleasant with the slightest hint of an accent. 'I should not have known it. You are not at all like her.'

'No,' I said. 'I am like my father's side of the family.'

'And does that please you?' The question came swiftly. Clever, I thought, because of what it could reveal.

'Not very much. I am said to favour my grandfather. I think it would have been in my better interests to take after Mother.'

He laughed, and I grew bold enough to look more closely into his face, taking in the strong features, the high-bridged, slightly hooked nose, the brows marked straight and heavy about dark, penetrating eyes.

'Your mother tells me that your father's family have property in the north of England and that for the present you are making your home there.'

It was the first confession of any intimacy between them.

'Yes, we have been staying at Clere Athel.'

'She tells me you are very fond of this place and that you have cousins there near your own age, whose company you much enjoy.'

I recognized this as a gentle prompt, an attempt to draw me out. But I had no wish to resist. It was a pleasure to me to talk about Clere Athel, and I told Mr Aucassin things I had never put into words before. I told him about the tall pines and their grace in any season, their long blue shadows on the snow and the soft sibilance of their topmost branches on a still summer day. I told him about the miles of sand that had pushed back the sea to a thin rim under an infinite sky. I talked about the family, too: how Grandfather knew the land so well that he could predict the yield of any acre to the bushel, taking into account not only the weather but the nature of the man who had sown the crop; how Grandmother had sat all night in the stable straw, cradling the head of a mare in foal; how it was Hugh's nature to be gay and affectionate and Charlotte's to be solemn and undemonstrative. I talked about Aunt Sophie and Cousin Rainbird. I even tried to describe Great-Aunt Ivlian. But I didn't talk much about Athel. It isn't easy to describe Athel.

I realized they were starting to serve the entremets, and I had talked almost continuously through Aunt Mathilda's long, stately dinner. Yet I never felt I was boring Mr Aucassin, because every now and then he would interrupt with a close question or an appreciative chuckle. And when I stopped for very shame, he at once began to tell me of his own enthusiasm for Lebanon.

'I understand so well how you feel. I, too, love a place. And it is strange, for this is not the land of my birth and yet I think of it as home . . . even as you find yourself drawn to Clere Athel. I think I was very much the same age as you when my father first took me to Beirut. He had to transact some business there, but when it was complete, he said to me, "Come, Pierre. No we are here we will take ourselves a small excursion and wonder at the cedars of Lebanon." . . . And so we made the two-day journey over six thousand feet up into the mountains to the Cedar Grove, and I fell in love with Lebanon among these magnificent trees which were famed even before Solomon was king. Believe me, nothing I have ever seen of the splendour of nature has moved me more. So at last I have built myself a home just outside Beirut, and whenever the pressure of business allows, I return there—to see the trees and listen to the waters of the Kadisha Torrent. Perhaps you will visit me one day and I may have the pleasure of showing you the beauties of my adopted country.'

Something in his manner of issuing this invitation, perhaps the very deliberate pause for my answer, gave it a special significance. Surely this was more than a mere politeness. It recalled me with a jolt from the enthusiastic flow of our conversation. Had he already proposed to my mother, and if so, had she accepted him? Was he in reality offering me a home, anxious to know whether I would make it difficult for her to leave England?

130

I tried to think quickly, to give the answer that might be of best service to her. But what if she did not choose to marry him and intended to make me an excuse for refusing? Then I remembered how they had looked together when they met in the drawing room.

I said, 'I am sure I would love to visit Lebanon, and if the opportunity ever arises, I shall remember your kind suggestion.' A proper, neutral answer, I thought, but it seemed to please him well enough, and watching him closely while the pudding was served, I saw his eyes search out my mother farther down the table and the almost imperceptible nod he gave her.

I had said good-night to Mother in the drawing room and was about to get into bed when Aunt Mathilda's maid brought a message to say Mother wanted me to go to her.

'Is anything the matter?'

I thought Flora looked knowing, but she was too discreet to commit herself.

'I don't believe so, Miss Justine. Your mother is in her room, and I'm to bring you a pot of hot chocolate in there directly.'

Mother's bedroom was on the floor below mine. I put on a wrapper and went down to find her brushing her hair. She looked remarkably young and pretty in the lamplight, with the froth of a lacey peignoir about her bare shoulders and the silky abundance of her hair hanging free almost to her waist.

'Come in, my dear. I hope I didn't fetch you out of your bed. It suddenly occurred to me that we have had scarcely a moment alone together since you came back from Clere Athel.' The brush strokes grew more vigorous. 'I have had so many engagements.' Our eyes met in the reflective depths of the mirror. Was I right in thinking her cheeks darkened? But the light in the room was deceptive from the pinky bowl on the lamp. 'I thought we might drink a cup of chocolate together.'

Not for me to point out that the night of a party, when we were already late going to our beds, was a curious time to remedy any such deficiency.

'Shall I sit on the daybed?'

'Yes, dear. . . . Ah, here comes Flora now. . . . Justine,

move the little table so Flora can set down the tray. Thank you, Flora. That will be all. Good night.'

Mother came over to sit by me while she plaited her hair. 'Shall I pour?'

'Yes, do. Now you must tell me all your news!'

'I haven't any news.'

'No news!' Mother frowned momentarily. 'Really, Justine! How difficult you are. . . . Of course you have news. What about the witenagemot?'

'You don't really want to hear about that, do you, Mother? Why don't you tell me your news instead?'

Mother looked startled. 'My news! Why I—How did you enjoy the party tonight?'

'I thought it was a very good party.'

Mother was watching me closely, and I did wish we could stop playing cat and mouse and that she would tell me directly what she wanted to tell me. But it was not Mother's way to come right at a thing. She liked to feel her way, judge the mood of her audience.

'And Mr Aucassin? You found a great deal to say to him. . . Did you like him?'

'Yes, he's very pleasant. He seemed interested in Clere Athel, so I told him about the family. Then he told me about Lebanon. He is very easy to talk to.' I waited, but Mother did not say anything. She was drinking her chocolate, staring over the rim of her cup at nothing in particular. 'He appears to be an admirer of yours,' I added boldly.

'What makes you say that?'

'Oh . . . the way he looked at you for one thing.'

'You saw him looking at me?'

'Often. And then he wouldn't be interested in Clere Athel or me if it weren't for you, would he?'

'Modest of you,' said Mother.

'Realistic.'

'You know, I don't think that I like this tone in you, Justine. You unbalance me. It isn't like talking to a child at all.'

'Well, I'm not a child now, am I?'

'It's this hanging around the stables at Clere Athel——'
she began doubtfully and stopped. 'Still, as you are so worldly-
wise all of a sudden, I may as well tell you that Mr Aucassin
has asked me to marry him.'

'Have you accepted him?'

'Not yet. He only asked me yesterday morning. I have told
him I will think it over.'

'But you are going to marry him?'

'Well, what do you think about it?' Mother asked sur-
prisingly.

'Me? But it isn't for me to say.'

'Of course it is. You don't imagine I would marry a man
you would dislike as a father. I want you to make your home
with us.'

'But . . .' I hesitated. I had been about to say that I would
hate to surrender Clere Athel in exchange for Lebanon; that
Mr Aucassin would never be a father to me, only my mother's
husband; that I would visit them often if only I might continue to call Lancashire home. I could not say any of these
things, for they would be unforgivably hurtful. 'I wouldn't
mind you marrying Mr Aucassin in the least,' I said. 'If you
will be happy with him, I shall be happy, too.'

Mother had half guessed what I was thinking anyway.

'Pierre is very rich, you know. There will be all the money
you want for travelling, and we shall probably travel a good
deal. You could go to Clere Athel from time to time. He has
promised to make you a generous allowance and settle capital
on you when you marry. He is a very openhanded man, and
to tell you the truth, I think he looks forward to having a
daughter he can indulge.'

'That is very generous of him,' I said rather awkwardly.
I did not want to hear her justify the marriage by talking
about money, so to change the subject, I asked when she
thought the wedding might take place.

'I haven't decided. Quite soon, I think. And quite quietly,
here in London, from this house.' She poured another cup of

chocolate. 'I shall have to write to your grandfather. He won't like it.'

'Why ever not?'

'He'll never understand how a woman who has been privileged to bear the name of Athelson could think of changing it.'

I was bound to agree. 'But it doesn't matter to you what he thinks, does it?'

Mother shrugged her elegant shoulders. 'I would rather he had wished me well.' She looked at me moodily. 'You won't let him turn you against me, will you?'

'Never!' I said staunchly. 'How could he? Anyway he wouldn't try. He isn't like that. You don't understand him.'

'Perhaps not. At least don't ever let him persuade you there is anything disloyal to your father in my marrying again.' She got up and went over to the dressing table, making minute and unnecessary adjustments to the array of cut-glass flasks and brushes, while she deliberately kept her back to me. 'When one is young and marries for love despite difficulties . . . well that is a very different thing. . . . One doesn't repeat that. It can be painful, and maybe one wouldn't wish to. The quality of love changes as you get older. Comfort and compatibility are the larger part of it. You understand?'

'Yes,' I said. 'I understand.'

Mother was married twelve weeks later, towards the end of March, 1906. They were going to spend a month in Italy and urged me to go with them. But I refused firmly, and Aunt Mathilda supported my argument that it would be far better if I returned to Clere Athel, at least until the end of summer, when Mother would have had time to settle in the new villa, now nearing completion.

So I waved her off happily, glad to see how assiduously Pierre attended to every detail for the ease of her journey, and then turned my attention to my own arrangements.

Just before she left, Mother had given me a bankbook, with a handsome deposit in my name. 'Things have changed now,' she said. 'I want you to go to Clere Athel feeling completely independent. You are a sensible girl, so I have given

134

an authorization that you may withdraw what amount you like, whenever you like, both in London and the branch in Lancaster. Take this letter with you when you make your first withdrawal.' I looked at the signature with the two flourishing capital letters. Mother's initials remained the same, only now they stood for Antonia Aucassin. Everything else, as she said, was changed.

There were even changes at Clere Athel, I was shortly to discover, although naturally these had nothing to do with Mother's second marriage, and they were not at first apparent when I drove through the village, with a cheerful greeting from everyone we passed.

The first intimation of trouble came when I had reached the Dower and was enjoying being fussed over by Mrs Rimmer.

'There's a note here for you from your cousin Athel. He said I must on no account forget to give it to you directly you arrived.'

A few scrawled lines on a folded piece of paper said, 'Grandfather in a foul mood. Don't come up to the house today. I'll come round to you this evening and explain. Don't want this to spoil your homecoming. Looking forward to seeing you.'

I looked at Mrs Rimmer, who had folded her lips meaningfully.

'What has happened? Why is Grandfather angry?'

'There's a troublemaker in the village—that's what's happened. Causing no end of a stir, the big good-for-nothing!'

'Who are you talking about, Mrs Rimmer?'

'Timothy Tyte, Bartholomew's younger brother—him that ran away to sea when he was thirteen years old. Brought grief to everyone the day he was born, he did. His mother died, and his father was never the same. Josh had always been a hard-drinking man—well, a forge is thirsty work, so perhaps one must make allowances for that—but after his wife was gone, he grew mean with it. Still, he did right by the boys, and he was always specially fond of Timothy. It was a terrible shock to him when Timothy ran off without a word, and it were eight years before ever a letter came to say where he'd gone——'

'Yes,' I interrupted quickly, 'but what is this man doing to make Grandfather cross?'

'What isn't he doing?' was the unhelpful reply. 'Well, if he isn't turned out of the village soon, I dread to think what will happen . . . all this wild talk! And there are those who'll listen to him, more's the shame of it. I'm sure I don't know what young people are coming to these days.'

'For pity's sake, Mrs Rimmer,' I implored, 'I cannot understand what it is all about. Do sit down and tell me the story properly.'

'No, no! I'm away to get your dinner. I'll not bring myself to repeat wicked nonsense. When folks begin to question the right of a good master to hold his own property, I begin to think I've lived too long. . . .' And she bustled off, muttering, to the kitchen.

When I had finished dinner, I went through into the drawing room. It was a chilly April evening, and the doors to the terrace were closed. I stared out at the silent fountain and the ornamental trees still with their poor bare branches and the winter moss making the trunks an eerie green in the unpromising dusk.

'There'll be a frost tonight,' Pegger had said, when he served my soup.

'Really, Pegger, that isn't very welcoming of you,' I had teased.

'Spring's late. There's nowt'll come on in t' garden if this keeps up.' He had made it sound as though the world would never bloom again.

Now, looking out of the window, I began to think he might be right. I was lonely and depressed, and things were not well in Clere Athel. I wished Athel would come, and the wishing brought him, as it sometimes miraculously does. There was a rattle of stones, and I looked across and saw him climbing over the garden wall to land with a thud among the lilac bushes, as he had done the first night I met him.

I fumbled eagerly with the catch on the door and ran out on the terrace to meet him.

'Justine!' he said, and he caught my hands and held them tightly in his own. I was confused because he said my name in a special way, giving it a sound and a meaning it had never had before so that for the moment I could not say anything. 'You're shivering,' Athel said. 'It's bitterly cold out here; let us go inside.'

'I'll ring for Mrs Rimmer to bring coffee.'

'Tell her to bring the brandy, too. I could do with something to warm my toes.'

Athel piled some more logs on the fire and moved two of the lamps. 'There now! That's more cheerful, and I can see you better.'

'Good! I hope you like what you see.'

'Oh, I do. I do. . . .'

'Well, I rather wish you wouldn't stare so; you're making me quite uncomfortable.' I laughed defensively.

'Your hair is different.'

'It's called a Grecian knot. Anyway I am eighteen now. I have to wear it up, you know.'

'Yes, I'm sorry I didn't send you a birthday gift. I do have one for you, but it's a surprise. You'll get it any day now, if Pegger performs his part.'

'How mysterious! Whatever can Pegger have to do with it? I brought you something, too. I don't intend to give it to you until tomorrow. I have presents for all the family, and I wanted you to open them together. Now, are you going to tell me what this trouble is that seems to have upset everyone so much?'

'Everyone?'

'Well, Mrs Rimmer sounds like Cassandra, but she isn't very specific, and I can only gather it has something to do with Timothy Tyte.'

'Yes, it has. Tim Tyte left Clere Athel when he was a lad, ran away to sea, and now he has come home again, with a hook where his right hand used to be and a block of wood between his ears. He doesn't know anything about the way things are here, but he rants on about social justice as though he had just invented it and he's been down every night at the alehouse, trying to stir up folks against the family.'

'But what does he want them to do?'

'God knows. He says those tenants who want to ought to be able to buy their land, and he talks about us perpetuating a feudal myth, holding them back from the reality of the twentieth century. It sounds quite impressive, and he comes with an aura of experience from the great, wide world, so some of the farmers' sons have been daft enough to listen to him. But his talk doesn't have any real meaning here. He goes on as though we were grinding the tenants into the dust and pays no mind to the fact that we only take peppercorn rents and some labour and produce. Anyway, I don't need to tell you. You know how things are and how I feel about them. It's only for Grandfather's sake that I mind. He takes it very hard.'

'So this Timothy Tyte is some sort of revolutionary?'

'I suppose that is what you would call him. He's a bitter man, without home or family, and I guess he just wandered back here to sponge on his brother. When he found his talk of other lands and other ways gave him some claim to attention, it went to his head, and now he sees himself as a leader of men, a sort of saviour of the agricultural poor.'

Athel stood up impatiently and crossed the room to stare down into the fire.

'What is Grandfather going to do about him?'

'I don't know what he can do. You remember how things are between him and Bartholomew Tyte—well, Bartholomew has a perfect right to have his brother staying with him and Timothy hasn't broken the law. He only talks.'

'Has he come face to face with Grandfather yet?'

Athel turned around, smiling faintly.

'No, that'll be the day! But several of the tenants have come up to the house, asking whether Grandfather would consider naming a price for their farms. They got the answer you'd expect, of course, and now they have formed some kind of deputation and requested a hearing. Fenn Haldane brought the news this morning, and I thought Grandfather would have a fit. That is why I left you the note. He'll have cooled off a bit by tomorrow. He's been looking forward to your arrival, but I thought he might take it out on you somehow.'

'Why should he? I haven't done anything.'

Athel sat down beside me, eyeing me doubtfully. 'No . . . but he wasn't very pleased about your mother getting married again. I thought he might bring that up and say something you would both be sorry for.'

'Oh, I see. Actually he wrote and said he hoped she would be very happy. I was quite surprised. The letter was perfectly reasonable, rather grudging perhaps, nothing more.'

'Well, it cost him something to send it, I can tell you! Grandmother and Mother and even Cousin Cuthbert all worked on him for days. We practically had to hold him down and put the pen in his hand.'

'How ridiculous! Mother has been a widow for years. Anyway, Grandfather ought to be glad she has married. Now he doesn't have to keep her. Or me, for that matter.'

'But that is just the point, as you very well know. Grandfather wanted to keep you both. He wants to keep us all.'

'He can't really afford to, can he, though?' I snapped, still thinking about Mother.

'This foreigner your mother has married, he can afford to keep you better than we can, I suppose?'

'Yes.'

'Money isn't the most important thing.'

'I never said it was.'

'Will you go and live with them in Lebanon?'

'I may,' I said curtly.

Athel stood up abruptly. 'Oh, to hell with you! You are always going or talking about going. I don't know what you came back for.'

I stood up, too, and we stared at each other bleakly. Then I saw something in his face that I could not resist, and I said, 'Athel, stop it. We're quarrelling, and I can't bear that. I'm sorry if I was hurtful—it is just that I sometimes feel torn between Mother and the family.'

To my relief Athel accepted this at once and smiled. 'I know. I ought to understand that. And I would if only I didn't . . . Oh, anyway, let's forget it. Pour me another brandy, and then turn me out into the cold night. You must be tired and I have to walk across the park.'

'If I pour you another brandy, you'll be staggering across the park. You have already had three. Whatever would Grandfather say?'

'He'd say, "Don't cross me, woman. Give me the brandy!" '

It was a good imitation of Grandfather's roar. Too good. And I wondered just how much of Grandfather there was in Athel's nature.

'Grandmother said I was to tell you to come in good time for lunch tomorrow. We could ride in the afternoon, if it is fine. I'll get my work done in the morning.'

'I should like that very much,' I said. 'What are Hugh and Charlotte doing? Will they come?'

'No,' Athel spoke carelessly over his shoulder. He was already striding across the hall. 'I shan't ask them.' The door closed, and he was gone without saying good-night.

CHAPTER SIX

'WELL, CHILD, so your mother has run off and got married.'
Grandfather's gruff greeting to me next day made it sound
like a piece of the most abandoned folly. 'And now you are
alone in the world you have come back where you belong.
Quite right. Give me a kiss!'

'I should like to stay here . . . perhaps until September, if I
may . . .' I began tentatively.

'What's that? Asking me? This is your home, girl. Never
let me hear you talk such stuff again. As for you leaving in
September . . . we'll talk of that nearer the time. It ain't
fitting for young girls to be travelling half across the world
on their own. And I tell you plainly, although your mother
writes that she wants you to join her later, it don't seem a
suitable arrangement to me at all.' He turned away to avoid
argument. In fact, I knew better than to give him one.
Grandfather detested open challenge, and the way to handle
him was to let the sleeping dog lie until the very last moment
and then sidle around it.

After that he made no further reference to Mother's marriage
and showed no interest in the details of it. But Grandmother
and Aunt Sophie were full of questions, and later I had to do
my best to describe Pierre Aucassin for them and satisfy them
on such points as where my mother had met him, the length

141

of their acquaintance, the size and quality of the trousseau, and the proposed range of the stables at the Lebanon villa.

I made a poor showing with the answers, and when this last inquiry defeated me utterly, Grandmother was quite disgusted.

'What a tiresome gel you are to be sure! You're hardly telling us more than Antonia did in her letter. Still it's plain she's landed on her feet, and I'm glad of it. Always said she had style, and a woman like that ought to be able to make life give her what she wants.'

Aunt Sophie giggled. 'It is really quite diverting to think Antonia took Dr McIntosh's advice after all. Do you remember how he prescribed a new husband for her? I think I must consult him myself!' I looked at her, surprised to see the sudden flush in her face and her eyes peculiarly bright.

Grandmother was looking at her, too, and there was a small awkward silence.

'Marriage may be infectious, but you ain't the type to catch it,' Grandmother said at last, and though the words were tart, enough, her tone was not unkind.

Aunt Sophie's flush deepened, yet she was not to be crushed. 'Oh, I don't know,' she said jauntily. 'I caught it once before!'

It would be ridiculous to say Grandmother gaped. She could not have done any such thing. There was always a trancelike stillness about that fine-drawn, fleshless face, with only the dark, bright eyes moving restlessly and sometimes kindling with pleasure at some private joke. But I felt that her *mind* gaped. Was it Fenn Haldane, I wondered, who had given Aunt Sophie this uncharacteristic assurance? It seemed unlikely she could have any other admirers without the family knowing.

I do not know whether Grandmother made her guess in the same direction, but—'Don't be a fool, Sophie! Above all don't let a young, impressionable girl hear you talking like one. Count your blessings, and be content as you are.'

About the middle of May it was suddenly summer, and the land, having overslept, became prodigal of green tendrils and lush, thrusting leaves. Days of brilliant sunshine, with warm evenings and light showers during the night, made us all cheerful, especially Grandfather, who was confident the men of Clere Athel would be kept too busy to pursue the uncomfortable issue of the deputation which he would not receive.

'I'll hear them at the witenagemot—not before!' he told Fenn Haldane. 'Every man may have his say there, and I'll have mine.'

But the rumblings and grumblings of the tenants persisted. The first hay crop was cut, and not even the long hours in the fields could tire the argument out of Timothy Tyte's closest adherents.

Pegger, at once loyal and critical towards the family, brought his alehouse news to Mrs Rimmer, and she repeated it to me with much dour shaking of the head.

'There's trouble over the labour the men have to put in on the home farm hay. Some are saying they won't give bidden labour any more, and that they must be hired for an hourly wage.'

'But they owe us the labour. They know perfectly well it is part of their rent,' I replied.

'Aye, I knows it, an' tha knows, and they knows it an' all,' said Mrs Rimmer, her dialect broadened as a measure of her outrage, 'but they're a nowty lot when they feel hard done by. And if you want my opinion Old Athel were wrong not to meet 'em. He should have talked to them face to face and cleared t'air.'

* * *

Athel and Fenn agreed with her. They had both been trying for weeks to get Grandfather to change his mind.

'You could call an extraordinary meeting of the witenagemot if you prefer not to go against custom,' Fenn suggested.

'Extraordinary!' Grandfather shouted. 'I should be damned if I didn't call it an extraordinary thing to hold the witen out

143

of season to please a ne'er-do-well son of old Josh Tyte.' His anger was frightening, his voice like the wrath of Thor, and he seemed to grow inches taller, which, considering he already stood head and shoulders above other men, gave him an almost supernatural advantage. In the face of it, Athel, who was quite six feet tall but still with the touching thinness of boyhood, seemed almost fragile. But he would not cower, and he would not bend. Instead, he would stand there, white as death, saying what he had to say in a steady voice, and only his hand, shaking slightly when he pushed back the stray lock of wheat-coloured hair from his forehead, betrayed what he was feeling.

Fenn Haldane could face up to Grandfather, too, though it was his way to bear the storm with a darkened colour and a sullen, dogged set of the mouth, waiting silent and resolute to have his say when Grandfather had blown out like a hurricane.

We had many such scenes about this time, and they usually raged over our heads either at mealtimes—which was not unnatural as the members of the family hardly came together at any other hours of the day—or just after, when we were taking coffee in the drawing room. Aunt Sophie would be reduced to tears and would leave us. Hugh would go as well if he could. It used to make him feel physically sick, he said, and I think his own nature being so easy and uncomplicated, he could not understand or forgive anger.

On the whole, Charlotte's reaction was the most surprising. She was so young, and yet she appeared to take no more than a detached interest in the proceedings. I was frankly afraid of Grandfather, although I tried not to show it, and I used to force myself to get up and fetch an old journal from the sofa table if we were in the drawing room or ask Grandmother for a second cup of coffee, braving his notice. When we were dining, I would eat unhurriedly and complete the meal no matter that the food became tasteless in my mouth and tormented me afterwards with the effort of digestion.

If the arguments wore most of the family down, it became apparent that they were wearing Grandfather down also.

Athel and Fenn had managed to get the hay in on the home farm, by summoning all the goodwill and diplomacy at their command, but nothing would make the men of Clere Athel take part in the customary pitchfork contest, and this was almost certainly the means of persuading Grandfather that he had been wrong.

Dearly as he loved every tradition of his people, the times when it was customary for him to give them gifts were his happiest, and the pitchfork contest was one of these occasions. The men would show their skill with the last load of hay, competing to see who could raise the most on a single pitchfork, and the winner kept his measure as a prize. It was an occasion for a lavish picnic, and there would be home-made sweetmeats for the children to take away and a keg of ale for the oldest competitor. Grandfather was really hurt when he heard the men did not want the contest. At first he would not believe it, but Athel convinced him, and it was then that he turned to Grandmother.

It was hard to understand what there was between Grandfather and Grandmother. Most of the time an outsider might conclude there was nothing at all. But in the moment when Grandfather was vulnerable he turned to her with uncertainty in his voice and said, 'Well, Cecily, what do you think about this?'

Grandmother did not fail him. 'I think you have handled the whole matter extremely well' was the prompt and emphatic answer. 'Very proper that you should keep them waitin' and wonderin' before you agreed to meet them. Now it turns up as sweet as you please. Can say that since they're prepared to give up a day which all—especially the children—enjoy, see they have a serious point of view. Deputations new-fangled things, and wouldn't know one if you fell over it, but the date of the witenagemot could be advanced, and you'll recognize their right to speak there according to custom.'

Not only was this a perfect opportunity for Grandfather to save face, but it was a sound suggestion whichever way you looked at it. The dreaded deputation, with its hint of demand

and its want of precedent, was the thing to shy away from, while in the tried and trusted framework of the witen, Grandfather was master and judge.

Grandfather gave the idea a rapid appraisal, and it was clear that he liked it.

His acceptance was cautious for form's sake. 'I have been thinking . . . there's no real reason why we shouldn't change the date of the witen if we've a mind to do so. And if we must face trouble, as well now as at the sad end of the year.' He chewed his lip thoughtfully and then looked at Fenn with a sudden gleam in the eye. 'Suppose—I only say suppose, mind you—that you were to tell our people that it would please me to feast them on contest day as I always do, only they can leave their pitchforks at home this year and the children can run races instead. Then in the evening we'll have the witenagemot. . . .'

Fenn nodded. 'It might do——'

'Might do!' Athel interrupted, throwing back his head with a whoop of laughter. 'Grandfather, you're incorrigible! You never miss a trick and there's no advantage you won't take, is there? You know that if they take your salt, there's many of our folk won't like to speak their minds so free at the meeting.'

'Well,' Grandfather growled, 'all's fair in love and war, and this is a bit of both.'

Athel nodded, his face grown suddenly serious. 'I know it, Grandfather. I understand.'

'What I'm wondering,' said Fenn, 'is whether Timothy Tyte will try to get into the witen. I'm sure he'd have come with the deputation.'

'Yes, and as most of our men feel unsure of their legal position as tenants, they'll want him there to give them courage,' Athel added.

'They've reason enough to worry about their position, when they come to me demanding that I should surrender land our family has had title to for nine hundred years,' Grandfather observed acidly. 'But that they should hide behind a hook-

146

handed, bar-rail politician into the bargain! All I can say is the blood's run thin in our people! Still'—Grandfather brought his mind back to the original question with an effort—'the possibility must be faced. Of course he has no right to attend, he ain't a tenant, nor a tenancy heir, not yet a cottager. But we don't want any sort of a fracas with him beating on the door or shouting through the keyhole. None of that nonsense!'

'No, indeed! And the fact is'—Fenn eyed Grandfather warily—'the fact is he may have a right to attend. He only needs one of the tenants to call him as witness to a cause, you know.'

'Damn!' said Grandfather. 'I was forgetting. Will they think of that, I wonder?'

'Like as not they will. And if they don't and come asking my advice as to how they can get Tyte into the meeting, I shall be bound to point it out to them.'

'The devil you will!'

'It would be my duty,' Fenn said simply. 'Of course, you could argue that he is not a fit witness, since he's virtually a stranger in these parts. But it would be a nice point. Custom has always been to give a liberal hearing to anyone.' He consulted some notes on a scrap of paper. 'I've a record here of two shepherds brought over from Houghton Beacon way in 1853, when a pedlar's daughter claimed she was'—he glanced uncertainly at me—'er . . . discomposed by one of our lads. Some of our folks heard the shepherds bragging in a tavern at Upstrand that they had . . . er . . . discomposed her themselves only a short while previously, and she not at all unwilling . . . I merely quote you this to show there is a precedent for complete strangers being admitted to the witen.'

'Oh, yes,' said Grandfather, with none of Fenn's scruples, 'but when a man's defending himself against a charge of rape, that is an exceptional matter. His good repute, even his freedom may be at stake. . . . Nevertheless, I take your point. And if Tyte *must* come, then let him.'

Clere Athel was both relieved and excited by the prospect of the witen at the end of May. There was a general upsurge of goodwill for Old Athel, who had had the grace to change his mind, and the invitation to the traditional picnic was readily accepted.

'Though God knows what they are hoping for!' Athel told me when we were alone. We were often alone these days, for Hugh was studying—preparing for his entrance in the veterinary course at Liverpool University—and Charlotte was helping Cousin Cuthbert with a new generation of toddlers in the village school. As I had little to occupy me, Athel suggested I should help him with the paperwork involved in the management of the home farm. I did not find it a labour much to my taste, but at that time I believe I would gladly have cleaned out the pigsties to please Athel.'

'Don't you think there's the slightest chance Grandfather will sell to the tenants of the bigger farms? Your mother seemed to feel he might.'

'No, not a chance. We talked about it when you were away. He sold his beloved gold then and redeemed the mortgage—the land is clear now. But when I asked him if it was his intention to sell any, he was appalled and reminded me of the old promise we made. "Don't you be the one to dishonour the Athelsons in the minds of our people," he said. Nothing would make him change his decision.'

'Why did he suddenly want to pay off the mortgage, then?'

Athel shrugged. 'The interest, I suppose. It always sounded an unbusinesslike arrangement to me, to borrow capital when you can raise it from your own resources. But then I don't think Grandfather knows anything about business. I only wish I did. Somebody around here ought to try and get us on a more economic footing.'

I shook my head. 'I can't imagine Clere Athel run on the commercial principle.'

'Well, I always seem to be reading in the journals that the big organization is the thing. It ought to be more efficient and profitable than a number of small units.'

'Then why doesn't it work?'

'I don't know,' Athel said fretfully. 'This is where I feel

the lack of a formal education, experience of the world.' He waved his hands helplessly. 'Perhaps we're trying to keep too many people; perhaps we should go in for more machinery. . . .' He turned to me with a sudden intensity. 'Justine, it frightens me that when Grandfather goes, I shan't know what to do. If I make the wrong decisions, families might go hungry. . . . Oh, I know there are some who could fend for themselves if I gave them their land. They might even grow rich. But what about the others with their little strips of market gardens and their bits of cottage industry? If I can't *make* the land keep them, they might starve!'

I felt frightened at the thought of the responsibility, but I said as cheerfully as I could, 'What nonsense! It won't come to that. When I first came here, you talked to me of all sorts of hopeful plans you had for Clere Athel. What became of them?'

'I hadn't given any thought to the practical details then. I was just like Timothy Tyte with his half-baked notions.'

Sooner or later Timothy Tyte had a way of insinuating himself into every conversation. I seemed to have heard his name a hundred times in the past month, and yet, curiously enough, I had never seen the man. Clere Athel is just that size of a place where if you are on the lookout for someone, you do not see him, but if you are trying to avoid an encounter, it is inevitable.

'Ah, yes. Timothy Tyte. Have you heard yet whether he will come to the witen?'

Athel nodded. 'I believe Richard Warrener means to call him. I only hope he will have the grace to put his views civilly.'

'Grandfather will be more than a match for him on any terms. I think he is a much harder man than you will ever be. Insolence won't hurt him.'

The hedgerows were sweet with white and red May blossoms when the day of the witenagemot arrived. I went walking early and climbed up to the top of Godwin's field. Even at nine o'clock in the morning the sun was hot across my shoulders as I stood on the hill. I could see the Warrener cows dappled by the light and shade of their leafy meadow. And since it was a festive day with no school, children were swimming in Little Rip.

I went up to the house about noon to find the family and the household staff assembled in the hall and Grandfather assigning the business of the day.

'Well, miss! And where do you think you have been? I expected you here directly after breakfast to make yourself useful. As it is, you have missed half of what I had to say. Never mind, never mind! What good to say you are sorry now? Sit down and be quiet.'

Grandfather and Athel, it appeared, would not be attending the picnic party or the games, thus avoiding the possibility of any undesirable encounter outside the witen. Instead, Grandmother would preside over the afternoon's events, and Hugh would organize the sports.

'And think on,' said Grandfather, 'that I want every member of the family alongside me at the witen this evening. I want a solid wall of Athelsons behind the high table. You, Cecily! Don't be telling me there's a mare foaling, for she must labour on her own. You, too, Sophia—as Athel's mother, you must be there——'

'Not Charlotte,' Grandmother interrupted. 'Charlotte's not old enough for the witen.'

Grandfather considered, frowning. 'Very well then. Charlotte is excused. But every other member of my family will attend.' And then a very interesting thing happened. Grandfather's eyes moved warily among us until they found Great-Aunt Ivlian sitting in the shadows of a stone arch at the back of the hall. For an instant he stared at a point directly above her head. '*Every* other member of my family,' he repeated.

The day passed amiably enough, but there was an air of waiting and with the strange perversity of human nature people showed their anxiety by too-ready laughter.

'They're feeling Grandfather's presence more because he ain't here,' Hugh said simply, another contradiction.

It seemed that all of us who had seen the day through were

a little tired by the strain when the witen opened. Perhaps that had been part of Grandfather's plan. Certainly no one looked as relaxed and vigorous as he did himself. Elegant, too, in his brown velvet jacket and ruffled shirt. He took his place with Athel on his right hand and Grandmother on his left. Then there was Hugh just below Grandmother and I next to him, and Aunt Sophie and Great-Aunt Ivlian at the opposite end of the table. Fenn Haldane and Cousin Cuthbert sat a little apart at a separate, smaller table, claiming a becoming impartiality.

We made, as he had wished, a good show of Athelson stock.

Grandfather knocked on the table, although the meeting was already fully to order and indeed sitting almost at attention. The tenants had struggled back into their dark Sunday best jackets, despite the stifling atmosphere, heavy with burning candles, and spotted neckerchiefs were already being pressed into service to mop the sweat under starched collars.

'There is only one reason why we have called this meeting out of season, and tha knows it reet well,' said Grandfather, without preamble. 'I hear of strange talk among you.' He scanned them and repeated the words slowly. 'Strange talk, indeed. . . . Yet even the wildest words may deserve attention, if they are spoken from an honest heart. And so I will hear you . . . as I have always heard you . . . even as my fathers heard your fathers. . . . Now, who wishes to speak first?'

Claimants for the honour did not immediately present themselves.

Timothy Tyte could only be the gaunt, brown-skinned man who had planted himself, legs asprawl, in the centre of the front row. I watched him, wondering whether he dared lead the assault party. A not unattractive fellow with a rakish twist about the mouth, floridly curling sideburns and bright-blue eyes, he hadn't the look of a man of Athel.

But it was Richard Warrener who opened the meeting, and I am bound to say he put the case for the tenants as well as any man on earth could have done. I am glad I heard him, for what came later was not so good. I longed to know what was going on in Grandfather's mind as he leaned forward, listening intently to this solid farmer with an honest, weathered face, talking with reason and dignity of his lifetime of labour and his hopes for his four sons. The hard fact for him was that the better the yield he won from the land, the more produce Grandfather wanted to take from him.

'Of course, I knows thee doesna want it for thee sen. I know it goes to keep t'old folk and pay for the new drainage scheme and the like, which is to the benefit of all. But the truth is you'd never bring yourself to up money rents the way you tak' kind, and yet kind's one an' all wi' money to me, for if I marketed it me sen, I'd 'ave brass and could reinvest it in t' land or put it by for t' lads. Now I'm asking no favours from you nor any man, but the right either to have a fixed rent, which I'll meet on quarter days, or better still a rent and a mortgage. No matter it were a struggle, I want to see that land mine in my lifetime. Many others hereabouts feel the same. That's our dream. But it never will come true unless you give us a chance, let us know where we stand and plan for ourselves from one year to the next.'

Approval and sympathy with these views were proclaimed in many parts of the hall when Richard Warrener had finished speaking. He mopped his face with a large blue handkerchief, then wiped the palms of his square hands on it and finally blew into it, and all this time Grandfather said nothing. The silence lengthened.

'I am thinking,' said Grandfather at last, 'of the succession of bad years you had when you first took over the tenancy from your father. I'm remembering what a struggle you had, when your sons were no' but knee-high to this table, and I'm recalling that you never went short of owt. . . . Now just suppose there was rent and a mortgage to be met and you came on hard times again. Would you expect to pay me interest on top of interest and see your debt mount up without the principal one whit reduced and the land no nearer being yours than it ever was, or would you not come to me looking for help, as you have always done? And how shall I help you, who have nothing myself unless you pay me what you owe? I tell you, Richard Warrener, that when the only relationship between two men is a debt, the world becomes a far harder place than you or any of our people here have ever known.'

'But I'm not in debt yet,' Richard Warrener protested, stoutly good-humoured. 'You've got me already behind wi' t'mortgage and going downhill fast. But 'appen I'll manage better than you think. . . . Furthermore'—he cleared his throat, just a shade embarrassed suddenly—'if you'll pardon the liberty . . . that is to say . . . well, we all know you've a job to mak' ends meet you sen, and with a steady income from the sale of some of the farms over the next twenty years or so, you, and young Athel after you, could set the home farm up better nor it's ever been.'

'Thank you kindly,' said Grandfather coldly, 'but I can manage my affairs without your advice. Now who else wants to say something? Very well, Arthur Parr, what's on your mind?'

Arthur Parr was probably in his early twenties, much less sure of himself than Warrener, and must be continually verifying that his feet were where he had left them. Nevertheless, he had his say. Clere Athel had clung too long to the old ways. There were machines to do the work for you now, even one that swept the dust out of your house and another that played like a full brass band inside a small box. Grandfather laughed a good deal at that, refusing to see any connection between 'such toys' and the business of the witen. But they did not like his mockery. There were other voices rising in a clamour to take up Arthur Parr's argument and put it better than he could himself. Things they had seen in Upstrand, things they had heard tell of in Manchester.

'Folks laugh at us and the way matters are run here, you know. They say we're a queer lot, inbred and daft in the head.'

'And do you believe them?' Grandfather asked sardonically.

They liked that even less, but William Leigh, striving to take the heat out of the exchange, said quietly, 'Well, there's no getting away from it; we are different from other folks, set apart like,' and everyone fell silent again at that.

It was then that Timothy Tyte leaped to his feet as though he could bear no more. Turning his back on us, he addressed the tenants in a loud, jeering voice.

'So this is the best account you can give of yourselves, is it? You get your precious witen, and all you can do is go clacking on about how different you are from other men. Well, you're different, right enough. You must be the only peasants left in England! And this farce'—he flung around on us, dismissing the family at the high table with a sweep of his arm—'this witenagemot! Is this the way for men to conduct their business?'

'Be silent!' Fenn rapped the words out with his gavel. 'You're out of order. You were not called to speak, and if you continue in that tone, you will have to leave the witen.' He nodded briefly to Grandfather, transferring the conduct of the meeting back to him.

Grandfather was staring at Tyte as though he saw the devil himself manifested in our midst.

'Now,' he said, 'now at last we are met. You have your arena and your audience. You have had a busy tongue among our people—now let it wag here, and I, Athel Athelson, will hear you.' He spoke softly. There was almost a lulling note in his voice.

Tyte bridled to the challenge. 'Oh, I'll speak, never you fear. And what I have to say will be a deal more to the point than what's gone before. You and your kind are nothing but a load of bloody tyrants!' He scythed down the family with his hook. 'You've bled these good people here for centuries so that you can live like lords in the big house. You talk about hard times, and I hear how you're supposed to have shared them. But have your hands ever been worked until they're raw, has your aching back ever bent under a load? No! You're a gentleman, and your sons are gentlemen! Let me tell you that when I ran away from Clere Athel, I was putting mile on joyous mile between me and everything you stood for. I never had much

154

education in your school, but I've learned some long words just the same. I know what a patriarch is, or says he is, and I know the word "despot," too, and I've learned there isn't a farthing's worth of difference between them!'

It was a curious experience to face this tirade. I noticed that many of the tenants were uneasy, and several made slight protesting movements, as though to disassociate themselves from it. But Timothy Tyte seemed to have forgotten their presence. It is to be doubted that he had ever felt a genuine call to be their advocate. They had their grievances, and in some inexplicable way his return to Clere Athel had put a spark to ready tinder. But the rôle he had chosen he played for his own reasons.

'You Athelsons think you are born to be leaders of men. You're not unique there. . . . I've met others like you in every province on the face of the globe, and there are plenty more sailing the seas, too, come to that. Well, what I want to know is: How do you come by this divine appointment to govern the lives of other men? Does God set his thumbprint on you in the womb? Are you endowed with rare qualities, gifted with greater wisdom, richer in understanding than the rest of us? Or is it not rather that you are greedy men, who know how to take more than your fair share and how to hold on to it in the face of justice and reason? Who said this land was yours, Athel Athelson, to sell or not to sell, and who gave you the right to rule these people as though they were serfs?'

These last words were drowned in an uproar of protest. Athel and Hugh were on their feet but could not make their voices heard above the din, and Fenn was hammering with his gavel, which might have been a feather for the notice anyone took of him.

Richard Warrener seemed to be in favour of throwing Tyte headfirst into Little Rip, and with four substantial sons and the mood of the meeting generally in support of him, it looked for a moment as if this motion might be carried by a strong majority.

I looked at Grandmother and Great-Aunt Ivlian sitting

impassively through it all and took my cue from them so far as I was able, but it was not easy.

Then Bartholomew Tyte loomed up at the back of the hall and began to push his way to the high table. People quieted down at once, anxious not to miss anything.

'Ah, good old Bart to the rescue,' Timothy said, angrily shaking off the Warreners. I thought there was relief in his voice. 'Bart will tell you I'm right. . . . Perhaps you'll believe him if you won't take it from me. . . . He has no more time for the Athelsons than I have.'

'Hush up!' said Bartholomew. 'You've shot your bolt here!' And to Grandfather he said, 'Athel Athelson, you know me, and I know you, so it won't come hard to you to know what I'm feeling. I've listened to our Tim ranting on over a jar or two of ale these past few weeks and I've never said owt, because as long as he was on about the land, he and t'others with him have had the right of it to my way of thinking. But hearing him tonight with his talk of tyrants and serfs . . . well, the kindest thing I can say is he's run mad. And since he seems to have insulted everyone here in the process, I'm sorry and ashamed for that. He'll be leaving my house first thing in t'morning, and he'll not come back to Clere Athel again, else I might tell a tale he'd rather have forgot.'

Grandfather looked around the hall. 'Very well. We hear what you say, Bart. There's no feeling between me and thee.'

Bartholomew turned to his brother. 'Come away, Tim. Tha's not wanted here.'

'I should think not,' Harry Leigh called out. 'That's done for us, reet enough. A fine witness *you* turned out to be. Now witen's gone for nothing!'

'No!' Grandfather interrupted sharply. 'Witen's not been wasted. Stay and hear me a moment.' He waited for the Tytes to leave, and when the door had closed behind them, he went on. 'You've heard and seen Tyte for what he is—a man full of envy and personal bitterness, a placeless wanderer come among us by mischance. He is nothing to me, and now I think he will be nothing to you. But because of him, you have spoken out your feelings about the land and now I will speak mine. . . . I do not own Clere Athel, and no part of it is mine to sell. I hold it because by so doing I make sure all here are fed and cared for. Which one of you could trust his neighbour to provide for him as I provide? When any of you falls sick, who calls the doctor and pays his fee? Who pays the taxes, repairs your property, sustains your widows, and clothes and feeds your orphans? In every community there are those who do well and those who fail—in Clere Athel as elsewhere. But have you seen the unprotected poor? Perhaps not, you are innocents in the midst of a world of suffering. You think you have little enough, but let me tell you there are children not two hours' ride from here who would beg for the scraps from your tables. I have seen children with arms like sticks hunting through the bins outside Liverpool eating houses for a mess of plate scrapings. You think your cottages plain and simple enough, I don't doubt, but they are dry and warm and well ventilated, and each one has its earth closet. How many other landlords could say the same? You work hard on the land, but there are men fighting each other like animals outside the dock gates in Liverpool and London, every morning of their lives, just for the chance to be taken on. If I were to parcel out the land and sell it, some of you would have fine fat farms to work. What about the others? I do not doubt that in time many of them would be coaxed to sell their strips of market garden land, and in time they could no longer feed a family. And the men would say they must look for work in the towns. It has been the pattern of other old villages, this drift away from the land to the promise of a new prosperity. Too often the promise is not fulfilled, and it dies instead in a typhus-ridden slum. I cannot bear that for any of you. I cannot let it happen.'

He paused, and it was so quiet in the old hall that you could hear the tick of pocket watches.

'Tyte mocked at the old manorial system . . . aye, and some of you here may agree with him. I do not say it was idyllic, and I do not say there were no abuses under it. Of course there were. Men are men. But at its best it gave folks a place, and therefore a security, in an interdependent community that was still small enough to care and provide for all its members. We have kept a version of that old system going here, it is true, and I am not ashamed of it. It has not been easy for me in my lifetime, fighting against the pressures of progress and change around us. Still, I have thought I did right by you, and because of that, I have had sound sleep and a good appetite. What Athel, coming after me, will do in his time I can't say. It may be he'll let you all go to the devil by your own road. And after what we've heard here tonight, I don't know that I'd blame him.'

He nodded to Fenn, who closed up the chronicle with a slam to signify that the meeting was at an end. The formula for the end of the witen was always the same, and from long habit Grandfather usually dispatched it like a perfunctory grace after a meal. But the words having an unwonted aptness, on this occasion he lingered over them.

'Now I call the close of this witenagemot, undertaking to hear deferred petitions at our next session and assuring every man and woman here of goodwill despite any attachment claimed against my own property or any word which may have——' He broke off as the door burst open. A boy called Ralph Weaver erupted into the hall and imparted some breathless announcement to a man in the back row. 'What the devil! What's he saying?'

'By God! He says Timothy Tyte has shot Rabbity Jake!'

'Where are they?'

'Down at t'alehouse.'

'Come on, Athel.' Grandfather was already striding towards the door. 'Horses?'

'I told lad on me way through t'yard.'

'Good boy! And the doctor?'

'Me brother's ridden off on Monday Sutliffe's hack for him.' We all hurried out to the stableyard.

Grandmother said, 'If Jake's in a bad way, someone from the family should go to Muriel.'

'Aye.' Grandfather nodded. 'But not you. You've had enough for one day.'

I could see Aunt Sophie in a flutter of dread lest it should be she.

'I'll go,' I said.

'Well, you're near enough Muriel's age.' Grandfather hesitated. 'All right then, if you've the stomach for it. Athel, take Justine up in front of you, and let's be on our way.'

CHAPTER SEVEN

CHAPTER SEVEN

MONDAY SUTLIFFE, who kept the alehouse, was doing his
best not to let the drama of the situation get the better of him.
When we arrived, he had Rabbity Jake lying on the cushioned
settle at one end of the bar parlour and Timothy Tyte penned
in at the other by the snarling lurcher. Muriel, with one child
in her arms and another at her knee, filled the air with
lamentation, which Jake's intermittent groans did nothing to
discourage, and the doorway and the street outside were
thronged with women, some with plaintive children roused
from sleep and others so old and infirm that they hadn't been
outside their own cottage gardens in years, but now offering
such advice for the treatment of wounds as would surely have
had them burned three centuries ago.

Monday Sutliffe was playing shove-halfpenny.

Grandfather made a rapid examination of Jake. He was a
grim sight with his shirt blood-soaked and torn from a wound
in the chest, and his face drawn and bluish-white about the
mouth.

'You've had a shock, man, but you're not going to die,'
Grandfather said.

The change was astonishing. Jake stopped groaning, and
his fluttering eyelids opened wide. 'Amn't I?' He struggled to
sit up.

'No, lie still until the doctor gets here.' He replaced the compress on the wound. 'What's that dog on about? Call it off!'

Jake signalled weakly to the lurcher, who left Tim Tyte with the greatest reluctance and slunk over to lie by his master, still maintaining an arrow of outraged fur along his lean back and continuing to watch his adversary with eyes full of hatred and fear.

I went over and put my arm around Muriel's shoulders. 'Don't you think the children would be better in bed? Grandfather says Jake is going to be all right, and we'll bring him home to you as soon as the doctor says he can be moved.'

'Aye, musn't move 'im till t'shot's out. But as soon as that's done I'll get t'cart out and bring him round to thee, gentle and easy like, never fear,' Monday volunteered.

Muriel was resolute, however. There was no moving her, though I did persuade her to let Mrs Weaver put the children to bed in her cottage next door. So we settled down to wait as best we could, all of us covertly watching the blood seeping through the compress, hoping that Grandfather knew what he was talking about.

Jake himself appeared to drift into unconsciousness, and things had quietened down considerably since Grandfather had made his presence felt among the onlookers, scattering them with firm orders to go to their beds and not sit up half the night talking about the affair to no purpose.

Grandfather now turned his attention to a grasp of the facts. Timothy Tyte, sullen-faced, slumped in his corner, was not the man to give them to him.

'Well, Tim Tyte? What have you to say for yourself now?'

'It was an accident. I'm not to blame.'

'You're saying you didn't shoot Jake?'

'I didn't shoot anybody. The gun went off. I'm saying no more.'

'Where's your brother?'

'In his bed, I suppose.'

The men, who had walked down after us from the house,

were standing about in groups in the moonlight outside. Grandfather went to the door and called for one of them to fetch Bartholomew.

'The rest of you go home. There's nothing to be done here. No sense in missing your sleep.'

He returned impatiently to confront Monday. 'Now, come along, man. You'll have to tell what it's all about. We must know where we are at before McIntosh gets here. He'll want the law, d'ye see? I can't handle him unless I know the exact truth of what happened. Think carefully, and tell me how it was.'

Of all the traditions cherished in Clere Athel, that of keeping the law out of its affairs was perhaps the most unanimously upheld. Homegrown justice was best, it was believed, and it was a long time since any other variety had been tried.

Monday heaved himself out of the close embrace of his chair and went behind the bar counter. He drew a pint of ale for himself and two more for Grandfather and for Athel before he answered.

'Well, it were this road. Parlour was empty most of t'evening with everyone up at yon meeting o' yourn. I was beginning to think I should have gone me sen, when in comes Jake about half-past eight and starts talking about whippets——'

'Whippets?' Athel queried.

'Yes, whippets. It seems he met a man from Rochdale trying to sell one at Upstrand market. Fellow told him how racing whippets was the go now and——'

'Never mind about that,' Grandfather interrupted impatiently. 'Get to the point.'

'I am doing. . . . Well, as I was saying, we're talking about whippets when in comes Tim Tyte, and I pour him his usual tot of rum at once, because I can see by his face he needs it. When a man's got that face on him, I make it a rule never to cross him or keep him waiting. He doesn't say owt, just drinks it straight down and pushes his glass across to me for more of the same. I give it to him, and I'm just hoping he'll sink that and go, when Jake has to open his big mouth. "What now, Timothy?" says he. "Drinking alone? I thought revolution was to start tonight." '

' "Hold thee tongue, Jake," says I. But damage were already done. Tim Tyte rounds on him like one gone mad. "Aye, sneer if you will," he says. "Your kind is parasites on t'rich, like rich is parasites on t'working poor. Happen the day will come, though, when you'll need to do an honest hand's turn your sen. Then you'll know what I'm on about." Well, Jake doesn't care for this, and his language isn't wanting of a colourful phrase or two when he's roused. But he keeps his temper. "You can rant and preach all you want," he tells Tyte, "but you'll never push the Athelsons out unless they go feet first." '

Monday took a long pull at his tankard to refresh his narrative. 'At that Tyte fair boils over wi' frustration. He strides towards door and wi'out a word of warning snatches up Jake's gun, which he's left propped against wall yonder, same as he always does. "Put that gun down," Jake says, very quiet. "No man touches my gun." "Might is right," shouts Tyte. "Happen Old Athel will change his mind when he looks down the barrel of this." I don't like the way things are shaping up, and I am keeping as still here as if I was painted on t'wall, but Jake is edging towards him gentle, and he says as how the gun is loaded and Tyte shouldn't be a fool. Then all hell breaks out. Yon lurcher takes a spring and fastens his teeth in Tyte's leg. Tyte reverses gun to club him on t'head wi' the stock, and Jake sees his chance and jumps on him.' Monday shook his head helplessly. 'I can't rightly say what happened after that. Lurcher sailed past me through t'air, and Jake was still grappling Tyte when there's a sudden crash and Jake falls backwards across that little table and I see he's hit. Tyte's standing there, looking dazed, and gun's on floor, and Tyte's saying, "It were me hook got caught." I take it to mean his hook got tangled with the catch or the trigger or summat and gun went off unintentional like. . . . That's all. . . . The rest you've seen for yourself.'

Grandfather did not take long to consider the evidence. 'It's clear then from what you say, Monday, that this was an accident. Tyte had no business with the gun but then'—he stifled Muriel's small outraged cry with a look—'Jake has no business bringing a loaded firearm into a public place and leaving it propped against the wall, where any young lad with a drop too much on board might take it up. Now just step outside wi' me, Monday . . . and you too, Athel. There's a thought or two I want to share with Fenn and there's not much time.'

While we waited, Muriel went over to kneel beside Jake and made pathetic, ineffectual dabs at his wound with the compress. Jake was unconscious.

'You rotten devil!' She turned on Tyte. 'I'd like to claw your eyes out with my own hands.' A sympathetic rumble sounded in the depth of the lurcher.

Grandfather came back, followed by Athel and Monday. Fenn and two of the Warreners were with them.

'Now, Tyte,' Grandfather said, 'we're going to say nothing about the struggle.'

Tyte's head jerked up quickly. 'Happen you're not! But I am. That's my defence!'

'Be quiet,' Grandfather snapped. 'We are going to say it was an accident, of course. But we are going to tell the doctor you were examining Jake's gun with his permission, that it went off when your hook tripped the catch, and that you were both outside on the green when it happened. The struggle makes it look far more serious for you, you know.'

Tyte's eyes narrowed suspiciously. 'But you're not bothered about saving my bacon. What's in it for you, that's what I want to know?'

Just then Bartholomew came in with Cousin Cuthbert.

'You've heard, Bart?' Grandfather asked him.

'Aye.' Bartholomew nodded. 'Well, Tim, so you've done it again.'

'He's done what again?'

'Killed a man.'

Muriel screamed.

'For God's sake, do something with that woman, Justine . . .

164

no, no, Jake's not dead.' Grandfather spoke quickly. 'Doctor'll patch him up good as new, and our only thought is keep a hoard of long-nosed busybodies out of our affairs. But you say your brother has *killed* a man?'

'Aye, he knifed a mess-mate in a brawl over a woman. He jumped ship in South America and signed on another under a false name.'

Timothy started up. 'You swore to me you'd never tell.'

'I didn't know you were going to make a habit of it.'

'Well, this changes the situation, doesn't it?' Athel said.

Grandfather scowled at him. 'I don't see why.'

'But the man's dangerous.'

'Plenty more like him running loose in the world. It's nothing to us so long as he don't stay in Clere Athel. Besides this was still a genuine accident . . . and I'm not having the whole business dragged into a court of law and happen all that went before coming out.'

There was a visible closing of the ranks, the Warreners agreeing with Grandfather and Fenn pointing out to Athel that Tim Tyte was no homicidal killer but a man who acted rashly when his temper grew violent.

'Think on then, Timothy,' his brother told him, 'better do what Athel Athelson tells you. An accident is one thing, but a struggle followed by an accident puts doubts into men's minds, and there's many a jury wouldn't give you the benefit of doubt.'

'Here's McIntosh.' Hugh stuck his head around the door.

'Hush now,' said Grandfather. 'Leave everything to me. Justine, take Muriel out. This is men's work.'

The dawn was already streaking the sky, a pattern of gold against navy blue, when they finally brought Jake home to Muriel's cottage.

'Here he is then, Muriel. Strapped up neat as a babe in a binder. Doctor says he'll be right as ninepence inside a fortnight, but he'll call in later, just to have a look. Jake's to lie flat in his bed, he says, and take nothing but milk with an egg or a drop of beef tea.'

Monday and Fenn carried Jake up the narrow, twisting cottage stairs and helped Muriel put him to bed.

'Now we can all get some sleep. Come along, Justine Athelson! Tha's last parcel we have to deliver!'

Yawning, I followed Fenn out into the yard and was glad to be lifted into Monday's cart.

'Did McIntosh ask many questions about the accident?'

'Never a one. Your grandfather told him the tale, and he just did his work and left.'

'And Tim Tyte?'

'He'll be gone from Clere Athel before you wake again.' Fenn chuckled. 'Old Athel's given him ten guineas to help him on his way.'

'Why did he do that? That isn't like him.'

'Oh, yes, it is. He wouldn't want any man of Clere Athel to have to beg his way. Not that Timothy Tyte needs much help. He has a clever tongue in his head, that one, and he'll soon talk his way into some likely situation. . . . Now here we are at the Dower, and there's Mrs Rimmer at the door for you. . . . Bless my soul, Mrs Rimmer, that's a mighty handsome nightcap, ma'am, if I may say so!'

The crocheted points fluttered with indignation.

'You may not!' she snapped. 'No gentleman should remark a lady's dress at this hour of the morning. . . . And staring is as bad.' She rounded on Monday Sutliffe. 'Come inside quickly, Miss Justine, and let's get you to your bed.'

*   *   *

It seemed that their disillusionment with Timothy Tyte had a subduing effect on the aspiring landowners, and for the time being at least, we heard no more grumbles. Tenancy dues were paid without protest, and Grandfather for his part made do with as little bidden labour on the home farm as possible. When harvest time came, he was determined we should manage without calling any of the tenants or their sons away from their own land. Hugh put his studies aside and joined

Grandfather and Athel, labouring in our fields from dawn to dusk with a handful of men. It was astonishing to see how much work Grandfather alone could accomplish, advancing through a field of grain, scything with great, wrathful strokes, his shirt open to the waist and stuffed into the top of an old pair of breeches.

'Begins to look as if we shall do it alone,' Grandmother said, one hand shading her eyes to view the work, the other quieting a sidling chestnut hunter. 'The only question that remains is whether your Grandfather will have a seizure before, or immediately after, the harvest is in. Ridiculous situation, of course. Typically Athelson. Tenants worried to death and want to help him, but too stubborn to come without being asked . . . and he too proud to ask them after what's happened.' She clicked her tongue impatiently at the restless mare and gathered up the reins. 'Oh, well, never could *tell* him anything.'

I laughed. 'He says never could tell *you* anything, either.'

She nodded vaguely. 'Very likely,' and was gone across the home park and over a hedge like the side of a barn.

In this battle of pride it could only be the tenants who gave in. I am sure Grandfather would have lost half his crop rather than surrender. Probably they understood this. Anyway, when the weather looked like breaking up, they came. Not in uncertain ones and twos, awkwardly and ungenerously, as you might expect in the circumstances, but every man and boy of the village in a whooping, cheerful throng, shouting for 'Old Athel,' in the fields at first light. And Grandfather, trudging out at the start of another weary day, found them waiting for him and threw back his head and roared with laughter, so Hugh said, calling them every name he could think of, cursing their obstinacy, and showing them his bandaged, blistered hands until the whole countryside rang with laughter.

Just in time, this help, as it turned out. Forty-eight hours later such a storm blew up as no one could ever before remember. The whole of the long, warm, moist summer seemed to explode above our heads, plaguing us for five days with lightning that seared limbs off trees in the home park and shrivelled the weather vane on the stable roof as though it were dried grass. Sometimes the storm centre wandered off for a few hours, and the cry of Grandmother's peacocks rang out eerily in the clammy stillness of an afternoon. But by evening its full fury would be back with us.

*   *   *

'Leave those accounts! They'll keep.' I did not know how long Athel had been standing behind my chair, hadn't heard the door open behind me because the farm office was a fairly flimsy wooden building and like a sounding box for the thunder overhead.

'But Grandfather said he wanted the vegetable figures this evening. . . .'

'Never mind. I'm going for a walk on the shore, and I want you to come with me.'

I did not argue any more but collected my mackintosh.

Athel did not have a coat. Only a thin silk shirt and a scarf tucked in the neck. 'It's going to pour any minute. You'll get drenched,' I said. The air was so humid it was an effort to walk along, like wading through lukewarm soup.

'At least we shall be able to breathe by the sea.'

After that we walked in silence. Athel carried my mackintosh over his shoulder but took no further notice of me. He was striding along quite fast, like a man with a destination and something on his mind, and I almost had to trot to keep up with him. I noticed we did not meet anyone along the way. It was growing darker, and they must have taken warning and gone to shelter before the next wave of the storm.

Athel was making for the place where the pine trees swept right down to the edge of the sand dunes. The pines were standing incredibly still against the dreadful bronze sky, and we saw them that way for an instant before they suddenly began to stir and sway.

'There!' Athel pointed triumphantly. 'Can you see?'

168

'I can feel it! A great rush of wind.'

'It will blow the storm out to sea.'

As though he had ordained it, a jagged crack of light split the sky above the grey line of sea.

'Look, there it goes! Now we shall see a sight. Nothing so splendid as a storm over the sea.'

The strong offshore wind laid a sudden chill across my shoulders, and I shivered. It was as though the warm, moist air were being sucked out over the sea with the storm.

Another explosion of the molten light, and another and another, we watched the burning prongs plunge ever closer to the sea until they stabbed at the horizon itself and we lost sight of them, and the thunder rumbled after them into the realm of echo and finally silence.

'Such a presence, a storm,' I said. 'I almost feel a sense of loss, watching it die.'

'It hasn't died. Only rolled off over the horizon to raise a hullabaloo somewhere else.'

I shivered again, increasingly conscious of the falling temperature.

'Better put your mackintosh round you. Here comes the rain on the back of the wind. We'll shelter under the pines.' Athel took my hand and pulled me up the soft, loose sand of a steep bank, until we stood under the trees. They grew very close together, and the silky carpet of needles underfoot still held a comforting warmth.

Athel kept hold of my hand, and we stood watching the rain whipping along the dunes.

'September.' He rang the word in a melancholy way. 'Autumn into winter. . . . Will you go away now with the swallows, I wonder? Will you chase the sunshine to some other summer place? I can't bear you to go again. . . . When you were gone last time, I walked down here alone and the wind in the pines and the waves on the shore were saying "Justine . . . Justine . . . Justine."'

I could not bring myself to look at him at once. I suppose I had never allowed myself to think of loving Athel in anything but a sisterly way until then. I sometimes think the mind is like a great untidy cupboard. We spend our youth throwing things into it, higgledy-piggledy, and the years of our maturity trying to straighten it out. Perhaps loving Athel in a deep and special way was there all the time, but it got pushed into the dark at the back, and I never took it out and examined it until that afternoon sheltering from the rain. Then from the way he spoke and the way he said my name I knew he had never loved me in the way he loved Charlotte and that my feeling for him had never been in the least like the cheerful warmth I felt for Hugh.

I said, 'I don't want to go away. But I haven't seen Mother for nearly six months. I don't know what excuse I could make.'

We looked at each other. There could be only frankness between us now.

'If we were married,' Athel said. 'Oh, Justine. . . .' His kisses left me shaken and exhausted, and when we drew apart, I felt humbled by the way he looked at me, conscious of my draggled hair with the pins falling out and my starched petticoats gone limp under a wilted muslin dress with a muddied hem. I couldn't get over the wonder of him loving me like that.

His expression changed, darkened abruptly. 'Grandfather. . . .' There was no need for complete sentences between us.

'You can't tell Grandfather!' I was suddenly afraid.

'I *must* tell Grandfather. I have to tell him sooner or later.'

'Later then. Not now. Grandmother goes to Yorkshire tomorrow. Wait until she comes back.'

'Grandmother won't help us.'

'She might.'

Athel shook his head, doubtfully. 'I don't see how she can. We'll have to face it out alone. . . . Perhaps he won't take it so badly. . . .' But of course he would. The only question was how far he would go to prevent us marrying.

The rain had stopped. 'I think I want to go home now,' I said. Fortunately it was one of those evenings when I dined alone at the Dower. I still went up to the house three evenings a week, and I always lunched with the family, but I was glad that I had resisted Grandfather's invitation to live with them. It suited me to have an independent establishment.

We had reached the wicket gate alongside the main entrance to the drive. 'Perhaps I *will* wait until Grandmother comes back. She'll only be away for three weeks.' Athel sounded painfully aware of his own weakening resolve.

'I am sure that will be for the best.'

'I'll come and see you this evening, after dinner.'

'No, not this evening,' I said.

The garden at the Dower looked fresh after the rain, and there was a new wanton beauty in the way the late-flowering shrubs spilled their drenched blossoms across the grass walks. I sat by the open windows and relived the sweet, frightening experience of the afternoon.

'Now then, Miss Justine! Sitting alone in the dark! What's the matter, have you a headache after the storm?' Mrs Rimmer, bustling in with a pot of coffee, made me start and blush for my thoughts.

'I had intended to write letters. . . .' She was looking at me suspiciously. I cursed the unwonted self-consciousness that had come upon me. Nothing would ever be the same again.

*   *   *

Grandmother was going to Yorkshire to visit her family home. It was thirty years since she had last made the journey and she was going because of Tamerlana Rose.

'Well,' Grandfather grumbled quite unjustifiably, 'the Hamlacks always were a clannish lot. I suppose this sort of jaunt is the kind of thing one must expect.'

Tamerlana Rose was the crowning achievement of Grandmother's life, a magnificent mare, more than sixteen hands of perfectly proportioned muscle and bone, with a long, lean neck, a fine head, and remarkable eyes that contrived to be at once reflective and humorous in expression. Grandmother told me Tamerlana was descended from the Darley Arabian, and although I am very ignorant of such things and this did not mean much to me, it clearly should have. At least I could recognize there was something exceptional about this creature.

'A great hunter-chaser,' Grandmother said, caressing the soft, quivering nose. 'In the right hands she might be the greatest of her day.' And so she was taking Tamerlana to the Hamlacks, which was hunting country. 'I shall ride with them myself, show her off at her best, and find a buyer.'

'Goin' huntin' at your age!' Grandfather was outraged. 'You're insane, Cecily! You want lockin' up. You'll break your bloody neck.'

But Grandmother was determined.

Over the next weeks Athel and I spent all the time we could together. It was hard to discipline ourselves so that the meetings were not *too* frequent, the pretexts for seeing each other at odd moments not too transparently feeble. Probably we were more cautious than we needed to be. I doubt if anyone had a suspicion that we were more to each other than we had been. And yet I could not look at him without my hands restless to reach out and touch him.

Except for one brief letter to say Tamerlana had travelled well, we had not heard from Grandmother for nearly four weeks. We were halfway through October, and Grandfather began to be very irritable because she did not come home.

Then, just after lunchtime one day, a stranger rode into Clere Athel with a message. Pegger, not knowing where Grandfather was to be found, brought the lad to me.

'Where do you say you've come from?'

'The Turk's Head in Upstrand, miss. Mr Wintershaw says I was to come direct to the Athelsons at Clere Athel and say the Hamlacks had called him on the telephone from Yorkshire. They're calling again at seven o'clock this evening and must speak to one of the family very urgent.'

'Telephone? *Telephone?* You mean one o' they voice machines?' Pegger was outraged. 'What would Hamlacks want speaking to Wintershaw on one of they things for. I can't make no sense of it; if you ask me, lad's daft in the head!'

'No, I'm not! Mr Wintershaw give me a leg up on his nag and says, "Go like 'ell. It's bad news and they mun come to the Turk's Head to take telephone call at seven sharp."'

'But the Hamlacks don't know Wintershaw from a doorstop; why would they talk to him?' Pegger persisted obstinately.

'Oh, do be quiet a minute, Pegger. I understand. They want to speak to us quickly, and we've no telephone here in Clere Athel. They traced one at Upstrand and got the message sent from there.' Pegger was still shaking his head. 'Well, never mind. Just take this young man to Mrs Rimmer and ask her to give him something to eat and drink after his ride and two shillings for his trouble. . . . I must find Athel.'

There Pegger was more helpful. 'Athel's just gone into Cuthbert Rainbird's house. I seen him not twenty minutes since.'

I was already running down the drive. Bad news. From the Hamlacks. It could only mean that Grandmother had had an accident.

It was almost as hard for us to persuade Grandfather that the message was genuine as it had been to get through to Pegger. We had tried to get him to consider a telephone for Clere Athel once, but he would have nothing to do with such an idea, and I do not suppose he had ever seen an instrument or understood how it worked.

The fact that Clere Athel men did not favour the Turk's Head, and preferred to drink at the Plough or the Drover's Arms on market day, made him all the more suspicious.

'Never been in the Turk's Head since I was a boy,' he kept saying. 'It's a damned fancy place, and the beer's thin.'

Athel was very patient with him. All at once Grandfather seemed querulous and old, and we knew that he was trying to stave off some painful reality already guessed at, though not yet framed in words.

'It must be serious.' Athel drew me aside. 'The Hamlacks

. . . well, you know they would never go to this trouble with the telephone business over a broken leg.'

'You'll go with Grandfather to Upstrand, of course?'

'Oh, yes. And I think it would be a good idea if Cousin Cuthbert came, too. If things come to the worst, it might be easier for Grandfather if he had someone older there.'

'Do you want me to come?'

'I wish you would! Ask Grandfather whether he wants you.'

In the end the four of us went, Grandfather seeming relieved to have company.

Mr Wintershaw was not unconscious of the importance conferred on him by his telephone, but it was clear from the way he received Grandfather that the name of Athel Athelson weighed enough to carry the day. Moreover, when Grandfather, with a sudden return of spirit, had finished giving him a concise opinion of this and all other modern scientific wonders, Mr Wintershaw was prepared to admit that his telephone could be a 'nuisance of a thing' with a tiresome habit of going off when one least expected it.

We were shown into the presence of the instrument—a room that served the landlord both as private parlour and office. It was just a few minutes before seven.

'We'll take a glass of your best Madeira for my granddaughter and brandy for the rest of us,' Grandfather said.

Mr Wintershaw was on hand to answer the summons when it came. He handed the earpiece to Grandfather and left us to ourselves.

'Who's there?' Grandfather challenged sternly. 'Who? *Who?* Speak louder, man, I can't hear you. Is it Howard? Just a minute. . . . Athel, I think it's Howard Hamlack, but there's such a damned, mincing little voice coming out of this thing I can't understand what he's saying. Can you do anything to make it louder?'

'No, I'm afraid not. Can't you tell him to shout?'

'Are you there, Howard? Can you hear me? Well, look here, you'll have to shout. What's that? You say you are shouting. . . . Go on then, I can just about make you out. . . . Cecily,

yes. . . . What about Cecily?' It was as though some unseen
hand passed over Grandfather's face, erasing the expression
of earnest concentration and leaving only a mindless blank.
He took the receiver away from his ear and stared at it for a
moment. 'I'm sorry'—he spoke slowly—'I didn't quite catch
that. . . . I thought for a moment you said she——' He was
listening again. 'I see. . . . I see. . . .' But his eyes were
unseeing. 'It might be better if I put young Athel on. . . . I
don't hear you too well again.'

Athel took the receiver from him. 'Yes. . . . Cousin
Howard? . . . Yes . . . it is a shock, of course. . . . Wait a
minute. I'll ask him.' He turned to Grandfather. 'Howard
wants to know whether you will have Grandmother brought
home or if they should open the Hamlack vault. . . .'

Grandfather had slumped, vacant-eyed, in a chair, but
anger revived him. 'Of course, she must be brought home.
She's lain beside me the larger part of her life; where else
should she lie in death?' He hesitated. 'Ask him . . . ask him
if she suffered.'

Athel relayed the question. 'I see . . . a matter of minutes. . . .
Did she say anything. . . . Oh, yes, of course. . . .'

'Well, did she say something, or didn't she?' Grandfather
tugged impatiently at Athel's sleeve.'

'She said, "I want to see it done now. And make a good job
of it." She was talking about Tamerlana Rose being shot.'

'No message for me?'

Athel shook his head.

He was talking again to Howard Hamlack, asking him how
soon he thought the arrangements could be made to bring
Grandmother's body back to Clere Athel.

I went over and knelt beside Grandfather, slipping my hand
into his. He looked at me. 'So like Cecily to die thinking about
a horse.'

The people of Clere Athel received the news of Grandmother's death in a matter-of-fact way. It was in the nature
of things that Athelsons should come and go. Moreover, it
seemed especially fitting to them that she should have gone

in the hunting field accompanied by her favourite horse. Old Tom from the shore, limping in to pay his last respects at the funeral, even went so far as to say it was 'reet grand to think on her riding Tamerlana Rose to meet her maker'.

Latter-day Athelsons had found a last resting place in a tomb dating from 1623. This was now opened up with its smell of death and moss and given a thorough sweeping. For the first time I saw the plaques to my father and my Uncle Athel, both buried far from home: 'In memory of Lucian, second son of Athel and Cecily Athelson, murdered by robbers in a foreign land.' The other plaque was much larger: 'In loving memory of Athel Athelson, son and heir of Athel and Cecily Athelson, killed while fighting in a war in South Africa. Father of two sons, Athel and Hugh, and a daughter, Charlotte.'

Grandfather took a long time deciding where to put Grandmother. 'It has to be a good-sized space for the two of us, mind. . . . No, not over there. . . . That corner is too crowded already. . . . No, that won't do, I'll not have Red Athelson with his knees in my back . . . fellow robbed his own brother of fifteen hundred pounds and then lost it all at cards! That won't do either because I'll have to go this side on account of my length, and that leaves Cecily next to Willie the Rake, and you know what they say about him!'

'No,' Athel said, interested. 'What about him?'

Grandfather glanced at me and grew vague. 'Oh, well, you know . . . chap was a lecher. . . . They say when he succeeded his brother, he even tried to claim *droit du seigneur*.'

'What's that?' I asked.

'Never you mind! But I'm not having him next to Cecily!'

When he did finally find a place in the right company, he chose the following inscription: 'Cecily Athelson, well-loved wife of Athel, 1835-1906. Two sons predeceased her. A noble horsewoman.'

CHAPTER EIGHT

OUTWARDLY Grandfather showed scant emotion when Grandmother died. I have said he reacted to the brief, first shock, but later there was a brusqueness in his handling of the arrangements, and he appeared to find the formalities of actually getting her into the ground more irksome than affecting. Nevertheless, he missed her. At mealtimes his eyes rested constantly on her empty chair, facing him at the opposite end of the long table, and he did not invite Aunt Sophie to occupy it, which was what tradition expected of him. There were no more tirades against her peacocks—the one idle fancy of her life—and when her horses were sold, the broodmares were pensioned off into a quiet field because she had loved them and often delivered them with her own hands. Most of the stock went to the Hamlacks, and most of the proceeds went to Hugh, which was just as she would have wished.

'Oh, yes, I am very sure he loved her. Perhaps he never realized how much until now.' Great-Aunt Ivlian brought a rare clarity of observation to bear on the conversation we were having. She had drifted into the Dower in time for an afternoon tea of Mrs Rimmer's hot buttered pikelets with raspberry jam. 'I came to say something very important to you . . . but I cannot for the life of me remember what it was. . . .'

We talked of Grandfather in the twilight of the November afternoon. Some days now he seemed an old man, almost failing. But his mood was unpredictable, and he could take you by surprise as though the life-force surged and ebbed in him like the tide along our shore. And his anger was as frightening as it had always been.

'Of course, I don't suppose any of our menfolk have ever loved a woman as much as they've loved our land and our people. And although I have read all the family papers in my time, I cannot call to mind a single love letter. One must suppose some of the wives would have treasured them if they had had them, so they ought to be there. . . . No, I doubt any Athelson was ever a wooer. . . . But they probably cut a bit of a dash in their way. Perhaps it was their looks.'

'Grandfather is still a very handsome man,' I said.

'My dear, when he was young, he was magnificent! I always used to feel it was terribly unfair that he, being a man, should have the best of the looks. . . . Now Cecily was never what you would call a beauty, but she had that special quality—one hardly knows how to describe it—she was exciting to be with. . . . One felt things *happened* when she came on the scene.'

I was curious to know how my grandparents had met.

'Ah, that was my mother's doing. She was a Yorkshire-woman, you know, and Cecily's mother was her closest girlhood friend. They always kept in touch by letter over the years —we have those letters and they are full of Hamlack history— I think our mother secretly hoped that Athel and Cecily might unite the two families, but of course my father would not hear of such a thing because the Hamlacks had no money and he wanted an heiress for my brother. Still he did let Mother invite them to Athel's coming-of-age ball. . . . There were scores of pretty girls there from all over the county . . . so much more company to choose from in those days, and the Athelsons still basked in the last of Eugenie's fortune. It was probably the final grand occasion for Clere Athel. . . .' Her mind wandered back over the years. 'There must have been sixty or seventy guests,' Great-Aunt Ivlian said. 'One did not count one's guests in those days, you know. There was always plenty of everything when one entertained.'

I exclaimed over the difficulty of accommodating so many.

Great-Aunt Ivlian laughed gaily. 'Oh, that was the least of our worries! We danced most of the night away. . . . The larger bedrooms were turned into dormitories, three for the girls and three for the boys. I remember I slept in that hideous old bed in the gold room—you know, the one with the dragons carved round the posts—and had a frightful dream that their scales were scratching me. It turned out to be the coarse lace on Cecily's nightgown, as a matter of fact . . . scratched all down one side of my face and left quite a mark!' She smiled roguishly. 'I warned Athel afterwards, but he took no notice! Of course, she couldn't help it—there were five of us in that bed that night . . . hardly room to breathe, let alone move. . . . I never *have* liked cheap, coarse lace . . . don't ever wear it, my dear. A garment is better left plain if one can't afford a good trim.'

I promised to observe this advice at all times. 'But if Great-Grandfather was against the marriage, how did Grandfather persuade him to accept Cecily?'

Great-Aunt Ivlian frowned over a choice of jams for her fourth pikelet.

'Matter of honour—haven't I just been telling you? Even if it started out as a joke, it was still a matter of honour! Besides, she was a very taking little thing.'

'But you didn't tell me anything about a joke or anyone's honour,' I pointed out patiently. 'You left that part out.'

'Are you sure you were listening? Perhaps you had your mouth full; it is very difficult to concentrate when you are eating.' She discarded her plate with reluctance. 'Oh, well . . . as I was saying, there was dancing after dinner, and you know your grandfather never has liked dancing. He and a few other lively souls like Cecily and Ned Landless and Walmer Prewett were out on the terrace, and my partner—Arthur something, I don't remember his name, but I do recall that we were just

179

forming sets for a quadrille, and he said let's go and see what they were up to because he thought we were missing something. They were laughing in a wild sort of way when we joined them and there was some talk—most improper, really downright shocking for those days—about what a man could do and a woman could not. Cecily said there was one thing she could do better than any man, and Athel said did she mean bear children, and she said no, ride. The men thought that was terribly funny, and Cecily said that if they did not believe her, she was willing to race any one of them there and then. They laughed a good deal more at that and said they were only sorry they didn't have their horses with them. Cecily was looking straight at Athel, and there was that mocking half-smile she had. "I suppose it is not impossible that our host keeps something in his stable!" And Athel bows slightly and says, "Yes, Miss Hamlack, I think I can oblige you." "Will *you* race me, then?" she asks, and to my horror I hear Athel say, "Why, certainly, if the stakes are attractive enough." ' Great-Aunt Ivlian paused to pass me her cup, and I refilled it. 'I wanted to call Mother and Father to stop it, but Arthur held me back and said I mustn't be a killjoy; it was bright moon-light, and no harm would come to Cecily. No one would listen to me, least of all Cecily, and by then Ned Landless had brought two horses from the stables saddled and ready. I'll give Athel credit for this, at the last moment he offered Cecily a good excuse to back out. But the next thing I know I am behind a bush helping Cecily off with her hoop and some of the half dozen petticoats we wore tied at the waist in those days, and Athel is on the other side of it explaining the course. Cecily chooses her horse and is up in a flash. "What's the wager?" Walmer calls. "Why, since my name will be lost after this, if I win, Athel must offer for me," Cecily says. "And if you lose?" I can still hear her gurgling laugh. "Impossible! But if I do lose, Athel can name his price." '

'Good heavens! I can hardly believe it of Grandmother. How bold!'

'Ah, you may smile,' said Great-Aunt Ivlian, smiling

herself, 'but believe me, I was frightened out of my wits. . . . Anyhow, away they went across the park with their black shadows flying after them, and who should step out on to the terrace but my father and Cecily's father with him? They wanted to know what the excitement was about, and of course, no one wanted to tell them. I certainly couldn't. I believe I had lost the power of speech at the sight of my father. . . . I seem to remember Walmer told him, and my father cursed Athel for a wild fool and said that if any harm came to Cecily, he would disinherit him. . . . I don't really suppose he would have done anything of the kind, but it sounded dreadful at the time. Then we heard someone galloping hard, and there was a dark figure skirting the lake at terrific speed. It was Cecily with yards of torn lace hanging from her beautiful ball-gown and her hair all over the place. She just slipped from the saddle as casual as you please into my father's arms. He said something like "Good God, Miss Hamlack! Whatever are you at?" And Cecily just laughed up at him and answered, "Why, sir, I was giving your son a riding lesson!" Athel came up then and walked straight over to her and kissed her hand. "So you have won your wager! Let me be the first to congratulate you on your prize." I thought Father would have a fit when the wager was explained to him, but Cecily Hamlack's father roared with laughter and said it was the finest thing he had ever heard. The announcement of the engagement was made the same night.'

'I don't suppose Grandfather ever dreamed he would lose the race,' I said.

Great-Aunt Ivlian shook her head impatiently. 'No, child! You've missed the whole point. I told you about the letters that passed between our mother and Cecily's. We had been hearing for years that the girl rode like a demon and could beat her brothers when she raced against them. Athel was no horseman nor ever pretended to be!'

*　　　*　　　*

There was no witen held that November. Perhaps in deference to Grandfather's bereavement, although this was not clearly stated, the villagers said they had no matters to raise, and Fenn transacted what little business there was informally. We looked forward to a gloomy Christmas.

For some weeks I had been summoning up courage to write and tell Mother that I was putting off my promised visit to her yet again. Her letters to me at that time were full of reproach for my long neglect of her and my replies were stilted and defensive. Of course, I could not tell the truth and say I was unable to tear myself away from Athel. In the end I wrote that, with regard to Christmas, it would be a sad one at Clere Athel without Grandmother, and Grandfather had particularly asked me not to be absent just then. This was the truth, but I sent it off with a heavy heart because I knew my own duplicity. For love of Athel I could even be thankful for Grandmother's death if it gave me an excuse to stay with him.

The new year began to unfold, and still no one seemed to sense any change in our relationship, although even Grandfather commented that Athel and I were nearly always together.

'What a help Justine could be to you in running the farm, if only she will not fly off and get married!' He sighed. For a moment a light of hope flickered in Athel's eyes, and I thought he was going to take this as encouragement to speak out. I shook my head slightly, warning him not to, for I knew that Grandfather was thinking of me only as Great-Aunt Ivlian might have been to him if things had been different. And just as well. 'Sometimes I think she is the marryin' sort, and sometimes I think she ain't.' Grandfather pondered me deeply. 'What do you think, Athel? She certainly seems to love this place as much as we do . . . try to keep her if you can.' It was incredibly painful.

'Yes,' Athel said later, speaking the words softly against my ear. 'I should like you to stay an Athelson all your life. Don't ever be called anything but Justine Athelson!'

Yet in another minute he had turned away from me. 'What

is the matter with me! When I hold you, I feel I could die for love of you, and yet I can't face up to one old man and tell him. . . . Am I a coward, Justine? Tell me the truth, for the love of heaven, do you think I'm a coward?'

I could not stand the anguish in him.

'Hush, no, of course not! You're not afraid of Grandfather . . . only of hurting him.'

'But you do think he'd get used to the idea in time, don't you? After all, it isn't unheard of for cousins to marry. It isn't forbidden. He'd come round to accepting it, wouldn't he?'

'Athel, I don't know. I only know I love you, and even if heaven itself forbade me, I should go on loving you to the last day of my life. . . .'

I spoke wretchedly, afraid for us both as I had always been since that first afternoon sheltering from the storm under the pines.

'I sometimes think . . . I mean we have only to hold on, to wait until we come of age. . . . No one can stop us then.'

But I took no comfort from this, and I doubt if Athel did either. We both knew that what the law said was neither here nor there. We would never make a runaway marriage in defiance of the family. Two other people in a like condition perhaps, but not us.

* * *

In February I had a letter from my mother saying that she intended to accompany my stepfather on a business trip to Paris the following month. She urged me to join them there and then travel back to Beirut with them. 'I beg you to consider carefully before you refuse me again, Justine. You are my only child, and your continued rejection of the home I offer you is extremely painful to me. . . . I do not insist that you should stay, but only that you should spare me a little of your time. . . . The villa is now complete in every detail, and I have made your rooms so beautiful. . . . If you say you will come, we could hasten our arrangements and meet you in Paris on your birthday. . . .'

My birthday. In just under three weeks I would be nineteen. It was nearly a year since I had waved good-bye to Mother on her wedding day. Suddenly I felt a great need to see her again, and on an impulse I got Pegger to take me into Upstrand and sent a message by the telegraph that I would be in Paris on the second of March without fail.

I meant to tell Athel the same evening, but an accident to one of the farm workers, who fell off a ladder while tiling a barn, prevented him from coming to the Dower. The next day he was gone to Lancaster on an errand for Grandfather, and the following day was market day. With one thing and another nearly a week passed before I had an opportunity to speak to him alone. Then, when I did see him, he was so happy and so full of his own surprise that I could not bring myself to break my unwelcome news.

All year Athel had been talking about the present he had *not* given me on my last birthday. It was to be something so special, apparently, only it would not come right, and the combined efforts of Bartholomew Tyte and Pegger and Athel himself had failed to make it work. It had been an entertaining puzzle to me, what they were at, and I teased them a good deal.

Now at last, Athel announced, their unremitting efforts had been rewarded—just in time for this birthday, but they were far too pleased with themselves to wait—and I must go on to the terrace and keep my eyes tightly closed and be surprised. Shivering in the damp chill of the late afternoon, I did as I was bid. There was a good deal of unfortunate language and the sound of something metallic striking stone. A peremptory call from Athel to 'Let her go,' followed, surely, by the gush of water . . . then a crash . . . more bad language. . . . 'Turn her off.' . . . 'Right, turn her on again . . . up a bit . . . a bit more. . . .' And then at last a fairy sound, erratic and yet with a sort of pattern to it, tracing a delicate beauty on the air.

I opened my eyes. The fountain was working, and balanced

triumphantly on the slight rise and fall at the top of the jet was a round, shining copper ball.

'It has a bell inside,' Athel said proudly. 'It's a fountain bell.'

'But how marvellous! I never heard or dreamed of such a thing!' I approached the fountain with wonder.

'No. Daresay you wouldn't have. It's an eighteenth-century toy. Had them in Italy, so I understand. Eugenie brought back the idea. . . . I found a drawing of it in her notebook years ago, when I was a lad, and there's an item in her account book to "pay Noah Tyte for his labour upon the bell for a fountain" soon after she moved into the Dower. But later there's another item "to pay Noah Tyte for further work upon a fountain bell, the which not yet fulfils its office." It looks to me as if poor old Noah never did get it to work. But we have, haven't we, Bartholomew? And Pegger's worked hard, too, changing the force of the jet!'

I looked from one to the other of them with great affection. Three men beaming their delight in the victory of their own ingenuity.

'I think it is the cleverest thing I ever saw,' I said. 'It must be the only one in England, and I have it in this garden to give me pleasure. How kind you all are to take so much trouble!'

And so we stood for a long time, listening to he merry tinkling, and Mrs Rimmer must be fetched, and Ellen. And Athel's gratification in my pleasure and mine in his was too sweet to spoil, and so I still did not tell him that I was going away.

The days had dwindled away so fast that there was barely a week left before I must leave Clere Athel. I had written to Aunt Mathilda that I would break my journey for one night with her, and she had replied that she would make the necessary travel arrangements for my journey to Paris and that Flora would accompany me. There was nothing left to be done except to tell the family and pack my things.

I decided to tell Grandfather at dinner that night. At least to make a general announcement would take some edge off the painful scene which must certainly follow when Athel and I were alone.

Grandfather came to table carrying a letter and looking mighty pleased over it. He could hardly wait for the soup to be served before he told us its contents.

'Here's news from the Sawards . . . remarkable interesting news it is, too. Saward's brother, Crispin, him that ran off to America and made a fortune, is coming home on a visit next year.'

We murmured politely and waited for more.

'Bringing his daughter with him . . . let's see . . . Sarah-Louise . . . there now, that's a taking name, isn't it? . . . Sarah-Louise. . . .'

There was a wary silence while we sought the significance of Grandfather's unwonted enthusiasm.

'Well, well!' said Grandfather. 'We really must tell Saward to bring them down to see us.'

I directed an uncertain look at Athel and saw that his eyes had hardened.

'Are they making a long stay in England?' I asked, because I thought someone ought to show *some* response.

Grandfather beamed at me. 'Saward says about a twelve month; then his brother must needs go back to see after his affairs. P t the daughter . . . ah, that's another matter! Saward tells me his brother has a fancy to find an English husband for her.' He chuckled. 'America may be the promised land of rich grain and cheap beef, but it offers a dubious selection of husbands: too many European immigrants whose antecedents cannot be known, too many predatory young men with their way to make in a new land. And Sarah-Louise Saward is an heiress, a handsome prize.'

'I should have thought it as likely a man would marry her for her money here as in America,' Hugh said cheerfully. 'Wouldn't do it myself because I haven't a fancy for a wife in any circumstances. But Athel won't turn his nose up if a bit of brass comes with a bride, will you, old chap?'

'Hugh! How coarse!' Aunt Sophie protested. 'I do wish you wouldn't talk in that way.'

'Ah, but apparently Crispin Saward don't object to an *Englishman* looking at her bankbook, just so his background is a decent one and he's a steady young man who'll treat her right and take care of her as he should.'

Impossible not to see the significance of his eyes lingering on Athel. But Athel would not meet them, keeping his head bent over his plate and continuing to dissect a trout with dedicated skill. He was ignoring the conversation.

There was an awkward silence, and I plunged into it, directing some trivial questions at Cousin Cuthbert, who did his best to spin out the answers.

A pair of roast ducks made their appearance, were duly shown to Grandfather, and then set down before Athel. In the performance of this comfortable domestic duty always required of the heir, Athel must break his unnatural silence, and I believe we were all thankful for it.

Athel accepted the carvers folded in a napkin on the big silver serving dish which Alfred brought to him.

'Shall I carve now, Grandfather?'

'Yes, do so.' He watched Athel's performance upon the birds with a critical eye, marking the careful arrangement of the portions upon the server, the division of the dark meat from the delicately sliced breast. But Athel worked quickly and neatly, and apparently there was no fault to find. When he had finished, one of the footmen wheeled forward a trolley with a bowl of water, and Athel washed his fingers while Alfred served the rest of us.

Usually Grandfather complimented Athel on the carving if he thought he had done well or at worst gave him a set-down.

'The Moselle,' Grandfather said to Alfred. Our glasses were filled. 'And now,' Grandfather went on, 'I give you a toast, to Athel. . . . Do you recall what Chaucer says of his young squire on the Canterbury pilgrimage? . . . "Courteous he was, lowly and servisable, And carve before his father at the table." . . . I give you Athel, who by dutiful diligence has acquired every skill I could teach him . . . including the art of dispatching a pair of ducks!'

We drank to Athel. Grandfather's smile was resting on him, and it seemed to me then, as it seems to me now, that he loved Athel more than he had ever loved anyone else in his life, more than his own sons. My cousin Athel was gentle without any loss of manliness, strong-willed and yet never hasty in his judgement, quiet of speech and manner, and yet authority was in his nature. He was such a person as anyone might love, not least a man who had helped mould him. And Athel loved Grandfather, even seeing his faults, the ruthless prosecution of his own will, the ferocious, unbridled rages, the possessiveness.

I could well understand that, too. When you had known Grandfather, you had known a man, slightly larger than life and therefore with the good and bad in him magnified in proportion, generous-hearted, mean, wise, rash, honourable, dishonourable.

I do not know how I kept up any normal conversation that evening, although I suppose I must have done so. I was preoccupied, crystallizing my personal dilemma into a series of neat, bald statements. Grandfather thought he had found a marriage prospect for Athel in Sarah-Louise Saward. He had taken the opportunity of reminding Athel of his duty—for what else had that curious toast been but a leaning on the yoke of love and obligation? Grandfather would never countenance Athel's marriage to me because our affinity must make the union unacceptable to the people of Clere Athel, who had obeyed the Blood Book for hundreds of years. Therefore, if I were determined to have Athel, I must alienate him from the people and the place he most loved and rob him of the rôle in life for which he had been prepared.

After supper Athel wanted to walk back with me across the park. But it began raining at the last moment, and I went home in the trap with Cousin Cuthbert. I am not given to idle speculation, so I do not say to myself, 'But for that sudden shower.' I do not see how the rain changed anything. Even if I had had the opportunity, I could not have talked to Athel about my fears for him.

So I spent the long hours of that night forming a dreadful resolution. When I went away this time, I must not return. I had to leave Athel. I said the words over deliberately to myself, and they frightened me so much that I grew cold. I began to shiver uncontrollably, and there was a breathlessness, a physical struggle for air, almost as though the thought itself could crush the life out of me. After a while I grew calmer and forced myself to concentrate on Athel and his needs. I would not put him to a test of love on my account and set one-half of him at war with the other. I knew his sense of duty towards the people of Clere Athel. Could I let him fail in that for me?

I had always a feeling of protectiveness towards Athel, inextricably part of my love. It was his pride, as for all strong men, to present a resolute face to the world and fight his doubts and fears inwardly and alone. I think such a man has a need —no, a right—to the emotional protection of the woman who loves him. I could not spare him the pain of our parting, but the agony of the decision, I could at least bear that for him. I made that my own.

The next morning there was a letter from Aunt Mathilda confirming our arrangements and suggesting that, if I felt inclined, I should travel to London directly and make several days' stay with her before going on to Paris. Coming so opportunely, this letter put a notion into my head, and I acted on it at once before I could change my mind. Here was the opportunity of instant escape at hand. It cut through the need to bear an anguished scene with Athel, to suffer reproaches because I had given no warning that I was going away, even the painful leave-takings. I am no hand at amateur dramatics, neither does the polite social lie come easily to me, but I managed to convince Mrs Rimmer that Aunt Mathilda's cheerful, chatty letter was news of the gravest kind, that Uncle Simon was taken suddenly ill and that I must leave at once, that very day for London.

We began to pack in frantic haste, so that I might catch

an early-afternoon train, and if Mrs Rimmer was surprised at the amount of luggage I thought it necessary to take, I contrived to convince her it was no more than adequate to the time of year, being spring and the weather likely to change. Moreover, I pointed out, the length of my visit was uncertain. Harry Thorpe was summoned to stand by to drive me to the station.

And what about a message up to the house, Mrs Rimmer wanted to know. Mercifully, Athel and Grandfather were the least of my worries, for they had an appointment to look over some heifers on a farm the other side of Beacon Hill and must have left Clere Athel early.

'Oh, never mind that for the moment. We will only throw Aunt Sophie into one of her alarms, and there is really no need. I will write her a note, and Ellen may take it up later.'

'Ellen ought to be going with you, to my mind. It isn't fitting for a young lady to make a long train journey without a maid. And how you'll manage your luggage I don't know.'

'I shall manage quite easily. There are porters, you know. Besides, I shall naturally take a seat in a compartment reserved for ladies. There really is no need to drag Ellen all that way.'

'Well, you know *my* views on these newfangled ways, and I'll remind you that your grandfather shares 'em. He won't like it, and he'll blame me. But you won't care for that!'

On an impulse I gave her a hug and pressed a guinea on her, which she was reluctant to take. I wanted to give her a better present but was afraid to arouse her suspicions. Later I could write and tell her that she and Ellen might do what they pleased with the clothes I had left behind.

For the time being, I said nothing about seeing my mother in Paris or going back with her to Beirut. These moves could seem to develop naturally once I was safely in London, and could be told more easily in letters.

I took a last, sad look around the Dower. It was hard to keep my good-byes casual, not betraying their finality. There were surprised looks as we drove through the village with my boxes on the carriage. I waved as cheerfully as I could, and everyone we passed waved back. 'We didn't know you were going away. Come back soon! Good-bye, good-bye!' *Good-bye, Clere Athel, I shall never come back.*

The old pier road winds across a desolate stretch of that coast, and the wind is mournful in the marsh grass.

Harry Thorpe found a porter at the station and let him do the work of loading my boxes on to a barrow. But he condescended to get my ticket and found me a seat in a compartment with a formidable creature of a severe 'governessy' aspect. I whispered that I would rather be alone, but Harry's glare silenced me, and I was lacking the spirits to make a fight of it. He seemed to sense this and decided to take charge of the situation.

'Pardon me, ma'am. Are you travelling to London?'

My unpromising companion reluctantly agreed that she was.

'I'm in the service of Athel Athelson, of Clere Athel, and this 'ere's his granddaughter, Justine Athelson, going to London urgent. Will you please to keep an eye on 'er?'

I sank under the crushing weight of this appalling introduction, yet it seemed to do more good than harm, for the forbidding face relaxed by a minimum movement of muscle, and the lady signified her assent. Perhaps she had a sense of humour. At least she read a book for most of the journey and left me to my thoughts.

Just before the train started out, I asked Harry to tell Athel that I would write to him as soon as I reached London. It was the only message I left, apart from the brief note I had written for Aunt Sophie.

'I hope you know what you're doing,' Harry Thorpe said, and his shrewd eyes were on me.

'I think so. I think it will be for the best.'

'Some things you can't run away from.'

'You can at least try,' I said.

It was no part of my plan to tell Aunt Mathilda why I had left Clere Athel in such a hurry. In the event I pleaded guilty to the lie of saying Uncle Simon was not well and told her

I did not know how else to escape without a scene with Grandfather.

'He is so difficult since Grandmother died. I haven't even dared to tell him I am going to Beirut.'

Aunt Mathilda said I was 'a very silly girl' and ought to have written and told her long ago if things were as bad as that.

'Fancy trying to keep you away from your mother. I never heard of such a thing. Your Uncle Simon and I would soon have come and told him a thing or two if we had known.'

'Oh, it wasn't as bad as that,' I said hastily. 'He didn't stop me from leaving . . . only discouraged the idea. . . . And I really was very happy at Clere Athel . . . once. . . .'

'But not any more?'

'No . . . no, I don't think I want to go back there.'

'Good.' Aunt Mathilda was approving. 'Your mother will be delighted. We always thought the Athelsons a very strange lot, you know, and she was terribly afraid they might be a bad influence on you.' She looked me up and down. 'But they don't seem to have done you any harm. . . . Now we have a few days to do some shopping for your wardrobe—not before time by the looks of it—and we can get your hair dressed by Narcisse. . . . Yes, I think on the whole your mother will find you grown quite creditable to her.'

I wrote to Athel and to Grandfather, almost duplicate letters, explaining that Uncle Simon had made a remarkable recovery and adding the news that since by a happy coincidence Mother was travelling in Europe at the present time, I had decided to go and spend some time with her in Paris.

Athel replied at once for both of them:

My dear Justine,

We were surprised to hear your Uncle Simon was better so quickly. We had thought from the way you flew off without saying good-bye that he must be dying for sure. I imagine your Aunt Mathilda is vastly relieved. Naturally you will want to take the opportunity of seeing your mother, and we will try not to be selfish and wish you back too soon. Only don't stay too long away. Grandfather sends his best wishes to your mother, and I add mine, and the affectionate regard of all the family.

Yours ever,
Athel.

It was lovely to see Mother again. She was now at the height of her looks, a radiant, elegant woman, who turned appreciative heads wherever she went. It gave me pleasure just to watch her, and I saw that my stepfather felt the same. Nothing could have exceeded his kindness to me, and when I told Mother that I had grown bored with Clere Athel, his pleasure seemed almost as great as hers in the prospect of my making a permanent home with them.

'Oh, Justine! This is marvellous! This is just what I had always hoped for,' Mother said, throwing her arms around me.

Over her shoulder I looked at my stepfather, who nodded and smiled.

'You make us complete, Justine. You make us a family.'

It was far more than I deserved from either of them.

And so I had said good-bye to Athel in my heart. I still do not know where I found the strength to walk away from him. Perhaps in a sense I never have. I was very young when I loved him, very immature, yet there was something damaging in that encounter, and I have never been ready to love again so completely. I am the tinder with the unstruck match. Green fruit of the orchard that falls from the trees in June. I cannot measure what it cost me. How can you measure the loss of the first fine vision of love and the pity of its sad wraith haunting you down the years?

Those who know me now praise me for my self-containment, my tranquillity. Yet sometimes still, in a melancholy season when the haunting is strong, I think of Athel. Then there is a wildness rises up in me that has the potential for every kind of folly, and I long to cry aloud, 'I loved a man once, a man who stood like a tree on his own land, and his hair was the colour of ripe wheat. I looked into his eyes and could have damned my soul for love of him. I am robbed, I am cheated. I am desolate, groping for the touch of his lips, yearning for the lost scent of his skin. Where is he now? What is he doing?' I have cried his name on many a hill and many a seashore and willed my soul away to cross three thousand miles and more and trouble his.

They say to me, 'How calm you are, Justine! How quiet. How still.' Ah, yes. I have tenderness left to me and quiet affection. But no ecstasy.

Part Three

Part Three

CHAPTER ONE

PIERRE AUCASSIN got up early—the habit of a lifetime—
and either rode or swam before breakfast. Failing the opportunity for such exercise, as was sometimes the case when he
travelled, he would walk. Later he would breakfast, attending
to urgent correspondence with his first pot of coffee, enjoying
his first cigar of the day with a second. He would not expect
to see Antonia before ten o'clock, an arrangement perfectly
agreeable to both of them.

The latter part of the morning was devoted to business.
Lunch was for entertaining business associates or being elsewhere entertained by them. Dinner and the evening were for
leisure, amusement, and close friends. This was the way Pierre
Aucassin had always lived, and the acquisition of a wife in no
way disturbed his routine, since he had had the good sense
to choose a mature woman well able to adapt herself to it.

Mutual friends were hard put to say who had the better
of the bargain. True, Pierre would be most unlikely to get
children by Antonia, but then perhaps he had never wanted
a family. He had been in no haste to get married. And there
was a nephew, his younger brother's child, orphaned when
his parents drowned in a yachting disaster. . . . Pierre had
given him control of the tobacco interests based on Cairo and
appeared to treat him as heir to the family business. On the

other hand, Antonia's tastes were cultured, and she was noted as a lively conversationalist with a quick wit, an undoubted social asset for a man like Pierre, who, though he had a sensuous appreciation of beauty, had never spared the time to cultivate any knowledge of the fine arts and who, for all his graceful manners, could be moody, even dour, when he was preoccupied.

He was in many ways a difficult man to know or belong to, a stranger in every country he visited, including his own. His reputation was that of a cynical, cosmopolitan merchant prince, a loyal friend, and a ruthless competitor. Certainly he was merchant before he was man, and a younger bride might well have complained of neglect. As it was, Antonia did not demand more attention than she got, and it is doubtful if she would have welcomed it. Widowhood had taught her how to arrange an independent social life, to fill the hours her husband devoted to work. He would not delegate. She did not ask it. Constantly charmed by her and liking both her self-sufficiency and her frailty, he gave her all the money she could want and approved the way she spent it. What more felicitous match can there be than that in which a man and a woman want from each other exactly what each is prepared to give?

Breakfast at the Aucassin villa was a meal of deliberate simplicity to be eaten on the terrace above tiered gardens stepping down to an opulent view; a unique experience, piquant with the contrasts of East and West. The food seldom varied. There would be a quantity of delicious small rolls, baked by the chef in the cool of the dawn; a glimmering pool of honey in the depth of an earthenware bowl; a dish of creamed cheese fragrant with chopped herbs; sherbet made from the juice of freshly gathered limes; and coffee brewed in the Turkish manner as well as the French. Then conceive a fine Persian carpet spread over the paving of the terrace and this modest, homely fare consumed in formal style, with a good deal of starched white napery and heavy silver upon the table. And finally, lest the sun should climb too early or the breakfasters descend too late, a canopy of blue silk was unrolled overhead and swagged and tasselled between gilded poles along the balustrade.

Justine, on the first morning after their arrival at the villa, chose to find her own way down the wide marble staircase and through the long, cool shadows of the salon to the terrace. She hesitated when she saw her stepfather alone and engaged with a letter. But he looked up and rose at once to bring her to the table.

'Mother is not down yet?'

'No, it is too early for her.'

Justine laughed.

'And I thought I had slept too late and you would both be wondering whatever had become of me!'

'You slept well?'

'Yes, certainly. Very well.'

'And yet there are blue shadows beneath your eyes.'

Justine raised a defensive hand to smooth away the telltale signs of the long hours before sleep came.

'Perhaps the fatigue of the journey. . . .' Her voice failed under Pierre's direct scrutiny.

'It has seemed to me, forgive me if I usurp the role of a father, that you have not looked quite . . . happy . . . since we met in Paris. Has it troubled you to put so many miles between yourself and . . . Clere Athel?'

Justine was startled by the accuracy of his observation. And yet her mother had appeared to notice nothing.

'No . . . no. Not at all. . . . Believe me, I am delighted to be here.'

Pierre sat back now admiring the girl's poise. Her voice was hesitant, but she kept it sure. But he was right. It was as he had always suspected. The child had a *tendre* for her cousin, the one she never spoke of . . . what was his name? . . . Athel. Now why had she run away? Was the union of cousins forbidden by Christianity? No, surely not. His own mother had been a Roman Catholic, his father born into the Muslim faith. Pierre Aucassin lacked a religious identity, as he lacked a national one, yet he felt certain he had heard of cousins being united in the Anglican Church. What was the barrier then? Money? His eyelids drooped indolently as they did when his mind was moving quickly.

'Will it trouble you if I light a cigar?'

'Not at all.'

'Hamid will be here to serve you directly. Will you help yourself to coffee?'

He watched Justine, liking the leisured assurance of her movements, the repose of her fine straight features and the tilt of her head. She would be an elegant woman in a few more years, make an ideal wife for the right man. He wondered idly what it would cost to buy Athel for her. It was a pleasant daydream to see himself playing the role of indulgent father. A signature on a banker's draft, and it might be done. So easy. Too easy. The realist in him reasserted itself. And what manner of husband did one buy for a girl with money? A woman might bargain her beauty and charm against a fortune, that seemed reasonable to him—but a man?

Pierre's thoughts were interrupted by the arrival of Hamid.

'The Aucassin *bigam* asks me to say that she will join you in five minutes. May I serve breakfast to the daughter of Aucassin *beg* now, or will she wait?'

'Thank you, I will wait.'

Hamid occupied himself discreetly with the coffee trolley, preparing a fresh infusion on the silver spirit burner with the deft, minimal movements of a long-practised craft. Hamid could have made perfect coffee in his sleep. In fact, he was not called upon to make it at all. He was more steward than servant to the Aucassin household, but he preferred to wait on the family himself. Only then could he be sure the task was performed to his satisfaction.

Antonia, aglow in a morning gown of pale-yellow chiffon, drifted out on to the terrace and kissed her husband and her daughter.

'Hamid! It distresses me to say there is a dead fly on one of the console tables in the hall.'

200

'The Aucassin *bigam* has a tender heart!'

Pierre spluttered into his coffee, and Justine looked up sharply, amused by the irony of the words and the gentle wonder of the tone in which they were delivered.

Antonia made a gesture of impatience. 'You misunderstand me deliberately, I think. I mean, of course, that I do not wish to see a dead fly in such a place. Please see that it does not occur again.'

Hamid shook his head regretfully. 'I cannot promise this thing. It is for Allah to appoint the time and place where the fly shall die.'

Outraged, Antonia directed an appealing glance at her husband, but he had vanished behind a financial newspaper and clearly intended to take no part. Only the newspaper shivered slightly to suggest a subdued enjoyment of the exchange.

'It is, however,' Antonia attempted again in a tone of dangerous sweetness, 'for you to appoint the cleaning staff and to see that they do their work properly.'

Hamid's eyes flickered over her briefly. With what, Justine wondered, intercepting the look, resentment? No. More like mischief, but a very adult mischief, as one who indulges a child.

She stared hard at him. His eyes were once more respectfully downcast, and he continued his attentions to the breakfast table.

'The hall was cleaned and polished this morning as it always is. I inspected the work myself when it was finished. There was no fly upon the table at that time. If a fly is struck down in a room after it has been cleaned, it may chance that the Aucassin *bigam* will see it before I do. I deplore this, but I cannot prevent it.'

Antonia, effectively vanquished by this argument, turned to Justine as one discovering a useful ally. 'You must forgive these wearisome household topics, my dear. The fact is we are much plagued by flies in this climate, and while Hamid can be tolerant of such a nuisance, I cannot.'

Justine murmured that she had not observed any flies in her own apartments.

'No. We burn some perfumed pastilles in the house which deter them, and we are fairly successful in keeping them out of the upstairs rooms. Now we shall change the subject, or I can eat no breakfast. You may go, Hamid.'

Pierre closed his newspapers. '*Thank you*, Hamid.' Impossible for Justine sitting directly opposite him not to notice the conspiratorial look and the wry smile that accompanied this more gracious dismissal.

He patted Antonia's hand affectionately. 'My dear, you have quite discomforted Justine, you know.'

'I? Why, whatever can you mean?'

'I will explain to you, Justine. Hamid's family has served mine for several generations. When I was seven years old, Hamid, who is two years my senior, was engaged as watchdog over me. Some watchdog. We were up to double the mischief together! He is Turkish, as you may have guessed. His family were warriors rather than servants, and in fact, his great-great-grandfather served mine as captain of the private body-guard which it was not unusual for anyone of substance to maintain in the East in those days. In the long years of my bachelorhood'—he paused to kiss Antonia's hand—'the long, lonely years, my best beloved, Hamid took charge of my house-hold. He runs it with a military discipline, and he is absolutely incorruptible. We never have any servant problem, and we are never cheated, because his eyes are everywhere watching our interests. There is no reason for Antonia to play the chatelaine. Hamid does everything far better than she could hope to do it.' Antonia opened her mouth to protest, but her husband silenced her with a firm pressure on the delicate hand of which he was still possessed and continued firmly, 'Further-more she knows this, and since she is your mother, and dear and familiar to you, Justine, you will be as aware as I am that she is secretly relieved. She has no taste for making preserves, ordering provisions, and chasing after idle servants with a broom, but perverse and feminine as she is, she will not admit this. Every now and then she likes to bustle after Hamid to show that she is conscientious and that this is her house. Hamid understands this. He is her very willing and devoted slave. I have no doubt he would die for her, but he has pride in his work, and he will not permit her to fault it unjustifiably. That, Justine, is how it is . . . is it not, my love?'

Antonia stared at him for a moment, then threw back her head and laughed, the warm, rippling laughter that was so irresistibly infectious. Pierre and Justine were certainly not immune. Deep in the shadows of the salon, Hamid smiled with satisfaction. The Aucassin *beg* had joy in his family. He had not been easy to please. The women of many countries had failed to please him. But Allah in his infinite wisdom had at last sent him one who brought him joy of the spirit and, to make up for his tardiness, a daughter fully grown, graceful as the willow, pale as the moon. He smoothed the smile from his face and went out to see if more coffee should be needed.

Of all the places one might run to put a lost love out of one's mind, it sometimes seemed to Justine that in her step-father's villa at Beirut she had chanced upon the best. There was still the heaviness, the sadness, but for a little more than half the time in every day she could at least pretend it was not there. The resident society was very amiable, largely French, and there was a good deal of entertaining. Moreover, both Pierre and Antonia had a wide acquaintance, who liked to travel and thought little of making the trip to Beirut for a visit, so the succession of house guests seemed never-ending. Artists, friends of Antonia's youth, a connection established when her father was alive, came to paint and in turn introduced writers, who came to write. Representatives of the *corps diplomatique*, with impeccable manners and suave conversation, came, waving introductions from Pierre's mother's family in Paris. And Uncle Simon and Aunt Mathilda between them sent so many people that Pierre observed somewhat tetchily that there must be hardly anyone left in England.

The villa itself provided every kind of diversion, too. There was a splendid library, a fine music room, one might ride or play tennis in the grounds, and for the first time in her life Justine was introduced to the pleasures of swimming—in a pool hewn out of solid rock and romantically ornamented with a grotto at one end and a slender waterfall at the other.

'My dear, do remind me to tell Hamid we want the Tapestry Room prepared the day after tomorrow, and . . . let me see . . . the one next to it will do—after all, she is his sister—then they can share the balcony.'

'Quite,' said Justine. 'Who is whose sister?'

'Oh, heavens! Didn't I tell you? Well, I can't remember her name; I've never actually met her. But she's quite famous. Writes travel books, doesn't she?'

'Does she?'

'It is in a letter here somewhere. . . . Ah, Pierre! *Do* come in, dearest. What is the name of Richard Engerard's sister for goodness sake?'

Pierre thought for a moment. 'Have I ever heard her first name? I don't think so. . . . Wait a moment. . . . V. Engerard. . . . V. E. Engerard. . . . We saw something she had written once on a bookstall in London. You pointed it out to me. *Seven Nights on the Back of a Camel*, as I recall.'

Antonia laughed.

'*Nine Days in Arabia!* Well, the V must stand for Victoria, what else?'

'Valerie, Veronica, Violet,' Justine suggested.

'Bother! I shall just have to find the letter then.'

'I imagine Richard Engerard is only coming to renew his acquaintance with Justine,' Pierre observed.

'But I do not recall ever having met him!'

'Justine, you must remember! He was at Aunt Mathilda's the night I introduced you to Pierre. He was sitting almost opposite to you and drinking in every word you uttered. Aunt Mathilda said he never took his eyes off you the whole evening and was hardly civil to his neighbour at dinner.'

Justine looked at her mother in astonishment. 'I have absolutely no recollection of him. What does he look like?'

Antonia was vague. 'Hard to describe, really. He must be

fortyish, greying hair, thin features. A refined face, but not handsome. He's an anthropologist.'

'Doesn't revive any memory.'

'His sister writes these travel books, as I told you. She wasn't there that night, but normally they go everywhere together. Rather charming, I think, wandering the face of the globe hand in hand in pursuit of learning.'

Pierre yawned. 'My dear, you make them sound a pair of first-class bores.'

'Not at all. Richard Engerard is very interesting to listen to . . . he has been to so many strange out-of-the-way places.'

'No need to extol him further! You have already said everything that is necessary to make him attractive to Justine. You have said he admires her. For a woman that is quite enough,' her husband concluded dryly.

Justine was out when the Engerards arrived. Having been foolhardy enough to pretend a polite interest in ancient Arabic literature, she had been captured by an earnest young lecturer at the American-established Syrian Protestant College in Beirut and carried off to see the treasures of his department. Unfortunately his enthusiasm for his subject was not in any degree matched by his ability to convey it across the barrier of Justine's total ignorance of the language. Furthermore, he insisted on completing the outing with a thorough tour of his college, which bypassed no bookstore or closet to which a key could be found. She had become uncomfortably warm hurrying to keep up with his long stride, her feet were aching, and she was bored to exhaustion when her escort finally returned her with reluctance to the villa.

She was slipping thankfully into a soothing bath when Antonia burst in upon her.

'I came to say *do* wear your most devastating toilette at dinner, my dear. It will be the most diverting thing for you to see the effect. I always think it is so good for a girl to have at least one mature admirer, so reassuring. And if he were to propose . . . not, of course, that he is a suitable husband, too old—heavens above, he could be your father—but a girl of your age will naturally like to be receiving offers. Coquetry is not your style, my love, I know, and I am glad of it, but it will give you confidence to have a man like Richard Engerard swooning after you.'

'Mother, I beseech you—stop!' Justine laughed helplessly from the depth of the marble bath. 'If you only knew what a dreadful day I have had. I doubt whether I can summon the strength to totter downstairs.'

Antonia sank into a chair. 'Not come down! Oh, Justine, he will be so disappointed. He could hardly take in a word I was saying to him when they arrived; his eyes were everywhere, looking for you. And when I said you were out but were sure to see them at dinner, his expression changed completely. It was quite marked. I saw his sister watching him, and I'm certain she was thinking what I was thinking.'

'I hope not,' said Justine with sincerity. 'Really, Mother, I don't know how you expect me to face the poor man after you have gone on like this. I shall feel horribly self-conscious.'

'Nonsense. We do not lack finesse, I think.'

Justine saw that her failure to participate hurt Antonia.

'I'm sorry. It is just that I was feeling so fatigued. Tell me, then, what I should wear.'

Antonia smiled happily again, and Justine wondered, not for the first time, at the charming contradiction of her mother's character. Many years of living in France had given her an air of Gallic sophistication, and yet sometimes she seemed to have an almost childlike simplicity, readily pleased, easily downcast.

So it was that Justine found herself, nearly two hours later, gazing into her mirror at a reflection she hardly knew. The pale aquamarine silk of her dress—one which Antonia had bought for her in Paris—shimmered and flowed about her. 'Like sculptured water,' the designer had claimed, when it was modelled for them. And Josette, Antonia's French maid, had arranged her hair high and smooth, coaxing two long spiralling tendrils to frame her face softly.

Antonia expressed her admiration. 'Perfect. A look of wistful fragility. I have some delicate filigree earrings which will complete the effect. Josette, take Justine to my room and find her those long silver earrings we bought in Vienna. You know the ones I mean. I must go down. We are unforgivably late. Follow me as soon as you can, Justine!'

'Oh, dear, do you mean I must go down to the salon alone?'

'Yes,' said Antonia with a small, satisfied smile. 'That is precisely what I do mean.'

In the salon Richard Engerard attempted to concentrate on what his host was saying. He was giving his views on the Ottoman administration, and they deserved a more attentive reception.

There was a brief flutter of interest over the arrival of four more guests, visitors to the British Syrian Mission. 'Is everyone here, now?' Antonia's voice could be heard asking clearly. 'No. Justine is keeping us waiting. You must forgive my daughter; she has been out all afternoon.' The bright chatter of introduction and establishment of common interest and acquaintance that goes on at such occasions broke out again. The sherry circulated once more.

Afterwards it would always seem to Richard Engerard that the salon fell utterly silent as Justine walked across the hall. In fact, he was the first to see her, having unconsciously taken up a position which gave him a clear view to the foot of the staircase. And the silence was a fiction, the fractional oblivion of a mind temporarily deranged by virtue of falling in love. Some people claim to hear violins, Richard Engerard heard . . . nothing, saw only Justine, and moved towards her like a man in a trance.

Antonia, watching them meet in the doorway, had the oddest feeling that what she had so lightheartedly contrived could not now be undone.

Justine, still with no recollection of the previous meeting, felt instinctively that the man moving so purposefully towards her must be Richard Engerard, but it was a relief when he identified himself. Perhaps he guessed that she had been preoccupied on the last occasion.

He was a little above medium height and rather thin, with a pale complexion and greying dark hair. Her mother had been right, she thought; he was not at all handsome. But he had a clever face, which was so much better, the brow wide and deep and scored by concentration, the eyes well lit, the mouth sensitive. Would she have seen this at another time, in another place? Possibly not.

After that first quick appraisal she was reluctant to meet his eyes so directly again. She found herself saying everything that was amiable in a careful voice. They went in to dinner together, and her fingers rested light as a whisper on his arm; even so she could feel the tenseness in him and was unaccountably moved by it.

It was the beginning of an interest she could never have foreseen or imagined.

At dinner he talked quietly to her of his current research, his interest in a religious sect, the Druzes, who had a community in the Lebanese mountains. There was an unostentatious parade of his modest achievements, the paper he had read to the Royal Society, the lecture tour of American universities, which he had turned down because he and his sister, Violet, had been on the point of leaving by camel caravan for Petra, a trip they had promised themselves for years.

'And was it worth it, your visit to Petra?'

Unhesitatingly, 'Yes. I am not really a talker. I do not believe I should have made out very well lecturing. The truth is I would rather learn than teach. In Petra I learned about the Nabataeans, who built it. Your stepfather would have approved of them, I believe. They knew how to build and guard a business empire. At least they guarded it successfully until they met the Romans!'

'What made you go by camel caravan? A romantic idyll . . . a string of camels winding, swaying across the sands. . . . Is there no other way to reach Petra?'

'No. No other way.' He was looking at her strangely. 'The desert under the stars should be seen by everybody once in a lifetime. . . . You should see it. . . . I wish I might be the one to show it to you. . . .'

Her mother was making slight, discreet signals to the women, and it was with relief that Justine received hers and joined the general drift out into the hall and thence to the music room.

'How d'you do. We didn't have time to get ourselves introduced before. I'm Violet Engerard.'

'Oh, Miss Engerard. Won't you sit here?'

Violet Engerard belonged to that division of the female sex commonly delineated as 'strapping' and 'hearty.' Of indeterminate age between thirty-five and forty-five, she was not unattractive with a pair of fine, bold eyes and strong features.

'So you're the girl my brother wanted so much to see again —you won't mind me, my dear, I am always direct—yes . . . I believe I understand. . . . You have a quality.' She looked Justine up and down, smiling to herself. 'Be the damnedest thing if he fell in love now at his age. He never was one to moon over girls. No calf love in his life. I don't believe he ever had more than a passing fancy for a woman—I'm not embarrassing you, am I?'

Justine laughed ruefully. 'Yes. You most certainly are!'

'Hmmph! You've a spark of humour in you, anyway, and that's more than can be said for most women.' She added as an afterthought, 'I suppose it would be asking too much for you to tell me how you feel about him?'

Between exasperation and amusement Justine said, 'Miss Engerard, I hardly know your brother. I found him very pleasant company at dinner, to be sure, but as to *feelings*. . . .'

Violet Engerard sighed. 'Well, I own I would like to see him married. You mustn't mind if I do what I can to further his interest. Now I never had a fancy for marriage myself— much too restricting. But a woman alone can always look after herself. It is her nature to contrive the comforts of life. On the other hand, a bachelor is a poor thing, especially when he gets older and past being a catch for anyone.'

Intrigued as she was by this unorthodox thinking, Justine was nevertheless thankful that the men joined them and put a summary end to her tête-à-tête. And she took good care to secure herself one of the solid British matrons for company, as the party prepared to admire Antonia's musical talents, hoping that a bulwark of bronze satin would deter Richard Engerard from trying to sit next to her.

It did, and he contented himself with a position from which he could observe her in profile, marvelling at the stillness about her as she listened to the music.

Antonia had all the latest scores, and there was a clamorous request for *The Merry Widow* waltz. She was smiling across the piano at Pierre while she sang, and the melody seemed to mean something special to them. Richard felt a sudden surge of envy. And then he was remembering the night when he had first seen Justine. She was sitting across the table with Pierre, and they were talking quietly, exchanging reminiscences in an intimate, easy way. Misunderstanding a casual observation by another guest, he at first thought it was Justine who was expected to marry Pierre. He watched her, admiring the soft contours of her face in the candlelight, the fine, wide eyes—were they grey or gold?—and their level, listening looks at odds with the almost indolent droop of the eyelids. She had seemed oblivious to his examination of her. A proud face he had thought . . . and a wilful mouth. But wilful to what? To kiss or to scold, to do right or to do wrong? He had looked at her face too long. Later, when he learned that it was Antonia who was to marry Pierre, a wholly uncharacteristic excitement took possession of him. He could not forget Justine, could not get her out of his mind. He must see her again, talk to her, know more about her. But she had gone. Left London altogether.

'"At seventeen he falls in love quite madly . . ."' sang Antonia. . . . He awoke to recognition of the present. Justine was bending her head to hear a remark made by her ample neighbour. How graceful the curve of her neck was! . . . '"At twenty-four he gets it rather badly. . . ."' This time he would not let her slip away from him so easily. It might be he had small chance of ever winning her, but at least he would risk the stakes. . . . ' "When a man thinks he is past love, it is then he meets his last love, and he loves her as he never loved before!"' . . .

*   *   *

The letter with the Liverpool postmark was heavy in Justine's hand. It was from Hugh. She was both eager and afraid to open it, and she carried it very slowly up to her own rooms to be sure of reading it undisturbed.

My dear Justine,

    Am staying in Liverpool cramming through the first month of vacation. But I went home last week-end, and I thought I had better write to you because there's the devil to pay there, and I think you ought to know about it. I could tell there was something up when I got there on the Friday night. Athel looked dreadful, and so naturally I asked if he was ill, and he slammed out of the room, and Grandfather roared that I had better go after him and see if I could get any sense out of him because nobody else could. He said he'd been impossible to live with for weeks, moody and off his food and snapping everyone's head off. . . . Well, you know, that's not like Athel. You can imagine how shocked I was when I found him and saw that he had been crying. Justine, I never saw Athel weep since he was nine years old. I accidentally stuck a pitchfork through his foot, and I remember he just cried for a moment, but he stopped when he saw I was frightened. Well, I'm not putting this very plainly perhaps, but you'll follow it because, as you have probably guessed, the trouble is over you. I never knew Athel and you . . . that is, we all love you and I miss you very much, but anyway Athel told me. He said it was a relief to tell someone at last. He thinks you've run away to Beirut and don't mean to come back. He said he would have followed you to France, but of course, he doesn't have the money to come chasing all the way after you to Beirut. He asked me if I could raise the wind from what Grandmother left, but I can't because that's sewn up, and I only get an allowance out of it. In the end (we talked half the night) I said he should tell Grandfather about it and ask him for the money. There was a terrible scene next day. Grandfather took it very badly. I don't mind owning I was listening behind the library door, but quite honestly I should have thought you could have heard them shouting at one another in Upstrand. Grandfather said he'd disinherit Athel and leave Clere Athel to me (not that I'd have it, of course), but Athel said to hell with that, he didn't care, and he'd take the fare to Beirut as wages for his work this year and never ask another farthing. Then Grandfather asked how he thought he would earn a living, and would he let you starve while he found out? It made Athel go very quiet. You'd have thought Grandfather might have let it go at that, but he didn't. He went on and on and on at Athel about heredity and responsibility, and Athel had stopped answering him. Then Grandfather begins to shout again that the whole idea of marriage between you and Athel disgusts him, and suddenly there is a terrible crash, and I burst in to see what happened and there is Grand father leaning on the table having some kind of seizure and Athel standing over by the window staring at him. The window was smashed, and I noticed that the big bronze horse that's normally in the middle of the library table was missing. (You remember that rearing horse? God knows what it weighs. I found it in the garden afterwards, and it took quite a bit of strength to lift it.) Athel said, 'He threw it at me. He could have killed me.' And then he just walked out and went to his room, and that was the last we saw of him that night. Well, I called Alfred, who fetched one of the lads up, and between us we got Grandfather to bed. I thought it was a stroke he had had, and McIntosh confirmed it. I told Athel next day, and he just said, 'Oh,' as if he didn't care. I asked him what he was going to do, and at first he said I should mind my own business. I said it was my business. He looked at me in a way I've never seen him look before and said, 'Do you want Clere Athel, then?' and I said I wouldn't have it at any price and then he said, 'Somebody has to have it. We can't just walk away from it. It's a burden to be handed on from one generation to the next.' He wouldn't talk to me any more. I asked him what he meant to do about you, and he wouldn't talk of that either. I don't know what you'll make of this. Grandfather seems to have lost the feeling in his right leg, but McIntosh says he isn't badly affected and should be up and about in a few weeks, if he takes things quiet. I've always thought he'd go in one of his rages. Perhaps this will be a warning to him. Actually, although I hate him for the things he said about you and Athel, I feel sorry for the old man. It's dreadful to see him looking so helpless, and I know you'd feel the same if you were here. Athel won't see him at the moment, and he's just going on about his work as if nothing had happened. There doesn't seem to be any pity in him. I hope for his own sake that he'll come round and forgive Grandfather. After all, blood's thicker than water, ain't it? And good or bad, we've all got the same blood. If you won't think it a cheek on my part to interfere, I wish you'd write to Athel and tell him straight one way or another whether you'll marry him. If you really have gone to Beirut to get away from him and don't intend to have him, it might make things easier for him to know that now. For my part I only wish you both happy. I don't know much about love, but I understand it's strong stuff and can weather a few storms. You can count on me either way.

Assuredly your loving cousin,
Hugh

There was a postscript over the last page:

On reading through what I have written, I see that I have not spared you. Still, I think you must have the truth to understand how things are here and to make up your mind about what you will do—H.

213

When she had finished reading the letter, Justine refolded it with meticulous care, then locked it away in the little ebony box with all the letters she had ever received from Clere Athel.

It would have been a comfort to cry, to cry for Athel, for herself, even for Grandfather. But the self-control which she had enforced so ruthlessly at each stage of her journey from Clere Athel to Beirut was now a barrier to that consolation. There was only despair at the catastrophe she had foreseen and failed to avert.

Downstairs in his study, Pierre Aucassin concluded the dictation of a business letter and glanced at his watch.

'That will be all, Grooter. You may sign that on my behalf, and when you have attended to the cables, take the rest of the day off.'

The secretary snapped to attention with his notebook. 'Thank you, Herr Aucassin, thank you.'

Pierre watched his erect retreating figure with a tolerant amusement. What an odd lot these Germans were—stiff as bristles on a wild boar—but they were punctilious in their duty, and he liked that, employing a number of them in secretarial positions.

'Grooter!'

'Yes, Herr Aucassin!'

'You will probably find Hamid in the hall as you go by; be so good as to ask him to come to me.'

'Yes, Herr Aucassin!'

Hamid padded in with his swift, quiet step.

'The Aucassin *beg* needs something?'

'Have you seen my daughter? The Aucassin *bigam* is lunching out today, and my daughter has engaged to be my hostess. He glanced at his watch again. 'The gentlemen from the Cinquecini company will be here in one hour. Will you remind her of the time?'

Hamid frowned thoughtfully at the toes of his soft leather boots.

'The Aucassin *beg* knows that his daughter has received a letter from England?'

'Yes, I saw it. What of that?'

'The letter keeps the daughter of Aucassin *beg* in her room, and she has sent away the woman who attends her.'

'She wishes to be private with her letter—this is not strange.' But he knew that Hamid never spoke without reason. 'Ask her if she will come to me for a minute. Say that I wish to confirm the time at which we will lunch.'

Justine went down to the library at once. Pierre noticed her pallor with alarm but did not refer to it.

'Ah, there you are, my dear. I wished to consult with you about our arrangements. Antonia prefers to use the petit salon when the party is small. I have given directions that the table shall be set out in there, and we will receive our guests in this room. Do you think one o'clock for lunch? They are due to arrive at a quarter after noon. . . .' He was watching her closely. She was perfectly composed. The eye of the cyclone can be almost as still. It will hardly lift the feathers of the songbird that crouches, panting in the branches of a tree a moment before destruction.

'Justine, my child! Is anything the matter?'

For a moment her eyes turned on him with a wild, lost look; then the smooth eyelids drooped over them defensively. 'Yes, I have had bad news of home . . . of Clere Athel, that is. . . . I do not know why I say home.'

'Will you tell me about it? Sometimes it is good to talk.'

'I would like to tell you.' She sighed. 'But there is so much to it, and then you might feel bound to repeat it to Mother. You see I don't want Mother to know now. It is too late for confidences, and she would only be angry and upset for my sake, and it will serve no purpose.'

Pierre did his best to conceal the alarm he felt. 'What precisely do you mean by too late?'

'She would think I should have told her how things stood between us before now. She would think I have been secretive.'

'It does not come easily to all of us to confide things when our feelings are deeply involved.' He shook his head, doubtful whether to press her further. 'It has sometimes seemed to me that you have a reluctance to talk about your cousin Athel. Can it be that this trouble concerns him?' He saw her startled reaction and went on quickly. 'If it does, you may tell me and be sure I will not betray the confidence to anyone without your permission.'

Justine hesitated. 'I do need advice. The truth is I have tried to do the right thing, but maybe I've made matters worse.'

'I think you should try to begin at the beginning,' Pierre prompted gently. 'Take your time. I am listening.'

Pierre was a good listener. He was sparing of questions and not impatient for the truth. In due time he received a fairly full account of the uncertain dawning of love that did not quite fit into the pattern, of the conflicting loyalties, the tormented indecision, the flight that was to resolve everything and had resolved nothing, of the painful conclusions that had now been reached.

'Justine, there is one important question I want to ask you. Do you still wish to marry your cousin?'

'No,' fiercely. 'No. I would never marry him now. There could be nothing but unhappiness for both of us.'

'What if I were to help you? Would a dowry make no difference?'

'No.' She shook her head decisively. 'You are so generous— I cannot tell you how. . . . But it would be no good. I know the way Grandfather thinks, you see, what his priorities are.'

'Then I suppose you will write to your Athel and tell him that you are not going to return?'

'That is what worries me—I don't know what to do. Will he believe me when I say I will never marry him, or will he be provoked into doing something rash? Might he not put himself into debt to raise the money for the fare and come out here?'

'Would he? But, my child, you know him better than I!'

'I cannot be sure. . . . Now if I were to convince him. . . .' She twisted her fingers together desperately. 'I believe I would never convince him unless . . . unless I told him I was going to be married to someone else!' There, it was out. The last resort that had occurred to her. The ultimate flight.

Pierre said cautiously, 'You mean that you would pretend you were going to be married. Wouldn't that be very difficult? The family would expect to see an announcement in a newspaper, to receive a formal communication from your mother. And they would send a gift, which would be embarrassing.'

'You misunderstand me. Of course it would be impossible to pretend such a thing. . . .' Her voice faltered.

'Justine, a few minutes ago I called you "my child" but I am reminded that neither description fits you. You will be twenty next birthday—no child, for many a woman is married and has two children at that age. Nor are you my daughter in truth and by blood. Therefore I will speak to you plainly as a woman of sense, and I will speak as an onlooker. You and your cousin Athel have formed an attachment which ought to have been predictable to older relatives. Neither of you had much opportunity for meeting eligible members of the opposite sex. But first romances seldom lead to marriage, and this is probably just as well since very few would provide the basis for a strong, lasting union. This is not to say they are unimportant. Sometimes they teach us something about ourselves.' He paused choosing his words. 'I do not think you should consider marrying simply in order to put yourself beyond your cousin's reach. Such a gesture has the'—he weighed a word again—'the touch of melodrama, and I feel it is not in character for you.' Justine smiled slightly, and he was encouraged to continue. 'You are already meeting a number of agreeable young men, and I have no doubt that in the not too distant future there will be one who can impress you more than the rest. Find one you can *admire*. It has always seemed to me that the most successful marriages are those between an admiring woman and a great-hearted man. Yes, that is what you must look for, a great-hearted man.'

'I used to think that of Athel . . . that he had greatness of heart.'

'Pah! A boy of twenty? Who can tell what he will become?

217

Look at him in ten years' time, and you may begin to know.'

She sighed. 'Perhaps I shall never know. Perhaps I shall never see him again.' She gave herself a determined little shake. 'Your guests will be here soon. I must go and change at once.'

'There is no need for you to come down to luncheon if you would rather not. We can plead a headache for you.'

'No. I am perfectly well and would prefer to be occupied.'

'You are quite sure.'

'Perfectly.'

Pierre rose and took her hand, tucking it through his arm. 'I will go up with you. At least we shall be quiet at dinner tonight. We are *en famille*. The Engerards will not return from Byblos until late tomorrow, and the next house guests do not arrive for nearly a week.'

They climbed the stairs companionably and paused in the gallery by the doors that led to Justine's apartments.

'You will not feel you must tell Mother?' Justine asked.

'No. I promised I would not. Besides, I believe you are right. She would be hurt and troubled for you, and I think that you are strong enough to resolve your own problems.'

'Am I strong?' For an instant her eyes were bleak with doubt, and then she contrived a tremulous smile which Pierre found deeply moving. 'We, Athelsons, you know!'

'I understand the English call it *noblesse oblige*.'

She shook her head. 'We call it self-preservation.'

CHAPTER TWO

JUSTINE had listened attentively to her stepfather's advice, but she did not take it. She had been too long accustomed to making her own decisions. And when, on an excursion to the mountains at Bait al Din, Richard Engerard proposed to her, she accepted him.

Later, questioning the wisdom of her impulse, she might blame the thinness of the air. Perhaps she had been a trifle light-headed. There was an extraordinary quality to the light, an almost metallic edge to it, and the setting—everything had increased the sense of unreality which made it possible to accept Richard almost as if she did so on behalf of someone else. As though the significant part of her, the real Justine, were absent at the time or had ceased to exist.

They had stood under a shadowed archway and looked out on the courtyard of the abandoned palace of Bashir II al Shihabi. Violet and Antonia were engaged on a tour of the formal apartments, leaving them alone, and Richard had been explaining the derivative sources of the architecture to her. Suddenly their eyes met on a level of mutual interest and sympathy, which can sometimes change the quality of a relationship between a man and a woman almost by accident. He reached out for her hand, and she let him take it.

Then he was saying, 'Justine, I love you. Will you marry

me? I know you don't love me. I am twice your age, and it seems a folly to hope that you ever could . . . yet I would do everything in the world to make you happy. . . .' She was silent for several moments, not knowing how to answer, staring at him as though she had never seen him before. He stumbled on, uncertainly. 'Of course, I am not a rich man. . . . Cannot offer you the sort of home you have here with your stepfather and mother. . . . A comfortable house in Devon. . . .' Justine heard little of what he was saying. She was wondering what there was about her that this man should be prepared to take her without love.

'Justine,' he entreated, 'at least say that what I am telling you does not distress you, is not unpleasant to you.' Almost despairingly he had pulled her into his arms. 'Forgive me . . . I do not know how to woo a woman. . . . I am awkward, graceless.'

Instinctively she had put her hands against his chest to push him away. 'But why?' she thought. It was comforting to be held so. His voice against her hair was muffled, but she recognized the anguish in it. 'I need you, Justine. When I am not with you, I am lonely for you.' Athel! The name rang in her head, a cry of her own anguish, an echo of Richard's. 'Richard is a fine, kind, clever man,' she told herself. 'And from this time I will be nothing to Athel.'

'Richard, Richard.' She detached herself gently and looked at him. 'If you are sure you want me, I will marry you.' His face had been transformed at once. She was ashamed of the effect she produced with so few words. Almost boyish in his exultation, he picked her up, twirling her around and setting her down before he kissed her. She had not disliked the experience. It was an amiable kiss. But it moved her not at all.

When Richard spoke to Pierre that evening, Pierre's reaction was one of consternation, which he did his best to conceal while he listened with a sympathetic expression.

'May I ask whether my stepdaughter has given you any reason to suppose that she entertains an affection for you?'

Richard hesitated. 'She was willing for me to speak to you.

She gave me to understand. . . .' Such phrases, such a tired, old formula of words with which to approach the skirmish of love. Where did they come from; who invented them? The truth was that Richard could not remember precisely what Justine had given him to understand in the courtyard of the emir's palace.

Mercifully Pierre interrupted his groping attempt at justification.

'Well, it is clear to me that you are an eligible husband for my stepdaughter in every way, except perhaps in regard to age, as you yourself appreciate. I will speak to Justine at once. It may be, also, that her mother will have some questions she would like to put to you.'

Pierre took care to speak to Justine alone before he went in search of Antonia.

'Justine'—his voice was stern—'I have just had an uncomfortable interview with Richard Engerard. You must needs know what about.'

'Yes, he asked me to marry him. I think it will be a good match. We shall do very well together.'

His worldliness did not prevent him being shocked. 'This is a very offhand way to take a husband. Why, you hardly know this man, and after what you told me only the other day, I must suppose you are simply taking the irresponsible course, against which I was at some pains to advise you. I feel it is my duty to stop you doing this.'

'No!' She stood up to face him with a sudden quiet determination. 'No, you must not stop me. I feel instinctively that this man is right for me. He does not demand the kind of love that I cannot give.'

'He is too old for you.'

'You wouldn't have made his age an objection if I said I loved him. I wish now that I had never confided in you.'

'So do I.' Pierre's agreement was emphatic. 'Oh, come, Justine! You cannot mean to go through with this. You have no feeling for the man.'

'Yes, I do. As a matter of fact, I admire him very much.

221

You said that was a good basis for a marriage.' Pierre scowled at her, but she was not intimidated. 'Furthermore, I find myself drawn to him. I like being with him. He's clever and interesting and——'

'And I would guess that he is vulnerable.'

'I know that, too.'

Pierre shrugged. 'You have put me in a difficult position. I still feel I ought to stop you but——'

'But you won't, will you? Really, I have everything to gain and nothing to lose.'

'That may be so.' Pierre sighed. 'I'm almost more concerned for Engerard, when I think about it. But he ought to be able to look after himself. . . . I cannot imagine what your mother will say, however.'

'You will only tell her of the proposal—nothing more?'

'No. It shall be as we agreed.' He turned at the door. 'I hope you will find happiness, child. In time.'

Antonia was pleased with the proposal but not with Justine's decision to accept.

'My dear, you might have done so much better for yourself. I had someone quite different in mind for you. And consider the opportunities you may have when we travel in Europe next spring. Far better tell him that you cannot make up your mind on such a brief acquaintance. . . . Ask him to give you time.'

'I cannot ask him for time to look around for something better!' Justine's voice was sharper than she intended.

'Well, it's only natural that I should want you to make the most of your opportunities, dear,' Antonia said reasonably. 'Any mother feels the same.'

'Yes, I understand. But there really isn't any point in waiting. I have made up my mind.'

'Oh, dear, you sound just like your grandfather when you talk like that, and I feel there is no reasoning with you. I do hope you don't mean to plunge into this with indecent haste. . . . You know there's *nothing* harder to live down than a wedding arranged with dispatch.'

Justine smiled slightly, and Antonia was surprised into the recognition of how seldom these days she smiled at all.

'I don't see any point in waiting until we can go back to London. I don't want to be married from Aunt Mathilda's house, if that is what you have in mind.'

'But she will be very hurt if you aren't married from there. She has always wanted it, you know. We might manage to be in London by Christmas, if you won't wait until spring. And goodness knows that gives us little enough time to prepare your trousseau.'

'I would prefer to be married here in Beirut. And I should think we could manage it in two months, say by the end of November. Richard has his work, you know. He will be travelling extensively in Syria over the next few weeks.'

It took hours of argument, but in the end Justine had her way. She said good-bye to Richard with relief. She was beginning to find the times they were alone together more of a strain than she had foreseen. There was more ardour in his nature than she had supposed, but she deceived herself with the notion that it would somehow be easier to handle him once they were married. In the meantime he would be safely out of the way until two days before the wedding.

She had, of course, written to Athel and was not kept waiting long for an answer.

My dear Justine,

I received your letter this morning and make speed to reply while I am still angry enough to say what I feel. It is a dreadful letter. A bad letter. What a struggle it must have been to write it. How almost impossible to send. It reads like a false confession, like some denial of a true faith for the basest of political motives. You say that Hugh told you what had happened, so you knew I had faced up to Grandfather at last—that the worst was over. Since his illness he has not referred to you, and it seemed to me that he might be prepared to accept the inevitable in time—especially since I shall be twenty-one next April. Have you so little patience? Have you no faith in our love? Do you really mean to go from my arms to the first man who asks you? You tell me little about him except that he is twice your age. Is that supposed to console me? You must have taken leave of your senses. . . . And now the hot fury has flowed out of me through my pen, and I am left empty and desolate, feeling the first chill of autumn in the air. Wanting you. I shall always want you whoever you belong to, and you will always want me, although you may try to say it is not so. Will you live a lie all your life with another man or come home to me?

It was not so very different from what she had expected, and yet Athel's letter was an unbearably painful experience. Unbearably? But it must be borne, and not only that, it must be concealed. She did not reply since there was nothing more to say.

Violet Engerard, through the hectic weeks of preparation, was an unexpected source of strength and even of comfort. She was determined that the wedding should pass off with as little to ruffle Justine's nerves as possible. Her shrewd eyes missed nothing, and intuition told her far more about Justine than Antonia would ever know, for all her motherly concern. When the preparations threatened to become too elaborate for Justine's liking, Violet would be on hand to say that 'Richard don't like a fuss either,' and when it was a question of where the bridal night should be spent, she was as sure as Justine was that Richard would rather they left at once on their journey to Damascus.

Damascus had been Pierre's idea and, he flattered himself, a rather good one. He had obtained the loan of a handsome house for them, from a business acquaintance, and they would spend two months' holiday there, before travelling back to England to visit Richard's father at the Engerard family home in Devon. He had chosen Damascus because there would be plenty of interest to see there and a whole way of life to explore that was strange to both of them.

'I can give you an introduction to several amiable families you may care to visit,' he told Justine. 'You will like to shop in the suqs, and there is the Great Mosque of the Umayyads and the Azem Palace to see. It is one of the oldest cities in the world, you know.'

'I think it is a splendid idea. You are so kind to us.' Justine accepted gratefully. 'Richard has a friend, an archaeologist, who is working in Damascus at the present time, and he writes to me that he is delighted to have the opportunity of meeting him again. He asks me to thank you very much.'

'Good! Excellent! You will be able to entertain this friend freely. The house is fully staffed, and I understand the cook can do you credit. Damascene society is very lively. Be sure to enter into it.'

Pierre was far too much of a realist to believe in romantic notions that a newly married couple wanted only solitude to be happy. He did not approve of the Western custom of a honeymoon in isolation, where the shortcomings of either partner might be the more intensely observed, and he was especially anxious to help Justine over the difficulties she must face when she found herself alone for the first time with her husband.

Uncle Simon and Aunt Mathilda made the journey with a good grace and were present among the two hundred guests whom Antonia had contrived to summon even at such comparatively short notice.

'I am so glad you felt you could come,' Justine said simply. 'Richard and I are both rather short of relatives, and every one is precious to us.'

'No Athelsons, I understand!' Aunt Mathilda made the sentence heavy with disapproval and dislike.

'Er . . . no. I'm afraid not.' Aunt Sophie had written kindly 'from all the family,' and Eugenie's prettiest table silver had been deposited with Justine's bank in London, a lavish gift by any standards and one that must have had not only Grandfather's approval but that of Athel, Hugh, and Charlotte also.

The bank had sent her notification on receipt of the deposit.

'Now let me see,' Antonia had at once been busy totting up the value. 'Twelve place settings with fifteen pieces to each set—that's one hundred and eighty pieces, Justine. That really is handsome of them! I wonder what it weighs?'

'No. No Athelsons,' Justine repeated firmly. 'Except me, of course.'

'And Richard's father didn't feel up to the journey?'

'No. He's quite old, I believe. Then there are his orchids. He cannot leave his orchids, you see.'

'Good heavens. Well, there are eccentricities on both sides, so it doesn't behove us to be critical.'

The stifling scent of exotic blossoms and a great deal of veiling. Justine looked at her reflection in the mirror, as she was dressed on the morning she was to be married, and wondered how many other brides had known the same moment with such heaviness of spirit. The rest of the day passed like a fantasy. She moved slowly through it, receiving small jolts of pain and a series of pale, blurred images. Her mother and Aunt Mathilda crying discreetly. The reassuring steadiness of Pierre giving her away, giving her cold hand to Richard. Too many people. Where had they all come from? How different it would have been to have gone as a bride to the little church in Clere Athel, to have made her vows with the whole soul and only those dear and familiar to listen to them.

'I, Richard Henry Edward Seaton. . . .' Who was this man? She had not even known half his names. When it was her turn to make the same vow, she thought: 'He knows I do not love him. I am not deceiving him. And God knows what is in my heart—I am not deceiving *Him* either.'

'With this ring I thee wed, with my body I thee worship. . . .' Richard's voice came from a long way off. It was wrong. No woman should ever go to a man in this way. It happened all the time, so they said, but it was a sin against nature. The words of the marriage service had faded, and she found herself listening instead to the voice of unbidden memory. 'As the apple tree among the trees of the wood, so is my beloved among the sons. I sat down under his shadow with great delight and his fruit was sweet to my taste. He brought me to the banqueting house, and his banner over me was love.' Yes, that was how it should be. Song of Songs. She was in the very land of Song of Songs. . . . 'Come with me from Lebanon, my spouse with me from Lebanon . . .' and she had just become Mrs Richard Engerard.

*   *   *

Old Athel lay in the vast canopied bed, which he had shared for the better part of his life with Cecily, and reviewed in his mind as many Athelsons as he could remember who had lain there before him. It wasn't easy to differentiate between the generations—so many having the same name—and when you were at the back end of your seventies you didn't have the same confidence in your memory. In this century there had been his father, Athel, and his grandfather, also Athel. Then there had been two that were easy to remember because they were second sons—Edgar Athelson, whose elder brother died after being trampled by a bull, and Willie the Rake. Old Athel could never think of Willie without chuckling over his misdeeds and the irony that life rewarded him well for them. He had committed just about every folly and excess a younger son could be expected to fit into a busy life. His army career was cut short when he was discovered in an unspeakable position with the wife of his commanding officer. Turned loose on London, he found the cards were kind to him and won a fortune at faro; but the dice were not, and he lost it at hazard. Eventually he was imprisoned for debt, and his brother, Athel, was dispatched to lead home the lost sheep. But Athel had caught smallpox in London and died shortly after returning to Lancashire, leaving Willie to inherit. Farther back than that, Old Athel became confused. Had Red Athelson slept in this bed? No, for he was the second of five sons. It was easier to remember the rascals! But *that* Athel Athelson, Red's elder brother, had died in this bed, secure of it until his ninety-fifth year. He was the one with the neat, rather round hand, who left such meticulous farm records behind. . . . Old Athel was dozing. . . . The sound of hooves stamping in the courtyard below his window woke him. That would be Athel returning from his morning round.

'I shall get up for lunch.' Old Athel spoke the words out loud, because then he was committed to the idea and he would do it. He sat up, feeling his head spin. Sickening! It always did that now when he first lifted it off the pillow. That was why he kept putting the moment off. The truth was he didn't have much faith in McIntosh. It might be that this lying in bed in the mornings wasn't such a good thing after all.

'Never been the same,' he said irritably, 'never been the same since. . . .'

He did not bother to complete the sentence for the listening silence of the empty room. Since the night Athel had told him he wanted his cousin Justine. What a terrible blow that had been! He turned cold to think of it. Shameful! No, perhaps that was too harsh. Their youth and innocence rose up in his mind's eye to defend them, and for an instant he regretted their unhappiness. But it was for the best. Athel had come to a better realization of his position; the boy must get heirs, strong, healthy heirs. . . . An Athelson must always think of the future, not the present, and love was—— He tried to remember what love was. Cecily. He had loved Cecily. He had bedded Cecily in this very bed. His sons, Athel and Lucian, had been born in it. He would die in it. Cecily hadn't died in it, but that was her own fault. He would die in it when he was ready, but not before he had seen Athel married. Nothing to stop him now. Justine was safely married to her anthropologist, and Athel had got over his sulks. A boy was young, resilient. A boy soon forgot. A wife would take his mind off his disappointments, and one day Athel, too, would lie in this bed. His sons would be born here, and he would understand that his grandfather had been right. Today was the twelfth of March, Athel's twenty-first birthday. They must be expecting him to have forgotten, but he had not forgotten. He'd tell Alfred to bring up the best champagne for dinner. That'd surprise 'em. He would like to have given Athel a present, but there was the heavy expense of the Saward's visit coming at the end of the month. Money. Now there was this worry about death duty. Never knew there was such a thing, but his lawyer, Houghton—a good enough fellow in his way—said it was so. Not likely he was mistaken. Death duty, indeed! The tenants had once paid feudal dues on death. What did they call it? Heriot, aye, that was it, heriot. They paid merchet on marriage and heriot on death. Now when tenants died, it often cost *him* money to bury them!

His thoughts turned on the Sawards. Good of Saward to put him in the way of an heiress for Athel. Perhaps he could get Hugh to take one of those buck-teethed daughters off his hands in return. What did they call Crispin Saward's girl? Ah, yes, Sarah-Louise. Such a pretty name, and she would be pretty, too, not like her cousins. No, God would be kind, and Athel would fall head over heels in love with her. The settlement she brought and later her inheritance would put all to rights. His head had stopped spinning now.

Fifteen hundred and five. It had just come to him. That was when this bed had been built. There was still the account in the family papers to prove it. Good, solid, English oak. No beetle in that! It would last another four hundred years, like as not.

There was a tap at the door, and Sophie came in.

'Good morning, Grandfather. How are you feeling today?'

'Very well. Very well indeed.'

'It's just after half past ten; would you like me to bring you some coffee?'

'No. I'm going to get up now.'

'Shall I send Alfred in? He wants to speak to you.' She hesitated. 'It's Athel's birthday today, you know, and Alfred is wondering whether you will want champagne brought up at dinnertime.'

He felt the disproportionate dismay of a child cheated of

some looked-for pleasure. Now no one would believe that he had remembered. He wanted to roar at her that Alfred should mind his own damned business and not go making suggestions above his place. McIntosh would not approve of him exciting himself, and Sophie would whine to the family that she was ill used. And in the end he would have to tell Alfred to bring up the champagne, and it would be ready and waiting at just the right temperature. Sophie was hovering nervously at the foot of the bed. He took a mighty breath and roared at her.

CHAPTER THREE

CRISPIN SAWARD was a man of genial, almost ingenuous appearance. And yet there was that about him—some subtle, animal signal—which suggested it would be foolhardy to trifle with him. He had arrived in America with twelve dollars and his worldly possessions in one small, shabby valise. Now, thirty years later, he travelled to Europe with his daughter on vacation, and it was necessary to take an additional suite to contain their luggage. He could not have told you at any given moment what he was worth. Money begat money for him. He paid other men to make it do that—but a hundred thousand dollars more or less? Who could say? One figure tonight, another when the market opened tomorrow morning. That was just the interest, of course. About the capital he was less vague. The first million he made was diversified in solid gilt-edged stock and property, and there was a trust set up for his wife, another for his daughter. He allowed no one to gamble with that. Crispin Saward would never go for broke.

The name of Athelson of Clere Athel had been familiar to him in his childhood. It was not readily forgotten. The Sawards were an old proud family, but the Athelsons? He remembered how people had held the very name in awe. A family that seemed to have grown up out of the very earth they farmed, undefeated by the upheaval of centuries of change going on about them. His brother was no great letter writer, but he had glimpses of the Athelsons over the years and was always intrigued by what he heard. Old Athel Athelson, who was said to speak at one minute with the coarseness of his meanest labourer and in the next with the hauteur of a feudal baron—he looked forward to meeting him—and the sister, Ivlian, who had given up the chance of a husband for a faith, only to sacrifice a hope of heaven for love of Clere Athel. He was prepared to wonder at her eccentricities as he had wondered at the Tower of Pisa. . . . 'Well, will you look at that!' . . . Gazing with something like colonial fervour at the trappings of a past and a culture he had so readily disowned.

Most of all, he wanted to see Athel. He had had a son once, himself. A fine, hopeful boy—there never was a better. Strong and full of himself, like a young stallion. Jonathan. It was just five years since he had lost him. They were blasting rock to put the railroad through. Someone's misjudgement. He had had the man dismissed as a matter of course, but there was no comfort in that.

It left only Sarah-Louise. And for Sarah-Louise he would have the best. The best blood . . . not bred thin and carrying disease like some of your fancy-titled nobility . . . the best looks . . . the best temperament, sturdy, stable, realistic, which to Crispin Saward meant bred close to the land, where hard work and determination paid off better than big ideas. He liked the sound of this Young Athel. If he should like the look of him, too. . . .

John Saward brought his brother Crispin and his niece Sarah-Louise to Clere Athel. He had intended to bring his most presentable daughter Millicent, also, since although he was resigning the hope of Athel, there was still Hugh, who might make a likely son-in-law. They said Hugh had brains and would be a veterinary surgeon in a few more years. It might serve well enough. But Millicent had taken the mumps. John Saward sighed and looked her sisters over for a last-minute substitute. But fond as he was of them, in the end he went alone.

He enjoyed driving with Crispin through Clere Athel and up to the heavy gates of the home park. He could see Crispin was impressed, and it was worth something to see his brother —fabled rich and almost a stranger to him—look and look again: at the people raising a wave for friends of the Athelsons; at the Dower House, elegant and impassive around its sweep in the drive; at the great trees of the avenue; and lastly at the house itself, standing with a haphazard beauty and a casual splendour in the soft light of late spring.

'Well, Athel Athelson, here we are! I'm pleased to present my brother Crispin to you at last, and this is my niece Sarah-Louise.'

For the first time in his life John Saward saw Old Athel leaning upon a stick. He was shocked by the change in his host's face, feeling instinctively that the recent illness, made light of in a letter, had in fact written death there.

To Crispin, however, with no recollections of the long-preserved prime of the man now confronting him, Athel Athelson was still a presence to remark, his great height emphasized by the low, vaulted ceiling of the entrance hall, the fierce eyes sunken under the boney prominence of their jutting brows more startling than ever, the imperious manner and gestures more noticeable in the unaccustomed langour that had come upon him since his sickness.

Where once he would have greeted such guests with a vigorous warmth, he was now affable but distant, like a man who kept something of himself always in reserve. Crispin was doubly impressed, thinking that here was a worthy opponent if he should come to face him across the negotiating table. He viewed his daughter's marriage very much in the same way as he would any important business merger, a question of how little he could give and how much he stood to gain. He knew Old Athel needed money, but he was not showing any eagerness. Crispin respected that and gave him credit for being cooler and more astute than he was. In fact, the two men brought to their acquaintance a considerable misjudgement of each other. But Athel Athelson made the more serious mistake. He *under*estimated the man he had to bargain with, taking Crispin Saward at face value for a guileless, plainspoken fellow, who had struck lucky in a new land. Never having tried to win a fortune in a competitive world, he had no idea of the qualities required or the sacrifice of principles involved.

Perhaps he was giving most of his attention to Sarah-Louise. She was worthy of it. A girl, just past her eighteenth birthday, of a fragile, slender beauty, with a delicate skin and silky red-gold hair. Old Athel's eyes narrowed; then he smiled. Everything about her rang a contrast to Justine, and this one was far the greater beauty. Wait until Athel saw her.

He was saying, 'I am sorry my grandsons cannot be here to welcome you. The youngest, Hugh, has his studies, you know. He will be here at the weekend. Athel is in Lancaster, but he will return by the time we dine. Let me introduce the rest of the family. This is my daughter-in-law Sophie; my granddaughter Charlotte. . . .'

The house seemed overlarge and faintly sinister to Sarah-Louise. She was frightened of Great-Aunt Ivlian, who wore such funny, old-fashioned clothes and moved so quietly and was always watching. And the servants stared, too.

But Athel, when he arrived, was a pleasant surprise. He seemed to sense her nervousness and went out of his way to put her more at ease, talking to her quietly at the dinner table, leading her with gentle questioning to speak of her home and of her mother, who did not care for travelling.

Crispin Saward intervened. 'The truth is my wife does not enjoy robust health.'

Old Athel raised his eyebrows, wondering whether there was something here he should know.

'She has a somewhat nervous disposition when on a journey and finds this impairs her digestion,' Crispin concluded heavily.

Sarah-Louise smiled down at her plate. This was almost the word-for-word explanation her mother had perfected over many years of not accompanying her father when he travelled. The statement lacked only the faint, suppressed yawn with which it was usually concluded. The only thing that had ever ailed Mrs Crispin Saward was a monumental laziness, aggravated by excessive wealth and alleviated only by a surfeit of romantic novels or an occasional hand of cards.

Athel saw the half-hidden, dimpled smile and approved it without much curiosity for the cause. He had thought it a poor little mouth at first, drooping and uncertain. The smile did wonders.

Crispin Saward watched Athel with his daughter, and his thoughts were wonderfully busy. Covertly he examined the tableware. Some solid silver, but most of it plate. His brother had spoken of better stuff than this. He considered whether it might have been deliberately kept out of sight for fear he should call it into settlement. No, more likely sold. There was evident dilapidation about the house, and the furniture was shabby. Certainly the Athelsons were hard up. Well, they had no need to worry. He wasn't looking for them to settle any money on Sarah-Louise, if the marriage should come about. On the contrary, he was prepared to give them a reasonably handsome sum, precious capital and no strings. The only thing he intended to take from them was Athel.

He looked at Athel Athelson sitting impassively in his high-backed chair at the head of the table. Did the old man know he was presiding over the last rites of his order, that the landed gentry had had their day, that the tide was running now for a new order, the getters, the dealers, and the men of business?

A fourth wine was introduced. Crispin Saward tasted it appreciatively. Old Athel still kept a fine cellar and an enviable table. The food in his own home wasn't one-quarter as good. That was Arabella's fault, of course. Crispin's bland expression was disturbed by a flicker of irritation when he thought of his wife. She really ought to take more interest in the house keeping. He wondered whether he might be able to buy Old Athel's cook from him.

Later, when the guests had retired to the dubious comfort of their rooms and Sophie, Charlotte, and Athel had been glad to follow their example, Old Athel lingered in the drawing room, staring down into the still-bright heart of the log fire.

He was not at ease in his mind, and he dreaded to lie sleepless in the empty bed upstairs. If only Cecily were there so that he could talk his doubts away with her. . . . He checked himself impatiently. . . . What doubts? Why should he have troubles when the future was bright and promising? There was just the matter of negotiation between himself and Saward to be accomplished, and the prospects for Clere Athel could look fairer than ever in his lifetime. . . . 'It won't do, you know.' He looked around sharply. Cecily's voice in the shadow-filled room? What a nonsense. Cecily lay quiet in her grave, away across the park. He had merely invoked her voice in fancy. . . . Nevertheless, it was just such a thing as she might say to start an argument. 'What won't do?' . . . 'Athel and the Saward girl.' . . . He let the imaginary conversation run on because it suited him to do so; he could stop it whenever he wished. 'What the devil do you know about it?' he challenged. 'Athel won't be happy with her.' . . . 'They seemed to get on well enough this evening.' . . . 'He's a good boy. He was being kind. Speaks just the same way to Charlotte, you know.' . . . 'She's a deuced pretty girl. He's fallen for her.' . . . 'You see what you want to see, but he hasn't forgotten Justine yet. You haven't given him time. You're wrong to push him into this marriage.' . . . 'I ain't pushing him. Athel will do as he likes. But heiresses don't come by the dozen, and if he knows where his duty and his own best interests lie, he'll have her.' . . . 'You didn't think of duty when you chose me.' . . .

'No, I damned well didn't! And the greater fool I was to heed heart instead of head. If I'd only listened to my father, I wouldn't have spent these years struggling to——'

'Athel Athelson.' Alfred stood in the doorway, holding a lamp aloft in a shaking hand. 'It's time thee and me were in our beds.'

Old Athel passed a confused hand across his forehead. 'Alfred. . . . Did I call out loud, man?'

'Aye, thee did.'

236

'God! I'm going nonny-witted.'

'Tha's just old, like me. I'll light you up to your bed.'

*   *   *

The early days of the Sawards' visit were pleasantly passed in an exchange of information about two contrasting ways of life. It was hard for anyone in Clere Athel to believe the half of what Crispin Saward told them of America. Could the farming really be on such a scale? Could a rancher ride for days and never see his own boundary fences? Was it possible to send meat across half a continent to market and still make a profit? Old Athel shook his head, implying not only wonder but disapproval. Nothing to do with America, he seemed to suggest, could surprise him more than the fact that people desired to live there.

Crispin withstood this superior attitude good-humouredly enough. He saw that the grandson did not share it. When Athel asked questions, they were intelligent and close, and he sought to learn something from the answers. In turn, he showed Crispin the farming and marketing methods of Clere Athel and his modest innovations, such as sending the asparagus to a retail outlet among the wealthy industrialists of Manchester. A contract to supply had brought better prices. He hoped to make another with an exclusive London food emporium and that the increased profit would more than cover the rail costs.

'Of course, I appreciate it must seem tuppenny-halfpenny trading to *you*,' Athel said with a deprecating wave of the hand for the books over which he had laboured so many hours.

'Not at all. I see you are a young man with vision enough to realize that a market needs to be cultivated as carefully as a crop. My guess is that any change you have made here, however small, has taken patience and determination. You are methodical in the way you work and keep records. I like that. There is always something to be learned from yesterday. Tell me what a company has achieved in the past five years, and

I can tell you where it stands today and what its prospects are five years hence. And I believe you are right when you say that even modernization is unlikely to make arable farming pay on such a scale as this and that the future in England lies in dairy farming. The ability to be right about tomorrow can make a man's fortune. It made mine.'

Athel shook his head ruefully. 'It isn't enough by itself, though. I think you need a bit of luck, and you certainly need capital. We have been building up the Red Poll herd over the years, but now there's no money for new stock. Besides, Hugh tells me I ought to think again about the breed. Red Poll certainly aren't the top of the table for a high yield. My father introduced them because he liked the look of them, and he'd heard that the butterfat content of their milk was better than what we had been getting. But I don't know whether it is, because I've no comparative figures.' He paused, suddenly aware that his enthusiasm and the pleasure of having someone like Crispin Saward to confide in had carried him away. 'I'm afraid I must have been boring you. . . .'

'Not in the least. I am most interested. You have given me something to think about.'

'Oh, you don't want to go thinking about my problems,' Athel said hastily. 'After all, why should you?' He was uncomfortable beneath the older man's searching eyes. Inwardly he cursed himself for having talked so freely. Did his confidences seem to commit him? Must it seem to Crispin Saward that like any prospective son-in-law he had been making a statement of his situation in order to elicit whether or not his suit was welcome?

Dully he understood at last that he had been committed even before he had met Sarah-Louise—perhaps even when his grandfather sent the significant invitation. If he had been determined to avoid the marriage, the only possible course would have been to absent himself from Clere Athel during the visit. Having met the girl, could he reject her, if she herself was willing? And on what grounds? On the grounds that she was not his cousin Justine, who had taken a scant eight months to forget him in the arms of another man. That wound was still too painful to be explored. Justine was married. If he must marry, too, then as well a girl who would please Grandfather and perhaps salvage the future of Clere Athel.

A strange way to choose a bride, he reflected bitterly, almost by default, by surrendering himself. But what use was it to take a stand when there was nothing left to stand for? Grandfather was failing. He could at least let him die happy.

From that time he began to pay more serious attention to Sarah-Louise, looking for qualities on which he might base a fondness. She was surely a beauty. Perhaps the sweetly trusting expression of this little heart-shaped face would help him forget Justine one day.

John Saward had to get back to his farm, but Crispin and Sarah-Louise were pressed to stay on.

'Nonsense! Nonsense! We won't hear of you leaving us yet. Why, you've only just come.' Old Athel collected the thin resources of his ebbing strength to appear jovial. 'I only wish we had more to offer you in the way of entertainment. But it is a real pleasure for us to have you here. Charlotte gets little company of young women near her own age, and I daresay she is not the only one who would complain if you take Sarah-Louise away'—this with a touch of archness and an anxious look at Athel. He wished he knew what the boy intended to do. Certainly no one could accuse him of rushing his fences, yet he was always attentive. There he was, teaching her bezique. And the two promising heads so close together. . . . By God, but didn't he begin to feel like banging them together, so they would get on and make a match of it? He wondered what Saward thought of the way things were progressing.

Crispin did not keep him guessing much longer. The rest having gone down to the village school to see the children give a concert, he took the opportunity to stay behind.

'Good of you to bear me company.' Athel Athelson was gruff, not sure if he was entirely pleased. It meant he would have to go a whole afternoon without a rest, and latterly he was always a trifle sleepy after luncheon. 'Usually go myself, of course. Our people expect it. But not quite up to that at the moment.'

'No. Well, I am sure they will make allowances. We are none of us able to keep up with all our obligations,' Crispin soothed.

He studied Old Athel covertly for several minutes, trying to gauge just how ill he was. His expectation of life could be a most significant element.

'Anyway, Athel is perfectly able to take my place.'

'I am . . . sure . . . he . . . is.' Crispin pronounced each word separately and with the slight alien New World drawl, which was always more apparent when he was abstracted. That was what the old boy wanted more than anything—that Athel should take his place and live like a lord on Saward money, with Sarah-Louise getting more little Athelsons. 'Athel . . . is a . . . fine . . . boy,' Crispin volunteered, in the same weighty tone.

Old Athel didn't like the drawl. It offended him. He merely nodded.

'A man who has raised a boy like that has a right to be proud,' Crispin elaborated. 'Very proud. I would be proud of such a son myself.'

'You had a son, I remember.'

'Yes, sir. Taken from me in a tragic accident that never ought to have happened. Well, you have lost sons yourself, so I needn't tell you what a blow it was to me.' He selected a cigar, cut it, and lit it with a spill from the fire before he spoke again. 'Of course, you had grandsons, which was a blessing. For my part, I don't mind telling you that I am a lonelier man since my Jonathan died than ever I thought to be in my life. That's why I look forward to the day when I can see Sarah-Louise settled and on the way to producing grand-children. I am a man of strong family feeling, sir. Enough said! You will understand.' He peered a trifle anxiously at Old Athel through the smoke of his cigar, hoping he had sounded the right note for opening up the discussion.

Old Athel had become very wide-awake. 'A man with

something to leave behind him must always look hopefully to his children and his children's children.'

So! He was too wily to make the first move. Well, that was only to be expected. He, Crispin, would have to make it . . . but he would also make the last. . . .

'I have been very favourably impressed by your Athel's manner towards Sarah-Louise. There is a delicacy in his attentions, a consideration of her extreme innocence and youth, which far exceeds what I could hope to find in most young men of his generation.'

Old Athel conceded this praise with a faint lift of the eyebrows. 'I should expect no less of him.'

'You set a high standard, sir, but believe me it is not general. Now Athel treats Sarah-Louise very much as I do myself, and if I may say so, I could wish no better or more tender care for her than that!'

Old Athel was relieved. If that was how Crispin Saward saw Athel's behaviour, then clearly no initial lack of enthusiasm had spoiled the boy's chances. On the contrary. But this fatherly business, this extreme propriety which won Saward's approval, was it the way of any Athelson wooing a woman? There had not been so much of the kid glove about Athel getting to an understanding with his cousin Justine when they were left alone together for a few minutes! That was the devil of it—he was so unsure of Athel. He had to get down to brass tacks with Saward now, and he still didn't know whether Athel meant to have the girl or not.

*　　　*　　　*

Amias Houghton was an unhappy man. In nearly forty years of legal practice he had never been called upon to draw up any document which gave him so much trouble as the betrothal contract between Athel Athelson and Sarah-Louise Saward. Hussey, Houghton, and Hoad had carried the burden of the Athelson affairs for the best part of a century. It had been Hussey and Hussey in the old days, but there were none of that name left. In his more melancholy moments it sometimes occurred to Mr Houghton that having worn the Hussey family into extinction, the Athelsons were now bent upon his own destruction. The only consolation was that when he had gone, they would get Hoad. He had never liked Hoad.

In the meantime, he must travel to and from Clere Athel, at the imperious summons of old Athel Athelson, who treated him as though he was a hired clerk and criticized every other word in his draft; and changed his mind a dozen times; and liked a provision and then slept on it and didn't like it; and modified it; and then pulled it to pieces; and finally threw it out altogether.

God alone knew what would happen if the marriage failed to take place and it came to litigation! The contract was a most improper document, most unworkable. Mr Houghton had said so a dozen times. Driven to exasperation, he had even cried, 'You pay for my advice; *why don't you take it?*'

But Old Athel had merely looked at him with those burning eyes of his and said, 'Ah, but then I haven't paid you yet, have I?'

And Amias Houghton, with an account for the past three years' work as yet unsettled, had lapsed into silence.

The fact that Old Athel was plainly a dying man, and now often forced to conduct the progress of the contract from his bed, did nothing to lighten the harassed lawyer's load. The will became involved. That was Saward's fault. He was pressing that the tenants be given their land under the terms of the will, and he had been strongly supported by Athel. In the end the old man had agreed. He wanted to pass on his inheritance just as he received it, but the gift of the farms would greatly reduce the amount of death duties payable on the estate, and there was a certain rightness that he should be the one to fulfil the old promise that the Athelsons would one day give the land to their tenants. Yes, Mr Houghton liked that. There was a kind of poetry in it, as he remarked to Mrs Houghton. But it made a deal of extra work.

Mr Houghton did not know what to make of Saward. His

role seemed a generous, almost a disinterested one. He was asking for no settlement on his daughter, and he was giving Young Athel an unsecured, interest-free loan of ten thousand pounds for investment in the home farm and improvement of the Dower House property, with a view to Sophie Athelson's future occupation of it. He was also undertaking to find the full amount of the duty on the estate which would be payable at Old Athel's death. Altogether the man seemed to be showing an extremely open-handed attitude to his future son-in-law and to be genuinely concerned to make the estate into a sound proposition, even before the marriage was completed. Why then, Amias pondered, did he feel a shadow of mistrust in the corner of his mind when he talked to Saward? He could see that Old Athel felt it, too. It was as if there was something they had both overlooked, something so simple and obvious that they could have it in front of them and yet not see it.

He was greatly troubled by the thought. He refined the wording of his own draft almost as obsessively as Old Athel did, and all the time Saward shrugged and smiled and for the most part readily agreed with them.

Saward had stipulated that the marriage should not take place for one year and that when it did, Athel must go to America for the ceremony in the presence of Sarah-Louise's mother and her mother's New Hampshire relatives. This year would give Sarah-Louise the chance, as he put it, to 'grow up a little' and to prepare her trousseau at leisure. Once promised, she would be able to go about more, safe from the attentions of that predatory species of fortune-seeking young men whom he had so long dreaded as a snare for impressionable girlish fancy.

On the wedding day, the loan of ten thousand pounds would become an outright gift to Athel, as it would on the death of either party before that date or upon the circumstance of Sarah-Louise breaking the contract through her own inclination. Should Athel break the contract, the sum of the loan and the amount to cover his grandfather's death duty—provided it had been advanced by that date—would be repayable on terms to be arranged in a fresh agreement between the parties.

It seemed to leave Athel in a strong position, whereby if he defaulted, he could make the repayments at any rate he chose, and it was a matter for remark that shrewd man of business as he was, Saward had fixed no time limit for the return of his capital.

The ten thousand pounds had been transferred into Houghton's anxious keeping, and at last Athel Athelson's will was sorted out and the new one ready for signing, along with the betrothal contract, on the next day.

'There's just one thing'—Saward had sought Athel out at the farm office and now they were alone with the glimmering sunset turning the whitewashed walls a delicate shade of pink —'about the contract. . . .'

'Yes?'

'I shan't sign it unless you give me your promise that when you come to America to marry Sarah-Louise, you will stay.'

For the space of a minute Athel was too astonished to answer.

'But I don't understand,' he said at last. 'If that is the only condition on which you will sign, why isn't it written into the contract, and why have you never spoken of it before?'

Crispin smiled slightly. 'Oh, come now! You're brighter than that, Athel. Would your grandfather have been likely to agree to it? . . . No, I've bided my time because the only thing I need from you is your word as an Athelson, your promise. I know you well enough to accept that. And your grandfather need never learn of it, because I think we are both aware he can't last more than a few months—certainly not a year.'

Athel continued to stare at him in bewilderment. 'Then if this was what you wanted all the time, why are you giving me money to improve the farm, pay the death duties, do up the Dower? It just doesn't make sense!'

'Yes, it does. You have your obligations to your mother, your great-aunt, your sister, your brother even, until he has finished his training. I appreciate that. I don't want you to come to us with home ties round your neck. If you set the farm up properly, Fenn Haldane can manage it for your mother, and the Dower House can be turned into the family home. It will be far more comfortable and manageable than the big house could ever be, no matter what was spent on it. Then you might sell that together with the home park. Men who've made their brass lately are sometimes in the market for the most unlikely properties if they've a wish to play the squire. . . .'

Athel shook his head. 'You seem to have it all worked out, but I can still scarcely believe that you are serious. You must realize that Clere Athel is my home and I love it. How can you expect me to leave it?'

'Well, I do. If not for my Sarah-Louise, then for your grandfather. Do you think he could stand the disappointment of his hopes falling through at this stage? And although he would never have agreed to my terms if he had known them, I am not giving him such a bad bargain. There will still be Athelsons at Clere Athel and a family home, and the whole community will benefit when it becomes a more workable proposition.'

'I might have achieved this myself in time.'

'And you might not. It's my belief you'd never break the old habits if you stayed.'

Athel began to see how skilful Crispin Saward's timing had been. The shock might kill Grandfather, who certainly could not have long to live, and the death duty would certainly require that some of the land be remortgaged, and what of the tenants then. And yet his spirit revolted against the unscrupulous force that was being used against him.

'Does Sarah-Louise know of this condition? What if I tell her I love her but I cannot do what you ask? How will she look at you then?'

'Don't be a fool. Sarah-Louise is a child. She will do just as I tell her. She won't question my judgement.' He laughed suddenly. 'I don't blame you for trying to turn the tables on

245

me, boy, but it won't work! . . . Look, I don't mean you anything but good. I just want you to come to America and make your home with us. . . . Athel, I want *a son*! I want *you*! I can *make* your future for you. You can have anything you want. What can Clere Athel offer you but a lifetime of debt and problems that have no solution? I offer you an honourable exit from an impossible situation and a brilliant future . . . not starting at the bottom as I had to, but at the top. . . . My God, what wouldn't I have given for such a chance at your age!'

'But I belong *here*.'

'A man belongs where his fortune leads him. It is a challenge he must take up.'

Athel scowled, and Crispin did not miss the fleeting resemblance to his grandfather.

'You put yourself to a mighty lot of trouble and expense to get what you want. What if I disappoint you? I doubt if I'm cut out for a life anywhere but on the land.'

'If land is what you want you can have it. Only make it land in my country. And my country now is America.' The tension went out of him abruptly. No need to press the boy further . . . leave the arguments in his mind to do the rest. He could already sense Athel beginning to slip towards him. He had won. 'Think over what I have said. You have until breakfast tomorrow to make your decision.' His voice, relaxing into its customary drawl, was gentle, almost indifferent.

*   *   *

Athel's reaction to the ultimatum Saward had given him was one of bitterness and near despair. Throughout supper he could hardly bear to look at the man, and directly the meal was finished he left the company without troubling to offer an explanation and returned to the farm office, where he might think undisturbed.

He seldom worked there after dark, but there was an oil

246

lamp kept for dull days. He found matches and lit it. And that was a bad thing to have done, for memories came flooding in with the light. He could see again Justine's head bent over his accounts on a storm-darkened day. He remembered the fragile lines of the nape of her neck and the wisps of escaping hair about it, incandescent in the glow of the lamp. She had looked up, and her eyes had widened, seeing him, trustful, full of pleasure at his coming, and he had known then that he wanted her forever, looking at him in that way.

Angrily he crushed the recollection. It was a mistake to let his mind play these tricks. Justine was gone, and it was to the future he must attend, not the past. He sat down deliberately in the haunted chair at the desk.

The sound of footsteps on the shingle outside interrupted his thoughts after a few minutes. The door opened, and Hugh peered around it.

'Hello. Thought I'd find you here. Can I come in?'

'Yes . . . yes, you had better come in, Hugh,' Athel said slowly. 'There is something I have to tell you.'

But when they were sitting across the desk from each other, with Hugh looking at him expectantly, Athel still could not bring himself to shape the words.

The silence lengthened.

Hugh watched him with increasing concern. 'Come on, then. What's up?'

'It's the contract,' Athel said at last. 'Crispin Saward says he won't sign it unless I agree to live in America permanently. He's given me until morning to think it over.'

It took Hugh several seconds to make sense of what he heard. The words were too improbable. And then—'Think it over! *Think it over*.' He gave a derisive shout of laughter. 'Of course, you told him to go to the devil. Well, we'll manage without his money. We always have before.'

'Oh, Hugh. Don't be so bloody silly,' Athel said wearily. 'We can't manage this time.'

'But you don't mean to say you'll consider accepting his terms. Why, it just ain't possible! And what about the family,

247

who need you? And our people trying to stand on their own feet for the first time—have you thought about them?'

'Of course I have,' Athel said desperately. 'I'm thinking about all of you and wondering what's best for you. I never think about anything else. I wish you'd stop shouting at me and talk this over in a useful way.'

'But I don't want to talk about it. There's nothing more to say. Why ever should Saward ask such an extraordinary thing of you, and why leave it until now? It doesn't make sense that he should give you the money to enlarge the home farm and do up the Dower if he had this plan in his mind all the time. I just don't understand the man.'

'Well, I'll explain if you'll only give me the chance. He wants me to leave the family in a comfortable way before I go. He thinks the Dower should be extended and turned into the family home and the house sold. He's a practical man, and he's worked it all out neat as you please,' Athel added with a certain grudging respect. 'As to his reasons'—he shrugged—'it appears he wants a substitute for the son he lost. He's prepared to buy me. I suppose we ought to be flattered.'

'Don't talk like that! It's a disgusting idea! How can you even think of letting yourself be bought and shipped like some steer he's taken a fancy to? And all as though your pride were nothing to you.'

'Oh, for God's sake.' Athel sprang to his feet in sudden anger. 'What do you understand of my problems, of the burden of being responsible for so many people? You think there's no choice to be made. That I can just do what I please and to hell with everyone else. Well, that might be all very fine for you.' He strode over to the window and stood looking out across the darkening meadowland towards the village. When he turned around again, his expression was unfamiliar, hard. 'I was fourteen when our father died, and there was never a day since when Grandfather failed to remind me of the duties I inherited. I was just a boy, but I had to stop being a boy and be a man because I was his heir. You went on your care-free way and were forgiven when you got into scrapes. I had to learn the running of the estate and mind my dignity, because it was said folks wouldn't respect me if I was wild. I don't know whether you thought I had the best of it because Clere Athel was to be mine and you had your own way to make in the world, but there has been many and many a time I would gladly have changed places with you.'

Hugh stared at him in surprise. 'I never knew you felt like that. I only saw how you loved this place and our people. It never occurred to me that you found it a burden. And when you even let Justine go, I thought——' Hugh stopped, biting his lip regretfully.

'Yes, what did you think then?' Athel demanded harshly. 'Did you think that was an easy decision?'

'No! Of course not. I know different——'

'I love her so much . . . even now . . . at this very minute . . . that it is painful to me just to say her name. I love Clere Athel, too. And our people. . . . Oh, for heaven's sake, Hugh try to listen to what I am telling you, what I am trying to tell you—and *understand*!'

Frightened by the anguish he saw in his brother, Hugh said, 'I am trying to understand, old chap, I am trying.'

'Hugh. I must go. There is no alternative. Grandfather doesn't have long to live. A few months perhaps. There is no money for death duties, and if I start mortgaging the land, I shall never be able to free it. There's no other way.'

'But are you sure?'

'Yes, I am sure. I've gone over it and over it in my mind. Please don't give me any more arguments. I can't bear it.'

Hugh shook his head miserably.

'I'm sorry,' Athel said. 'I don't mean to rant at you. You are as white as a ghost.'

'That's all right. It's just that I never saw such . . . *passion* in you. I don't know you when you're like this.'

Athel took a deep breath. He was suddenly calmer. 'I know. I'm sorry.' He smiled faintly. 'You spoke about Justine just now. I've been thinking about her this evening. You know it's strange, really . . . a woman and she has no part of this place, but she loved it just as much as I do.' He nodded to himself. 'I hated her once for running away. But, perhaps gradually, perhaps just tonight, I have come to understand what she did. You can leave all you love, if you love it enough.' His eyes gazed unseeingly across the room, but he grew more collected as he talked. 'You know how things are with the finances of the estate. We can no longer afford to lag centuries behind the rest of the country. We have to give our people the chance to turn their land into an economic proposition before we ourselves come to ruin and pull them down with us. I don't know what I should have done if Saward hadn't come along.' He sighed. 'Of course, in some ways I wish he never had. But he's a thinking man, and he said a sharp thing—he said it was his belief I'd never break the old ways if I stayed. There's truth in that. I have wondered what my part would be when the land was given away and it has weighed heavily on me. Could I change? I have been raised to order the estate. Could I change my attitude to our people? Could I be content to advise? I doubt it.'

Hugh interrupted him, frowning. 'But they will need advice. We've always supported them in bad years, protected them from fluctuations in market prices.'

'I know. But am I the one to do it? Would I not start by saying, "If I were you . . ." and end up, "God damn it, man, *I say* it shall be so"? And would they be able to forgive me such a lapse—them with their pride and so cock-a-hoop with their new-won independence? Or would they resent me?' His eyes met Hugh's in a long, level look. 'You might do it.'

'Might do what?'

'Might advise them. They could turn more readily to you.'

'Me?' Hugh gasped. 'But I shan't be here.'

'You could stay. That's what I am asking. I could go with an easy mind if only I knew that you would stay and be on hand if the family or our people had need of you.'

'But I can't practise here. This is arable land for miles around. Besides, as you well know, I planned to work with horses. I've always wanted to work with horses.'

Athel nodded. 'I know. I'm asking a good deal of you. You couldn't work with horses here. But there's no vet this side of Beacon Hill, and if folks follow the example of the home farm and go over to dairy farming and pigs, as I hope they will, there should be a practice of sorts.'

'You mean you are asking me to take your place? But I couldn't do it. I don't know anything about marketing and not much about the land either.'

'Fenn does. And just think what you could teach our people about stock. You have a great deal to offer them, perhaps more than I have, because what you *might* have been will not stand between you.'

'I should make a terrible mess of things,' Hugh said unhappily. 'And only think what Grandfather would say.'

'Grandfather will never know. I wouldn't go to America for at least a year, and we would have to be very careful not to betray the smallest hint to anyone of this so long as he is alive. . . . I love Grandfather, but he belongs to the past, the old ways. It falls to our part to sort out the future as best we can.'

'I can't bear it for you,' Hugh said.

Athel smiled. 'Don't worry. I shall survive.' He patted his brother's shoulder affectionately and walked over to the window again. The light had quite gone, and there was no moon. 'Ironic that it should be my sacrifice to go and yours to stay,' he said.

And so in the end the contract was signed.

'It will seem a long time until I see you again, Athel. A whole year.' Sarah-Louise sounded wistful. 'I shall forget what you look like, and I am afraid that when we meet again, we shall be like strangers.'

Athel encircled her with a comforting arm and gave her shoulders a reassuring squeeze. 'No, we shan't be strangers. I will write to you often and tell you how I go on here, and you will tell me your doings. You will be surprised how quickly the time will pass.'

Sarah-Louise sighed but managed a tremulous smile. 'Yes, there is that. We can write. Father says the post will only cost a penny after the end of September, and I suppose a letter will not take too long.'

'Not long at all! Why, now the *Mauretania* has the blue ribbon, the crossing may be done in under five days.'

'Are you good at writing letters, Athel?'

Athel hesitated. 'Not very. . . . But I will get better with practice.'

'So shall I. . . . Athel, you do love me? . . . I mean, you do want to marry me?'

'But of course I do. Why should you doubt it? Doesn't a girl as pretty as you expect to be loved?' Athel made his tone deliberately teasing.

Sarah-Louise regarded him, wide-eyed. 'It seems such a lucky thing that you should, when it is what Father wants and your grandfather, too, I think.'

'And you?'

'And I, too.'

The whispered words were hard to catch.

'Well, you see we are lucky,' Athel said heartily. 'We just are both born lucky.'

Four days later the Sawards left for Cumberland. They would make their farewells to their family and sail for America at the beginning of July.

There was a buzz of interest about the prospect of Athel's trip to follow them in the ensuing spring and some speculation as to what might be done at the house to ready it for its new bride. But it was surprising how quickly Clere Athel returned to normal and forgot about its recent guests. No realization that because of their coming the old pattern of life was broken for ever.

Athel proceeded carefully with his plans for the home farm and talked long, earnest hours away with his tenants, coaxing them to follow his lead and break with the tradition of their forefathers. It was not easy to revolutionize their outlook, and he was conscious always of the pressure of the passing months, knowing that it would be harder for each man to make the break when he stood alone, owning his own land.

The tenants knew now that this time was not far away. There had been a day not long since with Fenn out looking for men before it was light; stepping his horse gingerly along the rutted track at the edge of Warrener's wheat, his swinging lantern startling the hedge sparrows a full ten minutes before the night sky began to pale above the pine forest; on to Little Meadows to tap on the kitchen lattice, catching Ted Thrustleton just out of bed and buckling the leather belt about his trousers—'What s to do? Is it Fenn?' . . . 'Aye. Old Athel's had a bad night. He thinks he's going and wants to see you and t'others.' . . . 'How many others?' . . . 'Just the five farms and Coppin to represent the rest. Will you stop by for Siggie Thorpe?' Away to Orchard Farm to find Harry Leigh's wife brushing her hair by candlelight in the scullery. . . . 'Where's tha man? Tell him he must get up to t'house soon as mebbe.'

Alfred was waiting to meet them in the hall, fussing that they must strip off their muddied boots before climbing the oak staircase to Old Athel's bedroom.

They would have none of that. They guessed why they had been sent for. It was a proud moment, a solemn moment. They would none of them stand before Old Athel in their stockinged feet.

'If he wants us, he wants us as we are,' Richard Warrener growled. 'Now either tell him we're here or stand out of the road, man!'

Athel appeared at the head of the stairs.

'Is everyone here?'

'Aye.'

'Then what are you dithering about down there for? Come up.'

They filed past Alfred with triumphant looks, setting their feet with heavy deliberation on the patina of every tread.

Athel halted them at the door. 'He's much better now,' he warned. 'We thought he was going in the night, and he was bad when he sent for you. But this last hour. . . .' There was no need to say any more. Inside they could hear a familiar voice bellowing a string of curses.

'Get out of here, woman. Dear God, it's like being haunted! What are you at, now?'

And as the door opened . . . 'Athel! For pity's sake take your mother out of here. If she sets my pillows up once more, I shall have another seizure. Go on, Sophie, go away. You're not even halfways decent, and here's our folk must keep their eyes on the ground for very shame.'

Sophie, who had been up most of the night, gathered her wrapper about her with the remnants of her dignity and swallowed the plea that her father-in-law should not exert himself.

When she had gone, the men approached the bed. It was a big room, perhaps nearly fifty feet long. The two oil lamps left most of it swamped in shadow.

'Is it light yet?'

'Just about.'

'Then draw the curtains back . . . but leave the lamps.' Old Athel shifted irritably. After all, he would see the dawn of another day. He wished now that he had not been so hasty. He had been putting off the moment when he told the tenants that the old promise was to be redeemed at last, that he was giving them their land. He did not want to tell them. Whatever the justice and the sense of it, for him it was a defeat. Perhaps he might have waited another month . . . even two. And then again perhaps not. Athel was probably right when he said as well get it over and done with and Fenn had already left when he tried to retract the summons. Well, they were here. Warrener, Thrustleton, Leigh, young Arthur Parr, Siggie Thorpe, and Coppin. They stood close by the bed. He didn't like that because it meant he had to look up to them.

'Back off,' he said sharply. 'Stand over by the window where I can see you better.'

They did as they were told at once, understanding.

Propped up against a mound of pillows, Old Athel scowled at them across the room. All big men. Big men with strong, patient faces and steady eyes. For a moment he could almost hate them, resenting their strength and begrudging the depth of feeling they aroused.

'You have long known of our intention to give you the land,' he said at last. 'I have called you here to tell you that under the terms of my will I give each man the property he holds and works.' A faint sigh escaped them, but they were still waiting. What more did they want? 'We give the land freely, as a gift. You will have title to it and in good time may pass it on to heirs of your own choosing.' Still they waited.

Old Athel frowned faintly. They were simple men, but surely they could not have failed to follow what he was saying. They continued to stare at him intently.

All at once he understood. He had been ungracious. After so many hundreds of years it was not enough. He said slowly, picking his words with care, 'We do not give you the land out of the charity of our hearts but because you and your forefathers have earned it. We give you no more than your due. I say it is so.' He glanced across at Athel.

'And I say it is so.'

They smiled then and nodded. It was a simple end to a long contract. But it was fitting.

And miraculously, Old Athel's life flowed on, although now the great rushing torrent of it was slowed to a thin trickle that might cease at any moment. For days at a time he did not leave his room, although he would usually rise and sit in a chair in the late afternoon, watching out the window for Athel's return. He was eager to hear every detail of the progress that was being made, as anxious as Athel to see his tenants build milking parlours and found dairy herds. They would talk of the future, and Athel would explain to him the possibilities of group marketing, a scheme with the whole of Clere Athel focused on the supply of dairy products. Old Athel was both alarmed and intrigued.

'These are big ideas, Athel, big ideas,' he would say, shaking his head, but the hooded eyes gleamed. . . .

'How are you getting on with the old man these days?'

Hugh asked on one of his infrequent, lightning visits home. 'What does he say to the changes you are making?'

'He doesn't seem to mind. He takes a great interest, in fact —you'd be surprised.'

'Have you told him you've pulled the Old Mead Barn down? I bet he didn't like that.'

'No, even that was no problem when I pointed out that it was perfectly situated for the milking parlour and that I could re-use the foundations if I put in a good drainage system. He's coming into the twentieth century at a run.'

Mercifully, Athel had been given little enough time to dwell on the bargain that he had made with Saward. Always hard-working, the men of Clere Athel laboured that summer to the point of exhaustion. Everyone was short-handed. The farmers, who were taking their first tentative steps to follow Athel's lead, needed every penny they could lay their hands on to purchase dairy stock and readily dispensed with hired labour and even the assistance of younger sons, who were at once taken on by Athel and earned good money for building work at the home farm and the Dower.

But by the month of harvest it was clear that more hands were needed, and for the first time since the Dower was built, outsiders were brought in from Upstrand. Clere Athel folk hated to see good money leave the village in the pockets of bricklayers, carpenters, and the like, but building must be finished before the winter set in, and there was no help for it.

The extensions to the Dower were considerable. Athel had been at pains not to encroach upon the garden, accommodating the improvements in a wing built out into the home park. This provided for a trebling of the size of the original, rather mean kitchen, with additional staff quarters at the rear and a morning room and a modest library-*cum*-study on its frontage. On the second floor there were four new bedrooms and a modern bathroom, with a plumbed-in bath that had to be seen to be believed and was therefore exhibited to every man, woman, and child in the village on a series of specially appointed visiting days.

Such a summer. So many changes.

And now the contours of the countryside were once more etched in the charcoal and duns of autumn. It was November, and the witenagemot called for the following Thursday. Old Athel had declared his intention of presiding as usual, though he hadn't been out of his bed for the six weeks gone.

There was no strength left in him now. He lay in the Athelson bed and thought—between sleeping and waking—how short a tenure his had been. When he closed his eyes, he could smell a field of ripening grain in the sun, but when he opened them, the windows were darkening beyond the oppressive swagged curtains of burgundy velvet, and he was reminded that it would take him a long time to dress. The witen would begin in two hours or so. He heard the clock strike. He heard Hugh arrive . . . cutting it fine as usual, but he was a good lad, working hard, so Athel said. . . . He must ask him how he did with his studies . . . show an interest. He reached out for the bell rope at his head. It was an effort, but he made it. Two tugs. Alfred would take his time answering. The stairs were a problem to him, but one couldn't retire a man like Alfred. In his mind he climbed the stairs with him. . . . One, two, three—a rest . . . four, five, six—pause again . . . seven, eight. . . .

The sound of Athel Athelson's bell ringing frantically summoned the kitchen staff at a run and gathered up the family on the way.

Athel Athelson was dead, and they found Alfred kneeling beside him, tears streaming down his face, as he desperately chaffed the stiffening hand that rested on the counterpane.

'He rang, and I didn't answer him in time!' Alfred's wavering voice was high with anguish.

Athel put his arms around the thin, bent shoulders. 'Come away, come away. There's nothing you can do. See, his eyes are closed. He dropped off to sleep before you came. He died in his sleep.'

He handed Alfred over to Hugh. 'Take him downstairs and give him a brandy.'

'Oh, God!' Hugh said. 'I never said good-bye to him.'

'Grandfather wasn't the man for a deathbed scene with the family round him. Go on, take Alfred down . . . and Mother. Give them all a brandy.'

'What about the witen? Do you want me to send word that it's off?'

'Certainly not.' Athel's voice was sharp. 'I shall take the meeting. From this moment our people own their own land, and I can think of no more fitting occasion to tell them of it.'

CHAPTER FOUR

THE NEWS of her grandfather's death was more than a month old by the time it reached Justine. Sophie had written both to her and to Antonia by the same post and addressed the letters care of Beirut. But the villa had been closed up since the summer.

There was political unrest in Syria, as throughout the whole of the Ottoman Empire. The Turkish army had revolted against the Sultan Abdul Hamid, and Pierre thought it propitious to review his interests in those provinces where the cry of *hurriya* foreshadowed further trouble. He was not entirely out of sympathy with the young intellectuals he had listened to in Beirut, but too much freedom could be bad for business, and while these affairs occupied him, he dispatched Antonia to London, promising to join her for Christmas.

The political disturbance of government centres produced unpredictable reactions among rural communities, which only half understood what was happening. It became inadvisable, even dangerous, to travel in remote parts of the province, and Richard Engerard reluctantly abandoned his studies of minority religious sects. The secretive Druzes had continued to elude him, and in a mood of frustration and disappointment he had taken Justine off on a tour of Persia.

When Sophie's letters at last caught up with Antonia, she

sat down at once to write her condolences and to explain what had happened.

'You must have wondered, exceedingly at not hearing from us before this time. . . . I know how distressed Justine will be and that she will certainly wish to visit you while she is in England. . . . We are expecting them to join us for a family Christmas here with Uncle Simon and Aunt Mathilda. . . . The best I can do is keep your letter for her, since I have no address for Justine at the present time . . . they live like nomads. . . .'

She ran on, frowning over her own stylish script on the expensive, hand-cut paper.

Like nomads . . . literally like nomads. She only wished Justine and Richard would get a home together and settle down. Heaven knew, she liked to travel herself, but there was something unnatural about the feverish way they had kept moving about ever since they were married. A whole year— with Justine's lovely trousseau never out of the trunks and valises that followed her by camel or waited around in outlandish railway depots. She really must get Pierre to speak to Richard.

Justine and Richard did not arrive in London until Christmas Eve, having gone directly from Southampton to Devon to see Richard's father. Antonia was surprised and pleased to see how well her daughter took the bad news that awaited her. . . . 'Almost as though she barely knew the man and yet I had always thought her fond of him' she confided to Pierre. 'I was really quite afraid it would spoil Christmas for her, but not at all! She seems very high-spirited . . . unusually so, now I come to think of it. . . . Tell me, don't you find her changed?'

Pierre gave the question careful consideration. He had arrived on Boxing Day, still in time for much of the social festivity, the to-ing and fro-ing of tea and dinner parties, the occupation of the maximum number of theatre and opera house boxes. He sighed. 'Yes, I believe I do. Of course, one must expect a change after a year of married life. She has grown up. This is natural.'

'But I meant the restlessness, the *tension*. This is so unlike her. Do you think she is happy?'

'My dear! I have hardly had a chance yet to form any opinion. I have not seen her for two minutes, except in company. Perhaps the life they have been leading is not ideal, but then Richard has always been on the move. It will take him a little while to get used to the idea of settling down. It may be that now they are in England they intend to stay. Have you asked them?'

'I? No, certainly not!' Antonia said hastily. 'I thought that was something you might do.'

'Well, I suppose I might if the opportunity should arise naturally when Richard and I are alone. But in the meantime, why do you not ask Justine?'

Antonia looked doubtful. 'She has a way of turning aside a question. I don't know how she does it without being flatly rude, but one never seems to get anything out of her. Her father used to be just the same.'

By New Year, however, Pierre had other matters to concern him.

Hamid, left in charge of the villa, had written that things seemed to have quietened down in Lebanon, and the general mood was one of disillusionment with the bright promise of the revolution that had changed very little. Hamid's Turkish military connection, through the long tradition of his family, gave weight to his observations, and when he wrote 'The Aucassin *beg* may think the conditions ripe for counter-revolution and that in the end there is a possibility Abdul Hamid will be put off his throne altogether and in some haste,' Pierre paid close attention. A counter-revolution that failed could only strengthen the revolutionary party. He must at once return to the Middle East and conclude the deals he was making to free himself of assets that could become embarrassing. Now in the lull was the time to act. As regards their home, he expected conditions in Beirut to remain reasonably stable, and it was to be hoped that they might eventually return to it. But for the time being, he urged Antonia to seek out a suitable property in Paris. Very little urging was necessary.

The house party was breaking up. 'And what are you and Richard going to do now? Why don't you come with me?' Antonia suggested. 'Or perhaps you have plans to look for a house yourselves?'

Justine was surprised.

'Good heavens, no! Why ever should we do that? Richard already has a home. In Devon.'

'You're surely not going to live with his father and Violet, are you? Don't you want to make a home of your own?'

Justine frowned. 'I don't see the point. It's quite a big house, and there is plenty of room for all of us. Besides, Richard's father keeps very much to himself. He's always either in his conservatory or in his library, from what I can judge. And Violet is away most of the time.'

'What's the house like?'

'Oh . . . old . . . rambling.'

Antonia grimaced. 'Like Clere Athel!'

'No, it isn't as old as that. Quite comfortable really, and the gardens are beautiful. You must come and see it. We thought we'd go down there at the end of the week and get ourselves settled. Richard has to do some writing, so I don't think we could manage Paris at the moment.'

'Ah, well, at least I shan't be worrying myself to death about you if you put down roots in Devon. And I'm sure it's a wholesome place to raise children.' A sudden gleam came into Antonia's eyes. 'I suppose it wouldn't be because you are *enceinte* that you've decided to settle down?'

'Oh, no, not yet. Richard and I need to get to know each other better before we have children.'

Antonia raised the rarely used lorgnette and viewed her daughter with surprise.

'I should have thought a year of marriage would already have introduced a certain familiarity.'

Justine smiled slightly. 'But then we have always been travelling about and so much in company—I do not think one really learns to know anyone well under those circumstances. When we are settled in Devon, things will be quite different.'

'Different, yes!' Antonia said significantly.

'What does that mean?'

'Well . . . don't expect too much. The sad fact is that married couples who spend a disproportionate amount of time alone can soon bore each other to desperation. This is particularly dangerous for a woman. A man may be boring if he chooses, and if he is not also a fool, he will still be respected. But a woman has a positive duty to be entertaining. Be sure always to keep busy and to maintain as wide a social acquaintance as possible. Leave cards and accept every invitation you can fit into your diary. Keep well informed on current topics, and see that your opinions on everything are moderate. . . . Live your own life if Richard should neglect you, but when he wants you, always be there . . . smiling!'

It was virtually the only advice Antonia had ever offered on marriage, and Justine accepted it gracefully, even if she could not imagine herself acting upon it.

Recognizing that her relationship with Richard was far from ideal and that she herself was largely to blame for its shortcomings, Justine arrived in Devon with a high resolve and the best of intentions. There was a comfortable housekeeper already installed, a woman not unlike Mrs Rimmer, and Justine quickly came to good terms with her and made herself familiar with the running of Richard's family home. Tactfully she introduced those small modifications to routine and table which she knew would suit them better to Richard's tastes and preferences without disturbing his father. And when this was accomplished, she returned calls on the Engerards' neighbours as punctiliously as her mother could wish. Outwardly, she did very well. But inwardly she knew that she was failing her husband, and she watched him retreat more and more into his work.

At the end of February Violet came home on a visit, full of the book she intended to write about the castles on the Rhine and the avant-garde woman novelist with whom she was now sharing a flat on the Unter-den-Linden Strasse.

'Rococo, my dear, positively rococo!'

'The architecture?' Justine sought for enlightenment.

'No, no! This woman I'm living with. . . .'

And in the next breath. . . . 'Of course there is the damp, you know. . . .'

'In your apartment?' Justine asked in polite concern.

'Good heavens, no! In the last castle I visited. You remember I wrote to you that I had taken this dreadful chill that went to my chest . . . really I could hardly breathe. . . .'

But when she had unloaded her own news, the penetrating eyes were turned on Justine.

'Now I can't stay long. Two weeks at the most. I just came back to see how you were getting on and to take a look at Father. . . . Poor, old thing. He's very fragile. Do you find him a trial?'

'Gracious, no. I hardly see him except at meals.'

'Yes, his orchids *are* a blessing. Nanny used to say that he only took to them after Mother died. But we were very young then. I never remember a time when he didn't practically live in the conservatory. . . . How do you find Richard now you are married to him? . . . Go on, you can be honest with me.'

Justine laughed defensively. 'Oh, he treats me very tolerably. I have scarcely a bruise!'

'He seems to be buried in this book of his, and neither of you looks . . . relaxed. Is there anything wrong between you?'

'No, nothing. I think he is finding it difficult to discipline himself to writing. After all, this is the first book he has attempted, isn't it?'

Violet would not be satisfied with this. 'Do you find him pompous? He can be rather tiresomely didactic in manner. You should tell him so. I used to.'

'I don't mind that. I'm trying to understand the things that interest him.'

'*You* interest him. I would say you obsess him. I've noticed

264

he can't even walk out of a room without turning back to look at you.'

Justine was restless under the other woman's scrutiny, hugging to herself the truth that could not possibly be confided to anyone. Violet sighed, seeing that she would get no answer. 'Well, the fact is I sense some problem between you, but I cannot imagine what it can be. You are still very young, of course. . . . Anyway, write to me any time you feel the need to confide. I don't want to interfere, but I'll be happy to advise if I can. And you needn't think I shall be partial, either. I see all Richard's faults.'

But the fault was not with Richard, Justine thought ruefully. He had been kind, considerate, and patient with her, constantly finding excuses for her failure to respond to him. Nor did he fail to move her. There was a certain intellectual arrogance about him, and he could be brusque when his decisions were questioned—largely because he was nearly always right—but this was only the surface of his personality protecting a deep sensitivity. Gradually as the months had passed, she had grown to a new awareness of him, and there had been a memorable day more recently when coming across him unexpectedly in some unaccustomed part of the house, she felt a startled pleasure at the sight of him, a sudden lurch of the heart. Perhaps if he had seen and understood and taken her in his arms, then they would have crossed the barrier she had built up between them. He hesitated, she had thought he might. But the moment escaped them because she had shaken his self-confidence once too often before. He could only be patient and gentle and wait. He could not try again. They had reached the stage where she would have to go to him. And she knew that she must not do that until she was quite sure. Beyond any doubt, sure.

The letter from Athel arrived in the third week of March. Justine knew that he was due to leave for America some time in the spring and had already decided on a Honiton lace bedspread as a suitable gift for the bride. But she was quite unprepared for the contents of this letter, which stated with a startling brevity that since Athel would not be returning from America in the 'foreseeable future', the family home was to be sold and they would welcome an immediate visit from her to select any items of furniture or ornament that she might like to keep.

'Mother has stuffed the Dower to bursting point, and Monday Sutliffe is storing some of the things in the loft over his stables, against the time when Hugh or Charlotte may want them. But there are still so many dear, familiar old pieces. We would like to think of them staying in the family if you can find the space. Please come. I would so much rather we said our good-byes than wrote them. . . .'

She passed the letter across the breakfast table to Richard.

'I say, this is a bit of a shock to you, isn't it?'

She nodded. 'Yes, it is. I never dreamed the old house would go out of the family. I pictured Athel and Sarah-Louise making their home there and the whole place being done over and getting a new lease of life.'

'Doesn't give you much detail about why he intends to stay in America.'

'No.'

'Will you go?'

'Of course. I must . . . that is, if it doesn't inconvenience you?' The polite afterthought chilled him and made him adopt the same formal tone.

'Not in the least.' He hesitated. 'Perhaps you would like me to come with you? I am afraid it will be a long and tiresome journey for you to make alone.'

Was he waiting with some anxiety for her answer? Did it matter to him?

'Well'—she paused, choosing her words with care—'I don't know that it will be easy for them to put us up if the house is being dismantled. The Dower is quite small. I might share Charlotte's room if necessary, but if you come. . . .'

'Yes, we mustn't inconvenience them at such a busy time,' Richard put in quickly. 'Think no more of it. It was only a suggestion.'

266

'Naturally I do want you to see Clere Athel.' Justine's eagerness to compensate him betrayed her relief. 'As soon as I see how things are, I will arrange a visit with Aunt Sophie. I know she is longing to meet you. And Hugh and Charlotte, too.'

'What a pity I shall not have an opportunity to meet Athel,' Richard said, and his voice was colourless, rather flat.

'Today is Tuesday,' Justine said. 'I could leave the day after tomorrow.'

* * *

Athel had almost finished his packing. The wedding presents and the bits and pieces from the house that he was particularly fond of had already been crated and dispatched. Crispin Saward was paying the freight charges, and fourteen packing cases were even then crossing the Atlantic to a new home. Three trunks of Athel's personal possessions, corded and stamped NOT WANTED ON VOYAGE, were just waiting in the stables at the Dower, and there would be just one more box and the hand luggage to join them at the end of the week.

'I've just thought—what about your saddle and all those boots in the cloakroom?' Hugh stuck his head around the door of Athel's room.

'In the brass-bound box. That's the one I'm keeping for last-minute things that are too big for the valises.'

'Will they go in? Seems to me you're pretty optimistic about the dimensions of that box.'

'No. I tried the saddle earlier. It will fit.' Athel on his knees by his desk, in a litter of papers, grinned up suddenly at his brother. 'Look here! An IOU from Grandfather for fifty guineas. Do you remember that? He gave me the money for Christmas one year—in gold in a little chamois leather pouch. We'd never seen so much, and you and I were full of plans for the way we'd spend it. Then he borrowed it back on Boxing Day, and that was the last we saw of it!'

'By God! Yes, I remember. Years ago, that!'

267

'Nineteen hundred and two—it's dated.'

'What else have you got in there?' Hugh gestured at the desk.

'Oh, a load of rubbish. Nothing important. The family papers are in the two rosewood chests in the library at the Dower now. . . . You will keep an eye of them, won't you, Hugh? It would be such a pity if they were lost or allowed to deteriorate.'

'Never fear, Steward of the Records, that's me. Not a single account book shall perish while it is in my keeping.' He placed one hand on his heart and raised the other, intoning, 'I, Hugh Athelson, do solemnly swear to lay down life and honour— most especially my honour—in defence of these sacred— ouch!' Athel's blotter hit him square in the chest.

'Shut up,' Athel protested, laughing. 'And go and get us a pint of champagne. I'm as dry as a bone from the dust we've stirred up these past weeks. . . . By the way, is that bonfire still going at the end of the kitchen garden? I want to burn some of this.'

'Yes, it's roaring away. I'm just immolating a few million wood beetles in the shape of those rotten old benches from the hall.'

Athel's eyes shadowed at once. 'What do you think about the long table in there and the chair? They're both eaten away, too.'

'We can't burn those,' Hugh said quickly. 'Not among the rubbish. Our folk wouldn't like to see that. We'll just leave them where they are. You never know, the people who buy the house may take to the beetle, might make pets of 'em!' He was trying to cheer Athel by any means, anxious to take as much pain out of the parting as possible. 'Go on, take your stuff down to the bonfire, and I'll meet you there with the champagne.'

The cellar was in an uproar. Alfred was behaving like an operatic diva at a bad rehearsal, waving his arms and uttering shrill denunciations of the way the footmen were humping the wine about.

'What's going on?' Hugh inquired.

The men were sullen. 'We're supposed to get all yon over to Monday Sutliffe by lunchtime. He's shifted his own cellar round to fit this in, but he won't take kindly to being mucked about for longer than necessary.'

'Well, what are you standing around for then; get on with it.'

'It's Alfred. Just listen to him. Wants everything carried at an angle of forty-five degrees, and nothing to stand in the sun for five minutes while we come down for a second load. He's driving us mad.'

'Alfred, you must let them get on with it as best they can. Don't look if it's painful. Where's the best champagne?'

Alfred shuffled into a corner and returned with a magnum.

'That's not the best,' Hugh said indignantly.

'Well, it's all you're getting at this time of the morning,' Alfred said sharply.

'Oh, really? And whose bloody champagne is it then?'

'It ain't yourn, that I do know!' Alfred answered staunchly.

'But it's Athel who wants it, you old fool!' Hugh shouted back at him.

Alfred snatched the bottle and shuffled off, muttering dark threats among the cobwebs.

'Here you are, then. But the glasses have gone over to t'Dower.'

'Then we'll have to drink it out of the bottle, won't we?'

Alfred drew in a sharp breath of outrage.

'Poor old Alfred,' Hugh said. 'Don't take on so. You'll still have me, you know.' He turned and mounted the cellar steps two at a time.

'Whippersnapper, who wants you? . . . And don't run with that bottle!'

Hugh found Athel raking the last of his papers into the blaze.

'Here you are. No glasses, so I brought cups.'

'Fine!' Athel said. 'Get the bottle open, then.'

The champagne, much shaken, came out in a gush.

'Look out! You're pouring it all over the fire. Here are the cups.'

'Sorry. It's a bit out of control.'

'I've got one more load of stuff to burn. I'll just go and get it.' Athel gulped his champagne back. 'Pour me another cup while I'm gone.'

Hugh began to gather up the papers he had drenched and feed them into the heart of the blaze. One scrap attracted his attention. It looked like verse and was in Athel's handwriting. Just a torn page out of a lined notebook, the half of it charred so as to be indecipherable. Hugh had read what remained before he thought what he was doing:

> and the moon and the night clouds
> Flying, flying.
> When I dream of the girl who went unsped
> To an old man's bed
> And left me without my passion
> Just dying, dying.

Justine! The name seemed to flash across the page in front of him and Hugh started back, crumpling the paper into a ball and tossing it into the flames. He felt as though he had spied upon something secret and sacred. Athel, who thought all poetry was 'stuff' and scarcely ever read a book in his life except the ones Cousin Cuthbert had forced on him, Athel had struggled to frame his feelings for Justine in verse. . . . And tomorrow she would be here, coming to take her part in the forlorn ritual of farewell. How could Athel bear it? How could any of them bear the next few days?

*   *   *

'Is she here?'

'Yes, she is. But don't think you can go bursting in on her this minute; she's dressing for dinner. And you've only just got time to change yourself.' Mrs Rimmer was firm. 'Furthermore, no muddy boots cross my kitchen floor, so you can just take them off on the step, Athel Athelson, and go up in your stockinged feet.'

'You're very bad-tempered this evening,' Athel said mildly, leaning against the doorpost while he removed the offending boots. 'What's the matter?'

'Just about everything, and that's a fact! These ducks Rabbit Jake sold me have cooked up so tough I doubt anyone'll get their teeth into them, and there's Alfred refusing to let us have the wine because it's jogged up——'

'Now, now, don't get into a state. Your cooking is the best in Clere Athel, and you know it. Besides, we don't have to fuss on Justine's account. Where's the rest of the family?'

'That's another thing!' Mrs Rimmer exploded. 'Your mother's only just gone up to dress—been in my way the whole afternoon making petit fours and look at the mess she's left over there. You can just go and tell her to get a move on. Hugh and Fenn are in the drawing room drinking themselves silly on whisky,' she added with heavy disapproval.

Athel sighed. They were all feeling the strain. He had just spent a depressing afternoon with Old Tom in his hut out on the Moss.

Old Tom was dying, and knew it, and was glad because Old Athel was dead and the old ways gone with him.

'I don't belong na more,' he told Athel. 'Nor in a short time other folks won't belong neither. They'll drain away forever, like the sea left the Moss—the good, simple people with strong hands—and what is left will be grasping and greed on the one side and envy and bitterness on the other. Two sorts of people, where before there was only one. They'll breed their differences into their children, and there'll be na more love and respect between them, only fear.'

Athel had tried to persuade him to move into the village, where he could be properly looked after. But it was no use. Old Tom turned away from him in disgust.

'Shut the door as tha' goes!'

It was the same wherever he went in the village. He had

given them their land and their property, but they still felt betrayed.

Athel tiptoed out into the hall in his stockinged feet. The murmur of voices from the drawing room was interrupted by a familiar, fruity chuckle, betraying the fact that Cousin Cuthbert was now also at the whisky.

Then Athel looked up, and Justine was standing in the glow of the lamp at the top of the stairs. Suddenly, and quite irrationally, it was almost worth leaving Clere Athel for ever just to have the power of calling her back this one last time.

He wanted to take the stairs at a run, to reach out for her and enclose her in his arms as though she were the keep and he the castle wall that would never again surrender her. But he did none of these things, waiting instead with his white-knuckled hand gripping the baluster rail while she came to him, unhurriedly.

'You are going to be late for dinner. Better go straight up and dress.' Such mundane words for such a meeting. Her voice sounded husky. 'We can talk later.'

Athel moved out of her way. 'Later, then. There are things must be said.'

Justine nodded and passed him—they were careful not to touch—and Athel turned and followed the faint, sweet wake of her perfume up the stairs.

Despite the underlying tensions, the family united in a very creditable performance at dinner. Sophie was determinedly gay, Cousin Cuthbert proposed several toasts to mark Justine's reunion with them, and Hugh and Charlotte, the one anxious and the other curious, were discreet with their preoccupations. Everyone pretended not to notice Athel's impatience for the meal to be over, the restless toying with the forks between each course and his silence at the head of the table. He took little part in the conversation, ignoring remarks that were addressed to him, either because he was oblivious to them or for fear of further prolonging the meal, and his eyes rested sullenly and continuously on Justine.

'Upon my word,' said Great-Aunt Ivlian at last, rising at

the opposite end of the table, 'there are times, Athel, when you are even more graceless than your grandfather! Tell Alfred that we will take our coffee in the drawing room directly, if you please!'

After all, it seemed natural enough when Athel said that he intended to walk up to the house to fetch some inventory lists he wanted to work on and Justine said that she would walk up with him. The family offered them every assistance in creating the opportunity. . . . It was a fine, mild evening. . . . She must be anxious to see the old place again. . . . She had been sitting all day travelling and would be glad of the exercise before retiring. . . . Yes, yes, they all implied, only go and get it over and done with.

They walked side by side in total silence up the drive. It was not quite dark, but Athel carried a lantern to light the lamps. He did not offer Justine his arm, and she was glad of that, drawing her cloak closer, telling herself that the chill she experienced was in the spring evening and not apprehension of the scene that lay ahead.

The hall, without its tapestries or the glow of a fire upon the hearth, was dank and cheerless. Some of the oak chairs were shrouded with dust sheets and others, stripped of their velvet cushions and footstools, looked more gaunt and ugly than Justine remembered. Athel closed the door behind them and lit one lamp, which hung by a chain from the ceiling in the lobby. But he made no move to investigate any of the others, and Justine did not know whether she was deliberately left to stumble forwards in the near darkness or whether it was merely that the rest were unfurnished for use.

Athel walked over to one of the panelled window seats and sat down, resting his forehead in his hands. He said, 'Justine, will you ever know, will you ever guess how you have made me suffer?'

She moved to stand beside him, and her hand hesitated for a moment over his bent head and then gently caressed it.

'No,' she said. 'No one ever knows what the suffering of anyone else is like. But if I measured it alongside mine. . . .'

He looked up at her wonderingly. 'Then how could you do it?' Abruptly he stood up, close to her. 'Justine! My heart is beating indecent loud. Can you hear it?' She put out a faltering hand as though she would ward him off, and he snatched hold if it, pressing the palm against his chest. 'Feel it, then!' She struggled to free herself. 'Say yours beats the same!'

She implored him. 'Let us not speak of these things any more. We can only hurt each other.'

'Did you think we could meet like strangers?'

'No, of course not. But I thought we could meet and say good-bye like loving friends.'

'I can *never* be your friend. I am your lover. Nature intended me so.' He drew her close to him, and his mouth found her mouth in the dark, her resistance only a second's space, and then she clung to him, her whole body suddenly pliant in his arms. The feel of her said more than words. If a woman yields herself completely, a man knows the moment. Then the choice is his.

And what made Athel choose as he did? Was it the shade of Grandfather and all the other Athels that went before? Did they crowd into the dark hall and force him away from Justine with a united will from beyond the grave?

'And with your Richard? Is it like this with your Richard?' The words broke the spell. Justine steadied herself and turned away.

'Well?'

She was crying silently and could not answer him at once. When she did speak, her voice was almost steady and there was even a note of defiance: 'I am no harlot to have gone to a man without liking and respect. But if you think because I am a woman and inexperienced that I cannot imagine the difference between my surrender to him and the nights I would have spent with you, you are mistaken.'

She had to pause again but collected herself and went on fiercely. 'Don't ever think that I haven't loved you as you loved me. . . . I have. I have put your peace of mind above my own content. I would rather you hated me than suffered

274

for me. And I remember. . . .' She remembered so many precious moments. Athel on the top of a hayrick, laughing down at her with a straw between his teeth. . . . Athel with his hair wet and spikey from a swim in Little Rip. . . . His face that time he made the fountain bell work for her . . . a precious afternoon at the end of a long winter when they sat by the fire. She looked at him and thought: 'God help me, I have fallen deep in love and yet I am a poor thing with nothing to offer against the miracle and the beauty of him.' . . . 'Oh, yes, I have memories. And if that is all there is'—her voice fell away, trembling on the last forlorn words—'many women have less.'

It was not easy to recapture the spirit of their earlier relationship. Yet somehow over the next few days, with Hugh's and Charlotte's help and in the general disorganization and effort entailed in stripping down the house, something of the old camaraderie which had existed between Athel and Justine was re-established. At lease on the surface. What they suffered privately, what their innermost thoughts were, what the measure of their temptations, no one else at Clere Athel ever knew.

One afternoon the four of them rode together for the last time to the top of Godwin's field and looked down on Clere Athel. They were breathless at first, silent for quite a long while.

'I think it's rotten that you have to leave,' Hugh said at last. He looked at Athel. 'I have this grisly idea that if I left Clere Athel . . . if I pulled up my roots . . . I might rot away like a tree.'

'Oh, Hugh, don't!' Justine pleaded. 'How depressing. Besides, you are wrong. Maybe some families couldn't strike new roots, but we're made of sturdier stuff.' She gave Athel an anxious, sidelong glance, searching for the right words to comfort and encourage him. 'Why, the first Athel who came here adopted a new land and a new language and a whole new way of life. Any one of us could do that again.' An image began to shape itself in her mind. She turned eagerly to Athel.

'Do you remember how we stood on the shore once and watched that great storm pass over Clere Athel? The thunder was gradually growing fainter, and the black clouds slipped down into the sea. I said it looked as if the storm was drowning itself, that it was dying, but you said no, it had only rolled off over the horizon to raise havoc somewhere else. . . . Well, don't you see?' She looked around at them all intently. 'That's the way Athel is going. Not defeated, just like the thunder rolling out over the horizon!'

*　　　*　　　*

Great-Aunt Ivlian was quite shocked when she discovered that Justine had been in Clere Athel for four days without anyone volunteering to show her where her grandfather was buried. She at once gave orders for the tomb to be opened up and insisted on conducting the visit herself.

She walked, now, only with the aid of an ebony stick, and this circumstance, taken together with her trailing, mourning black, made her at once the most appropriate and least reassuring companion with whom to pay a social call on the dead.

Justine followed her down the mossy steps with some trepidation. The last time she had stood in the tomb, Grandfather's booming voice had filled it while he pondered where to put Cecily Hamlack. She could not rid herself of the notion that he was listening to them and might interrupt their conversation at any moment.

'There he is!' Great-Aunt Ivlian, swinging the lantern high, tapped her stick sharply on the stone and made Justine jump. 'We've given him a good inscription. I think he would have liked it.'

Justine read: 'Athel Athelson (1832-1908). The last of his line to hold Clere Athel. On his death he gave the land to his people in fulfilment of a solemn promise. His wife and two sons predeceased him. Two grandsons and two granddaughters survived.'

276

'Yes, I'm sure he would have approved of that.'

'A good man. A true father to his people—God honour him for that!' Great-Aunt Ivlian said, more in the tone of an injunction than an invocation. 'Do you want to pray for him?'

'Well . . . not here.'

'In the church, then. Come along.' Her trailing skirts drew a wake across the dust and the fragments of last year's dead leaves, as they climbed the steps once more into the sunlit land of the living. 'I will pray with you, but we must walk very slowly. Tell me as we go—what's he like?'

'Who?'

'Your Richard, of course! I didn't want to ask you in front of Athel, and this is the first time we've been alone. Are you happy?'

'Yes, I think so.'

'I'm glad. Your grandfather would have been glad, too. A pity about you and Athel.'

'Yes,' Justine thought, 'a pity.' Aloud she said, 'What do you think about Athel going to live in America?'

Great-Aunt Ivlian stopped, leaning heavily on her stick. Her eyes roamed across the churchyard, past the vicarage to the village and the fields beyond. 'He has his life to live. He is doing what he thinks is best—and not only for himself, mind you. He has always had a great sense of responsibility. I have remarked it ever since he was quite small. I admired that quality in my brother, and I admire it in you too, my dear.'

Justine was surprised.

'In me?'

'I think you did the right thing to go away when you did. It cannot have been an easy decision to make. And when we heard you were going to be married, I wondered if that, also, was part of the sacrifice. I thought of you constantly when I saw Athel reconciled with his grandfather at the last, the one to go on living and the other to die with serenity. . . . Now I am rested, let us go on. . . .'

They walked in silence for several minutes until they reached the north porch. Justine was too moved to speak. She

277

had never before had such a continuously lucid conversation with Great-Aunt Ivlian, and it was disconcerting to find herself observed so acutely by a figure they all had habitually over-looked.

*   *   *

Athel was sailing for America on the Friday, and it was therefore necessary for him to leave Clere Athel early in the morning of the previous day.

'And don't any of you think you're going to watch me sail, because you're not, and that's final! It will be quite hard enough to see England fade out of sight. Half the family on the dockside, and I shall find it beyond endurance.'

'All right, then,' Hugh said. 'Here's what we do. We give you a farewell party on Wednesday, and those who feel up to it can keep going through the night and wave you off at dawn.'

It was just what was needed. The idea put fresh heart into the people of Clere Athel. They would triumph over the melancholy of the occasion. They would make such a revel of it as must rouse the spirits of their dead ancestors, and the Song of Aethel would be sung like a battle hymn, among the drinking and the feasting.

Stripped of its furnishings, the house was not inviting, but the now untenanted stables and the barn had been newly whitewashed and made a cheerful setting for supper. Early on the morning of the appointed day—the spell of fine, mild weather continuing—a fire had been kindled in the home park and an ox set to roast, scenting the air with delicious promise. There was a coming and going with game pies and roast chickens and ducks and gingerbread and puddings, a bustle about trestles and boards for tables and plates, a supreme importance about Monday Sutliffe with his barrels of ale and Alfred with cases of wine.

Finally, when it was dusk, all but the very young, and the old women content to mind them, put on their Sunday finery and collected lanterns to light the way up the drive for the last time.

Athel was keeping watch outside the barn.

'Here they are. Hugh! Justine! Tell Mother they're here. Fenn, bring that chair forward for Great-Aunt Ivlian, will you? She can't stand all the time we are receiving. Where's Charlotte got to? . . . Now, who are the first arrivals? Why Jake and Muriel, by a short head! No work tonight then, Jake?'

'His traps'll be doing it for him, never fear,' said Bartholomew Tyte, directly behind them.

'A wagon coming. Looks like the Thrustletons . . . and the Leighs, too. By God, Ted, tha's got a load on board there!'

'Ah, here's our master butcher. Sam, Mother wants you to take a look at the beef, see how it's coming along.'

'That spit is five hundred years old and still in good working order,' said Great-Aunt Ivlian to nobody in particular.

There were to be many confused recollections of the night of that party, a number of stories beginning with the assertion that someone had said something to someone and had then been answered in a way that, for sheer spontaneity of wit in harmony with succinctness of language, would never be equalled. But alas, the *who* and the *what* were missing, leaving only the staunch witnesses prepared to be hanged if it wasn't the damned funniest thing they had ever heard. And no one in a position to pass sentence.

Could it really be true that Rabbity Jake, answering an urgent call of nature behind the barn, had stumbled on a roosting pullet, wrung its neck, and pocketed it out of sheer force of habit? And didn't he later, in the heat of the dancing, whip out the pullet's lolling head along with his pocket handkerchief and jig on, unknowing, with the evidence of his infamy plain for everyone to see?

The dancing itself was a part of the unreality of that night, making people unsure of what they had seen and not seen, said and not said, done and not done. It was not their custom in Clere Athel to dance. The men thought it undignified.

They preferred to drink, to sing songs and tell stories. They mistrusted the abandon of the dance. Yet the fact remained that they *had* danced.

It began with the hanging of the lanterns in the trees and Sir Roger de Coverley for the youngsters. That was reasonable enough. But what of the circles of eight that followed, and the polkas and the gallops that grew progressively wilder? That had been something else. And the men were the worst. A touch of frenzy in the fire-lit figures. Men like Arthur Parr, old enough to know better, leaping four, five feet in the air and spinning and whirling like savages striving to invoke old, elemental gods. Cuthbert Rainbird, himself a man of the cloth, snatching up his cousin Justine Athelson and heel-and-toeing with her as though his pumps were possessed.

'Whatever is going on?' asked Hugh in wonder. 'Fenn and I turn our backs for five minutes to make the wassail bowl, and when we come back, everyone has gone mad! What on earth is Cousin Cuthbert doing with Justine?'

Great-Aunt Ivlian watched serenely from her chair. 'I had no idea Cuthbert was such a good dancer. He has that quality quite often to be remarked in the heavily built of being exceeding light on his feet.'

Hugh regarded her in astonishment. 'But ain't it all just a trifle wild?'

It was Great-Aunt Ivlian's turn to be taken aback. 'Whatever is the matter with you, boy? They're only dancing!'

'Yes, but *why*? I never saw them do it before!'

'Perhaps they are exorcising the old and exulting in the new . . . or possibly it is the other way about.'

Hugh clapped his hand to his forehead in mock despair. 'Lord save us! That's too deep for me.'

'Feelings are deep,' said Great-Aunt Ivlian.

'Athel?' Hugh turned to his brother uncertainly. 'You ain't dancing?'

Athel was leaning one shoulder against the wall of the barn, his hands in the pockets of his breeches. The firelight revealed a faint, rather grim smile.

'Of course he ain't,' snapped Great-Aunt Ivlian. 'Don't you see? They are dancing *for him*.'

Soon after midnight the younger sons and daughters were sent home, since there would be milking to be done at first light and they must get some sleep.

The fire was stacked with fresh wood and the wassail bowl circulated while stories were told. By two o'clock most of the women had left.

'Are you tired, Aunt Sophie? Do you want to go back to the Dower?' Justine hoped the answer would be no, but she felt bound to offer the suggestion. 'I will come with you if you wish.'

'No, dear, thank you. We have so little time with him now. We will stay here. . . . Did Charlotte go?'

'Yes, she went with Mrs Rimmer. I think Great-Aunt Ivlian must have left at the same time. I don't see her anywhere.'

The older men had drawn closer around the fire. Athel sat in their midst with Fenn at his right hand and Hugh at his left.

The talk had been quiet and subdued for some time, as it is when men have wasted away the preliminaries and come at the heart of the matter.

Richard Warrener spoke. 'Well, Athel Athelson, this is a sorry day, and no man here but wishes tha would change thee mind.'

'Aye, Rick. But tha knows it's not as simple as that.'

'Some of us have been thinking . . . if it's a question of money . . . that is, we've taken the land as a gift, but there's nowt to stop us making some payment for it.'

Athel shook his head. 'Now, Rick, we've been over all this. No use to go through it again.'

'Aye,' Ted Thrustleton interrupted, 'but the fact is we're fair worried out of our wits at the state you're leaving us in. What about t'house. There's no knowing who'll buy it. There could come someone to make our lives a misery, throwing his weight about in Clere Athel and treating us like muck.'

Athel frowned. 'I don't see that you've any need to worry. You've the right to your land, free and clear. I've seen to that.

And Fenn will manage things for you. Hugh will be here and Mother at the Dower. Nobody could buy the house and then play the squire if you don't let him.'

'But t'house is slap, right in the middle of Clere Athel,' William Leigh pointed out. 'If we got someone who didn't like our ways, someone in county politics, you might say, well ... happen he could make trouble for us, one way an' another. . . . It worries us, d'ye see!'

Athel looked doubtful. 'What do you think, Fenn?'

'Happen they're right.'

'You never said anything before. Have you been thinking this all along?'

'Yes,' said Fenn simply. 'But I thought since you needed the money so bad I'd best keep my mouth shut.'

'But what else can I do except sell the house? The family can't live in it. It needs a fortune spending on it in repairs— you know that. Are you saying I should just leave it to rot away?'

'It'd be a sight of good brass gone to waste,' Fenn said grudgingly. 'No one would ask it of you.'

But they were asking. Athel looked at each man in turn, and the plea was in their eyes, half meeting his and not liking to, and in the stubborn set of their mouths. He thought of the need for the money, not least the modest portion he had wanted for himself, the price of a measure of independence from Crispin Saward. Sentiment and prudence wrestled within him.

And then—'Let it be as our people want.' They did not instantly recognize the voice that spoke out of the darkness, but the manner and the words were familiar. It was just such a thing as Old Athel might have said.

'Great-Aunt Ivlian?' Athel sounded uncertain.

She moved slowly into the fringe of firelight, its reflected glow emphasizing the gauntness of her features and dark-clad figure. Her eyes were fixed on Athel's face, and she spoke to him as though they were alone.

'You must tell them it shall be as they wish.'

282

'It needs thinking about. I have to consider the family.'

'There is nothing to consider. We shall contrive.'

'The income from the home farm may not be enough.'

'We will make it enough. And we will take eight more acres from the parkland.'

Athel brooded over this.

'I don't like to think of the house just rotting away, though. There's been shelter and good cheer within its walls for centuries. And birth and death and loving and laughing. . . . Just think of the Athelsons who have lived there.'

'I do. That is why it belongs to us and no one else. And I had rather see its timbers perish and lichen invade its stones than let a stranger call it home.'

They confronted each other across the dying fire, while the men gathered around it waited, tense. At last Athel made his decision. 'Very well, then. Let it be as you say. We will close the door on the house and leave it to the beetle and the weather. . . . Only think on'—abruptly he silenced the chorus of approval that greeted his words—'you take some of our burdens upon you with this last concession. Look after the church roof and the school building, and don't be expecting Hugh to provide from the little he has. Have a care for folk like old Mrs Parting, who have none of their own to fend for them, and Simple Sam—daft as a brush and a tinker's child, but it was our people found him by the road and brought him here and this is where he belongs. We have ever had a loving concern for you all. Do no less, one by another, in the future, than we would have done. And may God keep you and the land in good heart. . . . Now there is little enough time for sleep before daybreak. You'll be about your work when I leave so I'll shake each man by the hand and we'll say good-night.'

Their leave-takings were brief, a few of the phrases with which men dignify one another and a relationship, but they did not hurry over them.

When the last man was gone, Sophie and Justine began to collect up the tankards, and Hugh and Fenn to shovel sand over the fire. Even Cousin Cuthbert was not without a useful occupation, measuring out the remains of the wassail cup. And the small bustle contrived, by common consent, to afford Athel a kind of solitude.

It was a clear night and the moon very high. He was looking at the house in the moonlight.

After a while Great-Aunt Ivlian moved over to stand beside him.

'What are you thinking?'

'I'm thinking there's all the brass I had tied up in stones,' he teased her.

'Brass is for shopkeepers to jingle in tills.'

They were companionably silent for several minutes.

'You will not regret it,' Great-Aunt Ivlian said. 'Our people will remember that at the last you gave them everything you had to give, and they will love and honour you for that all their days. . . . No Athelson, no Athelson who ever lived,' she added fiercely, 'had the right to walk more proud than you.'

*   *   *

Athel was riding into Lancaster to catch the Liverpool train, and Harry Thorpe was going with him to bring the horse home.

It was a glorious April morning, almost unseasonably warm, with clear skies and a strong sun unfurling leaves before their time. A morning when the moist earth scents the air, and stirs, and heaves out small, white flowers in woods; and the willow warbler sings and the sandpiper whistles along the edge of Little Rip.

Athel ordered the governess cart brought around with the horses at eight o'clock, so that Great-Aunt Ivlian and Sophie and Charlotte and Justine could ride with him to the end of the village.

'You're never thinking to ride out?' Hugh was surprised. 'Why, folk have been waiting for you since half after seven.'

'You mean the children and a few dames in doorways.'

'I mean everyone.'

It was Athel's turn to be astonished.

'The men aren't on the land?'

'Not a one of them. Come on. Justine and Charlotte and I will walk with you. Great-Aunt Ivlian and Mother can follow in the governess cart, and Harry will lead the horses. That's the way it should be done.'

And that was the way they did it, walking out quietly through the park gates with Athel leading the way and the sound of the horses' hooves striking a hollow echo in the stillness of the empty lane. Past the school, unnaturally silent at this hour, and over the stone bridge. No one was in sight.

Athel glanced uneasily back at Hugh.

'They're waiting along the street. Go on.'

The little cavalcade turned the corner by the pond, and Hugh had not been mistaken.

Ahead of them, thronging the narrow, cobbled street, every man, woman, and child waited to honour Athel in a manner that seemed fitting to them, waited in silence to see him pass out of their lives.

The men had taken the time from the land, and that was no light thing to have done, and then, unsparing in the tribute they paid him, had everyone taken the trouble to put on his Sunday best suit and clean starched shirt and the flat tweed cap that covered him to church. Women had been up since dawn making the best of themselves and their families. Small boys had been held under the pump and scrubbed and squeezed into Norfolk jackets without remorse, and little girls had their hair teased until they wept. Old grannies, got up with bits of borrowed lace, were steered out into cottage gardens and propped in kitchen chairs and even old Mrs Parting, senile and bedridden for the past ten years, was brought out to recline on Monday Sutliffe's chaise longue, pinned into a blanket for decency's sake, with nothing much to be seen of her but the hair on top of her head. And even that curled up with the hot tongs and a pink ribbon tied into it.

Athel saw all this and, perfectly understanding what an effort such a show cost hardworking folk, missed no face with his gentle smile, either to left or to right of him as he walked slowly down the street. Then it was to be observed that as he passed by, the men, so proud that they would never have uncovered their heads for any master that asked it, were taking off their caps for the one who had resigned his rights over them.

They was no calling out or cheering. They would not have thought that seemly. They spoke his name quietly with a nod as men do in the north and make of it a greeting, an acknowledgement, a farewell.

'Athel.'

'Tom,' he answered.

'Athel.'

'George.'

'Athel.'

'William . . . little William and Roger.'

The women did not speak since it was not their place to do so. They smiled, and some bobbed unaccustomed curtsies, and some of the older generation cried quietly into best linen handkerchiefs.

When the road came to an end, Athel made his last farewells to the family, kissing Great-Aunt Ivlian's cold cheek, shaking Cousin Cuthbert heartily by the hand.

'Dear old friend and tutor. Have a care for my womenfolk.'

Sophie clung to him. 'You will look after yourself, Athel?'

'Of course, Mother, of course. Be brave, now. You can come and visit me by-and-by.'

He kissed Charlotte and embraced Hugh. 'By God, I shall miss you both. Write me often about the land, Hugh . . . and Fenn—ah, there you are, Fenn. Be sure to give Jake as much casual work as you can this summer. I believe Muriel is expecting again.'

Harry Thorpe brought up the cob, and Athel looked at Justine. He had left Justine to the last.

'Ride with me as far as the marsh.' It was not a question.

He lifted her easily on to the front of the saddle and climbed up behind her. One last salute, and then the villagers broke their unnatural silence. They sent his name ringing after him along the road.

Harry Thorpe cantered on ahead, and by the time Athel reached the bridge over the marsh he was already disappearing into the pine woods. Athel reined in and turned the cob. The village was hidden behind a coppice of willow. For a few precious minutes he was alone with Justine. Her soft weight was against his shoulder, and a strand of her hair blew across his cheek. He encircled her with his arms, holding her close.

'Look up,' he said softly, 'look up at Warrener's top field.'

Justine shaded her eyes towards the high ground. 'Yes, I see it. What has he got in there?'

'Winter barley. Doing well.' He spoke with simple satisfaction. And then . . . 'So beautiful, my land.' They enjoyed the prospect together.

'You must go,' Justine said at last. She gently unclasped the hands that secured her and slid from the saddle. 'You must leave today and I tomorrow.'

Athel leaned over her. 'If I were to get down and hold you as long and kiss you as hard as I've a mind to, I should never leave.'

'Don't do that.' Her eyes pleaded with him. 'Just go.'

'I love you.'

'And you are loved in return.'

For an instant she laid her cheek against his knee and then looked up at him, attempting a smile, holding out her hand. He took the hand and carried it to his mouth. There was a tender chivalry in the gesture, and the feel of the kiss in her palm was with her long after he had ridden out of her sight.